THE TALES OF AMERGIN
SEA DRUID

First Published in Great Britain 2014 by Mirador Publishing

Copyright © 2014 by Peter Green

First edition: 2014

Any reference to real names and places are purely fictional and are constructs of the author. Any offence the references produce is unintentional and in no way reflects the reality of any locations or people involved.

A copy of this work is available through the British Library.

ISBN: 978-1-910104-90-3

Mirador Publishing
Mirador
Wearne Lane
Langport
Somerset
TA10 9HB

THE TALES OF AMERGIN SEA DRUID

"THE JOURNEY BEYOND THE VEIL"

By

Peter Green

CHAPTER ONE:
THE TOWER OF GALICIA

Amergin's life will be spent in the search for the truth. He is the embodiment of the prophecy.

From the Tower of Galicia, as a young Milesian prince, one of the eight sons of Milidh, Amergin surveys the limitless expanse of the Northern Ocean.

The great journey prophesied by the tribal elders is about to begin. Steeped in mythological tales passed down from generation to generation, the Milesians have swept through Europe on a crusading quest.

Great Mediterranean civilisations have succumbed to the military might and magical forces controlled by the tribes and horsemen of Milesia.

Amergin embodies the vision and the restlessness of his people. The ancient tales, the collective belief that the warrior prince, druid, poet and champion of their nation will launch into the greatest adventure from the Northern shores of Galicia.

The elders and the mystics of the tribe have seen their visions become reality. The ancient tales of a tower built on the edge of an endless ocean, and from that tower a dream like vision of a distant place that is at the very heart of their consciousness, at the very core of their being, the root of their quest, fundamental to their reality, the source of all truth...

Imbued, instilled and impassioned by the quest for the truth, the young prince Amergin searched for signs on the northern horizon that will foretell the moment when the tribes of Milesia will embark on the next and the greatest phase of the legendary and historic journey.

The three eldest sons of Milidh, the King of Milesia, gathered at the foot of the great Tower of Galicia for an ordeal of strength and endurance. These three princes had been selected by the Chapter of Mystics.

The ones blessed with the powers and wisdom to confront the physical, spiritual and magical challenges ahead.

When the moment arrives, the champion of the ordeal will lead the Milesian tribes over the Northern Ocean to the Promised Land.

The three chosen sons, Eiremhou, Eimbear and Amergin, waited in anxious anticipation as the King of the Milesians arrived in regal procession. The shadow of the great tower lengthened as the sun set over the shimmering Northern Ocean.

Two of the prophesied signs were due. The summer solstice, when the sun reaches its northern zenith on the ocean horizon, and the shadow of the great tower reaches the Temple of Japhet, the place for the start of the ordeal for the chosen Princes of Milesia.

The second of the signs as foretold by the astronomers and astrologers from the ancient land of Scythia - a lunar eclipse as the full moon rises over the horizon of the Northern Ocean. The conjunction of full moon and total eclipse will give the coordinates for the great sojourn to the new land, the land of their dreams, mythology and ancient prophecy.

The third sign was in the hands and the destinies of the young princes. It was foretold in legend that the sons of the great King from Phoenicia, descended from Magog, the son of Japhet, the son of Noah, and the Queen, the daughter of the Pharoah, would pit their wits and their bodies in an ordeal of endurance and strength. The winner shall be declared on the day after the solstice. With the signs fulfilled and the declaration of a champion, the tribes of Milesia shall be in readiness for the greatest journey and the most challenging adventure to begin.

Scota, the Queen of the Milesians, surveyed the thronging masses gathered around the great Tower of Galicia and the Temple of Japhet. All eyes were on her as she walked in the company of Milidh, the glowing radiance of the solstice sunset gently confirming the belief in their hearts and the knowledge of their eyes, that before them was a dark skinned daughter of the great Pharoah Sona, a royal beauty beyond compare.

Milidh smiled knowingly at Scota, aware that his people adored and loved her, and would as soon follow her to the edge of the undiscovered world and uncharted realms, as they would him.

As the fiery globe of the solstice sun rested on the dark indigo horizon of the Northern Ocean, Scota gave the signal to her sons to ready themselves. When the last rays are extinguished the ordeal will begin. All of their youthful lives had been spent physically, mentally and spiritually preparing themselves for this moment.

As the vestiges of the light shimmered and danced and the crimson pink of the sunset slowly turned to the dark blue-black of the night, Scota raised her golden mace to the skies. The crowd roared in approval as the beacon on the great Tower fired to life. The princes knelt in homage before their king and queen, awaiting a royal blessing before beginning the greatest challenge of their young princely lives.

The ordeal before them could challenge them to the core of their being and threaten their very lives, but will ultimately bestow on the champion the honour of leading Milesia to the new world. The champion will have the wisdom and power of the ancients. He will be able to contact the spirit world, reveal the secrets of the cosmos and have a true sense of their destiny.

In Scota's words "The champion will embody the truth, even if he cannot know it."

Eiremhou, Eimbear and Amergin are royal siblings with all the traits, quirks and human conditions of any brothers.

Eiremhou, being the eldest had the innate and undeniable belief that he is the chosen one, the destined one.

Eimbear has a sense of the successor, but with limited patience, and a touch of the Machiavellian, an ingrained knowledge that he will have to manipulate his world, if ever he is to succeed.

Amergin, the youngest prince, has the heart of a lion, and a streak of wrecklessness. No expectation to rule, but the self belief and confidence in his own abilities. The mantle of potential ruler and champion will rest comfortably on his head.

Eiremhou was raised in the expectation of being king, and grew up as a pure bred aristocrat, groomed and trained in the manners of royalty, becoming the epitome of royal stock with all the associated airs and graces.

Eimbear surrounded his life with beautiful stories and cultivated beliefs. He had nothing to lose and therefore nothing to fear.

Amergin valued the beautiful things in life, embodied the wrecklessness of the artist, the restlessness of the warrior, and the philosophy of the poet.

This comfortable truth was seismically shaken by the announcement by Gonne, the supreme mystic to the court of Milidh that the cosmic alignment was such that Milesia had to find a great champion. The time had arrived for the ancient prophecy to be fulfilled.

Surely Eiremhou would be that champion, as the eldest prince? Not so, states Gonne and his Chapter of Mystics, cosmic revelations, and magical interventions have unveiled new truths. The prophesied signs are in alignment. The great ordeal would choose the champion, warrior prince and druid to lead the Milesians over the Northern Ocean…

And so it is written… and is in the stars… and the eclipse…

The first great challenge of the Milesian Ordeal is to harvest the fruits of the ocean, a race to gather sacred Goose Barnacles from the exposed reefs of Galicia, timing the entrance and exit between giant set waves heaving in from Biscay. Next to ascend the Stack of Ormond to collect the precious and rare egg of the Storm Petrel, then to dive to lung bursting depths to prise oysters from the deep trench of Rodiles. These are to be presented to Queen Scota on a silver platter, with an oath of allegiance and a declaration to the tribes of Milesia of their loyalty, and a promise to lead with honesty, bravery, fortitude and integrity.

The first test is seen purely as a physical challenge, to measure fitness, stamina, endurance and a willingness to push their bodies to the limits of their conditioning, all for the greater cause and the fulfilment of the prophecy.

All of Milesia knows the real tests are of the mind, their spirituality, their connection with the spirit world, and the wisdom and knowledge gleaned from the Chapter of Mystics. All of Milesia sees the champion as the one who can muster, and can corale the powers of the ancients. Collectively they sense the gathering magical forces over the distant Northern horizon, and the mystics have forewarned that these forces can be turned to good or evil. The correct choice of champion will enable the forces to be channeled to the benefit of Milesia. A wrong choice, a wrong decision, will ultimately determine the future of an entire race. The right choice, the right decision will take the nation to a heavenly paradise, harnessing the powers of the spirit underworld for good. The path is fraught, each turn, each move, can undo that gone before. A sensitive delicate balance, an equilibrium resting on choices made. The veil between the mortal and spirit-world can be shifted by indecision, inappropriate choices and human frailties.

The raging fire of the beacon on the Tower of Galicia lit up the dark, replacing the golden orange orb of the setting solstice sun.

The ordeal would run until the day of the lunar eclipse, forecast by the mystics, astronomers and astrologers.

The fiery beacon will be fuelled constantly by the Chapter of Mystics, overseen by Gonne. Should the flame be permitted to falter or be doused, then legend has it, the magical powers of the Sidhe will arrive on the shores of Galicia and the route to the Promised Land closed forever.

Gonne and the Chapter of Mystics sense that the magical powers of the Sidhe are increasing as the beacon burns. The beacon seems to be drawing energy from across the Northern Ocean, warning the Sidhe of the prophesied coming of the Milesians.

Further visions forewarn of the dangers of selecting the wrong champion. This will be the signal to the Sidhe that the Milesians are weak and the royal princes will be taken hostage and converted to the ways of the Sidhe.

Selecting the wrong champion is a death sentence to Milesia. Instead of a powerful leader taking their tribes to the promised world, the Sidhe will be channeled back to the Tower of Galicia and the lands of Milesia will be overwhelmed.

Either way a great battle is foreseen between the magical, otherworldly Sidhe and the invading wave of Milesians.

The only hope for the Milesian tribes is for the ordeal to select the destined leader and champion… The ordeal begins…

Each of the three stood transfixed at the edge of a powerful, surging, awe inspiring ocean. The rhythmic pounding of giant waves on sharp limestone rocks, resonated through their tense and braced bodies.

They have seen local fishermen risk their lives gathering the famed and precious Goose Barnacles that are literally worth their weight in gold. Only the extreme tides such as those at the time of the solstice will expose the harvesting reefs. Only when the oceanic swell is of such a wavelength, after traversing thousands of miles, does the fisherman have the time to reach the barnacle encrusted base of the razor sharp reef. Before the drawing waves regather, tower skyward and consume the exposed reef, and the vulnerable gatherer, if the wrong choices are made. Timing is all.

Each would go in turn, watching with baited breath as a brother would descend and make a death dash seaward. None were successful on the first attempt, each learning and refining their technique, watching the others and adopting their own strategy.

The gathered crowd, stood staring, on-watchers, with no influence on the outcome. En mass they took in breath as each of the royal princes timed the run for the exposed treacherous reef, only to exhale as the safety of the high tide mark, now warmly bathed in the early morning sun, was reached.

In the distance were the celebrating drummings of the solstice exuberances. All of Milesia were aware this was the dawning of the prophecy. Celebrations were slowly turning to the anxious reality that royal blood could be spilt this fateful morning. Life could be lost in the cresting of a wave. The destined warrior prince, champion and druid could be gone, consumed by the ocean. The prophecy could end, here and now…

Scota and Milidh watched on with resigned contemplation. This was a time for faith, a belief in the natural and trained powers of their offspring. They too were powerless. The forces of nature cannot be controlled, only harnessed, fleetingly and momentarily. Each meeting with natural energy has to be embraced, understood and absorbed, in readiness for the next encounter, and the next and so this will continue…

The parallels were not lost on Scota and Milidh. The first of the trials, although worldly and physical in nature, tested the future champion in ways similar to the forthcoming encounters with the magical otherworld forces of the Sidhe, encounters beyond the veil.

Each encounter will change, each encounter is life threatening and could fatally end the prophecy.

Eiremhou, the eldest, took up the gauntlet first, emboldened by his sense of destiny as the chosen one.

Timing his move, as the turquoise-emerald waters drained from the coral-like heads of the carved and sculpted limestone reef. White spume sucked and receded towards the low tide mark of the extreme solstice time. These strange shell creatures with goose neck-like stems live at the turbulent margins of the ocean, only found where cold water upwellings meet wave beaten zones, highly oxygenated and rich in plankton. They wave in synchronised dances in the pouring, surging surf.

Like a gaggle of geese moving in unison, the beak-like shells now glinting in the summer dawn, beckoning the unwitting harvester. This is the death zone. Drawing waters gather remorselessly, the tidal surge and readying giant set waves, as if a living entity, boil, fall and rise to the heavens. The moment is here. Eiremhou has split seconds to react and grasp the waving necks, stretching, reaching out, the prize in his grasp. Finger tips touching, his heel wedges into a razor sharp protuberance, slicing to the bone like a fisherman's knife. He flinches momentarily, the prize is lost. The white spume, now streaked with crimson, starts to fill the crevices of limestone. Eiremhou has a second to react, pushing off the reef. He takes off, like a false-starting sprinter. The all consuming surf projects upwards and outwards in a warping cavernous void. Eiremhou sucks in rarefied oxygen and throws himself towards a high tide crevice and wedges his bruised and beaten body tight into the reef.

Tons of water crash around him. The onlookers fear for his survival, inhaling deeply in empathy with Eiremhou. The explosive impact of ocean on sharp immovable reef sends shuddering sounds to the core of Scota and Milidh. Before they can react, in shock and disbelief, the wave dissipates and Eiremhou miraculously appears and lunges towards safety, just as the next gathering watery monster irresistibly crashes to land.

Eimbear breathed deep, taking volumes of heady ozone, seeing his brother fail, but fail bravely.

Naturally, as the next in line he felt this could be his time. He knew this was the first of many trials, and was aware that the natural order had been changed by the revelations of the mystics. The prophecy required a great champion to be selected by the ordeal.

Opportunity tinged with fear flashed through his psyche as he moved down to the ocean. His mind was consumed by the realisation that Eiremhou's failure enhanced his chances, and already he strategised a way to capitalise on his brother's failure.

To enter this gladiatorial scenario where man is tested against natures' forces requires total focus.

Before Eimbear knew it he was perched on the edge of the death zone. Flashing visions of Eiremhou's chances being dashed confused and distorted the clear thinking required by a champion. The first thunderous wall of white water swept Eimbear's feet from under him. As he fell, the axe-like lip of the next crashing wave drove him into the river of spume that flooded seaward from the refuge of land.

Volumes of heady ozone had long been used up as he was drawn, pitched and submerged in the seabound rip current. Half concussed by the driven lip of dense cold water, now his life flashed before him. Like a rag doll, he floated in the riverine rip, only to be drawn back to the zone where the ocean boiled, fell and rose as giant sets marched in from the horizon.

There was a collective exhalation by the tribes of Milesia as the young prince Amergin swam to the aid of his brother. Focused and fearless, he used the rip to get to his hapless brother. One more watery monster would be the end for him. As the behemoth of the ocean arrived, Amergin dove deep pulling the now near lifeless form of his brother with him. A real sense of oneness with the ocean, he knew they must get to the shallower water and avoid being drawn back into the breaking zone. The wave rolled and pitched forward, and deep under water he went with the liquid momentum. The surging white water rolled onwards. He held tightly on, embracing his brother, rolling again, surfacing to gain some ozone.

Again they rolled, gripping on for love and life, giving each other protection from the razor rocks.

He stretched out an arm looking for purchase to drag himself and the limp body of his brother away from the tidal zone. As he grasped the rock he realized he held the prize. The necks and beak-like shells of the goose barnacles. Praise the Great Spirit! His bravery and fortitude rewarded…

So the scene was set, the seeds of a new empire sown, survival the new instinct now. Whosoever the champion-elect may be, the realisation that one and maybe the one could be lost in an instant, a twist of fate, a moment of rashness…

The first trial and nearly all was lost, the royal princes returned to the Temple of Japhet to gather strength, to consult with the mystics, and connect with their divinities. All the brothers were very aware the ordeal had only just begun, and now there was a growing sense of a need for unity. If the challenges of the physical were to be overcome, they must now work together. Beyond that the challenges of the spirit will be personal, the meeting of magical and potentially dark forces on the path before them.

At the setting of the sun on this dramatic and traumatic first day, the three faced to the horizon as the heat of the star dipped into the cooling ocean. Amergin as the hero of the day spoke for them, addressing the solar deity Raqan.

"Great Spirit behold, our nation is in your power! The new land that you show me in my visions and dreams is nearing, bring the promised signs and take us on our great journey!"

Amergin turned to his brothers and implored them to be strong, to meet their destiny with courage, to be prepared for the immense challenges and dangers to come.

The tribes, the mystics and the royalty gathered again at the Temple of Japhet as the waxing moon rose in the northern sky. Scota and Milidh knelt in prayer before the deity Lunasa. The mystics led by their high priest Gonne, bowed before their deity, knowing the promised conjunction of Raqan and Lunasa is coming…

The chieftains and tribes of Milesia prostrated themselves as the first great ceremony of the ordeal began. Gonne stood before them, chanting as Amergin rose to start the ceremonial banquet. All of Milesia rose to join in the incantation. The mystics and the tribes chanted as one.

"May all the spirits bless and protect us, may all the strength of the gods be with you!", and in crescendo, "Amergin!!!"

At this point Amergin presented the elusive, sacred and highly prized goose barnacles on a silver platter to his Queen, Scota. Once again, all eyes were on this dark Eastern beauty as she tasted the much coveted delicacy, biting in to the neck of the goose barnacle, sea salted and spiced.

She kissed Amergin and smiled, in full knowledge that the prophecy was nearing, but in the bitter sweet realisation that one or possibly all of her sons could have been lost this day... the next challenge awaited...

CHAPTER TWO:
THE STACK OF ORMOND

In the mists of the bay stood the Stack of Ormond, a 400 foot precipitous outcrop of granite standing guard over its surroundings. A monument to volcanic forces and erosion, and now home to a myriad wheeling seabirds.The three stood on a carved platform, hewn into the cliff face, a place of ceremonial burial where the tribes connect with the ancestors.

The ocean surged below them, rhythmically, hypnotically filling the bay, aquamarine with brilliant white streaks of foam following the currents almost a mile out to the stack, shimmering in the heady mist of ozone and sunlight.

Amergin dived first, falling into a graceful arc. Silence then the tell-tale "shud" as he pierced the ocean 60 foot below. A ring of white-water and then he surfaced beckoning his brothers. Eiremhou and Eimbear launched themselves executing the same arc, surfacing almost simultaneously.

This time they were as a team, assuring survival and completion of the ordeal, the task to scale the vertiginous stack to reach the colony of storm petrels and return with the beautifully delicate egg of the storm petrel. This tiny creature of the ocean had become a potent symbol of Milesia. The dainty, fluttering of this tiny black petrel as they feed on the ocean surface, belies their powers of endurance, spending months on the ocean surviving all the tumultuous storms. The petrels symbolically represent the mortal struggles of their race. The powers of endurance required to fulfill the prophecy against the gathering dark forces.

They swam steadily and strongly towards the base of the stack, knowing that the only access point is at high tide. After this they would be confronted by a sheer, weed covered rock face, impossible to scale. At high tide a cove is filled and hand and footholds are reachable, an hour either way and the window is gone. As they swam in unison towards the towering, seemingly indomitable stack they were only too aware of the tide. They also knew deep water currents and shifting winds could affect tidal movements. The conjunction of sun and moon could massively increase tidal range... They all stroked deeply and strongly into the ocean, their goal in sight.

"Time and tide wait for no man!", urged Amergin as he saw his brothers catch their breaths, and interrupt their swimming stroke. All were powerful swimmers and had developed the low, steady, economic stroke of the distance swimmer, the anxiety, and the significance of the challenge weighed heavy on them. Amergin could see it in their eyes. Usually self assured and confident, the challenges, the near death experiences, had chipped away at their armour of invincibility. Amergin's talent of motivating, and his natural leadership skills would be key in this ordeal.

Nearing the jagged rocks at the base of the stack, all of creation seemed to be around them. They swam through the surging and cresting swell. The air above and the water around was full of bird life, gannets diving at break-neck speed to plummeting depths, kittiwakes launching from perilous ledges, puffins wheeling in eyeing curiosity, gulls of every description riding the thermals, forcing up and around the great stack. Gently, in the distance the black fluttering presence of the gracefully beautiful storm petrel.

Amergin drew his brothers attention to the diminutive bird, "Let the Great Spirit lift us to the summit of this great stack!"

The cove is full, timing the surge will be critical to reach the handholds. The echoing raucous cacophony of the sea-birds resounded around the sheer cliffs. One by one they hauled themselves on to the still dry refuge of the high tide ledge. South facing, protected from the sea breeze, the morning sun slanted in to the cove, basking on the ledges like grey seals, they rested and regathered their energies.

Restored, collectively their gazes studied potential routes upwards. A steep treacherously sloping ledge meandered skywards, around and out of sight, the only route, life threatening and challenging.

The weight of expectation almost crushing, the brothers embraced each other and yelled and roared to the heavens, "Great Spirit give us the strength to endure, in the name of the prophecy, and in the name of Milesia!"

Free climbing, steadily, handhold by handhold, foothold by foothold up the ancient granite stack, past the burrows of curious, brightly ornamented, clown-faced puffins, beyond the ledges of the tightly packed guillemots and razorbills, higher than the perilous perches of the kittiwakes and fulmars. The seabirds never see humans and are strangely indifferent, if curious, of the three beings ascending to the heights of the stack. The abundance of seabirds on neighbouring cliffs and the remoteness and inaccessible nature of the stack, make this staggeringly beautiful place a nature reserve, immune from the raidings and plunderings of the local tribes.

Only here in the most remote and most inaccessible places, can the nest of the storm petrel be found.

Skywards, silhouetted against the brightness of the mid-day, fleeting glimpses of the diminutive, jet black, storm petrels can be seen.

From the security of a high ledge, Amergin reached down to hoist Eiremhou to his side. Eiremhou in turn, reached down to help Eimbear. Again they rested, each breathing hard, their heaving chests straining for every thimble of rich ozone filled air.

From this point on it was very clear that only the most expert and brave of the free climbers should make the ascent. Eimbear conceded that he was at the limit of his skills, the near vertical slabs, narrowing to needle-like pinnacles, scared him. His resolve had been tested and finally broken. Only Eiremhou and Amergin would continue.

Now they were in competition. The choice of route of ascent was theirs. With no clear route, they now relied on their instincts to pick the fingertip holds, to wedge their bodies into claustrophobic cracks and chimneys, to swing from massively exposed overhangs, to scale the heaven touching pinnacle.

The sea breezes strengthened with the convectional heat of the early afternoon. The masters of the air currents, the fulmars, soared gracefully and majestically by, with a look of "Why are you here? Why do you do this?" Amergin and Eiremhou knew only too well…

In the distance a vortex of frenzied gannets plunged deep into the ocean. The ebbing tide had brought a shimmering, silvering shoal of mackerel into the bay. On cue, a large pod of common dolphin charged in to the feeding zone, diving deep, surfacing, coralling, swiftly and precisely, a time of plenty.

Eiremhou had found a climbing route, and was making good headway. Amergin had chosen a route with an insurmountable overhang. He had to back track and wasted valuable time and energy negotiating and moving to a route with a clear line to the peak.

Amergin saw Eiremhou above, now at least five body heights further up the peak, scaling the pinnacle to the North side of the peak. Amergin chose to go to the pinnacle on the South side of the stack. In a flash of realisation, he was reminded that this was not a race to the top, but a challenge to find the delicate egg of the storm petrel. The southern route was the right choice. There perching precariously, glinting in the afternoon light, wedged into a sheltered rocky alcove, was the prize! The parents must be out over the ocean, the egg still warm in the incubating glow of the sun.

Now, in his clutches, he carefully placed the egg into the pouch attached to his waist belt. Instantly he began the descent. He saw Eiremhou traversing towards the nesting area.

Way below, Eimbear was making his way down, he saw Amergin making his descent.

In the spirit of brotherhood he shouted up to Amergin, "By the blessing of the great spirit, you have found the prize! Bring it back safely, for the sake of the tribes of Milesia!"

On the distant cliff edge, the gathering tribes roared in unison as they witnessed the princes descending.

All the princes were descending safely. Who would deliver the prize safely to Queen Scota?

Scota and Milidh embraced each other. Milidh sent the message for the royal barque to make ready.

The royal barque would intercept the brothers on their swim towards the cliffs.

Amergin was only too aware that the descent could prove to be the most dangerous. Focus was all now, to find the route back to the ledge… safely.

Eimbear waited on the ledge. He would help his brothers in to the ocean. The long, arduous, energy sapping swim would begin…deep, steady strokes, efficient, breathing deeply. Amergin realised he was in the tidal race, drifting away from the cliffs. He knew he had to compensate for the current, tacking so he would arrive at the deep water mooring where the royal barque would drop anchor. He estimated an hours strong swimming.

He surveyed the horizon. No sign of the vessel. Turning his head to breathe in air, he witnessed Eimbear easing his elder brother into the ocean from the ledge. Eiremhou quickly got in to his swimming rhythm, forcing through the ocean. About two minutes behind Amergin. Choose the right tack and the time could be made up. The race was still on…

If Amergin boarded with the prize in tact, he was the champion, and the dive to the deep of Rodiles pure ceremony.

Amergin paced himself, cognisant of the valuable prize he was carrying. The mantle of champion was in his grasp. Eimbear sensed deep within that Amergin was destined for this. The omens were undeniable.

Eiremhou could not reconcile that his younger brother was fated for this.

Eiremhou could not catch Amergin, if anything the lead was stretching. Amergin called to the gods, "Give me strength. Give me the wisdom to be a great champion!"…

On cue the royal sailing vessel with its Phoenician designed sailing rig, bright red against the deep blue, appeared, cresting majestically towards the deep water mooring.

Spurred on, revitalized, enthused with new vigour, Amergin surged on, digging even deeper his swimming stroke visibly lengthening. He could hear the cheering on the cliffs. He saw his parents standing on the prow of the vessel, waving him on…

A crew member threw rope netting over the side. Gonne, the head priest of the Chapter of Mystics took up the sacred conch and blew a ceremonial blast, as Amergin grasped the netting. Rung by rung Amergin hauled himself upwards and on to the deck… the finishing point.

A mighty roar resounded around the sheer cliffs and out into the bay. The tribes of Milesia rejoiced, on the verge of finding a true champion…

The full moon rose over the northern horizon. The mystics gathered in the silver light, waiting, patient, the moment of prophetic truth in the ether, tomorrow night or the night after? The celestial signs are in alignment. Surely the time has come…

Amergin rested contentedly, his body relaxed in sheer exhaustion, his heart joyfully elated, his mind drifting in to quiet dreamful oblivion. The slanting silver light casting deep shadows, a green mysterious world started to emerge from the depths of consciousness. A serene flowing feminine form came in to view. Long golden tresses wrapped around his dreaming body, and soft tender finger tips caressed his gently heaving chest. An inner peace, through his body, his heart, and his soul, massaged to near ecstasy, he heard the words seductively murmoured, "I am waiting for you Amergin. My people, the Tuathan Guardians of Light are waiting for you. Be careful on your journey. The dark Sidhe also await you. Be careful of their dark magic, they can steal your soul, and you and your people will be lost."

In that moment, from deep dreaming sleep, to wakefulness, a vision of the most beautiful creature he ever beheld flashed before him. He stared into deep rich amber eyes. He noticed a small fleck in the iris.

He became that fleck, and felt he was falling into a cosmos of amber... "Sceine!!" he cried out...

And the slanting silvery light washed over his countenance. Amergin turned to see the full moon framed by the Tower of Galicia, and the ocean and stars beyond.

Now awake, he stirred slowly and took a cooling sip of water. All of his senses knew the dreamlike vision was of the world that awaits him ...

Straightaway he went to meet with his mother, Scota. She of all people would understand the significance of this vision. Scota could commune beyond the veil, into the other world. She is blessed with the wisdom of the ancients, and will be able to interpret Amergin's vision.

Scota informed Amergin that until now the powers of the good Sidhe were guiding Milesia onwards.

Now, under the influence and the collusion of Gonne, the high priest of the Chapter of Mystics, the path forward for Milesia is threatened by the dark Sidhe.

"Nothing is as it seems", Scota forewarns her questioning son. She pours a glass of golden rich apple liqueur distilled from the fertile valleys of Asturias. Given almost as a potion to the apprentice... "The veil is thinning and stretching, be sure to see clearly that which represents genuine good, and to dismiss that which is manipulative and malevolent."

The balcony on which they sit is directly in view of the Northern Ocean. Amergin sips the rich liquor and stares to the distant horizon. He tells his mother of the vision. She understands... Scota has had similar visions before she met Milidh. When travelling through the vastness of the North African deserts. She knew with absolute certainty her path was being guided by the ancients. "It would appear Amergin that your path is so destined."

She embraced her son and whispered gently to him, the echoed words, "Be careful on your journey Amergin, there are dark forces trying to foil your every move."Scota looked knowingly into her sons eyes. Here was the champion of the Milesian tribes, someone who has the physical strength, the spiritual connection and would ultimately be able to meet magical forces with powers of his own.

"Go now Amergin, go to meet your brothers, dive to the deeps of the Trench of Rodiles, and we shall celebrate the gathering of the final prize. We shall surely anoint you as Champion of Milesia", Scota's heart filled with pride as she embraced Amergin once more.

Amergin walked through the woods surrounding this palacial residence. The ancient woodlands with moss covered boulders, reminded him of his dreams, if that is what they were, where he became immersed in a green world, with slanting silver rays penetrating the deep shadows. He expected to meet his dreamlike queen at any time. His heart beat furiously and his mind raced. His stride lengthened, emboldened by a sense of destiny, his mother's path, his own path... merging into oneness.

He felt the ancients guiding him... He was living the prophecy... He knew he was the destined one...

The day dawned on the final challenge of the ordeal. Once more the princes met on the edge of the ocean, the challenge to dive to the lung-bursting limits of their endurance, the prize, the deep water oyster of Rodiles, a delicacy that had cost the life of many an adventuring waterman. Not only legendary for its size and flavor, but also the libido enhancing qualities, the ultimate gift of a suitor to their loved one. Very rarely, the Rodiles oyster will serve up a pearl of extraordinary quality, luminosity and brilliance. A pearl said to have otherworldly powers, a symbol of complete purity, bestowing the power of clairvoyance on the owner.

The three plunged in, arcing in a common trajectory, piercing the blue-green water, gliding with momentum into the serene depths. The Trench dropped away before them, deep and mysterious. The light struggled to penetrate in these nutrient rich waters.

All three exhaled as one, lungs emptying, buoyancy decreasing, stroking onwards and downwards.

 Bubbles of exploding air burst to the surface, all the onlookers aware of the ticking time.

Scouring the seabed for the tell-tale white brilliance of the mother of pearl, Eiremhou struck lucky, prising the oyster from its rocky womb, pushed off the sea-bed, and glided up to the light.

Eimbear next, he pushed Amergin out of the way as he grabbed an oyster shell. The Machiavellian streak showing, he hoped his brother would return empty handed, the ordeal unresolved. Amergin was disturbed by his brothers actions. Where did that come from? No time to dwell, his lungs bursting, he could see the prize...

Eiremhou surfaced first, thrusting the shell to the skies. All those gathered on the ocean's edge, roared in approval. Soon Eimbear burst triumphantly to the surface. All awaited Amergin...

Seconds passed, then a few more. Amergin with the prize, and he would be champion...

Seconds or was it minutes? The crowd moved restlessly. Was that a grimace or smile on Eimbear's face?

Deep below, Amergin was entering a state of narcosis. Every sinew and corpuscle strained to tear the shell from its limpet grip. A vision flashed before him... long golden tresses and an amber cosmos enveloped him. "Amergin, I am waiting..."

The shell broke free, and he pushed off the sea bed. He seemed to be taken with the current, unseen forces guiding him and coaxing to the surface. He thrust upwards, the shell broke the surface, but he hardly had the strength to find the surface himself. Eiremhou sensed the danger and swam over, just as Amergin surfaced his face in contortion and agony. "I have the prize!" he screamed with a deep intake of oxygen.

He looked over to Eiremhou and smiled, "Thank you brother!" The onlooking crowd roared and cheered. Scota and Milidh held each other in a tight embrace. The royal entourage began chanting and dancing. The tribes of Milesia were exultant drumming there celebratory beat across the land.

Amergin swam to the shore with his prize, his brother Eiremhou swimming by his side. Amergin looked up to see Eimbear in the company of Gonne. That deep seated sense of unease came over him once more...

Milidh took Amergin's hand and hauled him on to dry land. In one movement he stepped on to land and thrust the prize in to the air. The onlooking crowd erupted again, and as one started chanting his name "Amergin! Amergin! Amergin..!"

Scota grabbed him and kissed him on the cheek, "You were always destined for greatness Amergin." She hugged and embraced him, "Milesia will follow you to the new world."

Amergin presented the prize oyster to her, and she quickly and skilfully used her royal knife to open this majestic shell. She gasped! Before her was the rare, luminous, white brilliance of a pearl of Rodiles.

The legendary pearl giving the owner powers of clairvoyance. She in turn presented the pearl to Amergin. "You and only you will understand the powers of this pearl. Use it wisely in the journey to come. You are blessed with the purity of heart and spirit. Follow the path before you."

Gonne, the high priest of the Chapter of Mystics, walked over to Amergin. Instinctively Amergin hid the pure white pearl. Gonne stretched out his hand to offer Amergin an engraved crystal amulet on a gold chain, as witness to the warrior prince becoming the honorary leader and head druid of the Chapter of Mystics.

Amergin looked down at the pearl. In the presence of Gonne, a strange transformation occurred. A dark swirling cloud of pigment appeared in the pure white brilliance...

The physical challenges of the ordeal completed and overcome. Now the champion must expose his soul and connect with the spirit world. The true champion of Milesia will endure, will be enriched, and granted otherworldly powers. Any weakness, any flaw, could mean the losing of your mind, the closing of the third eye, and the connection with the Great Spirit severed.

Gonne spoke to Amergin before he embarked on this final spiritual challenge, "The ancients have sent visions to the Chapter of Mystics of a powerful leader, imbued with the magical forces required for the fulfilment of the prophecy. You must have complete faith and belief in your abilities and your destiny Amergin. Should you falter, show any weakness, then you will be seen as an imposter. Then the route to the Promised Land will be closed forever. The prophecy ended."

Amergin acknowledged the warnings, strange to have come from such a person as Gonne...

The procession of the Chapter of Mystics, led by Gonne, took Amergin deep into the ancient woods.

Amergin again found himself in this green mysterious landscape. Warped and twisted yew trees rooted in strangely sculpted limestone formations. Each outcrop covered in a deep carpet of all consuming moss. A winding path took them further and further into the dense, verdant woodland. Shafts of guiding sunlight showed the way, penetrating the canopy, taking them deeper and deeper, the sound of birdlife now quietening as they went into denser and denser ancient woods.

They finally arrived at the Pool of Cerces, a deep black body of fresh water, the surface of the water like a mirror reflecting the surrounding trees, trunks and branches. The mystics lined the edge of the pool.

Amergin stood on a limestone outcrop that gave him an aspect straight to the depths of this mysterious portal to the otherworld. Legend has it that such portals are connected in a web of earthly and divine dimensions.

The powers bestowed on the destined one by communing with the spirit world through the deep waters of the Pool of Cerces will enable the prophecy to be fulfilled.

Used incorrectly the Pool of Cerces will channel the dark forces through the veil. Milesia will be overwhelmed and inundated.

The ceremony began, orchestrated by Gonne. Amergin looked across the reflective expanse of the pool.

The mystics chanted ancient sacred verse. Each chorus drew his gaze deeper into the pool. He felt his very life force being drawn into the watery portal.

Amergin understood the nature of this challenge. He allowed his energy to be drawn deeper and deeper into the Pool of Cerces. The reflective surface represented the veil. Beyond this he would be communicating with the spirit world, gaining insight for the coming journey. He needed to feel synergy with the forces beyond the veil, and sense acceptance.

All he could sense was his his life force inexorably draining away, pouring into the vortex of the dark pool.

He remembered Scota's words, "All is not what it seems."He realised he was being tested, a test of his ability and suitability as a champion of the Milesians.

He knew he had to surrender to the spirit world, to commune.

He was disturbed again by a sense of malevolence. The echoing words, "Be careful on your journey!", resounded in his consciousness.

Momentarily, he resisted and questioned the process, spiritually raising himself above the veil of the pool's surface. Amergin became lucid, clarity swept over him like a cold torrent. Across the pool a shadowy figure seemed to orchestrate the sacred ceremony. Gonne was influencing the flow of energy, using his mystical powers to invite the dark forces from deep within the pool.

Amergin knew he had to resist, and counter Gonne's influence.

He summoned all his inner strength and resilience, calling the Great Spirit for help.

He prayed for a peaceful intervention.

This time he drifted gently into the vortex, falling into an amber cosmos that seemed familiar to him. The spirits were guiding him, coaxing him, nurturing him and accepting him… the malevolence had gone. For now at least…

A searing white light and then hallucinogenic visions, thoughts, words and images filled his senses.

He was being shown the way…

The spirits were gracefully accepting his presence, sharing their powers, blessing him with magical gifts.

Amergin knew he was in the presence of the Divine, the Divine in nature.

Gradually, he rose to the mirrored surface of the black pool…

He felt golden tresses releasing him, and gentle finger tips caressing him as he broke through the veil…

"I am waiting for you Amergin. Be careful my love…"

CHAPTER THREE:
THE ALIGNMENT

These are poignant, mindfull times, a significant and symbolic era.

The mystics studied the darkening skies as the full moon rose over the Northern Ocean.

"Is this the time for the prophecy to be revealed?"

The ancients have foretold of this moment. The signs are in alignment. The warrior prince chosen... the champion elected... the druid Amergin anointed...

The nation is in a state of readiness, prepared for the great journey ahead. The challenges of the unknown await them...

The tribes of Milesia are gathered around the Tower of Galicia.

The royal family and the mystics are gathered and stare transfixed from atop the Tower of Galicia.

Will the astrologers and astronomers, the seers and the sages, be right in their predictions?

Will the secrets of the cosmos be unveiled?

Milidh turned to Scota, "Never has our nation been so close, never have the revelations of the prophecy been so tantalisingly near!"

Scota smiled knowingly at her king. His profile silhouetted against the diminishing, waning light. She sensed this was the time, her body charged with electric excitement and anticipation.

Amergin stood proudly next to Scota. Silently, patiently, they stood staring into distant space.

The full moon cast its golden glow, low over the horizon, a shimmering path of light on the ocean cascading its aura over the expectant masses. The moon climbed higher into the Northern aspect, gold turning to a starker silvery-white light.

There was a collective gasp! A black shadow bit into the moon. A quiet murmur of astonishment swept like a rushing wave over the awe struck crowd. A steady crescendo of noise built and the tempo increased. The eclipsing shadow crept across the face of the moon. Amergin felt his pulse racing. The long awaited alignment. The signs of the prophecy were upon them.

He felt his mother's hand grip his. Neither could take their eyes off this magical, natural spectacle.

He heard his father yell in approval and encouragement, urging the eclipse on and on...

Eiremhou and Eimbear simultaneously turned to each other. They studied the reaction of their younger brother. They saw Amergin reaching out to try to touch the moon and the eclipse.

He was visibly strengthened and empowered by the alignment, the energy of the moment and of the cosmos surged through his very being. Amergin's countenance and posture were uplifted, elevated and energised by the eclipse.

This was his moment, and his nations...

In the diminishing light of the ever waning moon they witnessed a strange phenomenon from the northern horizon. An aurora borealis warping, pouring, merging spectral colours, strange wrapping, permeating light fell over the awaiting throng. Gonne and his Chapter of Mystics recognised the aura of the Sidhe, and fell to their knees in unison. They collectively meditated as though communing with an all embracing power. They were all aware of the fine balance, the delicate equilibrium, the shifting veil.

There was a need for harmony, the need for real communication with the other world. The Mystics knew these forces had to be placated and humoured, or else they will never be contained.

At the time of full eclipse, at full dark, at full shadow, it was said the veil was at its thinnest and vulnerable to penetration and malevolent intrusion.

Amergin now became the conduit. He stood strong. Powers were shifting through the veil in both directions. He became the fulcrum. He was the portal. If the powers of the Sidhe felt weakness, and the wrong choice of champion, then the tribes of Milesia could be overwhelmed.

As totality fell, Amergin sensed his powers were being tested to the limit. He felt the forces of the dark and light whirling in the vortex of the eclipse. He sensed a malign influence was trying to deflect and defy his efforts. The dark at its fullness, he prayed to the Great Spirit for assistance.

Gonne fell to his knees, visibly weakened and drained. Amergin knew the first encounter of the legendary journey had begun. Gonne was to be a powerful adversary in the mortal realm.

The austere and stark white-silver light of the waxing moon now felt comforting. The strange light of the aurora had receded. The sense of enlightened spirituality restored, Amergin called his loyal followers together. The Chapter of Mystics, the tribal elders, his royal siblings all gathered on the edge of the Pool of Cerces. Plans for the great journey were made. The gathering prepared themselves... they were the children of the prophecy, much depended on them...

Amergin walked alone through the woods, on his way to the Temple of Japhet. He drew inspiration from nature. He had the ability to commune with the Divine in nature, and to tap into the reality of the world around him. The trees were in their full verdant glory, lush green, resplendent in the summer light. The morning and night time mists pouring in from the ocean, cooled and condensed, watering the ancient woodlands. the twisted and magical forms of sacred yew trees. The sky-touching evergreen forms of the centuries old pines. A deciduous wonderland colonised in copses by opportunistic conifers. The roaring, rustling leaf canopy, the gentle swaying and swishing of the rushes, tinkling streams flowed fresh and clear into the ever-stretching lakes and pools, interspersed with the distant thunderous booming of the Northern Ocean.Nature's choir, a symphony on earth, clearing his mind, cleansing his body. Amergin needed true clarity. As a true diviner he would seek out the portals to the spirit world. His mind, body and soul felt in tune. As he walked he sensed a deeper knowledge, a spiritual wisdom. He began to sense the way forward.

He arrived at the Temple of Japhet and spent long hours into the night, praying and meditating.

Once more he felt he was being irresistibly drawn by a beautiful enlightened being, drawn beyond the veil, drawn across the Northern Ocean...

The following morning he scaled the heights of the Tower of Galicia and scanned the horizon.

Amergin prayed to the Great Spirit, and gave thanks, "I know the way! I am ready!"

Scota arrived at the tower. She too knew her son was ready. She and her husband would follow Amergin on his destined journey. She summoned her messengers, "Go tell the fleet to make ready. We sail tomorrow!"

Amergin and Scota sat in quiet contemplation. She had full confidence in the wisdom and resourcefulness of her son, but the unknown dangers worried her.

There was a clamour of activity at the Port of Jaisur. There seemed to be an innate sense of what to do, of what to prepare. The waiting over, all went about their duties in earnest, without questioning.

Amergin was heartened by his peoples unity, he had delegated well. The tribal elders took charge of the provisions. His royal siblings marshalled the manpower, ensuring the best crew and captain for each vessel in the assembled flotilla. Each crew member was provided with clothing suitable for the vagaries of ocean sailing. Waterproof layers, clothing for the warm latitudes, as well as for the cooling weather of the Northern Ocean.

Every man a mariner to the core and all highly trained in battle skills. An awesome fighting force was being assembled. Weaponry of all types, iron and bronze spears and swords, finely tuned cross-bows, plated armour. Each vessel was geared up with boarding and siege machinery.

Milidh gathered all the captains and the officer class for a final strategic, motivational talk. He wanted his leaders to be under no illusion as to the immensity of this challenge and the dangers confronting them.

Scota gathered the all female Xantha, a fiercesome, highly trained group of warriors with a legendary reputation. Scota is their spiritual as well as military leader. With finely tuned and honed fighting skills, each of the Xantha has been personally groomed by Scota in the magical arts. Their skills of premonition will be the key to sensing and pre-empting any infiltration. Scota knows that the Sidhe are steeped in the black arts. She is only too aware Amergin will need all the support he can muster when confronting them.

Amergin climbed the Tower of Galicia for the last time. He had just left the gathering of the Chapter of Mystics. They blessed the fleet for the forthcoming sojourn. Still he felt the unease. He needed to find clarity. He had to have the Chapter of Mystics on his side to succeed in his mission. He knew the high priest Gonne had already been infiltrated.

He climbed higher up the tower, and as he arrived at the top and surveyed the far distant northern horizon… Was that mist? In a deep rich amber haze, he saw, or was he imagining he saw, a slowly, serenely, beckoning form of a hand. And from the ether, a sensual voice, "Come Amergin, come…"

Amergin stoked the fiery beacon atop the Tower of Galicia for the last time. The flame would endure until sunrise the following morning. At that time the fleet would embark on its perilous journey.

The Milesian tribes would leave the Galician shores potentially for the last time.

Amergin returned to the flagship of the flotilla. In his well equipped master's chamber, he summoned his officers. Each captain on each vessel did the same. Navigators were briefed, and all the officers reminded of their duty.

On the sound of a mighty resonating conch, Amergin, his fellow captains, the crews, and all the tribes of Milesia turned to the still blazing beacon on the Tower of Galicia. Milidh, Scota and the Chapter of Mystics knelt in homage to the Great Spirit as they chanted their prayers. All of Milesia fell to their knees as one, "O Great Spirit we beseech thee, grant us the strength to endure, to find the true way, and fulfill the prophecy…"

Later that night, Amergin slept fitfully. The journey, the perils of the ocean, the shifting veil of the spirit world, flashing visions of beauty, Sceine wrapped in swirling amber mists, the promised lands of the prophecy, and there in the darker shadows of his dreams, an apparition of Gonne. Always the dream ends in the swirling rich amber vortex. He is drawn deeper and deeper…

The deep resonating sound of the conch, blown by one of the mystics signifies dawn. Amergin jolts upright, "This is the day of the dawning of the prophecy!" he internalised. With a deep sense of an adventure just beginning, he surfaced on deck, and with poignancy and synchronicity, the breaking morning sunlight washed over the Tower of Galicia. Within minutes the beacon was extinguished, the fuel gone, the adventure had begun. The sojourn, the great journey was upon them…

A creaking of the dry, salted, ropes and timbers, a ruffling of sails, as sheets were tied and mooring lines released. A shifting of the boom as the first gust filled the mainsail, and the tiller turned with the prow pointing seaward.

"Magnificent!" exhorted Amergin aloud. Gracefully the flagship began to glide out through the mirrored sea. Each harboured vessel in turn began to release from their moorings. Poignantly each prow pointed to the Northern horizon.

The fleet, a hundred strong, tacked en masse and soon they reached the harbour entrance, the Port of Jaisur resplendent in the warming sun.

Each thirty strong crew, on board each vessel, turned to see loved ones waving them farewell, waving them onwards to the promised-land, to the island of destiny. Exhilarated, happy and honoured to be on such a journey, but deeply saddened to be leaving their loved ones. Tears of joy and sadness welled up in their eyes, their hearts bursting with excitement, but breaking with heartache, joyful anticipation with underlying anxiety of the unknown.

The open sea soon rallied their thoughts and emotions to the task at hand, the first strong windward tack into the freshening westerly ocean breeze. The vessels leaned into the tack, the Port of Jaisur, the Temple of Japhet and the Tower of Galicia steadily disappearing into the distance.

Like a well oiled machine, the fleet manned by a race of mariners, danced synchronicitously between the dipping and rising wavelengths of the deep ocean swell. The weather and sea gods were smiling on the mariners of Milesia that day. The portents were good. Amergin smiled and shouted encouragement to his crew.

Once away from the familiar landmarks, Amergin took charge of the tiller. He knew the way. He would navigate by his instincts and senses, following the path of the sun, the wind and the flow of the currents and tides. The coordinates of the lunar eclipse had been marked on astral and planetary charts descended from Tolemei and the ancient astronomers. Occasionally he would consult with one of the mystics onboard the vessel, and look to strengthen his spiritual guidance by referring to the tomes "Biblios" and "Spirituu" and theological references to their place in the cosmos. Always there would be a representative of the Xantha on deck and one of the Chapter of Mystics. Between them, Amergin hypothesized, they would provide guidance and an early warning of any changes and shifts in the otherworldly veil. Changes and shifts that will present real danger to the fleet...

A pod of white-sided dolphin surfaced, danced and leapt in the bow wake of the flagship, the lowering afternoon sun sending rainbows in the spray of each cresting wave. At the last hour of daylight Amergin took out the astral charts, and with each flash of a mirror sent out coordinates to the next vessel.

He watched as the message flashed down the line of the fleet, now spread majestically to the southern horizon.

He envisaged each captain, Milidh, Scota, Eiremhou and Eimbear receiving and acknowledging the signal, setting their course by the charts and the first flickering stars and planets appearing in the darkening skies. As the sun finally extinguished over the north-western horizon, a gust of wind came unexpectedly from the south-west. Each of the vessels of the fleet leaned away from the gust, their white-cream sails of elegant Phoenician design flexing, now tinged with the roseate palette of the setting sun.

The pink, red and orange hues fringing the white fingers of cloud caressing the horizon were now showing indigos and violets as dusk approached. A tell-tale band of mackerel flashed, white, stratospheric clouds moved quickeningly towards them, and beyond a darkening shadow crawled ominously into the skyscape.

Xomas, the diligent and faithful first officer was justifiably concerned. They and the fleet were heading into the night with potentially the first storm of the journey approaching fast. "We need to be fully prepared", he urgently advised Amergin, "the strength of the storm is unknown…"

Afiente, the mystic resident on board the flagship, concurred with Xomas. Amergin sensed this mystic was of good heart and spirit, unlike his high priest Gonne. Accordingly, Amergin instructed Xomas to light the warning beacon sending word to the fleet of the impending storm. Each captain on each vessel had sensed the change. They were all only too aware that they were facing the fury of mother-nature.

However, Amergin was disturbed by Afiente's final comment, "You need to be wary my Lord, that this oncoming storm may be used as a veil to conceal even darker, greater, and more sinister powers of the Sidhe."

Lolling, rolling, gliding, cresting and riding each wave moving from West to East, sailing ahead of the chasing storm. The wind was strengthening from the south-west, pushing the entire fleet onwards to the unknown.

Dark has descended. The moon seems to hurtle through the scurrying clouds. Stark silver-white moonlight catches the surging, cresting and sometimes breaking waves. Silver-white horses appear across the now turbulent ocean. The sleek white-sailed vessels tip and twist with each ever strengthening gust and building swell.

Amergin, and his first officer Xomas, stand braced and now lashed to the tiller. With each surging swell, they line the bow up and surf from crest to trough. The storm rigging now in place, the fair weather sails furled. The crew sent below for safety. Amergin and Xomas stay with the tiller. This will be a long night, concentration of the essence, one lapse and the ship could be broadsided and lost.

The sea and tide are running high. Monstrous squalls appear as black walls in the moonlight. They arrive with venomous force, sheer through and are gone into the distance. Xomas keeps an anxious weather eye on the south -west horizon. Amergin grips and hangs on to the tiller for dear life.

Suddenly a strange lull befalls the fleet. Terese of the Xantha came up on deck. Xomas studied her as she swayed over to the tiller to discourse with Amergin. A proud, athletic beauty, a warrior to the core, her usual calm exterior was now flustered and anxious. A member of the fearless and fiercesome Xantha, she now appeared scared. She urgently confided with Amergin, as he continued to fight with the cresting waves. "My Lord, I have sensed a shift in the veil, the dark forces of the Sidhe are breaking through under the mask of the storm!"Her voice carried with the now screaming wind. Amergin caught the occasional word, but the message was brutally clear. As Amergin turned to relay the warning to Xomas, Terese shouted the alarm, "On the south-western horizon! Look!! They come!!!"

Now they all looked. A black wall on the south-western horizon, a dark shadow extended to the ocean.

The horizon was moving!! Amergin too sensed the dark forces of the Sidhe at work.

Amergin instinctively lit the distress/warning beacon at the stern of the vessel, and instructed Xomas to get the crew to lash everything down and batten the hatches.

The entire fleet were warned and braced for danger. All the captains of the fleet, Scota and Milidh, the royal princes, knew they were in danger. They saw the oncoming squall even in the blackness, as the moon broke the cloud cover. They also saw the swirling, heightening, body of dark silver moving as one with the ocean. They collectively knew that this was no natural event.

Each vessel turned to face the squall and an immense raging rogue wave. All rigging was stripped and everyone bar the essential crew sent below. All hatches and portholes were tightly secured.

The captains and first officers were lashed to each tiller. They were in survival mode. The lives of all depended on their ability to keep straight on to this tsunami like wave.

Amergin gripped Xomas's arm and looked into his worried eyes, "Be brave Xomas, we must call on our innermost strength. and pray to the great spirit for our salvation. We are not alone!"

The vessels stripped down and everything secure, strengthening gusts of hurricane force started to tear in.

Amergin and Xomas bent low into the storm force conditions. The flagship lined up to take the brunt of the storm on. They would be the first to take the wave on. Amergin resolved not to release the tiller as long as there was a breath of life in him. At the last moment he lashed the tiller into position. The prow, the tiller, the keel must be in line as they push up the face of the rearing aqueous monster.

Onwards, surging, gathering, rearing, five times mast height, the rogue wave came...

It seemed to be a living entity, intent on their demise. The flagship climbed and climbed, lined up, prow pointing skywards. If the wave crested they were gone. Amergin shouted above the tempest, "Great Spirit save us!!!" To the heavens they rose. Up and up, Crashing, breaking, roaring.Timbers straining, the vessel flexing, they punched through, piercing the lip of the wave. Tons of thunderous water and foam washed through, the deck awash. Amergin and Xomas, still braced and lashed, kept the tiller steady.Straining every sinew and muscle.White with effort and strain.

The ship finally fell into the turbulence of the trough. Amergin quickly unlashed the tiller and took control, ready for the swirling aftermath of the watery behemoth.

Amergin watched as the tempestuous squall and the silver black wall of water went crashing on. This was something demonic and unnatural. He knew that the elements were being ushered and conjured by unseen forces, against the Milesian fleet. He prayed for the rest of the fleet, as one by one each vessel rode out the storm front. Massive waves still followed the first monster. The eye of the storm still seemed to be gathering, a malevolent force cutting a swathe through the fleet. The next ship punched through the near cresting lip. Fortitude was required. The royal vessels made it through, Scota, Milidh, Eiremhou and Eimbear all unscathed so far.Far away on the South West horizon, a glimmer of hope, a chink of light, the back of the storm front.

Amergin kept praying. One more boat appeared over the back of the monster wave, one more to safety.

He'd lost count now, how many had made it? How many of the fleet had got to safety? At that moment he saw the wave rear up, drawn up to the blackness above, the final act of their evil tormentors.The storm and the Sidhe in conjunction, the wave and the squall in full collusion.

Oceans of water pitched and crested, a tumbling furious waterfall consumed two of the vessels of the fleet. Nothing they could do. The wave swept them over broadsides, pitching and rolling. Masts snapped, they rolled again, and were pushed deep into the wave, and were sunk, disappearing without a trace.

Only later did objects and remains start to surface. Not a person was found. No survivors. No bodies.No one. It was as if they were taken from this world. Consumed, buried in a watery grave. A frightening and foreboding thought flashed through Amergin's mind. He was reminded, how as a young prince and contender for the Milesian champion, he was warned by the Chapter of Mystics, that the wrong choice, a wrong move, would permit the Sidhe to take lives away. The Sidhe would then possess and own these unfortunates. These lost souls would then turn against their own, a fate worse than death…

Amergin prayed for their souls…

In the quiet, as the rolling storm, with its dark vortex of weather and waves, dissipated and subdued, the crews on all the surviving vessels came tentatively up on to deck. Blinking and scanning around like frightened prey after the predator had gone. The dark of the night now lifted, penetrated by the everlightening dawn. Xomas, Terese and Amergin stood in shocked silence, knowing they had been in the presence of dark and threatening forces, and survived. Others had not…"The Others" as they became to be known were destined for an eternal soul-less existence in limbo.

The wind gradually eased, and soon the warming light of morning wrapped comfortingly around the fleet. Amergin instructed Xomas to contact each vessel by the signalling mirror and say, "I am Amergin, your Druid of the Sea, your champion and warrior-prince. You have been brave, you have survived this ordeal. The journey continues. We have endured the dark tempest. The Great Spirit has given us the strength and the wisdom to survive. Today we will pray for the lost lives and souls of our fellow Milesians, we have been tested, and we have endured. We must give thanks to the Great Spirit. Our hearts and our spirits must be as one. We must unite on this our greatest journey."

The captains on the surviving vessels replied in return, each swearing allegiance to Amergin and the cause.

The ocean settled into a rhythmic, relaxing swell once more. The prevailing Westerly winds filled the now re-rigged sails. Amergin took the helm and sailed on, leading the fleet onwards to the Northern horizon. The warming sun and fresh breeze gladdening his heart, restoring his tested but unwavering faith.

He ordered the crew to bait and cast the long-lines. He prepared to have a feast this evening to bolster the spirits of all. The first of many yellow finned tuna took the bait and were soon hauled in.

All the vessels fished for the feast that night. "Xomas break out the pitchers of Xanthia, the liqueur from the sacred groves of Galicia! We will feast and toast to the Great Spirit. From adversity, our faith will be strengthened. Tell all the crews to feast, give thanks and to unite as one nation!"

A clear midnight sky stretched to infinity. Constellations revolved in their majesty around the one constant, Polaris, the Northern star. Amergin gazed to the distant heavenly void, the white, misty, creamy, dreamlike, swathe of the stars and planets of the galactic edge, a myriad of stars, more numerous than the grains of sand on the now distant Galician beaches. Stars twinkling in the high atmosphere, some pink, some blue, some reflecting the light from the shimmering ocean.

Replete with a plentiful feast, Tuna fresh from the long lines, the ceremonial liqueur washed down with the fresh Tuna blood.The Great Spirit toasted, the singing and chanting of the crew drifting over the now lulling ocean. Amergin sipped the sacred liqueur and rested on the mattress of coiled rigging and rope at the stern of the ship. Sipping, savouring and still focusing on the Northern Star, constant in the slowly rotating universe. The sky dark, the moon still not risen, slowly sipping, the hypnotic lilting motion of the deep ocean, he slipped in and out of wakefulness and consciousness.

From the deep recesses of the distant cosmic void, a feathering frond like finger of white gaseous elements. A pulse of plasma sent and shot, spurting through the heavens.The pulse wrapped around the Northern Star and warped straight towards Amergin. A vision surrounded him. A voice permeated his being, "Look for Jascinthus, the great Blue Whale. Watch for his giant blow over the morning horizon! This will be your guide. Do not be deceived by false mirages sent by the Sidhe. The Blue Whale will be your guide until the moon is full once more."

The pulsing plasma warped and gathered overhead, the risen new moon, in a spectrum of white silver to rich amber. He felt the plasma surround and wrap around his dreaming and gently inebriated body and mind. Again he felt his heart being massaged. His mind overcome, he sensed great ecstacy and joy.

"Amergin, I am with you my love…"

A vision of great beauty… and he was awake…

Sceine was waiting for him. He saw the Island of Destiny in his dreams. She was leading him to the promised land of the prophecy. She was guiding him. They must be watchful…

CHAPTER FOUR:
WRECKERS OF THE DARK

"There! A giant blow on the northern horizon! That is the way!" Amergin hurriedly took the tiller from Xomas and guided the flagship in that direction. On cue this magnificent creature of the ocean breached. No mistake now. An explosion of spray as the sea once again consumed the whale.

Amergin turned to Xomas "This is truly a monster of an animal, larger and heavier than this vessel, we must follow until the moon is full in the sky. We have been sent a guide."

With each arching graceful motion, the Blue Whale sped onward, occasionally diving deep and signalling with the massive fluking tale. Fortunately, a freshening southerly wind filled the fair weather rigging on the vessel and they sped onward, in harmony with the giant blue cetacean.

Behind them, the fleet stretched out in a long curving formation. Amergin mirror-signalled to each of the vessels, soon all of the fleet were made aware of his intentions.

Day followed day, on and on, further into the limitless blue ocean. Immense distances were covered each day. The southerly wind blew strong and sure. Their guide, the Blue whale, took them into the unknown.

The moon would be full that night. Amergin took readings on the astral chart, as the darkness fell.

How much further would the great whale take them? The answer would soon be given...

After days of sure and constant sailing, the friendly southerly wind dropped out and calm befell the fleet. The giant whale was to be seen no more. All the watchmen on each vessel scanned and scoured the horizon for the tell-tale blow, or a fluking tail. Nothing...

Somewhere down the line of the fleet was heard an anxious cry, "To the east! Look to the east!"

From the darkening eastern horizon over the now becalmed and glass like ocean, came a white rolling, dense bank of sea fog. One by one each vessel disappeared into the smothering, eerie, blanket of humid, dank, lightless, all pervading sea fog. Each watchman sounded a periodic blast of a conch to let each other know of their whereabouts.

The sound of the conch bellowed out into the mist. Strangely muffled but echoing and resonating.

Amergin and Xomas checked with the watchmen, perched high on the cross spars, "Any signs out there, any signs to show us the way?"

"Only the sounds of the conches from the rest of the fleet my Lord", they responded, "Nothing else, no wind, no light, no ocean sounds, nothing but stillness, nothing to give us our bearings."

In the eeriness they waited, floated and drifted. No direction, no signs. Amergin had heard of the vast fog banks that can sit in quiet isolation for weeks, becalming mariners for weeks at a time.

The days went by, just the sound of the conches, and the occasional cry out from a nearby vessel, as if the crew needed comfort in the knowledge that they were not alone.

The frustration of no movement, not a breath in the rigging, no point of reference, imagined or real, soon turned into despair. The ancient mariner's tales circulated around the crew, tales of doldrum madness, strange imaginings, creatures of the mind and deep-ocean taking over reality.

Amergin went below deck to converse with the representative of the Chapter of Mystics, Gyon. He requested that Terese of the Xantha join them. They all agreed that this mysteriously eery phenomenon was not entirely natural. They must be on their guard. Malevolent forces could intrude into weakened minds. Confusion, havoc and irrational thoughts and actions are their enemy now...

Amergin trusted Gyon, but he needed Terese to reassure him that he was getting pure, honest advice.

Gonne however, the high priest of the Chapter of Mystics, he did not trust. Amergin knew there was evil at work there. Amergin asked Terese to watch him, to use her telepathic skills to keep guard over him, to forewarn him of any malevolence at work...

Deep in the gunnels of Milidh's vessel, the head priest of the Chapter of Mystics, Gonne, sat in deep meditation, chanting ancient verse. He was surely descending into the deepest of trances, and was calling on the spirit world, calling on the dark Sidhe to come forth.

Throwing runes into the pentogram etched into the decking of the vessel, a dark indigo colouration, and shapes formed above. Gonne collapsed in a shamanic trance, losing consciousness, his job done.

The dark Sidhe was summoned. They were emerging through the veil...

Scota stood on the prow of their vessel, next to Milidh. Suddenly her senses were jolted.

Danger was coming! Milidh her royal soulmate saw her demeanour change, her pallor whitening. He gripped her hand, and knowingly told all the watchmen to be ready, to be alert.The forlorn sounds of the conch still resonating. No sign yet of the brewing danger.

Drifting ever onwards. Still no break in the dense fog bank, still no breath of wind in the sails, still no ocean sounds. Just the mournful resounding conch...

Terese went to Amergin, she too was aware of the threat, she felt Gonne's evil intent. She warned Amergin of the imminent threat... Amergin went to Xomas at the tiller. He took charge and once more braced himself.

Unbeknownst to the captains of each vessel in the Milesian fleet, an ocean drift began to steadily separate the vessels. Imperceptibly the resonating sounds of the conches changed as the distance between the vessels grew. The vessels at the tail of the fleet were being drawn to the East.

A watchman cried out unto the fog. Was that a light yonder?! An occasional flickering, then a flash and then in the distance the sound of booming surf!

There was no warning! They had no control, the strengthening drift, a current from nowhere!

The vessels at the tail of the fleet were caught, trapped, being drawn to their doom.

The captains of three vessels sensed the danger. They panicked! They turned towards the flashing light. Surely a warning sign, the light again! In unison they turned their tillers.

They turned their vessels looking for an escape, but in reality they turned directly on to the reef. Wreckers! Timbers creaked, cracked and snapped. A deception, they rolled, they were immersed, and were sunk. Desperate cries of drowning crew, sounding ship bells, and the conch resonating, and now smothered in a roar and boom of crashing surf. Three ships sent to their doom by wreckers of the dark Sidhe, lost without trace!

The rest of the fleet could only hold their course, relying on the sounding conches resonating in the eeriness of the fog bank.

Tears of despair ran down Scota's face. She did not know who had perished, maybe one of her own sons? How many lives had been taken? She understood that this was no natural threat. Experienced mariners had been tricked, deceived, and sentenced to death by the Sidhe, and they were helpless. She fell to her knees and prayed for salvation, prayed for a break in this foul denseness, prayed for a breeze to cleanse the ocean and this demonic fog bank.

Scota ordered the watchmen to keep chiming the ship's bell, and sounding the conch, warning the others that there was still danger while the fog lingered.

Each ship had its own distinctive bell, its own distinctive sounding conch. Amergin recognised the cadence and resonance of Scota and Milidh's vessel. He too knew that the danger continued while the malevolent mist persisted. No one knew which of the vessels perished on a reef they hadn't even seen.

He cried out into the denseness, "Help us Great Spirit. Bring us clear of this malevolence."He too fell to his knees and prayed. All of his crew followed suit. Xomas, Terese, the watchmen, Gyon, the whole crew fell to their knees. They all wanted freedom and to be released from this peril.

"I hear you Amergin…", and into the mist came a rich amber hue, moving mysteriously, wrapping around their senses. Amergin looked upwards, the mist swirled gently at first, then with a steady rhythmic beating, started to clear. Was that doldrum madness? Did he see an enormous, pure white swan beating powerful wings, fanning the fog away?

A glimpse of another vessel in the near distance, and their spirits rose in unison. Their sails were filling, and with another strong downward beat the mist cleared. The fleet came into view, the rigging straining in a strengthening breeze. The clearance! Amergin was blinded by a shaft of low slanting sunlight.

The vision was gone, the mist had cleared, and the ocean had come to life. Amergin stared to the heavens. He filled his heaving chest with freshening oceanic air. He yelled for all his crew and the rest of the fleet to hear, "Thank you Great Spirit, thank you!"

Mirrors flashed the reflected light of the day around the fleet. They were gathering to assess their losses and grieve the lost souls. Amergin stood high on top of the prow, beckoning his people to come to him.

Gyon, of the Chapter of Mystics blew the conch long and resonantly. They were gathering to be together, to raise spirits and to lay out a plan for the continuing sojourn.

One by one, ropes were thrown from ship to ship, reed mats between each hull to give protection from the buffeting of the low southerly swell. The fleet would drift in unison for a few days, while the wind blew gently, but steadily on course.

Milidh and Scota's vessel pulled up tight, a makeshift walkway on to Amergin's vessel. He lashed the walkway tight and grabbed his father's hand as he came on board. Embracing him, "Father, it is good to be together. We must make ready for the stormbound, cooler latitudes!"Scota stepped on board next, smiling uncontrollably, her beauty shining through, "My son, we have been tested, but we prevail and are strengthened! I am sure you have felt the forces battling to overcome us."Amergin embraced her tightly and lovingly, gently kissing her cheek. Scota's wisdom will be essential when confronting the otherworldly spirits.

The next vessel tied alongside, and the next, and the next. Eiremhou strode purposefully over, giving a strong brotherly hug, "Brother we fight another day!"Amergin held him tight, "Brother, we fight many other days!" Eimbear's vessel was already tied up, but no sign of him. Amergin's brow started to furrow with anxiety. There! Eimbear was assisted to the deck by two crewmen. He was injured. Amergin greeted his compromised brother, "Eimbear how!?"

"The storm, my brother, I was lashed to the tiller.Teimo saved me from the great wave. "Amergin had mixed emotions, relieved that his brother was safe, but Eimbear's trust was in doubt.

A giant raft drifted northwards. Tied, lashed and bound, side to side, prow to stern, the fleet of Milesia together, symbolically and spiritually. From the prow of the ship, Amergin conducted a memorial service for the souls lost at sea. Drifting and communing in silence, all bowed their heads, bitter sweet emotions, survival, but at what cost? Martyred for the cause … all in the name of the prophecy…

Gonne, the head priest of the Chapter of Mystics, lit incense and chanted ancient incantations for the martyred souls. Amergin felt his hackles rising… Where was Gonne sending those lost souls to?

Scota sensed it too. She took over the ceremony, delivering the final prayer in memorial of the lost souls of the martyred warriors.

Scota scattered dried flowers into the southerly wind. They became airborne, delicately landing on the ocean, drifting northwards to the Island of Destiny. A tinge of roseate pink proclaimed the dusk. The crews of the entire fleet contemplated in complete silence as the sinking sun touched the horizon.

Amergin imagined he heard the burning orb being extinguished, just as a sole bottlenose dolphin arched gracefully out of the ocean, silhouetted against the now violet and orange sky, and disappeared without a trace…

CHAPTER FIVE:
TIMES OF CHANGE

Unbeknownst to the advancing Milesian fleet, the mystical, legendary lands of the prophecy are in turmoil. Far, far to the north, earlier invasion forces are in collision. The mythical, magical Tuatha are battling against an earlier fearsome invader, the Firbolg. The Firbolg had divided the promised-land into provinces. The greatest of these provinces, Muintear, was held by the legendary warrior chieftain Gann. A war of cruel attrition against a seemingly irresistible Tuathan army blessed with magical powers had left Gann and his army weakened. His people were now dispersed around the land. Those not killed, had been driven to the far distant corners of the island. The mighty province on the western fringes of this prized and beautiful island finally fell to the forces of the Tuatha.

The Tuatha were in league with the spirit world, they had been able to penetrate the veil between the spirit world and the mortal realm. Antiem, the high king, used the spirit world, the Sidhe, to enslave and ultimately enlighten the pagan Firbolg. However his sons, particularly the cruel and acquisitive MacCuacht, had formed a pact with the dark Sidhe. The pact gave MacCuacht delusions of grandeur, believing that he was the High King in waiting. In reality he was being controlled increasingly by the dark Sidhe, turning darker and darker as the years went by. His brothers MacCuill and MacGreinne were younger and easily led. MacCuill, however, questioned his brother's cruel and dark ways.

MacGreinne was totally under MacCuacht's influence, and undertook all of MacCuacht's commands without question.

The favourite of the High King Antiem's siblings was Sceine, his beautiful wondrous daughter, as pure as a mortal being could be. Like Antiem, she had ingratiated the Guardians of Light. She was an enlightened being able to use the magical powers of the Sidhe for good. In Antiem's mind she was the natural leader, she embodied the true spirit of the Tuathans.

En route to the high mountain fortress of Sliebh Mis, now the stronghold of the Tuathans in this province, they scaled the highest peak in the land, now named Corran Tuathail, to survey their captured lands. They looked to the West, across a majestic mountain range and over to a shimmering silver ocean. They had battled the Firbolg and endured, but they all were acutely aware of the force that approached. From the highest peak they could see the vastness of the ocean. They had sent emissaries of the Sidhe to contact the coming tribes. MacCuacht used his increasingly malevolent ways to deter the adventurers from the South.

Sceine communed through the veil to contact the seafaring newcomers. The Guardians of Light, the enlightened Sidhe, confided with Sceine that an enlightened being named Amergin, a sea druid, blessed with powers given to him through the veil, was destined to arrive on this island.

Sceine sensed she was destined to be with Amergin, and together they would confront the dark forces of the Sidhe led by her very own brother MacCuacht in the mortal realm.

Sceine rejoiced with her brothers, the victory over the Firbolg was theirs, the last mighty province under their control. Sceine was torn by the fact that this had been a victory at all costs. MacCuacht cruelly subjugated the Firbolg, huge losses were endured.

Antiem, the High King was furious. He, like Sceine, wanted to use the powers of the Sidhe for good, for healing rifts, for appeasing, bringing light in to the new world. Antiem and Sceine wanted this, an island of the imagination, an island of the divine in nature, a unified place, a place of peace and harmony.

Antiem was known as a peacemaker, the great redeemer, a unifier, but he was betrayed by MacCuacht.

Antiem had called for all the Chieftains of the Firbolg to meet on the sacred causeway in the far north of the island. Antiem planned to propose a life of peace with the Firbolg, to join forces, to settle, and permit their tribes to mix, grow and go forward.

This was anathema to MacCuacht. He despised his father's plan. He had designs of his own, delusions of grandeur, an insatiable desire to be High King.

The gathering on the sacred causeway was undermined and betrayed by the treacherous MacCuacht.

He called on the dark forces of the Sidhe to bring grief and havoc. The dark Sidhe in the form of a black silver monster from the depths of the Northern ocean, reared up and swept the gathering Firbolg off the wave cut volcanic platform. Gann was the only Firbolg chieftain at the meeting to survive this treachery.

Antiem, the High King, had been severely wounded when battling with the Firbolg, he now returned to the mountain stronghold of Sliebh Mis.

Sceine nursed her wounded father in the mountain fortress. She had made the journey as soon as she had heard about his life threatening condition. This place was a fortress amongst the soaring white-tailed eagles, precarious and perilous to get to, but once here a haven. Precipitous peaks, sheer cliff faces, paths teetering on mountain ledges, easily protected. Few would have the knowledge or audacity to scale these heights.

Antiem had been a mighty leader and fierce warrior in his time. Recently his authority and leaderhip had been undermined, his legacy was waning, the time had come for him to pass his title on…

Sceine knew that his life was coming to an end. This high place was to be the grave of the High King.

Antiem was furious that MacCuacht had betrayed him, bringing the honour of the Tuathans in to question. Antiem was going to make most sure that MacCuacht would not become High King.

An untrustworthy High King in an alliance with the dark Sidhe was too much to countenance on his death bed.

Antiem asked Sceine to move him to the highest chamber in the fortress. A favourite place of his, overlooking the indescribably beautiful mountain chain as it swept in glorious majesty to the gently shelving beaches and the infinite ocean beyond.

While Sceine was nursing her ailing father, he turned to her, "I believe in you and trust you Sceine, I have a strong sense of your destiny. I know you will act instinctively and from the heart, and do what is right for Tuatha. I have given instructions to the priesthood, that on my death you and your brothers will be given a province each to rule over. There will be no High King, or Queen. I give you first choice of province. I sense that you will use the powers of the Sidhe for good. Tell me your choice."

Sceine took no time to respond, "Thank you father, I choose the Western Province of course. Here where the greatest power sources are found, where the veil is closest, the province bordering the ocean. Where I am destined to be and where I am destined to meet the sea druid Amergin!"

"You are welcome Sceine. This majestic province, bordered by the ocean and warmed by the prevailing south-westerly winds and currents, is yours!"

On her knees, by her father's bed, Sceine grasped his hand. It felt frail and brittle, not the strong grip that had hugged and embraced her in her youth. Pale and resigned to his fate. She talked quietly to him about the distant tribes that journey to these shores. She talked of the rifts occurring in the tribes of Tuatha. How the veil is torn and the Sidhe torn into the enlightened ones, the Guardians of Light, and the darkened Sidhe, who she fears is being led by MacCuacht in the mortal realm. She goes on to tell Antiem of the being of immense, courage, heart and magical powers that she sees in her dreams.

This being, the Milesian sea druid Amergin is her destiny. Together they will battle the forces of the dark.

Antiem smiled and agreed, "Be sure that your brother MacCuacht is the leader of the dark Sidhe in this mortal realm. I have seen his work, witnessed his treachery. He tries to draw your brothers in with him.

I think MacGreinne is weak willed and will ultimately join him. MacCuill is on the cusp and is tempted by the power offered to him by MacCuacht. I hope his honesty and purity and integrity will shine through, like yours."

Sceine confided in her ever weakening father, "There comes with the

Milesian tribes, a mystic of unimaginable powers. He is corrupt and evil. He already communes with MacCuacht across the Northern Ocean."

Antiem reassured her, "You will be vested with the powers of the High Priestess of Tuatha. You will go to the Temple of Xhara in the east. You will be anointed by the Guardians of Light. You will have powers to match this mystic. There will be no High King or Queen, but you will be the spiritual leader of the Tuathan tribes. I sense you are the purest and wisest of them all Sceine. You will use the powers of the Sidhe for good"

"I have already communed with the Guardians of Light. They have sent messengers to counter the powers of the priest Gonne, and the Machiavellian MacCuacht. Many of the souls have been lost to the dark Sidhe already. There is a time of huge change ahead, and a threat from within that could be even more damaging to the Tuathan way!"

Antiem gently squeezed his beautiful daughter's hand, and looked deep into the rich amber eyes, he focused on the mesmerising fleck in her right eye, momentarily he was taken to another world, he was in awe of her beauty and power, "I knew you would understand... You are ready Sceine... I must rest now..."

Sceine rose and as she left her father, she looked out over the view across the mountains and to the distant sea. This was Antiem's last resting place, a view for eternity... Her destiny awaits her...

The cooling mists of Sliebh Mis rolled over the summits and filled the valleys and corries. In the waning evening light, the Tuathan royalty gathered to witness and honour the passing of a great king.

The High King Antiem had departed this mortal coil. His soul had moved through the veil and joined the enlightened ones. He always fought the good fight. Sceine felt his presence looking on the gathering of family, friends and yes, foe.

The provinces of the island of destiny now had ruling princes and a princess ... Sceine of the Western Province, and High Priestess of Tuatha and representative of the enlightened ones, The Guardians of Light.

The princes, her brothers, knelt in deference to the High Priestess, their partners beside them.MacCuacht with Eiru, MacGreinne with Fodha, and MacCuill with Banba.

The mortal representatives of the Sidhe prayed for her and blessed her with the magical powers of the spirit world. Antiem looked on from beyond the veil and smiled...

The cooling mists in the valley seemed to part as a last gesture of the day. The distant views beyond the mountains and to the infinite ocean began to colour with reflective golds and deep rich ambers. Nature commemorates the passing of a great king and a good soul.

The new day would see a new order, a new regime. How would the new way be without the steadying hand of Antiem? MacCuacht felt the power in the new blood coursing through the veins of Tuatha.

Sceine was conscious of change, and the darkness rising...

The royal gathering travelled to the east this day, across their lands and to the spiritual home, the Temple of Xhara. This would be an investiture of Sceine as High Priestess of Tuatha. The word was out...

The road to the Temple was lined by a joyous populous, Priests in religious regalia, warriors in full armour, children waving flags, everyone cheering Sceine on.

Prayers were given, sacred incantations offered by the earthly representatives of the Sidhe, clad in white linen, their faces covered by the cloaked hoods, mysterious and otherworldly. Once more Sceine could feel Antiem's presence, guiding her and welcoming her to this sacred place. Here the veil between the mortal realm and the spirit world was so thin as to be almost nothing.

Sceine was dressed in a beautifully elegant white linen dress, decorated with gold thread. She felt empowered, strengthened, wonderfully alive and energetic. Her priesthood walked with her as she climbed the steps to the Temple, and was taken to an ornate chair at the entrance to the Temple, the gateway to the spirit world. The priesthood, her family and her people knelt before her. She was conscious of MacCuacht, she knew he resented her father's decision to give her the Western Province, and more vehemently resented that she was High Priestess, and the powers that gave her.

However, he knew he was next in line...

Sceine felt her powers growing the longer she was at the Temple of Xhara, the veil was so close...

She listened intently to her brothers acclaiming her as the High Priestess. Her powers of insight and clairvoyance so heightened now, she knew from this moment that she will never be able to trust MacCuacht again.

The Priests of Xhara raised a silver chalice, filled with the purest water from the holy well, to her lips. New powers surged and coursed through her body as she sipped the sacred fluid.

The priests chanted in unison, "Is she welcome!?"

The gathered throng replied, "Yes!!!"

"Is she the High Priestess of Xhara!?" the priests questioned the crowd.

"Yes!!!" answered the excited gathering, strongly, loudly and clearly.

"And so it shall be!!" with this the priests circled Sceine, each one anointing her forehead with the purest holy water.

Sceine closed her eyes. She could sense a spiritual and energetic connection with the spirit world.

She could feel her dear departed father looking serenely down on her.

She could feel the connection with the divine Guardians of Light. Sceine had become a conduit to the spirit world. She felt the life giving force and the power of goodness flowing through her.

Overwhelmed and overcome, she steadied herself, and sat in the ornate ceremonial chair.

An exquisite amber pendant on a long, graceful silver chain was placed around her neck. "The Pendant of Xhara!" she exclaimed. The pendant reflected her rich amber eyes.

She noticed a fleck grew in the amber pendant, a mirror image of the endearing and beautifully shaped fleck in the iris of her right eye.

Sceine also noticed as her gaze fell upon her brother MacCuacht, the fleck in the pendant grew in size, and deepened in darkness. The Pendant of Xhara confirmed her suspicions that MacCuacht did indeed channel the dark Sidhe through the veil.

The Priests of the Temple of Xhara joined Sceine in prayer. They prayed for the people of Tuatha.

They prayed for an eternal equilibrium to be maintained between the mortal realm and the spirit world.

The High Priestess and the Priests of Xhara were the mortal representatives of The Guardians of Light.

The Guardians of Light journeyed from the spirit world through the veil bringing life giving radiant light to the mortal realm. They were the pure ones, the good Sidhe.

The Priests of the Temple of Xhara were only too aware that events, natural or manipulated could unleash the dark power of the Sidhe. The annals of the Tuathans were interspersed with periods of dark and light. Cyclically and periodically there were dark ages where the veil had been thinned and breached. These cycles were growing more frequent, the dark ages longer. With each dark cycle civilisation, culture and heritage were affected. Morality, creativity and spirituality were all threatened.

The priests warned of an event that could irretrievably breach the veil and place the enlightened world in darkness and despair.

The priests took Sceine deep into the Temple, away from earthly distractions. This was a time for contemplation and meditation. The Guardians of Light came through the veil and accompanied her to the inner sanctum where her induction continued. Amazingly, deep in the Inner Sanctum grew a beautifully formed tree, The Tree of Life, a universal symbol of truth and enlightenment found in most earthly religions and cultures. Here in The Temple of Xhara, the Tree of Life was the conduit between the mortal realm and the spirit world.

Sceine was guided to a natural hollow in the midst of spiralling roots. The Priests of Xhara gathered around her chanting, calling all enlightened beings from all the provinces to unite together in the common cause. The cycle of life was turning. The enlightened ones must be united in thought and spirit.

Sceine and the High Priests communed with the Guardians of Light across the veil. Together they sent a message warning of a dark nemesis that threatened the way of the light. They called upon all the enlightened beings to face this nemesis, to confront the dark forces, before it is too late.

The cycle of life turns remorselessly and time is of the essence…

CHAPTER SIX:
EMISSARIES OF THE LIGHT

A roseate tern skimmed and soared, chasing the updraught of each cresting and surging wave, dipping occasionally without hesitation to pluck a briny morsel from the ocean larder, skimming, soaring, dipping to the northern horizon. Amergin watched this plucky, hardy yet delicate and fragile sea bird in total mastery of the elements as it skilfully winged its way over the vast ocean, a lone messenger, daring to confront the forces of nature with total confidence and acceptance.

"This is the way!" shouted Amergin, "Xomas call the Council of Elders together. I believe I have found a way!" The conches sounded across the raft of vessels, still gently drifting in the Southerly breeze and ocean currents.

Each captain of each vessel, the tribal leaders, the royal party of Scota, Milidh, Eiremhou, Eimbear, and the representatives of the Chapter of Mystics, including the sinister High Priest Gonne, and Terese of the Xantha, leader of the amazonian warriors, made their way to the deck of the flagship.

Terese stood next to Bith, one of the representatives of the Chapter of Mystics. She sensed in him a good being, one of the enlightened ones. They acknowledged one another and turned to watch Amergin as he arrived at the helm.

Amergin embraced his family in turn. All were full of gratitude and thanks for having survived the challenges this far. Scota spoke quietly to Amergin, "My son you are proving to be the true champion and the bravest of leaders. You must be aware of the messages and warnings that are permeating through the veil. Be wise and be sure of your next move. We are being summoned by the Guardians of Light. We are being beckoned to the promised land."

"Mother I know this, and in answer to this call, I propose to send an emissary to meet the representatives of the Tuatha in the promised-land. Their response and actions will guide us along the right path, giving us time to regather our strength and resources."

Amergin turned to his loyal subjects, greeting them and hailing their success so far, "My loyal and brave people, you have endured grave and testing challenges. Your resolve and courage is immeasurable. You must be aware that the greatest challenges are yet to come. For this reason I have decided to send emissaries to test the way for us. I ask for volunteers to go deep in to world of the Tuatha and assess the forces of dark that are gathering…"

Terese of the Xantha and Bith of the Chapter of Mystics stepped forward immediately, in unison. Amergin smiled, recognising in these two a powerful and synergistic combination.

Terese's powers of clairvoyance and finely tuned senses would complement and enhance the magical and spiritual powers of Bith.

Bith, a longstanding priest with the Chapter of Mystics had the foresight and vision to undertake such an arduous journey. He had witnessed and learned much as he journeyed with the Milesian tribes, on a course of invasion through successive Mediterranean countries. It is said that his ancestry goes back to the original tribes of Noah. His bloodline is so strong that his fellow priests have declared over time that he is a living manifestation of the prophecy. Amergin knew that Bith was a perfect choice. He had total confidence in him.

Terese of the Xantha was also an ideal choice. Her powers had been refined and strengthened over time by the best teacher, Scota.

Amergin addressed the gathering once more, "If you are all in agreement then Bith and Terese will lead the way for us. They will take our vanguard to the promised-land, to our island of destiny. Please support them and give them the crew and resources they need. We will adjourn and meet at sunrise to send our brave ones into the unknown, may the Great Spirit bring them back safely!"

Amergin instructed Eiremhou and Eimbear to help select the crew and make the vessel ready for the journey.

Scota, Milidh, Bith and Terese joined Amergin below deck. Amergin was disturbed to see the Machiavellian high priest Gonne, talking to Eimbear. Instinctively the hackles on the back of his neck rose. He wondered how they were conniving and conspiring?

Amergin knew the powers of the dark Sidhe were gathering…

These before him are the purest of the pure. They all knew the urgency of their quest.

They were being called by the Guardians of Light, messages sent through the veil, to come soon, and at all costs. Scota and Milidh were deep in conversation, "You are aware of the imminent threat my son. Our tribe, our nation and the promised-land are all in grave danger. If Bith and Terese fail in their mission, then you must be prepared for the onslaught to come. You and I must go deep in to the earthly portals, join with the spirit world, journey beyond the veil, and commune with the Guardians of Light."

Amergin looked in to his mother's eyes. He studied the countenance of this magical and inspiring woman, "I am resolved to do this dear mother. By the will of the Great Spirit I will be ready!"

Amergin reinforced this, "I have felt the connection through the veil already. I have been called by an enlightened, beautiful being, a kindred spirit who I feel I am destined to be with. The Guardians of Light will bring us together. Only then will the prophecy be fulfilled!"

Scota held her sons hand, sensing the power and strength of will coursing through his veins, "Good my son! We will go now to meet the others, to ensure the best are being selected for the vanguard. After this we will pray together. We will commune with the Guardians of Light and travel deep beyond the veil!"

A strange sort of democracy was at work in the selection of the vanguard. Each named five, the brief being to blend marine skills with those of the warrior. The vanguard would have to be the most potent force. The vanguard needed to represent the enlightenment of the purest Milesian, and have the strength, courage and wisdom to face the dark powers of the spirit world.

Eimbear and Gonne chose the same crew, the outcome already being influenced by the dark Sidhe.

Scota pointed this out to Amergin. He responded by saying, "Better the devil you know!"

Bith and Terese will have the wisdom to use this knowledge to their advantage. They will be able to see the workings of the dark Sidhe first hand."

"A calculated risk" Scota retorted. Decisions were made and Bith, priest of the Chapter of Mystics and Terese of the Xantha were informed of their crew. They were satisfied that they had a potent force.

"Tomorrow at sunset!" declared Amergin, "Your journey commences!"

He studied the gently heaving, glistening ocean... A roseate tern skimmed, soared and dipped... a lone messenger heading north confronting the unknown...

The chosen few, the emissaries of Milesia, would reconvene on the vessel "Fintan" at sunset, in readiness for a dawn sailing.

The Chapter of Mystics performed a ceremonial blessing of the vessel to prepare them for their sojourn into the unknown. Bith, as a priest of the Chapter of Mystics, and now as the messenger for his nation, led the ceremony, chanting sacred verse, welcoming the spirits of the ocean to be one with the vessel Fintan and her crew. "Give them safe passage, and find sanctuary in the new land."

Terese and her Xantha looked on, and chanted in chorus with the priests from the Chapter of Mystics, and those assembled, "Great Spirit hear us, defend us from evil, lead us safely to our destiny, bring peace to our people and the new world!"

Bith and Terese knelt before Milidh and Scota to receive a royal blessing. Milidh pronounced "Go safely and go in peace!" Scota continued, "May the Guardians of Light look over you on this perilous journey." Amergin embraced both Bith and Terese. "Go now. Be ready and may the Great Spirit protect you both!"

He knew how important they both were to the cause of Milesia.

They looked at each other and then to Amergin... They sensed a powerful connection to the spirit world and the Guardians of Light. They were being called. They were fighting for the cause of the Light.

Amergin inspired them with the words, "You will be like an arrow shot from the light, to penetrate the veil and enlighten a darkening world. Go my brave ones, go!"

Bith and Terese boarded the ship. Amergin watched, his gaze drawn to the horizon.

As they disappeared into the gunnels of the vessel, a gust of southerly breeze wrapped around him, seeming to whisper, "Amergin I am with you, I await your emissaries... be patient we will soon meet..."

Sensing his destiny, he was visibly shaken. He came back to reality... as the first of many shooting stars that night flashed across the northern horizon...

Under the clear starlit sky, Amergin sat in quiet meditation on the prow of the flagship. Minutes blurred in to hours. Scota sat next to him. She began to chant in the language of the ancients. Strange guttural, hypnotic tones, combined with the steady slow undulations of the ocean, drew Amergin deeper and deeper into a world of constellations, deeper and deeper into a heavenly cosmos. Dimension upon dimension, sliding, warping, weaving, morphing... He became aware of his hand being held... Who!?...

Scota continued to chant... trance inducing, taking him deeper... the gentle Southerly breeze wrapping sensuously around him... a hand caressed his, guiding him, taking him... away from the ship, high above the ocean.

A soft, glowing, amber radiance from another dimension ... a veil of mist, of spectral energy... gossamer soft, sensuous and caressing... His heart, head and soul were energised... taken to a blissful, overwhelming, orgasmic state... his body sensuously wrapped by a veil of pure, radiant, loving and enlightening energy . His hand caressed once more, being guided and drawn into a dimension beyond the veil..."My love, I am your destiny. The Guardians of Light give us their blessing... We will be together soon... and so it is written... and is in the stars..."

Amergin felt his hand being squeezed tightly. This time it was Scota. Scota realised the affinity that Amergin had with the Guardians of Light. She also sensed the sacred feminine entity that called him over the Northern horizon.

Scota was reminded of her own life journey, and how she was destined to meet Milidh, "You have found your spiritual soul mate Amergin, the bond is so strong, the draw irresistible. I can sense that. But now, this morning, you must send your brothers and sisters to meet their fate!"

Amergin arrived at the Fintan just as the mooring ropes were being untied. Sails unfurled, the vessel straining to break free from its tethers.

Amergin gave a hearty encouragement to Bith, Terese and the crew, "May you have fair weather and the good grace of the sea gods." He embraced Bith and Terese, "You will be in our hearts and the Guardians of Light will be watching over you."

For all the bravado of this impressive, if rapidly assembled crew, the tension was palpable. The time for planning done, each went about their tasks. Mariners, warriors, side by side, all for the cause, the fulfilment of the prophecy...

Amergin helped to untie the gangplank ... they were away! The vessel set free, unleashed. The sails filled, Fintan soon leaned in to the freshening breeze. Amergin raised his hand to salute them, "Farewell my brave ones... to a safe return..."

A lone roseate tern soared and dipped in the cresting wake of the vessel... they would have company while they headed north...

Bith checked their bearings, making sure the heading was correct, navigating by the sun and the stars.

The sun was now risen and warming the faces of the crew. Encouraging them onwards, they were all transparently clear about the nature of their journey. They were the pioneers, the adventurers, the explorers.The vanguard venturing in to the unknown.

Terese took her turn at the helm, guiding the vessel through a gently surging, now benign ocean, occasionally having to wrestle with the tiller as an unannounced gust swept through. She constantly surveyed the northern horizon, looking for any tell-tale changes that would forewarn danger.

Her clairvoyant senses were telling her the veil between the spirit world and the mortal realm was close and getting closer as they headed north.

They were all on full alert, looking for any minor disturbances, any unusual disturbances or phenomenon.

Bith inspected this fine, sturdy vessel. He gathered the crew together to praise them, and keep their morale high. They had enough provisions for at least one lunar cycle... surely enough for them to reach the promised-land. He regularly prayed to the Great Spirit for a safe passage. Days went by, the prevailing winds kindly pushing them northwards. They were making good progress... until...

One fateful morning whilst on watch, Terese heard chanting coming from the prow. In the dim light of the dawn, a group of five meditating, calling... she immediately recognised them as the five that Gonne and Eimbear had selected. She instantly knew they were summoning the forces of the dark...

She hailed the watchman over, "Go and fetch Bith! Be quick! We have very little time!"

Bith was on deck before the watchman hailed him, just as the first and strongest gust yet hit the Fintan broadsides. As a mystic, Bith had sensed the malign ceremony - the ritualistic summoning of the dark forces from beyond the veil.

By the time Bith stood with Terese at the helm, the ship was rolling in an increasing sea. The sails were being buffeted by more and more frequent gusts.

"Reduce to storm rigging!" Bith bellowed to the crew. The horizon darkened, a silver- grey line approached from the north, speckled with white cap crested waves.

"Brace yourself Terese, our nemesis arrives!" he grabbed the tiller with her, turning straight on to the oncoming storm front.

Moving so fast they hardly had time to react... a maelstrom of wind and rain, giant hailstones tore sheer through the storm sails. Thunderclaps overhead, lightning striking the mast, deck and rigging simultaneously. The vessel Fintan was being torn asunder. The storm seemed to rage forever, but in reality was over in minutes. Bith, Terese and the loyal crew were hurled to the deck by a final furious vortex. Air was sucked from their lungs, nearly suffocating, gasping for breath, as the front roared through. Senses stunned by an electrical field discharging along the vessel.

Suddenly, there was quiet, a stunned silence...Bith prone on the deck of Fintan, saw demonic apparitions writhing in a wall of all consuming mist rolling over the ocean. In the aftermath of the storm front, strange sea creatures swam through the ocean. The creatures and apparitions were real yet not real. They surrounded the vessel, beasts of the air and the sea.

They were helpless, looking on in stunned silence. The masts had been snapped like kindling, the sails shredded. Now an eerie calm, not a breath of wind, the sea mist enveloped them, and slowly, inexorably, the vessel Fintan started drifting in an ever increasing ocean current...

"We are being taken northwards, but I know not where!" Bith exclaimed, "This shroud of the otherworld has us in its power!"

Terese felt the tiller being manoeuvred by an otherworldy force, "Wherever, whatever this is, they have control, the helm is theirs!"

The mind numbed, you questioned your sanity, and your place in the universe. Only those with the strongest faith would survive with their integrity in tact.

Bith conjectured, "This must be the terrible place, the place of legend where souls are taken and converted to the dark Sidhe!"

Terese responded, "We must be united, our spirits must remain undaunted. Amergin selected us for a reason. Together we must call on the Guardians of Light!"

Bith was galvanised into action, "Gather around me, all of you!" the concern and anxiety showed on his face and in his voice. He began praying, delving deep into his psyche, drawing on his magical powers as a priest of the Chapter of Mystics. A lifetime of training will be needed now as they have never been needed before... Fail and they were lost!

"Great Spirit, protect us!!!" he chanted, the crew following, repeating. Together they prayed, without unity they would be lost forever...

The strange mist continued to roll and boil. The apparitions sapped their minds of their will to resist.

"Weaken and you will fall prey to the dark Sidhe! You must stay strong, we must unite!" urged Bith.

They gathered in unison calling the Guardians of Light. Calling the Great Spirit to protect them…

Amergin started awake, his dreams disturbed. A cry from the void! His adventuring vanguard in trouble! He leapt to his feet, and bounded up on to the deck. Racing to the prow of the flagship, he stared towards the northern horizon, no signs… but he knew there was trouble…

Scota too had woken and was up and watching the northern horizon.

The soft glowing light of dawn was no comfort to them now.

Amergin studied the raft of vessels drifting, bound securely in the prevailing Southerly.

"The time for Milesia was coming!" thought Amergin, "Bith and Terese were sent to negotiate, to find a peaceful way… but now is the time for the warrior! Xomas sound the conch! Our emissaries are in grave danger. We must call on the Guardians of Light!"

The sound of the conch drifted and resonated from vessel to vessel…

The crews of each vessel came up on deck. They all turned to the northern horizon chanting in unison.

Scota and Milidh began chanting ancient sacred verse.

Amergin chanted, "Great Spirit, protect our people. Come to their salvation!"

Eiremhou, the Chapter of Mystics, all the loyal Milesians knelt in prayer, chanting this again and again!

Bith of the Chapter of Mystics and Terese of the Xantha chanted with their vanguard, keeping their faith, but all too conscious of the malign energy unleashed against them.

They saw their vanguard weakening, it would not be long before, one by one they would be taken, their souls lost to the dark Sidhe. They battled the mist of apparitions that swirled and consumed them.

The vessel Fintan floated in currents being controlled by demons.

Suddenly Bith saw a vision, a vision of evil, the High Priest of the Chapter of Mystics, Gonne, was orchestrating and manipulating the apparitions, and controlling the ocean currents! In that same vision Bith saw three darkly shrouded women, mysterious and malevolent. They were in league with Gonne. They were in league with the dark Sidhe on the island of destiny. They all worked against the vanguard.

They were summoned to destroy a mission of peace… but who were these three?!

Bith knew that he would soon be meeting these agents of the dark…

The mist was impenetrable now, the ghostly apparitions haunting and disturbing.

"Was this hell? Is there no salvation!?" Bith cried out, as he witnessed members of his vanguard weaken and fall. Minds numbed, spirits weakened, bodies taken, souls lost...

There! The five selected by Gonne and Eimbear in a shamanic huddle, they were the conduit for this malevolence, the channel for the dark Sidhe...

Bith joined Terese in prayer, they were at their limits, they prayed, they chanted, they called the Guardians of Light, "Surely there must be a way!?" They implored the Great Spirit, "For Milesia and for the prophecy!"

Bith could take no more, he must act! He unsheathed his normally ceremonial sword.

Bith was sworn to peace, as a mystic he had vowed never to take life! He realised the lives of all on board were threatened...

"Come with me Terese! We must take these five traitorous vermin! They are the connection. They are drawing the dark forces to us!"

Terese of the Xantha was always ready for battle, always ready to fight for the cause! Terese tore into the five. One already clutched at his side and fell to the deck, her bloodied dagger raised and lunging towards the next victim.

Bith threw himself at the next one, grappled with him and was able to stun and wound him.

Terese's next victim was fatally wounded. He stumbled, was unbalanced and fell over the side of the vessel, as it drifted inexorably north in an unnatural ocean current...

As the body fell into the swirling sea mist, Bith anticipated the tell-tale splash into the veil of the ocean. But there was no splash! Not a sound! The body was consumed by the boiling and swirling mist of apparitions. With this, the remaining sinister traitors took flight and threw themselves overboard.

No splash! The bodies just disappeared into the impenetrable mist. The haunting apparitions continued to swirl around the vessel.

Bith sensed a difference now, the conduit broken. A light flooded in from the North, penetrating the mist. Beginning with a dark rich amber glow, then the white light surrounding an ethereal, beautiful female form...

Bith questioned, "Was this another apparition?" Then a voice came, "Bith of the Chapter of Mystics and Terese of the Xantha. We will watch over you for the rest of your sea voyage to the island of destiny. Beware. You are still in grave danger!"

The female form swirled into the impenetrable mist and was gone, the amber glow dissipated and the mist thinned. The apparitions were absorbed into the ocean, the tormenting shroud faded away.

Bith embraced Terese and a shaft of sunlight burned through the mist, bathing the vessel with normality once more...

The vanguard gathered again. Strangely the bodies of those who had fallen were gone, lost souls, taken beyond the veil by the forces of the dark.

In shock, mourning those lost, they gathered to witness the unfolding view of a distant coastline on the north-eastern horizon.

This was the land of the prophecy, the island of destiny. A land still shrouded in the thinning but still eery mist.

Under the power of the damaged and shredded sails, still drifting in a southerly breeze, and guided by a drifting offshore current, they approached closer and closer to the promised-land. Huge promontories taking the full brunt of the open ocean swell, crashing, surging surf, deep green to azure blue to cobalt turquoise to brilliant white breakers. Rays of warming light penetrating and spiritual illuminated stacks of jagged igneous rock. Huge slanting slabs of darkened, weathered, ancient red sandstone gleaming and reflecting in the slowly searching shafts of sunlight. Angel rays for those seeking sanctuary in this stormbound, weather-beaten land.

Slowly, diffidently, warily they edged the vessel closer. Following the rolling motion of the swell, they edged under mighty 600 foot cliffs. Staring upwards to exposure inducing heights, the crew suffered from vertigo attempting to get some scale and perspective from these monoliths.

Drifting further northwards the cliffs gave way to a sweeping bay. The shoreline stretched and curved to eternity, pounding breakers curling, cresting and detonating on to pristine white beaches.

The air a heady cocktail of ozone and sea spray intermixed with a twist of sea salt and seaweed.

They breathed deep, instinctively filtering the essence of the sea and the new land.

They scanned the endless sweep of the bay for a deep water haven and safe anchorage... beyond an impressive dune system, a huge spit of sand was pummeled and pounded by incessant surf.

Beyond that an outpouring of fresh water, siltier, sandier coloured indicating a rivermouth and potentially safe anchorage. Around the spit and in to the estuary, the deep water invited the Fintan up the beckoning channel. Travelling waves pushed along the river banks, slowing and filling all the time, finally, the calm slickness of the outflowing river.

Now under the power of the oarsmen, they rounded the first bend. Pristine white sands gave way to verdant, emerald green fields and soft rolling hills... Haven...

The keel of the Fintan pushed appreciatively into the soft sinking silt. The tide was still ebbing. The vessel would be safe until the next tide. Bith and Terese were proud to be the first Milesians to set foot on this island. Carrying and dragging heavy mooring ropes to the river bank. These were tied around the trunks of ancient yew trees. Trees that had seen a thousand years of storms, carved and sculpted by prevailing winds, their branches twisted and tortured leaning away from the gales. Trees that could tell the tale of many waves of invaders over many centuries, would secure their vessel, temporarily at least.

Bith was particularly conscious of those who had travelled before them, and more worryingly, conscious of those who waited for them… He gathered the crew under the shelter of the sculpted yew trees.

Were the trees listening? The swaying and creeking branches applauding and encouraging his rallying speech to the vanguard, "We are the emissaries of Milesia. Even with the horrors and misfortunes that we have experienced, we must be cognisant of why we are here. We are here as peacemakers, our last resort is to be warriors. We are destined to be here, we must do whatever is necessary to bring our tribes safely here."

A body of warriors remained to protect the vessel. The rest gathered provisions and weapons and began their journey inland, following the meandering river.

Everything appeared new and verdant, a pristine and beautiful land. They marched on, searching for signs of life and civilisation. For half a day they marched, eventually arriving at a steep sided valley swathed in ancient deciduous woodlands. Beyond the valley, the mountains rose into the far distance.

They followed a steeply ascending path. At the head of the valley, they climbed to a ridge that gave them a panoramic vantage point.

Here, Bith decided to make camp, nominating round the clock watchmen, to warn of anyone or anything approaching. As dusk descended he looked up towards the mountains, at the base of the highest peak, atop a huge granite outcrop, he saw a single light, then a trail of lights, weaving their way down the mountain track. They had been observed…

Dusk descended into the dark of night, the trail of lights getting ever closer. From the ancient woodlands nocturnal wildlife curiously watched. Silhouettes of nervous red deer moved through the trees. Bright eyes, reflected, flashed and disappeared into the dark.

Other creatures of the night, like moths drawn to the flames.Bats predating in the spreading firelight.

Sparks, smoke and ash filled the air. The trail of lights grew ever closer…

A mist of condensing, oppressive, cool night air formed and gathered in the lowest places.

Streams of colder mountain air rolled down from the surrounding ridges. Their vantage place was consumed. They could see nothing now. They were helpless, defenseless. They could not escape. The oncoming horde had them trapped.

They heard them long before they saw them.

The steady military step, the metallic clank of armour against spears and shields, and swords being drawn from scabbards. Voices pierced the night air. Lights surrounded them. Figures and shapes took form. Reminiscent of the mist of apparitions at sea, ghostly figures appeared through the swirling fog.

Three raven haired women, dressed from head to toe in a cocoon of radiant, luminescent fabric.

Bith knew them, these were the Witches of Hawardden so feared and reviled... the three seen in league with Gonne when at sea.

They all instinctively took a step back. They had seen their powers at work, they were afraid for their lives, afraid for their souls. They had seen their friends lost at sea.

A voice came from the shadows, "We have been sent to talk to you. You must try to understand our ways..."

Terese thought to herself, "You have come with your dark army. You have taken the souls of our warriors. We have seen evil in you. We have seen the dark Sidhe in your actions!"

Before the thoughts had formed, a reply was forthcoming, "Terese, I am Banba, I hear your fears. Would you not protect your nation from an invasion force?"

Bith had already felt the witches probing his mind, delving deep into his innermost thoughts. Just being in the presence of these sinister women was endangering them. He spoke to the others, "Close your minds, these beings are of the dark Sidhe. Let them in and you will be taken... lost...Protect yourselves!"

Bith was trained in the art of mind control. The others were physically strong, but he feared for their vulnerable minds...

He realised there was little point in trying to appease these lost souls. He had come as an emissary of peace. These dark beings saw them as invaders... In a conventional sense they were. However in a universal context they were saviours, the defenders of the Light.

Bith talked to the witch known as Banba, "Our tribes are coming to this island of our destiny. I have been sent to try and find a path, a common way. I have been sent in peace."

Banba stood motionless, expressionless. She communicated telepathically with the witches known as Eiru and Fodha, "These mere minions believe they can save themselves and their kind. We must humour them! Take them to Hawardden, from where they will never return!"

This time Bith heard their thoughts. He also heard the words, "Never trust them, you are in grave danger!" Words that came from beyond the veil, subconsciously he and Terese knew this and believed this.

Banba spoke, "Bith of the Chapter of Mystics, and Terese of the Xantha," They knew exactly who they were! "You must travel with us to the high mountain fortress of Hawardden. You will stay and engage with us."

Banba abruptly clapped her hands. The witches Eiru and Fodha signalled for the creatures of the dark to encircle Bith and Terese and their vanguard. Without a word they were being filed into the ranks of the dark army and were being marched to Hawardden.

The glowing embers of the campfire soon disappeared into the distance.

They walked with their captors, they had no choice. They already knew that the mission was lost... A peaceful way was never going to be found...

Up and up they marched. After a few hours marching, they were scaling the imposing granite cliffs that protected the high mountain fortress of Hawardden...

Bith and Terese were in complete acceptance of their mission, which was now to escape to warn Amergin...

Dim lights shone from the fortifications, the castle towering over the precipitous cliff face. The drawbridge creaked downwards over a bottomless crevice, giant chains easing out. "A place of no return?" speculated Bith. Were they hostages, prisoners or emissaries?

The appearance of the witches changed like the light. Sometimes they were sensuous and alluring, the raven hair, pale skin, sinuous form wrapped in figure hugging radiant fabric. Other times they were hideous and ogreish. Maybe this was deliberate to disorientate them. Nothing was real, nothing was certain...

Terese too felt the assault on her mind. Who were these women, horrific or beautiful, sensuous or hideous?

They were taken to a high vaulted banqueting hall where a massive roaring fire, a furnace of heat, threw waves of heat and light into the dark flickering shadows. They were offered seats of baronial proportions, covered in bear skin.

Banba welcomed them to Hawardden, "Please drink and have sustenance. Later we will show you Hawardden. You will see the futility of trying to escape!" She clicked her fingers and creatures of the dark, in hooded robes brought food on wooden platter and rich golden amber liqueur in silver chalices.

They ate unusual, unleven bread with veins of green moss rippling through it. They sipped on the liqueur made from crushed and fermented wild oak apples, followed by pungent mountain goat cheese, smoked and spiced with herbs foraged from the steep mountainsides.

The three raven haired witches talked quietly, obviously deliberating on Bith and Terese's future.

One of the witches floated over to the decanter holding the golden amber liqueur. She spoke, offering more of the 'liqueur of life', "I am Fodha, the partner of Prince MacCuill." She introduced her 'sisters', "You have already met Banba, wife of Prince MacGreinne, and here is Eiru, wife of MacCuacht."

They were all incredibly beautiful, if somewhat sinister, but there was something more about Eiru.

Bith thought that there would have to be some X factor about the woman who has the 'heart' of the dark one, MacCuacht. There was something though, that Bith could not place...

Fodha continued to pour the rich liqueur, "Please enjoy! We will talk soon..."

The rich golden amber liqueur 'brewed and fermented over generations in the grounds of Hawardden' slipped smoothly down... too smoothly! There was a heady instantaneous hit, inundating the senses. Bith felt dangerously off guard. Terese too, was intoxicated by this potent concoction.

The food, the drink, the roaring fire and the comfort, Bith suddenly felt himself sinking deeper and deeper...a voice from the spirit world, "Be careful do not trust them!" He was already no longer in control...

Was that his imagination? Fodha was gliding over the stone slabbed floor! Not touching the ground, she floated, constantly changing, from a beautiful sensuous raven haired woman to a hideously warped creature. All in an instant, smiling, shape shifting, her body wrapping around his... he was being taken, drawn in to a realm of dark shadows and lost souls... his power, his energy slowly being lost to the dark Sidhe...

Bith called on all his earthly and otherworldly powers! He was a priest of the Chapter of Mystics surely he could not be taken so easily! He fought. He lashed out at the raven haired temptress. He pulled her to the ground, he tore at the luminescent fabric of her gown, "Was he so weak to the sinister charms and magic of these witches?!"

In that moment there was a burst of radiant penetrating light coming from beyond the veil...

Fodha's form morphed from the rapturous beauty back to the hideous. She repulsed him – he felt her influence waning, back and forth from dark to light. His lifetime of training saving him... but the dark forces finally overwhelmed him... he fell in to a deep, deep sleep...

When he came too... he was out of the mountain fortress. He was on his own, back by the smouldering embers of the camp fire on the ridge where they first met the three witches of Hawardden.

No sign of Terese of the Xantha, "No! By the Great Spirit! That cannot be!" he sighed.

Bith looked up towards the high mountains, the fortress, the three witches... another world, another dark dimension. The mist had cleared, the sun just beginning to rise above the mountain ridges.

No time to dwell! He must go! He questioned the events of the night... did they really happen?!

He must return to the vessel Fintan, before the all enveloping mist of the night returns, before the dark forces find the vessel and the crew protecting it. There is no doubt the witches will come for him...

He found the path winding along the upstream river and began the meandering descent to the sea.

He took one last look towards the high mountain fortress, "Terese!" he whispered under his breath.

He soon found the place where the black valley bog water met the slowly eddying and pushing briny sea water, "Nearly high tide!" thought Bith out aloud, "Perfect timing, the vessel Fintan will soon be afloat!"

Bith pressed on towards the rivermouth. The incoming tide was creeping steadily up the river-bank.

Familiar territory now, he rounded the last bend in the river, and "Praise the Great Spirit!" there was the vessel and his loyal crew. They stood guard by the now gently floating Fintan, moored securely to the same warped and twisted yew trees.

Bith ran the last hundred yards, startling the crew, who raised their swords and pikes in reflex defence. Instantly they recognised Bith, they ran to him, yelling for joy, hugging and embracing him!

"Quietly my good men," Bith trying to calm them, "We must make ready the vessel Fintan. We are in peril. Terese is lost to the dark. A terrible evil tries to possess this land!"

Bith reckoned that with another hand's depth of water, the now surging tide would lift the vessel. He hurried the cohort on board. They all instinctively took position to help safely negotiate Fintan away from the shore. Bith untied the mooring rope, half a hand's depth should be sufficient.

He looked anxiously inland, scrutinising the distant river bank, his gaze darting from sea to mountains.

All quiet! The crew gripped the oars and made ready to push off in an instant. The tide surged and the keel broke free of the sand bank. Synchronicitously, each and every oarsman leaned in to their oars with all their might. Soon they were gliding into deeper water. Their spirits lifted their souls free!

The sea journey began, emotions elated! The journey of survival, and flight to warn the others!

Bith took command at the helm, he steered them in to mid-stream. The oarsmen pulled strongly, deeply, and with intent. They ventured into the widening estuary, away from the grip of the now racing tide.

They began to feel the freshening breeze out in the open sea. Bith ordered the sails to be unfurled.

The mainsail fell in to place. The tide pushed in vain, trying to return them to the river bank. The oarsmen pulled again, the well built, well designed vessel responded in kind.

The outflowing river water eventually won out, they broke free of the eddying tidal race, and started to plane in the open ocean.

Bith, looking up at the mountains once more, caught a glint of a reflection in the corner of his eye.

He steered the vessel further out to sea, another flash of sunlight on metal, the metallic glint of sun on weapons and armour. The army descended from the fortress of Hawardden, the three witches urging them on. Surely they were too far away now!?

Onwards into the open estuary, they felt the sea breeze strengthen. The skeleton crew unfurled the foresail and lashed it into position. On cue a gust forced into the now billowing sails. The crew prepared for the first tack…

The open sea! Surely freedom now!

They all looked back to see the distant figures rounding the last bend of the river.

The NorWester strengthened again. They tacked again.

Bith imagined that he could hear military commands drifting over the waves...

Sailing South now, back to the Milesian fleet, one of the crew pointed to smoke rising from the estuary.

Within minutes a beacon in the mountains fired up, and within minutes of that a beacon on a promontory to the South of them was lit. Warning beacons sending messages around the coast!

Bith knew they must sail into open sea... They sailed on and on into the limitless ocean, not knowing where the threat was going to come from. Their minds started to play tricks on them, they were powerless.

Bith steadied himself at the helm, concentrating on the task of sailing and navigating. Immersed in the roar of the ocean and the gusting breeze, he took the final bearings from the disappearing land.

Soon the horizon was nothing but ocean, and the sun dropping in to the evening sky. The first evening star appeared through the colours of sunset, twinkling ever brighter in clearing night air.

"Good, a clear night!" thought Bith out loud, "Good for navigating..." He watched as the indigo night sky darkened and constellations appeared one by one. Bith gave thanks to the ancient ones who have given him the training in astral navigation, and the wisdom and knowledge of the cosmos – now converted into practical, survival skills of navigation in the vast expanse of the ocean.

The course set, the weather fair, his mind drifted, dreaming of his people, and the reception he would receive on his return...

Bith estimated two to three days sailing, with this wind and this sea state. Perhaps Amergin and the Milesian fleet will have drifted further north than anticipated? Maybe they are sailing to meet them at this very moment? He ordered the watchman to be extra vigilant...

It was a dark night, no moon, the constellations blindingly intense. The universe unfolded before them, the edge of their galaxy, a glowing white milky path leading them to the safety of the fleet.

Bith began to relax. He organised the duty rosta, four hour shifts at the helm, four hour shifts on watch. His seafaring skills were unrivalled, perhaps only matched by the Sea Druid Amergin. The crew had faith in him. They were driven on by the prospect of meeting their fellow countrymen.

Gnawing at the back of his mind, Bith knew his message was vital... Amergin must know of the dark forces that strive to take over the Promised Land!

At the end of his shift, Bith took one more look to the northern horizon... All seemed quiet.

A shooting star flashed over the north-eastern horizon... almost in a direct line with the mountain fortress of Hawardden. A disturbing thought troubled him, "Where was Terese? What on earth had become of her?" Another shooting star! Always from the north-east he observed...

He settled into a makeshift bunk on top deck... ready for any eventuality... but he must sleep...

Another shooting star sped overhead... "That was closer ...!"

Lulled into a somnolent state with the lolling and rolling of the vessel. Drifting... drifting...

"Where was Terese? What had become of her?"

Tortured, flashing memories. His brave companion gone! Had she been possessed by the three witches? If so, better she was dead! He feared their powers of mind control and shape shifting.

He bolted straight upright! All her thoughts, all their plans, were now in the possession of the dark forces of the Sidhe... He was leading them straight to Amergin!

Another shooting star, followed by a warping, morphing cloud of high altitude plasma...

The ocean suddenly took on a brooding, menacing presence. They no longer had any forward motion...

Bith shouted at the crew, "Make ready! Be prepared!" the crew instantly on their guard.

Another shooting star... the vessel seemed rudderless, directionless... They waited...

From deep within, Bith sensed a spiritual connection, "Terese!!!"

A message came to him, a voice... "Forgive me, Bith. I could not resist them... I am taken, possessed. I am one of the dark Sidhe... You have no choice... be one with them... or die!"

Bith knew he had no choice... If he was taken, all the wisdom of Milesia would be in the grasp of the dark Sidhe. A way to Amergin would be completely open. The magical and spiritual powers of the Guardians of Light compromised.

Bith solemnly called his crew, and explained their lot. He asked for a moments silence to honour Terese. Then prayed for her soul, "May the Great Spirit give her peace and sanctuary!"

A darkening front started to encroach from the north-east, extinguishing each star, each planet and each constellation, one by one...

Bith rallied his crew, "Brace yourselves my brave ones, I tell you what needs to be done if all is lost... I will fight to the last, with all my power and strength... Should the cause become futile and all is lost, I will dive into mother-ocean and be taken by her, rather than be consumed and possessed by the dark Sidhe."

Fully armoured the crew knew they would sink rapidly and without trace, out of the reach of the dark forces, gone forever. Should they fight too long, they will become possessed, destined to be one of the army of lost souls for eternity...

Stoically they stood, without fear, resigned to their fate.

The North Star was soon extinguished. They had lost their guiding star. Resolutely they faced into the unknown.

They would never lead the witches and the dark Sidhe to Amergin. That would be a fate worse than death! Bith questioned, "But what of Terese? Would she lead them to Amergin? He must be warned!"

The rolling, all consuming cloud of cold condensing mist and swirling plasma soon reached the vessel Fintan. Beasts and denizens of all shapes and dimensions filled the thick acrid air, demons of the dark. They could not be defeated...

Bith took the lead. In a defiant gesture, he hurled himself into the ocean.

The crew followed bravely and unquestioningly.

Bith's armour took him rapidly into the depths, light glinting on sword and breast plate, plunging, down and down.

His last breath leaving his now dying body, he felt his mind going into unconsciousness, his mortal body sinking into the abyss.

He became aware of a divine radiance from below. Still falling deeper and deeper...

Now hallucinating, in his dying moments, he saw a vision, a face. It was Terese! A gentle smile upon her countenance, she was enveloped by a golden, amber light. Terese had been able to contact the Guardians of Light!

In his final moments Bith knew that Amergin had been warned. His mortal life had not been in vain.

The ocean abyss was now a rich amber cosmos... he was still falling and falling into the eye of Mother Ocean. An eye with a mysterious dark fleck that drew him in, and in, falling deeper and deeper...

CHAPTER SEVEN:
THE WRATH OF MACCUACHT

Amergin now knew that the forces of the dark Sidhe were waiting for him and the Milesian nation.

The voyage of the prophecy had taken on a new dimension... the avenging of the lost souls of Bith, Terese and the vanguard of his most loyal and brave Milesians.

The fleet that had waited patiently for the return of Bith, Terese and the vanguard, now started to make ready. Ropes untied, sails unfurled, sheets fastened... the anchors were raised, the entire fleet jostling and readying into position like a stallion waiting for race orders.

Amergin held the Milesian flag aloft, a flag embodying the prophecy – a tower, a flagship, the Northern Ocean and constellations guiding their way. Once raised, the fleet sailed towards the Promised Land...

Only yesterday evening had the Guardians of Light visited Amergin in his dreams, they brought the message from Terese. She had been fleetingly able to free herself from the control of the three witches and send a warning, "The dark Sidhe have been awakened and are forewarned! They inexorably take control of the promised-land! The Guardians of Light, represented in the mortal realm by the High Priestess of Xhara and Princess of the Western Province, Sceine, wait for you!"

Amergin visited Scota, the Queen of the Milesians, his mentor and muse, "Mother I have seen Sceine again in my dreams. She is an enlightened being of such great beauty. She is surely the one I am destined to be with. So it is prophesied! Together we will challenge the reign of the dark Sidhe. Apart, the Promised Land is doomed!" Scota acknowledged this with a smile and knowing nod of her graceful head.

The prevailing south-westerly winds strengthened, filling the billowing sails. The Milesian flags straightened, pointing their course. Amergin felt his heart and spirit bursting with energy, passion and belief in the cause. The Great Spirit was guiding him to his destiny!

Sceine returned to her high mountain fortress of Sliebh Mis. The Western Province will be the battle front. Her blessed father knew this when she was given the choice of province to rule over!

Word came from the north that the Milesian emissaries, sent by Amergin, had been either possessed or martyred! They had encountered her brothers' wives, the three witches, at the mountain fortress of Hawardden. They had done their dastardly worst! MacCuacht must be proud of them!

Sceine was relieved to know that a message had been given to her destined one, Amergin. She had gone to Amergin in his dreams. They met together beyond the veil. They were as one…

MacCuacht, her dark brother, had announced that he would be visiting the fortress of Sliebh Mis.

He wanted to pay his respects to his father once more. Sceine saw her brother as the real threat. She sensed that her brother was increasingly the representative of the dark Sidhe in the mortal realm. Treachery ran through his veins. He had disobeyed his father Antiem whilst in the Northern Province, incurred the wrath of the Firbolg, and incited the demons of the dark Sidhe.

MacCuacht was visibly incensed when Sceine was granted the Western Province. The most powerful of all the provinces, and anointed the High Priestess of Xhara. Surely as the eldest, he was the rightful heir.

Antiem, however, had seen through his eldest sons' malevolent ways. He had deliberately broken the Kingdom up in to provinces. No one sibling had total authority or control. Antiem had anointed Sceine as High Priestess of Xhara, effectively the spiritual leader, because she was the purest of heart, and only she could truly connect with the Sidhe Guardians of Light.

The wrath of MacCuacht was to be feared. Sceine's very life was in danger!

Their meeting was arranged for the following day. Everything was to be choreographed! Never was Sceine to be left on her own with MacCuacht. Her most loyal guard would chaperone her all the time.

That evening she prayed and meditated, asking for the Great Spirit to guide her and to give her the strength needed on her journey of destiny.

The arrival of MacCuacht and his hordes was heard long before they were seen. The regular, monotone, trudging, march of fully armed and armoured soldiers, climbing the narrow, precarious, perilous track high into the mountains of Sliebh Mis. An occasional sharp, staccato, military command cracked the cool, silent mountain air. A substantial force for an informal gathering, and for paying respects, thought Sceine. The high mountain fortress of Sliebh Mis was on high alert!

MacCuacht arrived at the drawbridge. Sceine instructed all weaponry to be deposited at the gatehouse. She counted thirty soldiers armed to the teeth. Each one was disarmed, and then ushered in to the barracks, and a heavy guard installed.

MacCuacht smiled at his sister, feigning the greeting of a much missed brother.

Sceine was unnerved to see the presence of Eiru… not what she expected! What were the intentions of the witch? Her very presence distracted the royal guard… her dark lustrous beauty, attired in a shimmering cocoon like gown.

Eiru stepped forward and bowed courteously before Sceine, "I am sorry for your troubles. Your father was a great man, and a guiding light to us all!"

Still unnerved, and now in shock, Sceine thanked Eiru for her condolences. Even more unexpected was the withering, resentful glare Eiru received from her husband.

Sceine, quick to recognise a potential ally, responded promptly, "Thank you Eiru! His light still guides us! His wisdom and his spirit will surely light up our lives for a long time to come. He will oversee us to our destiny! Praise the Great Spirit!"

They gathered that night to give their respects to the High King Antiem. This was the first time Sceine had been in the presence of MacCuacht since Antiem's funeral. She could feel the bitterness and resentment.

MacCuacht kept Eiru close beside him. Sceine felt her unease as well... they must talk!

Sceine instructed Sinbar, the master of the royal guard, to take MacCuacht and his commanders on a tour of the battlements and to Antiem's war room. The war room was a sacred place, exclusive to Antiem, where he planned and strategised the military campaign to overthrow the Firbolg.

MacCuacht was intrigued. This could be an opportunity to discover sacred secrets about the Firbolg, secrets that could be critical in the machinations of the dark Sidhe in the future.

He followed the diplomatic Sinbar. Immediately Sceine approached Eiru and asked her to join her on the high balcony, to enjoy the last remains of a dark purple, crimson light over the western horizon. Deep black shadows crept into the valley. Eiru spoke first, "You have inherited the most beautiful and most majestic of the provinces. My husband is most envious."

She had broken the ice. Sceine was encouraged, "Yes, this is the most glorious of places and the most powerful of provinces. My brother has every right to be jealous!" Sceine offered a glass of the mountain berry liqueur 'GraniaX' to Eiru. Sip by sip they were relaxing in each other's presence. The High Priestess of Xhara, Princess of the Western Province, vulnerable and exposed, opening her heart and mind to a witch implicated in the loss and corruption of the emissaries sent by the destined one, Amergin.

"I must do this!" thought Sceine, "I must find out whether she is enemy or perhaps a most valuable ally."

"I appreciate your sentiments towards my dear departed father. I sense that my brother, your husband, does not harbour the same feelings, "pointed out Sceine.

"Where do her allegiances lie?" she thought.

Before the thought had parted from her, the answer was being given...

"I have lost faith in my husband. His ways are controlled by the dark Sidhe!" Of course she is a mind reader, one of the three witches, who can probe the very recesses of the mind. Yet Sceine known for her powers of extra sensory perception could not penetrate Eiru's thoughts. "A skill that has presumably kept her alive in the presence of MacCuacht and her sister witches."

Eiru continued, "I have seen my husband sink into the mire of the dark Sidhe. I have seen him succumb, lose his way, sell his soul to the dark Sidhe. I have seen him use those powers ruthlessly and mercilessly on his enemies, the Firbolg. He will not stop there. MacCuacht is prepared to infect all the portals across the known world, he is prepared to unleash the dark Sidhe, and vanquish the Guardians of Light."

All that Sceine had suspected of her brother, and knew deep within, was now confirmed. But how could this witch be an ally when, she was implicated with the demise of Bith, and the loss of Terese?

Again the answer was forthcoming almost before the thought was formed,"When I encountered Bith, I felt the force for good, and my soul was bathed in the spiritual white light of the Guardians. I sensed the one who comes after him, the one that is destined for this land, destined to be with you. I felt the power of the spirit world, the good Sidhe, and their universal life force."

Sceine looked deep into Eiru's eyes, she could not read her mind, but could see the truth before her. Eiru continued, "I released Bith in order that he could take his chances in returning to the Sea Druid Amergin, hopefully to warn the Milesians of the impending onslaught by the forces of the dark. I permitted Terese to commune with her Xantha sisterhood, and ultimately with the Guardians of Light. This, before my raven haired sisters took her soul in to the dark realm."

"This is exactly how it was!" thought Sceine, "I have an ally in Eiru!"

Eiru smiled, just as an almighty hammering on the ancient oak door to the balcony shattered the peace and quiet contemplation of the moment.

Eiru grabbed Sceine's hand,"I cannot be found here! Alone in your company! He will suspect. He already has his doubts about my allegiance to the dark cause. Sceine you must trust in me…!"

With that her silver shimmering cocooned form and raven hair, morphed and changed and transformed. Feathers of light, silver to white, circulating, swirling… bursts of photonic light… powerful wing beats… a great white tailed eagle was airborne… and soared from the balcony, over the battlements and was gone into the darkness of the night…"A shape-shifter! Magnificent! Such a magical, potent being! Such a powerful ally!" mused Sceine.

Now to deal with her black-hearted brother…

The hammering on the door continued,"Eiru, are you in there?!" Sceine's brazen sibling remonstrated.

Sceine quickly removed the glasses and the pitcher of GraniaX, and slid the bolt of the door back. She prepared for his interrogation, "There you are brother. How was your tour? I hope Sinbar was the perfect guide. Father's war room is intriguing is it not?"

Thrown by this performance, and he in turn could not read Sceine's mind, "Yes it is… Where is my wife?" Flustered, and not a little confused, he strode into the room, searching the shadows. Before he could become the inquisitor, "Eiru was tired after the journey. We made our acquaintances and then I showed her your chambers. And you, you must be tired, and we have much to do tomorrow, "she ushered MacCuacht out of the door and towards their chambers, "I thank you for visiting and coming to pay your respects to our dear beloved father…"

MacCuacht was put off balance by this consumate performance. He turned and with a typical dismissive gesture left to seek out Eiru.

That night the Western Province bathed in the full and potent light of a harvest moon. The spirit of Antiem seemed to be omnipresent. All at Sliebh Mis were restless. The enlightened beings felt a dark and treacherous force in their presence. Each time a scudding cloud partially obscured the shimmering moonlight, Sceine started in her slumbers. She looked deep in to familiar shadows that now seemed threatening. Each dark recess seemed to take on other worldly qualities. She tossed and turned, reliving the encounter with her conspiratorial brother. And Eiru was she a kindred spirit?

Sceine needed further reassurance that she was a friend to the Guardians of Light, and not on some surreptitious mission with the other witches of Hawardden. She sensed that Eiru was truthful about her disquiet over MacCuacht's dark dealings.

Shifting, slanting shadows caught her, now wakeful, attentions, the stark silver light of the full harvest moon diminishing over increasing, gathering, clouds. The heavy, ornately decorated drapes, half enveloping the window frames, billowed in a sudden gust. A storm front approaching, high altitude moisture particles diffracted and refracted the white moonlight into fractured rainbows of light.

Sceine sat bolt upright as the next gust blew the drapes horizontal. The moonlight now blocked by a swift moving sihouette, pirouetting in a beating frenzy of wings, talons and feathers. Feather tips and white tail became a translucent, silver cocooned creation, reflecting the last vestiges of the stormbound moon… Eiru!!!

Sceine had instinctively thrust the tip of a jewelled dagger at the jugular of this interloper.

"Sceine, I did not mean to scare you. You are safe!"

Sceine still needed to be convinced of her truthfulness. "Tell me why you are here! Be honest and be convincing!" Eiru read the intent on her face in her mind. "At this very moment MacCuacht is in collusion with the demons and denizens of the dark Sidhe. When the harvest moon is obscured by the oncoming storm front, he will go to the ancient portal of Hushinish. He will summon the dark Sidhe, and the onslaught will begin…"

"This is as I feared Eiru… thank you for the warning! I must get to Hushinish before MacCuacht!"

"I will take you. Nothing is faster than the mighty white-tailed eagle!" declared Eiru.

Beyond the ramparts and castellations of the fortress of Sliebh Mis, high above the Ridge of Thormond, on a rocky outcrop, overlooking the entire Western Province was the ancient configuration of standing stones, the Portal of Hushinish. The portal aligned with all the other portals on the island of destiny, a network of lay lines across this magical, powerful land. The Western Province had the most powerful and strongest connections to the spirit world. MacCuacht marched there now...

He knew that Hushinish was the source of her power in the Western Province, the place where the Guardians of Light could be summoned, to protect and defend the enlightened ones. He also knew that the portal was most vulnerable at certain times of the year, such as at the harvest moon, or when the kingdom was in transition, as at the time of Antiem's death.

The threatening storm will be the distraction he needed. The harvest moon will be obscured, and the veil of darkness will give time to channel the forces of the dark Sidhe. This would not be a temporal shift, but a permanent change. The universe of the dark Sidhe will pour forth from the Portal of Hushinish, the connection with the Guardians of Light broken forever.

Sceine was aware of the danger. The portents were aligned for MacCuacht to make his treacherous moves. A dark, menacing storm front, twisted and rolled on the still moonlit western horizon. Time was of the essence. "You must take me now Eiru! MacCuacht approaches Hushinish! The darkness arrives! Go!"

Sceine watched as Eiru's body shape shifted and transformed. The lustrous translucent silver cocoon garment warped and morphed. Molecular and photonic light exuded from her very being, the brightness almost unbearable. Sceine turned her eyes away, her retinas burning. An explosion of light and her shape was transformed. The dark haired witch of Hawardden had become one of the mightiest raptors ... the white-tailed eagle!

Gripped by talons, they soared over the battlements, high into the leaden skies, away from Sliebh Mis. Sceine focused on the distant horizon, the Ridge of Thormond, and beyond that the rocky outcrop of Hushinish.

There! Way below them, traversing the Ridge of Thormond were MacCuacht's foraging soldiers. They were on course for Hushinish, and in time for the zenith of the full moon.

Eiru with her avian super senses had seen them and with a few powerful wing beats ascended into the high altitude clouds to avoid detection.

Sceine felt uneasy, she was being taken into the darkening, moisture laden storm wall. The dark forces were gathering. All her senses screamed to be returned to the comforting evening light.

Over the ridge and away from the line of sight, Eiru swooped down, dropping like a stone out of the clouds.

Silver shafts of moonlight picked out the rugged outcrop of Hushinish.

All the peaks and summits, every significant feature seemed to point and pay homage to this sacred place. Every lay line, sacred and magnetic, spiritual and otherworldly, converged here. The stark silhouettes of the standing stone circle of Hushinish stood up on top of this mysterious place, a portal that brought the veil from the spirit world into the mortal realm.

Only beings with a pure royal blood lineage could open the portal. MacCuacht and Sceine were such beings. Those blessed with the key to a portal were intended to use that key for the enlightenment of their race, the key to enter a universe of pure light and of unbounded good. Antiem their royal father would be turning in his grave if he knew the intentions of MacCuacht!

MacCuacht planned to open a black universe, void of light, bereft of goodness. His soldiers of dark, some of the army of lost souls, were within striking of the Portal of Hushinish. MacCuacht strode onwards, his goal in sight. The evening light diminishing, the storm approaching, the moon nearing fullness, the moment arrives. He looked around… the distant fortress of Sliebh Mis… all quiet and unaware. He had deceived his sister, her trust in him misplaced… but that pleased him.

His upper lip twisted in to something vaguely reminiscent of a smile,"This was his time! This was his rendezvous with the dark Sidhe, nothing to stop him!" So he thought…

The shadows of the standing stone fell into alignment, the gate stones stood dark and sinister, black against the oncoming storm. The moon rose in completion of its cycle, above the outcrop. The moment was at hand.

MacCuacht strode determinedly towards the stone circle. Standing between the gate stones, reaching skywards to touch the capstone, he would become the key. Here where the multiverses touch, he would choose the darkest. The mortal realm sentenced to eternal damnation, the Guardians of Light to eternal darkness. In his mind he was there… No one to stop him!

The moon at fullness, the storm wall approaching. The silhouette of her brother… time stood still… everything in alignment…

Sceine could feel the energy flowing, the universes touching. She sensed the Guardians with her. She felt their presence guiding Eiru as she beat her mighty wings. With powerful down beats she landed Sceine directly in to the stone circle, in reach of the gate stones. Immediately she straddled the giant Bluestones and reached skyward to touch the capstone!

"Impossible!" screamed MacCuacht. He struck out to stop her… Her hand brushed the Bluestone, fingertips touching, charging, energising. White light poured forth, a divine radiance, a universe of love …

Sceine stood defiantly before her now demented brother, "In the name of Antiem, you are banished from the Western Province, never return to Sliebh Mis!"

MacCuacht recognised the nemesis that was his sister, cowed but not defeated, he was visibly shaken,

"The dark forces still gather my beloved sister… I shall return!"

The radiance repulsed him, his aura darkening even now…

Eiru appeared in human form and disappeared in to the darkness…

MacCuacht reluctantly retreated to the Ridge of Thormond.

Sceine looked up to see the storm front dissipating… to be replaced by clear skies and constellations sparkling brighter than ever… the moon continued into the next lunar cycle…

CHAPTER EIGHT:
THE GLINT OF AN UNBLINKING EYE

Amergin stirred from a deep slumber. He was one of those fortunate beings that could sleep well regardless of the adversity. The memories and infinite flashes of other realities were still with him as he stirred from a dream of kaleidoscopic detail. Colours, universes, recognisable and unrecognisable beings, diaphanous tendrils of a dream state clung to him as he came back to a state of wakefulness.

He has drifted to a place where universe collided with universe. He had seen Bith of the Chapter of Mystics, and Terese of the Xantha battling valiantly. His heart sunk at the loss of them in the cold light of day.

Still struggling to distinguish reality from surreality, the visions of the dreams thinned and disappeared. But as the first rays of bright morning sunlight burst into his quarters, he had seen a vision of Sceine standing defiantly in a great portal, channeling light, a living conduit of pure energy…

Amergin's heart missed a beat, his mood and spirit uplifted. His body coursing with renewed vigour, his mind clear and the way forward clearly mapped.

Fully awake now, in tune with the day unfolding before him… a fresh oceanic day, a bright clear light. A steady south-westerly breeze and a gentle undulating sea state, the clarity of the early morning light gave an infinity of vision, "How good it feels!" exclaimed Amergin, "Let us find the promised land!"

He hung manfully on to the rigging as the royal vessel rolled in a steadily growing swell. He braced himself, and smiled in exhilaration. The bow broke a cresting wave, sending a fine, cooling, refreshing spray over his body. Amergin stood momentarily in a rainbow of sea spray, caught and illuminated by the low, crystal clear dawn rays of sunlight.

The early shift, led by Xomas, was now aware of his presence. They smiled with Amergin and in unison yelled, "To the Promised Land!"

One of those days when the ocean was alive and energizing, the tell tale living vortex of deep diving Gannets announced the presence of vast shoals of fish. On cue from the south-west came a charging, surging, pod of Common Dolphin, hundreds of them! They all watched in awe, as they leapt through the ocean, elegant, dynamic masters of the ocean, feeding and joining the frenzy with the diving Gannets.

Amergin instructed the crew to cast out long lines. This day they will feast, and the hold will be filled to the gunnels, "A blessing heaven sent!" delighted Amergin.

Looking back along the line of the fleet, he saw each crew starting to fish. Instantly fish were being hooked. Flashing, electric shoals of mackerel threw themselves at the hooks. Ten at a time they were landed, hooks gouged out, gutted and placed into trays of sea salt ready for curing. Food for the journey!

"Provisions for the battle ahead!" contemplated Amergin, "these fishers of men will need sustenance and all their strength for what is to come!"

Xomas came over and stood by Amergin commenting on the bountiful ocean, "There, my lord, a pod of Pilot whales coming to join the feast! This is a rich feeding ground. There seems to be an upwelling here, maybe a sign that we are moving from deep ocean to a shallower coastal shelf. I will tell the look-outs to be extra vigilant!" Amergin nodded in agreement as he watched the Pilot whales surface and feed on the starboard side.

Then the whole crew cheered in exuberance as a giant of the ocean appeared on the port side. A loud and voluminous blow that forced upwards twenty feet, "A Fin whale!" yelled Xomas, "one of the benign giants of the ocean, filter feeding in this rich upwelling from the abyss."

They both could see the place where the colder waters from the deep met the warmer waters of the continental shelf. The white line of turbulence and spume spread northwards to the far horizon.

"Tell the crew to be vigilant Xomas!" instructed Amergin, "Communicate with the rest of the fleet, we will tack to the north-east, and tell them to be prepared!" On the port side, the giant of the ocean seemed to be aware of their plans, and with a mighty blow, dove deep into the abyss, never to be seen again.

Far into the distance another filter feeding giant of the ocean appeared on the starboard side, a Minke whale, dark and mysterious, occasionally surfacing and then diving deep.

"This ocean is the richest I have ever seen!" announced Xomas, "A good sign, we must be close...."

The fleet now turned into the north-east. The Minke whale continued to arc and dive, quietly feeding in isolation.

"Heartening!" declared Xomas, "A sign of fine weather and fair sailing."

"Hopefully!" agreed Amergin, "We must remember the foe we face at all times!"...a solemn subdued warning, the exhilaration of the day punctured by reality. In the dwindling light of the evening their sense of foreboding was confirmed. The watchman exclaimed loudly, "Killer Whales on the port side!" These were not gentle giants of the ocean! They were the top predators. Killers by name, killers by nature! Not even on their sturdy vessels were they safe! Many a tale of ancient mariners told of Orcas broadsiding and sinking unsuspecting vessels.

Amergin, Xomas and all the Milesian crews watched anxiously as the pod of eight Orcas powered through the ocean. They went ahead of the fleet. They were heading directly for their unwitting, unassuming prey. The benign filter feeding, yet elusive Minke Whale.

Amergin stood on the prow observing, in quiet awe, the eight Orcas surrounding the Minke.

Surrounded and prevented from diving deep, the Minke headed out for the open ocean, trying to out run the Orca, size for size, the individual versus the pod. Baleen versus toothed whale, the odds were stacked. The Minke surfaced and thrashed its massive fluking tail. Shallow dives and thrashing tail, racing to deep water. Waiting for the junior Orca to make a mistake, a lapse in their hunting strategy…

The largest Orca bull charged at the Minke, trying to turn it over, trying to drown it…Once turned over the pod would close ranks, keeping the giant submerged, death would be quick.

Totally outnumbered, time running out, the Minke panic stricken, charged a juvenile Orca! An irresistible force meeting an almost immovable object!

Mass and sheer force won out, the Minke whale head charged and lifted the juvenile right out of the ocean. In the confusion the Minke whale sent out a giant, defiant blow of sea air and in one motion surfaced and then dove deep, deep and way beyond the reach of the frustrated Orca. The pod dove in unison. They were gone for minutes, but Amergin knew the Minke was in its own realm now.

All the teeth and brutality of the Orca were to no avail… here the Minke could dive deeper, stay under longer, and disappear into the twilight of the abyssal depths.

Amergin stepped down from the prow. What a spectacle, the chaser and the chased, the predator and the prey, outnumbered but not outfought!

A poignant tale of cetaceans, the parallel of Milesians versus the dark Sidhe was not lost on Amergin.

Xomas stayed at the helm while Amergin made sure the entire crew, were on alert. "Keep watch, my brave ones. The Orcas have been thwarted. They may turn their attentions on to us!"

Amergin returned to his quarters. The evening light steadily diminishing… still no sign of the Orcas…

In the gunnels of the wooden, clinker built vessel, the energy and constant percussive sounds of the ocean were filtered out. A crashing wave became a noise of gentle buffeting. The wind through the rigging became a sonorous low pitched lullaby. "A good contemplative place!" thought Amergin. He needed it… his tribe were on the cusp of a great journey. To connect with the spirit world, he liked to clear his mind and let his thoughts pour forth in a stream of consciousness.

The thoughts came forth in poetic lyrical form. His thoughts, his dreams, his emotions, his love and his faith in the Great Spirit…

"Purify your heart...
Turn away from the material world, and look deep within.
Find your true self, your immaterial agent of thought.
Assimilate to eternity, to the unity within.
Your body a reflection, an image, that counts for nought.

Unity linked to beauty, to goodness, to truth.
Original unity, mystical nothingness, the form of the good,
Intellectually, intuitively, anchored to a universal truth,
Celestial hierarchy, the soul, the intellect, the mystery of the Great Spirit"

Amergin's philosophical and poetic contemplations were jarred back into reality..."Orca! Orca!" the watch man yelled. The pod had returned, thwarted and frustrated by the Minke, but still in chase mode... the hunt was still on!

Amergin commanded the crew, "Remain at your positions! Be steadfast and we shall endure!"

He hurried to the weapons store and quickly handed out eight foot pikes. They would be ready to lunge at first sight of an Orca.

Amergin recalled the tales of ancient mariners that told of Orca leaping clear out of the ocean and broadsiding unsuspecting vessels. Shattering wooden hulls and splintering masts, and then preying on the crew. "Surely this vessel is built too strongly? Surely the Orcas would not attack one of a fleet of vessels?"

Xomas sounded the ships bell, warning the rest of the fleet to be on high alert until the danger was passed!

The pod of Killer whales divided and cruised powerfully through on both sides of the fleet. They were looking for weaknesses...

They had all watched as the Orcas hassled, harassed and cajoled the Minke. Again they probed, they tested. They were the prey! These massive cetaceans were cunning, deadly and threatening!

At the end of the line of the fleet, they dove in unison. They had reconnoitered and assessed their prey and now they contemplated their attack...

A murderous silence fell around, only the sound of the ship's bell.

On high alert, all of the crews were armed with pikes. The vessels closed ranks in a well rehearsed naval manoeuvre. They presented a united front, pikes in readiness, to their speedy, deadly aggressors.

Amergin looked down the line of the fleet, he saw his brothers Eimbear and Eiremhou, and Scota and Milidh, all stood, pikes in hand, on the prows of their respective vessels. Amergin had a very uneasy feeling about this... These were top predators with deadly intent. Mariners' tales were one thing, but for a pod to take on an entire fleet! This had the feel of a dark conspiracy. Other forces were at work here...

From the depths, dark and foreboding, came an intense high pitched wail, like the sound of a Banshee. This sent shivers up the spines of all the Milesians. The Banshee was deep in their psyche, to them it meant that a life would be taken that night... the portal to the spirit world would open and emissaries of the dark would snatch a soul for their own evil intent...

"Be ready my brave ones!" shouted Amergin. He braced himself, pike facing towards the depths. As one, the pod of Orcas, flexing every muscle and sinew, burst through the surface intent on a kill!

A powerful bull exploded out of the ocean immediately in front of Amergin. Amergin was consumed by a frothing, seething avalanche of aerated white water! All eight Orcas were airborne in an orchestration of assassins. They breached in unison with calamitous effect, belly flopping as an entity, sending half the ocean, so it felt, in a monstrous wall of foaming brine straight at the flagship.

"Brace yourselves!" Xomas yelled, as half of the crew, in self survival mode, let go of their pikes and grabbed rigging, the others dropped to the deck like stones.

Only this morning, Amergin was reveling in the glory of the day, the cooling spray of the breaking ocean. Now! A mighty weight of water fell on him, knocked him from the prow, flooring him heavily and painfully. Winded, wounded and bedraggled, half concussed, he frantically grabbed a loose sheet lying on the deck. His safety line as half the ocean drained from the deck. Like live bait dangling from that line, he held on with all his strength, for dear life! Washed out over the railings, he stopped at the extremity of the line – just as the jaws of the massive bull Orca snapped shut, a hair's breadth away from Amergin's exposed torso! With a glint of an unblinking eye, the monster disappeared back into the deep.

Serrated teeth and sheer jaw power had snapped Amergin's pike clean in two. "That could have been my body!" thought Amergin, "So close!" His senses recovering, but still in shock, he anxiously looked around. The ocean still receding, he saw one poor soul taken in the torrent of sea water, his arms flailing desperately, before the jaws of the same unblinking monster snapped together, dismembered in a gory instant...

Other crew started to get to their feet as the tide receded. Xomas hung on bravely and steadfastly to the tiller. Amergin went to him, they were speechless. Instinctively they knew they had to act fast!

They peered down into the depths, only a trail of spiraling spume in the liquid slabs of turbulent dark water showed any indication of their hunters presence, a swirling stream of oxygenated crimson, the only remains of the brave crew man. "The Orcas will return!" Amergin was sure of this. These deadly top predators will be merciless!

Amidst the turmoil, they must react calmly, their lives depended on it.

Amergin remembered the plight of the Minke whale. Their response too, must be strong, forceful and effective. There will be an instantaneous glimmer of a chance against the hunting Orcas. They must take it, but how?!

Amergin and Xomas mustered all their marine skills and survival instincts…

They would form a raft, close ranks, strength in numbers, just as pelagic fish shoal to confuse their predators and maximise their chance of survival.

Just enough light to mirror a message, the word flashed around the fleet. They immediately began to close ranks. They knew one charge from an Orca bull would be sufficient to sink a vessel. They were in grave danger. The fleet was spread out still, the line exposed and vulnerable.

"Orca!!!" screamed the watchmen on a number of rafting vessels. Instinctively they braced themselves, pikes to the ready! The last vessel in line was the weak point, exposed and vulnerable, like a forlorn isolated cetacean…

Separated from the core fleet, they were the target! This time the Orcas charged in one irrepressible line. Six of the Orcas breached as one, crashing into the ocean and sending an all consuming wall of white water to the port side of the vessel… It lurched and rolled, exposing the hull and the keel. With this, the remaining two of the Orca launched into the heavens, propelled by their massive fluked tails. They landed with an almighty, shuddering crash and huge downward force on the weaker timbers of the hull. The sound of fracturing, splintering, cracking timbers could be heard throughout the fleet. The crew of the floundering vessel were in the water and scrambling for their lives, trying to climb on the overturned hull. To no avail! They were as lambs to the slaughter. One by one, Orcas charged, and charged again. One by one the frantic crewmen were mercilessly plucked from the rolling overturned hull, nowhere to hide, like stranded seal pups in the shallows of some desolate beach.

A body blow to the entire fleet, they all whinced and recoiled at the sheer power and devastation. Amergin grabbed the ship's bell rallying the fleet, the message urgently sent to keep rafting. Xomas, sickened to the pit of his stomach, leapt from rail to rail as each vessel drew in, lashing the vessels together and telling each crew to lash the eight foot pikes facing outwards in a protective rampart of bronze spear heads.

Amergin in survival mode called to Xomas, "Breath is life! Instruct each vessel on the outer raft to soak their rope fenders in palm oil." Amergin hoped the slick of oil will hinder the Orcas, hampering their breathing, and irritating their eyes. An act of desperation to keep the monsters at bay…

The palm oil soon began to ooze into the ocean from the saturated rope fenders. A glistening, smothering, suffocating slick covered the surface of the ocean, spreading ever outwards.

The last vessel in the line had been sacrificed, giving the rest of the fleet time to defend against the onslaught. One desperate martyr clung to the overturned hull. Amergin had to turn away as the unfortunate man threw himself into the ocean in a desperate bid to reach the rafting fleet. Never a chance! With an appalling upward motion of gaping jaws, he was taken.

The jaws snapped shut, severing his torso and flailing limbs. The poor soul gone!

An occasional diving sea bird succumbed to the oozing slick of palm oil – never to fly again!

The fleet felt as if they were in the bloody final scene of a macabre carnival act, as the leader of the Orca pack rose imperiously out of the slick covered ocean, with a mighty flexing thrust of the fluking tail, rolled in mid air and with an awful snapping of jaw and teeth, tried to pluck one of the watchmen from his lookout on the outer raft, disappearing beneath the waves with that demonic set grin and the unblinking eye staring back at his fearful audience.

"This cannot be all nature Xomas!" conjectured Amergin, "This has to be driven by more sinister players. This has to be the dark Sidhe at work!"

Amergin's faithful comrade in arms had to agree, "I have heard of mariners' tales of old, but nothing quite like this. Nothing so orchestrated, so macabre, so evil…"

The last remains of the crippled and broken vessel sank into the void, an unceremonious sea grave for the brave crew. The eerie murderous silence returned, the ever thickening oozing slick deadening the sea's surface. Time stood still, the dreadful waiting. When will the Orcas return?

Amergin's attention turned to the vessels lashed into the outer raft. He recognised the figures deep in fraternisation, the untrustworthy High Priest of the Chapter of Mystics, Gonne, and his headstrong, unruly and now suspicious brother Eimbear.

Amergin waited until they returned to their own vessel. He leapt from vessel to vessel checking for anything out of the ordinary. Sure enough, he found lashings untied, pikes thrown to the floor, and where was the watch?! More worryingly he spotted the palm oil saturated rope fenders drifting away from the fleet. There was a breach in their defences! There is an enemy within!

Amergin's stomach churned. A concoction of fear and deception unsettled him. He was right to be fearful, in the distance a rigid dorsal fin of a giant Orca! The killers had returned!

The deception cut him to the core… his own brother! Deception by Gonne was by now a given, his corruption well known, but deception by his own blood line!?…words and emotions failed him. They threaten the entire mission, and the lives of his loyal mariners.

The upright, posturing, sail-like dorsal fin sliced through the ocean surface, heading straight towards the now place of weakness, where they had no defences."Orca!!! To your positions!" fully animated Amergin added, "The defences are down here! Make ready! We are under attack!"

Xomas was the first to react. He had been watching Amergin inspecting the defences…Amergin braced himself at the exact place where there was a breach, pike pointing seaward.

The Orca bull meant business. The tip of the dorsal fin sliced the sea, submerged and was gone! "He charges!" A powerful submarine thrust of the tail fluke threw up an eruption of boiling sea.

One of the crew, slow to react whilst tying a new fender, lost his footing. He was a stride away from the safety of the deck. Amergin cried out" Hurry! You have no time!"

Torpedo like, the Orca projected up and out of the ocean! In one calculated, rolling motion, lunged at the panicked crew man with evil intent and ferocity!

Amergin was shocked! Such evil! Such intent!

The Orca plucked the crew man off the dangling fender, a tender morsel in a sprung man trap, that snapped violently shut. Falling to the depths, the ocean stained blood red...The same dark swirling turbulence... then silence.

The crew and Amergin were in shock... they froze momentarily...

Amergin sprung into action, "Get the defences back. Soak the fender with oil. Lash the pikes in position!"

He knew the rest of the Orca would soon follow. In that moment he saw the rigid dorsal fin cut through the surface... seconds away he calculated at the speed of the attack. Another crew man was in the line of attack, tying one of the fenders... just a stride away from safety! "Not again!" Panicked Amergin, "Not this time!" he screamed out. This brute must be stopped!

Adrenalin coursed through his veins, he took his life into his own hands and threw himself on to the fender... just as the giant bull Orca flexed its mighty tail, projected into the air towards the defenceless crewman. Amergin lunged out with the bronze spear-headed pike, and as the monster rolled he sunk it deep, just behind the unblinking eye. A perfect strike! The harpooning pike caused the killer whale to veer, the jaws snapping shut on thin air. The giant bull fell back into the slick covered ocean.

Amergin held on tight to his comrade, as the water receded, soaked yet relieved, still in shock, the two of them were hauled to safety.

Xomas took over, seeing to the defences, soaking fenders in palm oil and lashing the pikes into place.

Amergin and his fellow crewman sat in a haunched recovery position, breathing deeply, watching the ocean. Their senses bruised and battered, but still alert to whatever might come next.

Amergin regained his composure, and stood next to Xomas. Staring out to the horizon, "What now!?" Xomas knew they had only gotten a respite. Surely the Orcas would return!

The light of the day almost extinguished now, it was nigh on impossible to see anything. Amergin ordered the archers to assemble at the prow of the flagship. He instructed Xomas to throw a fender soaked in palm oil overboard, letting the currents and the wind take it away from the fleet, and to where an Orca dorsal fin was last spotted. The fender was far enough away when Amergin ordered the archers to shoot fiery arrows, setting it alight.

The blazing fender cast an eerie reflective glow over the ocean, giving them at least a chance of observing the Orca pod. As darkness descended Amergin was aware that the odds shifted in the favour of the Orcas. While the drifting fender continued to burn they might see an oncoming charge. Even so the odds were stacked against them at night. The Orcas' super senses and honed predating skills left them nigh on helpless, defenceless and at the mercy of these mighty predators.

The crew watched, straining their night vision to its limit. Amergin and Xomas looked for any movement, any dark silhouettes of the upright dorsal fins. The flames from the drifting fender flickered, the palm oil nearly burnt out, the illumination diminishing. "Look, to the south!" Xomas grabbed Amergin's arm and pointed, "Just there, the entire Orca pod!"

Sure enough, barely visible, the dark sinister silhouettes of a number of upright dorsal fins, hardly moving, they appeared to be circling around an injured bull Orca. The fin of this Killer Whale had become lopsided. The others were slowly circling around the bull Orca, moving it slowly out into the deep ocean. This was the injured Orca bull, harpooned by Amergin, it was being nursed and coaxed away from danger... the killers were moving away!

The flames on the fender raft flickered into the descending darkness. Extinguished finally as the circling pod of Orca disappeared from sight, nursing the giant Orca bull.

One more battle in the name of the prophecy! The fleet relaxed and continued to drift quietly onwards, the crew in shock, nursing their wounded souls, grieving for their comrades.

Amergin moved slowly and deliberately from ship to ship, clambering deck to deck, rallying his fellow Milesians, praising their bravery in the face of adversity, saluting those that had sacrificed their lives in the name of the prophecy.

Amergin embraced each of the captains, imploring them to raise their own and their crews' spirits.

The next day he would lead the fleet in a commemorative ceremony, mourning their passing but celebrating their lives and their brave deaths. The Chapter of Mystics and the royals would give their blessings.

That night as the crew rested, Amergin and Xomas took the watch in turn. The fire on the raft well extinguished. A new crescent moon rose over the northern horizon and Venus in the west heralding the dawning of a new day. Every cresting wave, in the increasing South Westerly, resembled surfacing Orca in the mind's eye. Vigilance mixed with foreboding. How many encounters will it take? How many life threatening ordeals? How many of the crew will be lost?

Amergin drifted fitfully into a worried sleep... What of the Guardians of Light? He dreamed fleetingly of another place... where great standing stones dominated the horizon... A blinding, searing light from a portal to the spirit world... a beautiful enlightened being standing astride the gatestones... Sceine!

Amergin woke slowly, knowing now that the battle was being fought on all fronts and over all horizons. This is the time of confrontation, the time for endurance. Personal courage will be needed and faith in their cause.

Amergin felt his father's hand on his shoulder, "It is time my son. The dawn arrives. We are all gathered to commemorate our lost ones, and then to begin the next phase of our journey of destiny."

Scota took her son's hand. Eiremhou and Eimbear walked in procession with the representatives of the Chapter of Mystics. Gonne, the sinister High Priest, raised the conch to his lips and blew with all his might. The sonorous, mournful, resounding notes filled the cool dawn air. They all fell to their knees in prayer as the first rays of sun burst over the eastern horizon.

Milidh met the dawn with a discordant chant, calling upon the Great Spirit to guide and protect them.

Scota sang to the gathered fleet in a pure voice befitting such a royal beauty. The fleet harmonised in chorus. They could collectively feel their spirits lifting. Their hearts, bodies and souls healing...

It was Amergin's moment, he stood proud and strong, projecting his voice loud and clear. As the warrior prince, poet and sea druid he delivered a rallying speech to his fellow Milesians...

CHAPTER NINE:
THE MESSAGE OF ENLIGHTENMENT

The Divine is absorbed into nature when the Guardians of Light enter the mortal realm. The spiritual and the physical combine, never to return beyond the veil into the spirit world. The life force grows and evolves. All living beings and creatures are irradiated with this energy.

Sceine, as the High Priestess of all the enlightened beings can commune with creatures of every kind. She can command them to do her will. Together they will act in the force of good.

The High Priests of Xhara were aware of her growing powers. Her energy shone like a beacon across the verdant and beautiful Western Province, and over the vast and limitless Northern Ocean.

Sceine, as a beacon of pure and radiant light called the enlightened ones to her land. Sceine rested quietly at the Portal of Hushinish. She had won this battle against MacCuacht, the representative of the dark Sidhe in this mortal realm. She had released the pure energy of the Guardians of Light from the Portal of Hushinish. The equilibrium between the Guardians of Light and the dark Sidhe had been restored. The Portal of Hushinish was in her power, for now at least.

MacCuacht had been repelled, but she knew he would return, he would come again...

There will be a time when he will try to usher the dark Sidhe through the veil and take Tuatha into a dark place. Once there, the dark Sidhe will prevail for the entire cycle known as "Xustra" when planetary influences and the ever increasing trajectory away from the influence of the sun cause the veil between the mortal realm and spirit world to thin and become vulnerable to intrusion and corruption.

The cycle known as "Xustra" begins at the coming equinox, when the balance is tipped and the time of the dark prevails over the time of light. The cycle lasts for a thousand and one years...

Sceine senses that the veil thins now and draws ever closer to the mortal realm. The existing portals in the mortal realm are being compromised and darkened, and even more worryingly newly created dark portals are sucking the very life force and natural Divine energy out of the mortal realm.

This inexorable process continues to strengthen.

The balance tipping slowly and seemingly inevitably. The coming equinox will be critical… She is destined to be with the one known as the Champion of Milesia, the Sea Druid Amergin. He will be key to her and her nation's future…

Sceine took heart and strength from the evidence before her. The Portal of Hushinish was so strong and so pure, so enduring. She rejoiced in this place, revelling in the beauty… the luxurious, verdant growth.

A living place abundant with wildlife, the air filled with the raucous cries of birds of all kinds. Sceine felt growth and life in the air, the "Divine" emanating from the portal. She touched the capstone once more and felt the energising charge earthing through her body… pure life, pure goodness…

She channeled her thoughts into the ether, telling all, human or animal or spiritual, to be strong, pure and faithful, "I am here for you. The moment arrives when we must all rally, rise and unite against our darkest foe."

Sceine knew that only in unity would the Island of Destiny prevail. She felt the presence of the prophesied one, only now venturing out of the deepest ocean, only now about to encounter the dangers so feared. Sceine sent a message to her destined one on the wings of a pure white swan.

Out of the ether, above the radiance of Hushinish, the gloriously rising swan soared into a glowing amber mist and was gone. "My love, I send you this most beautiful of creatures to guide you, to bring you to me, safely."

Sceine called on her priests to meditate and pray, to connect with the Guardians of Light. They sent messages of encouragement, counseling and advising their priests and their faithful to show bravery and fortitude in the face of the sinister Dark Sidhe.

Even now the portals at the extremities of their land were beginning to be compromised, coming under the influence of the dark forces. Priests and priestesses were witness to the savage forays of MacCuacht. They saw Divine life forms being drawn back into darkening portals. Lured in and lost forever. These lost souls were turned against the Guardians of Light. The portals were literally becoming black holes, insidious and threatening, preventing everything from escaping. Divine light was sucked back beyond the Veil. Growth was halted, the vibrancy of new life deadened.

All kinds of strange events were happening all over the land. Strange forms were appearing where the creative life force met the destructive dark forces. The very essence of life, the genetic makeup, was morphed and deconstructed. Here was a strange limbo zone where heavenly forms morphed into demons and denizens of the dark. Here was a place of lost souls, who were then sent on missions of destruction beyond the veil…

Such deconstructed apparitions were sent to seek out Amergin… the dark Sidhe were aware of his coming…

Only the intervention by the Guardians of Light would save the unsuspecting Milesians.

Sceine summoned the priesthood once more… they must act quickly!

Over the distant ocean, many horizons away, out of a rolling amber mist, flew a white feathered form of perfection. Amergin was the first to see this white winged wonder... meant for his eyes only...

Mysteriously, magically, his mind and his senses were filled with the sensual sounds of the woman of his dreams and visions, "My love, I send this most beautiful of creatures to guide you, to bring you to me safely. "The long necked feathered beauty came to him from the same amber cosmos that he fell into in his dreams...

Samhain, the most gifted and connected of Sceine's priesthood spoke first, clearly explaining the predicament confronting them, "The Milesians have far to travel. They are spiritually bruised and impaired. They have encountered grave dangers, and now confront the strengthening hordes of the dark Sidhe. Turning to Sceine, "I fear that MacCuacht now knows of your predestined meeting with the Sea Druid Amergin, the champion of Milesia. He will try to mastermind and engineer Amergin's downfall. It is critical that the poet warrior is protected, to ensure that you will meet."

This was Sceine's worst fear! How can Amergin be protected?

MacCuacht was most certainly aware of their fated meeting. He had shown his hand at Hushinish. MacCuacht was wounded but undeterred, mentally scarred but his allegiance to the dark Sidhe ever strengthening. The Portal of Hushinish was under the control of the Guardians of Light, but for how long? The tide seemed to be turning. Darkness was encroaching on all the portals. On his return to Hawardden he schemed and contrived to find a way of entrapping Sceine and the Milesian champion Amergin.

MacCuacht's cohorts marched eastwards to the high mountain fortress of Hawardden. The army of lost souls seemed to know no fear. They were enslaved and indoctrinated, following MacCuacht to the death. Their ranks swelled all the time, every confrontation turning more poor souls... the Firbolg, Bith and the vanguard... Even Terese of the Xantha! A mighty recruit! She convinced MacCuacht of the inevitability of his victory. If such a steadfast, ardent supporter of the Milesian cause can be manipulated, then who will be able to resist?

Arrogance was a major chink in MacCuacht's armour, he dangerously assumed that the dark Sidhe were invincible. His arrogance blinded him to the reality that even though bodies and minds were lost to the dark, the hearts and souls could be redeemed, in some at least...

MacCuacht could feel the very life force of the enlightened ones diminishing. Every portal they passed was capturing light and drawing it back through the veil into the darkening spirit world.

There were an exceptional few, who when exposed to truth and light could be saved... Eiru was such a being. She had been converted to the light. She only now had to peer into the cold, unseeing eyes of her ex partner to realise he was forever lost, forever darkened. The light and life was gone irretrievably. Her world was now threatened by him.

Eiru had seen through his deception, his lies, the horrors perpetrated on the Firbolg and his unfaithfulness to Antiem. The deciding factor was the deception of his beautiful, loyal sister Sceine. She was the embodiment of the light, the epitomy of goodness, love and compassion, traits that were long disappeared in MacCuacht.

Eiru felt compelled to help Sceine, even if it meant turning against her "husband." The witches! What of the Witches?! Banba and Fodha were mind readers and clairvoyants and shape shifters like Eiru. They were black witches, dark and devious. They scared Eiru even more than MacCuacht. They had tapped into a vein of the darkest magic. Eiru will have to protect herself. She must cloak her thoughts and guard her actions. Once installed in the fortress of Hawardden she would find an opportunity to escape and join Sceine. Eiru knew the time had arrived. Sceine will need all the help she can get.

The army of lost souls marched onwards, through the Gap of Varna, around Lake Neidin and there towering before them the mountain fortress of Hawardden in the Iveare mountain range. The track narrowed, and the line of soldiers thinned as they wound their way up the mountain trail.

Eiru found herself walking next to Terese of the Xantha... "A powerful, beautiful, amazonian woman" thought Eiru. She wondered about her, she had been converted only recently, and as a member of the Milesian vanguard must have been intensely loyal.

Eiru looked into Terese's eyes, they seemed to have that familiar cold, soulless gaze, but she was so recent... Perhaps there was a way to redeem this lost soul. She would try all her potions and spells once they were back at Hawardden. She must try before escaping to join Sceine.

There was a gathering of the clan that night, a great banquet for the returning forces. Not a celebration, but a collective scheming. Hushinish had been a set-back for MacCuacht.

His brothers MacCuill and MacGreinne, showing their own Machiavellian streaks, questioned his authority. They both, MacCuill in particular, had found his treatment of the Firbolg and his disloyalty to Antiem, their much loved father, very distasteful.

The banquet roared on, much of the Mead of Banna was quaffed, the company getting rowdier and rowdier. There was tangible disquiet in the camp, brother accusing brother...

This was the perfect opportunity for Eiru to make her exit. She searched for Terese. Eiru was so intrigued by her...

Terese sat with a group next to the huge open hearth fireplace in the vast entrance hall of Hawardden. The fire blazed, sending out flickering, jumping, threatening shadows around the great hall.

Eiru stood next to Terese and offered her a glass of the rich amber mead,

81

"My husband has asked me to talk to you Terese. He believes with your background and experience, you could be of great value to us in the coming times, "she lied, "come, let us talk."

Terese took the glass and quietly sipped the mead. Eiru had laced the mead with a potion she used to enhance her own powers of clairvoyancy. She hoped the potion would be absorbed into the innermost recesses of her mind and body, infuse into her blood, and promote her own life spirit to the surface.

Eiru waited patiently, looking into the still blank eyes. There! A flash of life, a gleam, a glimmer of an expression! Eiru smiled gently at Terese, she did not want to startle her and alert the others. There again! A glint, a glimmer... There is hope! Eiru probed this time, "You are aware of the Milesian Sea Druid Amergin. He comes to meet with our High Priestess Sceine."

"I am,"uttered Terese, "I am aware of his coming..." This time like a bolt of electricity, her face broke into an expression of life, her eyes lit up. She looked around with a quizzical expression questioning where she was... "Take another sip," Eiru offered more mead, raising her glass to her lips. Terese sipped again, and again... the headiness of the mead and the potion, raising her senses, her life force returning, akin to someone emerging from a deep sleep, and the strangest dream, or nightmare as in this instance.

Terese blinked, searching for reality, turning towards Eiru...

"Hello Terese, it is good to see the real you. Do not be alarmed, you have been on a long and terrible journey into the dark. Now you are coming back to the light,"comforted Eiru, "Please be calm. I am your friend. You are in danger!"

Terese took another sip of the mead and potion. Sip by sip, moment by moment, she was returning.

Heartened by this, Eiru took her by the arm and led her to the balcony overlooking the lake and valley leading into the Gap of Varna. The freshness of the mountain air and the quietness of the night revitalised Terese. She was a fighter by nature... very few could resist the dark Sidhe this way. It was a testament to her bravery and fortitude. Eiru smiled...

Inside the banquet hall, raised voices continued to disturb the gathering. MacCuacht fought with his brothers. They were questioning of his ways and reticent of taking the same dark path.

The more time they spent with MacCuacht, Eiru knew they would be lost... The darkness of the soul is contagious... you only had to look at the witches Banba and Fodha. They were lost, the darkest of the dark, a formidable force of black magic, clairvoyance and the power of shape shifting.

Eiru was more concerned about the witches than MacCuacht at this stage. They were more likely to sense her errant ways. They may read her mind or even Terese's thoughts.

Eiru, quickly and clearly, explained what she was about to do... "We must leave! We must join Sceine!"

Minute by minute, moment by moment, Terese was rejoining the living. Eiru shielded this transformation, casting a spell on those around her, stunting the senses of MacCuacht and the witches. They would hopefully be gone before anyone realises.

Eiru described her shape shifting powers to Terese and in that moment walked with her to the edge of the balcony... golden trails of deconstructed molecules and dissipating matter. Her shape unraveled and morphed. Forming and reforming, a powerful downdraft, swirling forms, a beat of a feather, a kaleidoscope of gold and amber light, feather tips and white light, great talons gripping, white tails soaring... Eiru and Terese were gone... into the quiet of the night.

No one sensed their leaving. They flew high, on their way to join Sceine...

... Sceine discussed the urgency of finding the Milesians and protecting their champion Amergin with her priesthood. These emissaries of the light must help her to find the destined one. She knew that Amergin and his tribe were strong and fearless. He had been bestowed with great powers from the ancients, like herself. But to confront the dark Sidhe in unfamiliar territory, they were like lambs to the slaughter!

She felt Amergin's presence. Although he was still many horizons over the ocean away, the connection was growing... her senses were alive, her very soul lit up with the prospect of their meeting, kindred souls on a journey of destiny. Ancient lovers from past lives, reincarnated and coming together in full cycle, to meet again.

Together, the enlightened nations would be strong, a force to be reckoned with. Separate they were weak and ripe for the taking. They must stand and unite or divide and be conquered!

Long into the night, they delved deep into their consciences, searching for a way... Samhain urged his priesthood, "Be creative use your imaginations! If we are obvious then the dark Sidhe will be ready for us. We must be more cunning, more devious than our adversaries."

The absolute truth, agreed Sceine. Amergin must be protected!

Something distracted Sceine. A disturbance in the night air! A movement high in the still night sky!

There! Again! A steady rhythmic beating of wings... She stepped away from the gathering, stealthily disappearing into the darkness.

No one noticed her leaving. No one had heard the distant, but ever nearing, soft but powerful rhythmic sounds. A wing beat, then silence, another beat, a rush of cold night air.

"What is this?!" Sceine climbed to the highest vantage point. Now away from the lights of the encampment, her night vision strained to pick out the far hills, and the faintest light of the tip of a crescent new moon, rising over the horizon. The slenderest, faintest crescent casting a lunar glow.

Against this luminescence she saw, or at least she thought she saw, an eagle rising and dipping over the line of hills, the rhythmic beating of wings rising to a crescendo. Sceine grabbed a blazing torch from the encampment. She sensed the arrival of an extraordinary being. Closer, closer, she could feel the downbeat of powerful wings. Against the crescent moon she could see an eagle, white tailed with a huge wingspan... but there was something else, a human form gripped in the mighty talons.

Sceine knew now that this was Eiru! But who was that with her?

Downdraughts of air, cascading photonic light, as the eagle descended and touched ground. Morphing as it alighted, she was wrapped in beating wings, eddies of air, and a spiraling vortex of photonic energy... Eiru arrived... and who is this beautiful, amazonian woman with her?

In an instant Sceine knew, "Terese of the Xantha!" she proclaimed, "How could this be!?"

"We have come to join you Sceine, "Eiru introduced Terese, "Terese was lost to the dark Sidhe, but she is strong in mind and in spirit, she has rejoined the enlightened beings of our beautiful world!"

Sceine embraced Eiru and Terese. She was heartened and strengthened by their arrival. Sceine marvelled at the timing of their arrival. Just at the moment when she and the priesthood were looking for answers as to how they were going to protect the Milesians and the Sea Druid Amergin.

"Come. Your timing is perfect!" Sceine took them to Samhain and the priesthood, who led them all in prayer, "We thank the Great Spirit for bringing you safely to us. We and the Guardians of Light welcome you, your strength and talents will be invaluable to the cause. We praise you! We give thanks to the Guardians of Light. May the Great Spirit bless you and give you strength in the ordeals to come."

The makings of a plan began to form in Sceine's mind. She suggested that they should all retire for the night. A fresh mind and a fresh approach needed now...

Sceine gave thanks to the Guardians of Light, her spirits raised she drifted into a deep slumber. Soon dreaming of her destined meeting with Amergin, drifting beyond the veil, floating through an amber mist, she was with him. Their bodies entwined, hearts pounding. She held him. He touched and embraced her, soothing her. He was in her dreams, they felt so real. Ecstacy and bliss... as soon as the night had come...the morning arrived! She turned to greet the light, a smile swept over her face, joy and happiness permeating every inch of her outstretched body. Sceine relived their tender moments. She was overcome with expectation and anticipation...

Far, far away, many horizons over the limitless Northern Ocean...
Amergin prayed and meditated, composing a lyrical poem as he did so...

As he wrote he started drifting beyond the veil, journeying to meet his destined one...

"White Swan"
The impossible rising of a white winged beauty becomes an airborne softening of beating feathers.
Frond tipped gossamer, dipping sending ripples to ether, frailty and strength, fusion of the angel and the beast...

Leaving the black, swirling waters, circling in aqueous, soaring overhead, mighty and glorious, long necked and sensuous.
Paired for life, a formation of flight, wing tip to wing tip,
Menacingly graceful, passions on fire, a feather to the lip...

River's bend, a place of refuge, safe haven to rest,
A bed of Sceine and Amergin searched and now found.
For life, mated, satiated, quintessentially love bound.
Beyond human compare, a realm of senses so blessed...

She guided him, coaxed him... Journeyed with him beyond the veil...

The power and intensity of his dreams, real yet not real! This beautiful being that he was yet to meet, controlled him, overwhelmed him and excited him. In joyous ecstacy he greeted the dawn and reached out into the ether with a comforting hand. The same smile swept through his relaxed and expectant body. The amber mists of an all consuming dream thinned and dissipated. Once again he was falling into an unfolding universe, down and ever down into a dark fleck of a strange, wondrously beautiful eye.

Each and every finely honed muscle flexing and relaxing, they smiled together, yet still so far away...

They both sensed the moment was coming... they both came from a spiritual place and rejoiced in their togetherness...

Amergin came too... abruptly! The day dawned bright and glorious...

MacCuacht yelled at his brothers, "She cannot have gone! Find her, bring her to me or you will suffer my wrath!"

The two remaining Witches of Hawardden looked on in bewilderment, "Eiru, surely not!?" How could they have not sensed her leaving? They were surely as one, pledged to the same path. They joined the brothers, searching the imposing castle and its vast grounds. They searched and they searched... Not a trace!

Another mystery unfolded... Terese of the Xantha... She too was missing!

MacCuacht stormed and raged around the castle... No mortal was safe until that rage ebbed! Never had his brothers seen him in such a black tempestuous fury.

He would get answers and surely he would get revenge. Someone would suffer this night!

MacCuacht summoned the captain of the guard, his elite body guard, "Sirez! Gather your men. Bring me those that were on guard this night!" Sirez wasted no time, he was fully aware that his life and the lives of the guards were on the line. He had seen poor souls thrown over the battlements before now, to become the awful pickings for the Vultures of Mis. In allegiance with the dark Sidhe, they descended from high and distant eeries, their shroud like forms gliding in to clutch and snatch and to devour the dashed and broken corpses of the wretched victims of MacCuacht's fury.

Sirez noticed the vultures were soaring again…Nervously, he and his men stood before MacCuacht. Sirez's attention was drawn to the pallor of his sinister master, deathly white with ever darkening veins. As he questioned the guards, no answer was forthcoming. MacCuacht became even more tormented. The veins on his temples, his neck, the back of his hands and his furrowed brow pulsed and darkened. No one was safe!

He interrogated each of the guards in turn. His voice reaching a crescendo, as one by one they pleaded ignorance, shedding no light. None of them gave the information MacCuacht craved. The last guard to be dragged before him was visibly and physically in shock! Reduced to a quivering wreck by each searching and probing question, this poor wretch was clearly and transparently not to blame.

But his demeanour enraged MacCuacht. Showing weakness in his eyes was as good as confessing guilt.

Sirez stepped swiftly between his master and the shaking wreck of a guard, "They know absolutely nothing my lord!" he interjected, "I am sorry that we are none the wiser!"

Only this action saved the guard from becoming the next feast of the awful Vultures of Mis.

The interjection seemed to disarm MacCuacht, just as a giant shroud of a wingspan flew up and over the battlements, the indescribable ugliness of a Vulture of Mis. This distraction, ironically, saved the unwitting guard from a death even more dastardly than the living death he already endured, as one of the army of lost souls.

Surprised and relieved, the guards were ushered away from the battlements. Sirez swore on his life the guard would be doubled and preparations to be made to send insurgents into the Western Province to find Eiru and Terese. The retaliation for the betrayal by Eiru would be swift and vengeful!

The remaining witches suspected that Eiru had used a spell to shield her actions, and a potion to revert Terese of the Xantha back to the enlightened realm. The witches pondered and connived, they would produce a counter spell that would allow them to track Eiru, and potentially turn Terese once more.

Sure enough they found traces of Eiru's metamorphosis, the disturbance in the photonic continuum as a result of her shape shifting magic. Magic that only Eiru and her sister- witches possessed.

They were aware now that Eiru as a White-tailed Eagle had gripped Terese in her talons and made their escape.

The witches informed MacCuacht of their discovery, and how Eiru could lead them and the dark Sidhe to Sceine. Unwittingly, Eiru could have given MacCuacht the very lead he needed! The ultimate betrayal could become the ultimate indiscretion. Maybe even the key to unlock and turn the portals of the Western Province... A twisted and sinister smile now convulsed across the deathly white countenance.

Ever darkening veins pulsed excitedly and expectantly...

The arrival of Eiru and Terese of the Xantha in to their fold heartened Sceine.

She felt the tentacles of the dark Sidhe ever nearing, but there was still time and hope...

The enlightened beings must act in good faith, standing against the corruption and malevolence of their evil foe.

The Tuathan tribes had fought long and hard to prise this verdant and sacred land from the grip of the primeval Firbolg, to bring light, equality and fairness to a land forever in the dark. Sceine's dear departed father Antiem had given his life to the cause. To liberate the people of the Island of Destiny from the smothering, controlling slavery of the Firbolg and bring light, equality and justice to a land forever in the grip of oppressive, militaristic overlords.

The women of the Firbolg were mere chattels, possessions of the Firbolg warriors. The Shamen of the Firbolg had unleashed the dark energy of their aggressive male deities. All the warriors of the Firbolg were indoctrinated, brainwashed and controlled. They were fodder for the infection of the dark Sidhe.

The Shamen of the Firbolg had opened portals with their rituals and ancient ceremonies. The primeval dark ages of the Firbolg were now replaced with even darker forces.The battles with the Firbolg had been cruel, atrocious affairs, a war of attrition with no winners.

Many lives were lost. The hateful acts of war had fed into the spirit world and awakened the dormant dark Sidhe. During the dreadful deeds of battle, every scream, every terrible death, a soul was lost, drawn through the veil by the dark Sidhe, feeding a slumbering evil entity. The crusading adventures of the Tuathans galvanised the dark energy of the spirit world. The Shamen of the Firbolg were catalysts, their warring forays became the life blood for the dark Sidhe.

The treachery of MacCuacht and the terrible awful deeds all in the name of enlightenment fed directly into the portals of the spirit world. MacCuacht and his crusaders at the forefront of the slaughter became infected by the dark

Sidhe first. The darkness consumed them, their way was lost. They were the emissaries of evil now. An army of unholy beings, lost souls, was created. They were intent on a perpetual crusade until all this sacred land was converted and lost to the dark cause…

Sceine knew MacCuacht was such a being, she sensed his anger and rage at the loss of his beloved Eiru. They must be ready…

To have Eiru and Terese in their fold was a blessing! She could learn much from them. Their insight and knowledge could be critical. Eiru in particular had the direct connection with MacCuacht. She had witnessed his conversion. She knew the depths of his darkness and had a sense of his scheming malevolence. Terese of the Xantha had been taken, crossed the veil and gone deep into the dark spirit world, and returned. She was saved by the magical powers of Eiru.

Sceine sensed the danger in relying on the newly returned Terese, but she was fundamentally a good being. The infection of the dark Sidhe could run deep into her psyche, into her very DNA. Sceine knew that MacCuacht and the two witches would be doing their utmost to return Eiru and Terese back into the darkness. Maybe the all consuming rage of MacCuacht would be the distraction she needed?

The tribes of Milesia were nearing. The poet champion Amergin will need their help and protection. They came over the ocean over the distant Western horizon, while to the east the dark forces were mustering… the moment of truth nears…

Sceine called her priests to her. She knows they must return to the high mountain fortress of Sliebh Mis. The defences of the great fortress must be prepared.

Eiru and Terese of the Xantha will journey to the western coast to meet the Milesians. They will become part of a plan to deceive MacCuacht. Their lives will be at risk, they will be in grave danger, but they are the bait, the lure to distract the forces of the dark, whilst MacCuacht in his rage and anger seeks Eiru. She and Terese will give Amergin and the tribes of Milesia a window of opportunity to arrive safely on the Island of Destiny. Sceine counseled Eiru and Terese of the Xantha, impressing on them the need for secrecy.

Sceine also marshalled a force of her best warriors to go north into the vanquished land of the Firbolg. The mission was to win the hearts and minds of the more enlightened Firbolg. They would attempt to give help to the downtrodden, provide sanctuaries for the homeless and bring fairness and equality to the women and youth of the Northern Province. Under the leadership of Septiem, an inspirational priest, they would bring light where there was once dark, faith where there was hopelessness and peace after generations of war and intimidation. The message would travel with Sceine's priests and warriors like windblown seeds. The message of enlightenment will take root and flourish. The gentle, peaceful way of the Guardians of Light will hopefully endear itself to the downtrodden and war torn Firbolg…

MacCuacht and his army of lost souls, guided by the raven haired witches Fodha and Banba were in pursuit of Eiru and Terese, in the belief that they would lead them straight to Sceine...

MacCuacht's way was in stark contrast to the way of the Guardians of Light and Sceine. His dark threatening ways would pander to the animal within, to greed, to selfishness, to the craving for power, for personal possessions, to the addictions of the human condition.This, all at the cost of the soul and the heart and to love. He will draw in the weak, suck the humanity from their souls, corrupt them and ultimately destroy them. They will be lost, transformed and changed forever.

In his world the portals of Divine Light will become sink holes of the dark, feeding off the frailty and weaknesses of the human condition. Beacons of Divine Light will transform to black holes draining and sucking the goodness, love and pure spirit out of the land...

The coming morning witnessed the movement of Sceine and her faithful out of the camp. She returned south to the high mountain fortress of Sliebh Mis... Eiru and Terese went west to the ocean... Septiem went to the Northern Province to meet with the Firbolg...

Sceine kept constant vigil to the east. This is where MacCuacht will be coming from.

The trail of deception had been laid, with Eiru and Terese as the bait. Fuelled and driven by blind rage, MacCuacht would give Sceine valuable time to retrench. Sceine had instructed Temes, one of her loyal priests, to commune with the Guardians of Light at each portal en route, and then to place a guard, to best ensure that the portals remain in the power of the enlightened ones. Each guard was in the possession of a Bluestone key hewn from the Quarry of Izion, the purest source.

They were under instructions to take the key stones through the portal and beyond the veil to the spirit world, should they come under attack from MacCuacht. This would ensure the portals would close and not come under the influence of MacCuacht and the dark Sidhe.

MacCuacht, his brothers and their wives, the raven haired sisters, the Witches of Hawardden, marched onwards, tracing the steps of Terese and Eiru.

The Guardians of Light were alerted to their coming. They would take the form of beasts of the forests and raptors of the air to harry and deter the army of lost souls. The thinning veil left the portals vulnerable. The guerilla tactics and their enlightened magic would hopefully prevent the dark army from drawing malevolent forces through the veil.

"They go to the west my lord," sensed Banba, wife of MacCuill, "They will meet the Milesians and the destined one Amergin!"

"Perfect!" exclaimed MacCuacht, "We will take them and Sceine in one fell swoop!"

From out of the blue, a falcon fell at electrifying speed, stooping with talons bared, ripping the fleshy cheek of Sirez, the Captain of the Guard. He screamed in terror and in excruciating pain. Blood streaming, lost soul dark, over his body armour. A second Peregrine Falcon came in like a lightning bolt, straight out of the sky. No sound, no warning, just the high speed "thuk" of the collision as MacCuacht's second in command took another hit! A gash the length of his forehead opened up, and flowing dark crimson poured out. He fell to the ground clutching his torn, loosely flapping flesh. A third hit! As he fell, talons sliced through the exposed jugular artery, more dark fluid pulsed out of the torn conduit. Sirez writhed in agony, he screamed for help! There was panic and pandemonium all around! His fellow guards closed ranks – but too late! The falcons were gone! Mere specks on the horizon, as Sirez squirmed in his death throes...

MacCuacht reacted with typical rage, his deathly white pallor and darkening, pulsing veins revealing his fury. Not sorrow for the loss of one of his colleagues, but pure anger and indignation at being defied and outwitted. His heart was of stone, no emotion, no grieving... He knew the Guardians of Light were responsible for the attack... but the guerilla tactics had the hallmark of his beloved sister Sceine.

MacCuacht exploded with rage, "The war continues dear sister! We shall meet very soon...!"

MacCuacht left Sirez's body at the side of the track for the hideous Vultures of Mis to devour.

The army of lost souls moved on, but even the most hardened, the longest turned, looked skywards now. There was still fear deep within their stony souls. Existence was still precious.

A group of Sceine's elite guard too looked skywards. Far in the distance, they saw a wheeling vortex of preying vultures. They gave notice of a death, and the oncoming army of lost souls. They agreed, "Half a day's march to the east! We must be ready!"

The elite guard arrived at the first of the great portals on the route westwards to the ocean. Their leader Thiorn held the purest Bluestone crafted from the Quarry of Izion aloft, and rallied his troops, "Come my brothers! We fight for the cause of the enlightened ones! By the Great Spirit we shall protect this portal!" From the gunnels of the portal, through a mysterious, majestic cave system poured a glowing golden amber mist, enveloping all, swirling and rolling into the mortal realm. The elite guard stood in jaw dropping amazement. A shaft of radiant white light burst through the veil and illuminated the valley and woodlands in the vicinity of the portal.

The Bluestone inserted by Thiorn into the portal, into the womb of the land ...white light irradiated all around... The Guardians were in their presence... They all waited with trepidation for the army of lost souls to arrive...

CHAPTER TEN:
THE TEMPLE OF THE SUN

Days of endless drifting in a becalmed, benign ocean was now broken by the first gusts of a blustery, lively south-westerly. The sails billowed and Amergin gave the order, "Untie and be ready to tack!"

The fleet jostled, all vessels were separated and ready to sail. The next gust would take them, one by one, into the infinite blue…

No further encounters with the Orca. The Milesian fleet had settled again. They were strengthened once more and ready for battle.

Amergin too was heartened by his sensuous clairvoyant dreams… his destiny awaited him…Emboldened, life coursing through him, he gave the order, "Make sail to the Promised Land!"

He noticed a cloud formation in the form of a beauteous siren, beckoning them, leading them… The wind stretched the cloud into a long, elegant, sensuous arm, with a finger pointing to the northern horizon. The next gust took the fleet onwards. They tacked into the north-east. Amergin sensed in his bones, "Two days sailing…"

The beckoning, beautiful cloud formation rolled and reformed, morphed, reshaped and was gone. "Sceine!" uttered Amergin under his breath, "I will be with you soon!"

The defiant prows of the Milesian fleet pushed through the rising swell. An occasional set wave broke over the deck, giving a pleasing, cooling shower to the deck hands. High above in the rigging, the watchman atop the mast undulated in ever increasing amplitudes as the growing swell and strengthening wind pushed them ever onwards.

Amergin sent a message to all his captains in the fleet, to have the watchmen on duty and all on full alert. Land could be sighted at any time! They must expect the next onslaught from the dark Sidhe…

A distant pod of chasing common dolphins broke the surface, racing over the horizon! Arching, leaping, and forcing through a turbulent ocean. A shoal of frenzied mackerel their target. "Bring out the long lines!" shouted Amergin enthusiastically, "We will feast tonight!"

As he said this, he realised that this could be their last feast on the ocean. They must stock up, feast tonight, and salt the rest, ready for their journey to the Promised Land.

Tens, dozens, hundreds of shimmering, electric blue-silver and rainbow coloured fish were hooked and pulled out of the giving, bountiful ocean, stunned, gutted, cleaned and salted for storage in the holds of each vessel. Prize specimens were kept back and prepared for a satisfying feast for the crew that night.

Amergin and his royal family were reunited on his vessel that night too. A strategy for landfall was required. It was agreed that Milidh and Scota would heave too off the coast. They and their crews would be in the second wave, once a secure landing place was established. Amergin, Eimbear and Eiremhou, the warrior princes, would lead the way. They made battle ready... all of the Milesians were in battle attire... they were so close now. It would be foolish not to expect the unexpected...

Amergin wished his royal kin well, "May the Great Spirit be with all of us. May our paths meet again soon, and may our landings be safe!" They embraced and left for their own vessels.

Amergin rested quietly, regailed in full armour. The night slowly descended, he drifted in and out of a fitful sleep. Reality and dream world fused and joined... the thinning veil, portals of radiant light, a sublime, beautiful being... His senses were inundated, overwhelmed...

Suddenly his thoughts turned to Eimbear and his alliance with Gonne the High priest of the Chapter of Mystics! He was awake now! An unusual motion, as if another vessel was tying up! Bolt upright, he swung swiftly off his bunk and instinctively made for the darkened space behind the door. He knew he was in danger! The heavy mahogany door creaked slowly open, inch by inch. The tip of a Milesian sword appeared in silhouette through the growing gap, the unmistakeable steel, the royal crest on the shaft. "How, can this be?!" Amergin shoulder charged the door, crushing the assailant's arm. The sword dropped to the floor, they wrestled momentarily. It was Eimbear's helmsman Yatez!

Grappling with him, he grabbed his arm and threw him to the floor, and then Amergin cracked him with the butt of his sword. Yatez lost consciousness and fell like a stone to the floor. The sound of the struggle raised the alarm. Xomos and the watchman burst through the open doorway. Senses bristling and swords drawn, "My lord are you safe?!" Xomos anxiously asked.

"Yes Xomos, all is under control," and Amergin threw a decanter of water over the prostrate, concussed form. Amergin grabbed him, picked him up and pressed his forearm against his windpipe. Yatez regained his senses, floundering he shook the water off his face, "Where am I?" He was dazed yes, but that uncontrolled look? "How did I get here?" He was totally confused, literally in the dark, thought Amergin. Yatez had been placed under some kind of spell... he did not know what he was doing.

"You have been sent here to assassinate me," said Amergin pointedly, "What do you know? Who sent you?." Yatez shook his head once more, "I don't know... I can't remember a thing..."

"Throw this man into the brig, Xomos!" ordered Amergin, "We will question him later, in the light of day!" Amergin knew it was pointless interrogating him now... he was still under the malign influence of his master... Everything pointed to Gonne and Eimbear. Maybe he was infected and controlled by the dark Sidhe!

Amergin and Xomos took the helm together. They needed fresh air, space to think, and a place where they would not be overheard. They knew the vessel Yatez came from, and his association with Gonne and Eimbear, but they had never witnessed such power over a subject before.

Amergin speculated, "As we near the Promised Land the veil is closer and they are able to channel greater and greater dark energy from the spirit world. We will meet land in the coming days, we must expect the worst!" Xomas agreed... He looked out into the early morning light... He saw in the distance huge thunderheads rising above the horizon. Water colour mirages, white pale misty high altitude clouds with a dark menacing underbelly, towering over and dwarfing the fleet as they headed north-eastwards.

The fleet rolled and dipped into the following, increasing swell. The prevailing south-westerly pushed them ever onwards...

Further into the distance, many horizons away, even larger thunderheads appeared. They were the bell weather, the indicator of land, of a mighty mountain range, where moisture laden oceanic air meets mountainous contours. Amergin went below, no words were needed, the most vigilant of watches now required. The cresting bows of their wooden vessels throwing more and more spray. Occasionally the bow watchman got a drenching. His oil skins glistened wet in an abstract patterned accumulation of drying, crusty sea salt on his back. Wetted and encrusted again, he ducked into bigger and bigger breakers. Wind freshening, sails billowing, vessel leaning, they were forcing onwards.

Xomos waved the bow watchman back to the mast for safety, exhilarating sailing as they reached for the north-eastern horizon. One of those bright, fresh, inspiring oceanic days with crystal clear visibility! A blue-green, light turquoise seascape against a wide panoramic, cerulean blue, expanse of sky, they headed north where distant thunderheads were building and brewing. They had company now, great black-backed gulls and fulmar petrels swooped and dipped in the white cresting, rolling wake, tipping their wings in acknowledgement of the onlooking crew as they soared past overhead.

They gracefully flew in a wide ranging arc away from the racing vessels, only to rejoin their avian brothers and sisters in their exuberant wake riding.

"A sure sign of land!" mused Xomas... he peered and squinted into the horizon, "There! Land ahoy!"

A jagged, still distant, but majestic promontory thrust seaward. Too far away to make out features and relief, but close enough to sense of the scale of the sea cliffs. Rugged, inhospitable, rock formations and a huge breaking swell. Certainly no place for landing! Xomos tacked to the north again, the ever nearing land mass seemed to be drawing the wind around, backing to the south-east.

Amergin and the rest of the crew joined Xomas to witness the first spectacular glimpse of the Promised Land. All of the crews on all of the vessels in the entire Milesian fleet, mustered on deck to savour and enjoy the view. A view that didn't disappoint... The light, the ocean, the colours, the sound, the cloudscape, the energy, the place, the spirit... their destiny! There was a collective exhortation in awe of the place, and the realisation that they had arrived...

Amergin smiled inwardly, and breathed deeply, in relief and appreciation of bearing witness and being present at such a significant and momentous occasion. Amergin turned to Xomas. They were speechless and in awe of the moment and the place.

A tear dropped from Amergin's cheek, falling like glistening dew towards the ocean, only to be picked up by the gusting, petulant south-east wind, and then lost in a mist of sea spray in the wake of their vessel.

The joy of the moment was hijacked by a warning beacon lit on top of the distant precipitous headland. They had been spotted! A chain of beacons soon dotted the horizon. The defending tribes were warned of their arrival!

The south-easterly wind grew in strength as they neared the headland. It was being funneled and channeled by the high cliffs. They were being taken towards the jagged rocks and monolithic slabs of ancient red sandstone, the currents, tides and turbulence converging at the exposed tip of this great promontory. A mariner's graveyard... They worked in unison, each helmsman searching for a safe refuge... tacking, furling sails, responding instantly to confused and strengthening gusts and a building tide ripped swell. The irresistible ocean meeting the immovable land mass, a place where weather, time and Milesian destiny collided.

That same wind trying to take them on to the unforgiving rocks and submerged reef was slowly bringing the distant brewing thunderheads towards them. Darkening clouds, towering over the mountains and ascending to the heavens, had turned from the water colour mirages to the torrid, thick turbulent, elemental forces of nature. Real and dangerous! Tide, time, wind and weather and this force majeure were on a collision course. The Milesian fleet were taken northwards by a tidal race and gusting gale force winds. They searched along the coastline for a place of sanctuary, a place to land safely. Amergin took the helm, Xomas by his side watching...

Ploughing into wave troughs and cresting swell they forged ahead, the tidal race grabbing and controlling all the vessels of the fleet like flotsam at the whim of the ocean.

Following wind and flooding tide combined to push them to the north. On the horizon, two islands with pointed cathedral spire pinnacles, the tops of huge seamounts, shimmering like mirages.

Amergin had seen these monolithic islands in one of his amber misted dreams. This was the sign he needed! Instantly he tacked to the starboard, heading for the coast. Xomas was concerned, he urged Amergin to stay offshore, "With this tidal race and gusting wind, we will be in danger of being dashed on the rocks Sire! I see no place of refuge here!" Amergin turned to his first officer, "Have faith Xomas! The Great Spirit is guiding us! I have seen this place in my dreams..."

Amergin held securely on to the tiller. The entire crew relied on him, the fleet took his lead. Their fate was once more in his hands. Xomas strained to see the distant horizon – another monstrous headland loomed into vision. Offshore were the two island bastions, sea temples to the gods. Through the sea spray and mists of waves crashing into reefs and headlands, there appeared to be no place of refuge, no sanctuary, no safe harbour.

Amergin pressed on with total self belief, steering straight towards the tip of the nearest headland.

Xomas strained to see through the mist and spray. Then he realised that the first headland was actually an island! The roaring waves crashed into reefs and dissipated into a deep water channel to the north of the island. The deep water channel between the island and the imposing headland to the north was that sanctuary, was that refuge, was a place of safe haven, "A miracle!" shouted Xomas joyously.

"No, destiny Xomas!" hailed Amergin, "Destiny!"

One by one each of the vessels of the fleet entered the deep water channel... beyond this a sweeping bay came into view. Once safely in to the bay they dropped anchor, safe haven for now... Protected from the wind and swell they were able to take stock and take in the distant land and majestic mountains. Amergin looked to the distant mountains, and seeing the ever darkening, towering thunderheads, wondered how safe they really were...

The Milesian fleet rested quietly in the vast, calm expansive bay...

The sheer beauty of the place, sweeping golden beaches with the muted roar of distant crashing swell...

Headlands and hills stretching as far as the eye could see, greens of every shade, emerald and viridian hues... Shafts of scintillating sunlight swept over the land, searchlights illuminating and brilliant white light highlighting luminescent green swathes of pasture, woodlands and forest...

Dark shadows followed rapidly as fleeting clouds obscured the sun, only to be followed again by sunbursts illuminating a patchwork of glorious, verdant, magical landscapes...

Amergin watched in wonderment as one such searing searchlight swept from turquoise sea, to bleached white cold water coral sands to emerald pastures. His heart leapt for joy, and his spirits soared as he surveyed this heavenly panoramic vista. The adversities and trauma of the sea voyage receded and the horrific memories with their encounters with the dark Sidhe were soothed and eased.

"This beautiful, magical, mystical place shall be named after the one I am destined to meet, the woman in my dreams, 'Sceine'. This is now the Bay of Sceine!" declared Amergin wholeheartedly.

He continued to watch the searching shafts of sunlight as they travelled across the vast 'Bay of Sceine'.

In the distance he could make out a river mouth, pouring into the ocean. It seemed to connect to an upper lake that now emptied with the receding tide. The river mouth was fringed with verdant green pastures. Another shaft of sunlight swept through, miraculously illuminating an ancient megalithic monument standing in proud isolation on an escarpment to the East of the bay, three magnificent giant standing stones. A temple to the sun, the three carved Bluestones in alignment with the rising sun. They were also in alignment with the distant mountain range where the towering, darkening thunderheads ascended to the heavens. Now they were encroaching and threatening to extinguish the bright and illuminating 'angel shafts'.

"We must make for the estuary, and from there we will climb to the Temple of the Sun. We must hurry we have been given a sign. Look how the eastern horizon darkens! Our nemesis comes from there! We must prepare ourselves!" Amergin instructed Xomas to send the message to up anchor, and the oarsmen to row for the river mouth…

Amergin was fully galvanised and animated. Wonder at this inspiring place was being replaced by reality. His survival instinct still strong and robust!

The oarsmen on each vessel pulled in unison. Straining and stretching every sinew and muscle in their flexing bodies to get the fleet and the tribes of Milesia to a place of refuge.

The shifting searchlights had now become stationary spotlights as the sun lowered in the western sky. Meanwhile the eastern horizon darkened. The daily battle between the light and the dark commenced.

 Fair weather and bright light meeting foul weather and darkness, the shifting, slipping rays of sunlight sent shafts of illumination into the distant darkness. An incandescent veil of refracted and diffracted white light diffused into spectral colours of the rainbow in the misting darkness of the encroaching thunderheads. Not a rainbow but a rainwall! The encroaching front became a red, orange, yellow, green, blue, indigo and violet weather wall. The descending sun sent protective, warming rays of light into the invasive, intrusive, intimidating storm front, still, the one blazing, brilliant shaft of sunlight spotlit the gigantic standing Bluestones of The Temple of the Sun. The oarsmen rowed steadily and strongly to the south side of the estuary. Amergin's vessel slid silently into the soft sinking sand of the river mouth bar, Eiremhou's vessel next, then Eimbear's.

Soon the rest of the fleet had landed. As soon as the prows touched the haven of the Promised Land, the expeditionary forces leapt on to terra firma. The full force brought the provisions ashore, soon making camp and setting the defences. They were strategically camped at the foot of the escarpment with the gargantuan standing stones of the Temple of the Sun overlooking them and guarding them.

Amergin gathered his brothers, the representatives of the Chapter of the Mystics, including Gonne, at the Temple of the Sun. They knelt in prayer, placing their hands on the rough igneous Bluestone granite of the standing stones. In quiet contemplation, Amergin looked around. The location of the Temple of the Sun was breathtaking. Lay lines from all distant points, mountain summits, river valleys, sky touching offshore islands, all aligned here. The power, the energy, the spirit, the connection to the Divine, all was here. Amergin and his tribe had been drawn here, a portal to the spirit world where the veil between light and dark shifted and thinned.

Amergin led the gathering in prayer, "Great Spirit we beseech thee, grant us your protection and give us the power and the strength to overcome the forces of the dark. Connect us to the Guardians of Light and give us the courage, fortitude and integrity to face our dark adversaries…"

"All hail to the Divine!" was the response from the gathering.

Amergin stepped away from the temple and looked east… from the ocean to the river mouth, to the winding river valley, beyond the upper lake, over the verdant pastures and lush lowland woods, to the mountain ridges and lofty summits. An extraordinarily beautiful place… now a place of challenge and adventure, a place of flux with evil posturing and threatening… here would be the beginning of the battle for the Promised Land. All the portents, all the omens, all the signs had brought Amergin here… his quest continues.

CHAPTER ELEVEN:
THE MAGIC OF DERWYDD

MacCuacht marched on, he and the witches following the traces of the fleeing Eiru and Terese.

Overhead the rolling and boiling thunderheads tracing every step of MacCuacht and his army of lost souls. The glowing light of the late evening sun filled the carved glacial valley ahead, catching the the summits of the mountain peaks above. To the north, the cloud piercing summit of Cadris caught the full intensity of the setting sun. Like a sleeping giant resting and basking in the rays, light reflected from the uppermost slopes on the southerly side of this breathtaking mountain. Light from the west penetrated deep into the long and undulating valley meeting the cascading reflected light from the majestic peaks. The high terraces of evergreen conifer forests trapped and diffused the cascading glowing light. A fine mist of swirling rain descended from the leading edge of the clouds towering to infinite heights above Cadris and her sister peaks. An effervescent kaleidoscope of rainbow colours illuminated the higher slopes. A wall of hallucinogenic mist announcing the arrival of a darkening, threatening storm front...

MacCuacht surveyed his forces as they descended deeper and deeper into the valley. He was feeling stronger and more powerful than ever. The tribes of this land were increasingly turning to his cause. Ever increasing numbers and his foe in apparent disarray... MacCuacht did indeed feel strong!

They marched on through the vast conifer forests. Giant pines standing resolutely, as their high canopy swayed in the cold north easterly mountain breeze. The cold air plunged into the valley, in a temperature inversion produced by the intensifying storm system. Even the elements were turning as MacCuacht and the army of lost souls marched through the valley.

The shadows of the giant conifers lengthened and darkened. High above the canopy, the swirling wall of spectral colours began to dissipate to be replaced by an all permeating golden amber glow.

Unknown to MacCuacht, ahead lay the nigh on impenetrable ancient deciduous Woodland of Derwydd and beyond Derwydd the first of the great portals of the Western Province, Machlleth.

Machlleth was guarded by Thiorn and his elite guard, who awaited the coming of the dark one...

The army of lost souls marched westwards towards the ocean, before them the notorious Woodland of Derwydd. Even the dark infectiousness of MacCuacht could not prevent their unease.

They had all witnessed the permeating deep amber glow before. They had witnessed the shocking death of their esteemed second in command, Sirez. The writhing death throes were fresh in their minds. The darkening shadows, the deepening amber glow, disturbed even their twisted and demented minds.

The solitary, giant evergreen conifers seemed to feed off this nervous energy. In the diminishing light, darkening shadows and descending, strange amber mist, the conifers appeared to close ranks. The passage through became a maze, no clear path, no western light to guide them. The brewing, boiling storm clouds above the canopy of the woodland also deadened and absorbed any ambient light. Even the children of the dark felt suffocated. The forest barred their way, an impenetrable barrier. Now their disturbed minds began tricking them. The amber mist drugged their senses. Solitary, ancient pines were moving! Hallucination or reality!

The army of lost souls genuinely lost! The weaker souls and those who had been turned to the dark more recently were terror stricken. Some panicked and bolted into the woodland. They crashed into abrasive, resin soaked trunks. The mind altering sap clung to their flesh, sharp needles pricked and punctured exposed skin. Lowering branches scraped and scratched. Roots twisted, tripped and trapped them. In confusion, darkness and hallucinogenic madness they thrashed and battled through the maze, flailing into the darkness until they collapsed in quivering exhaustion!

MacCuacht, MacCuill and MacGreinne, and the two raven haired witches stayed close together through all the confusion and mindwarped frantic delerium..."Brother!" screamed MacCuill to MacGreinne, "We are surely on a demonic mission! MacCuacht is possessed! I fear for us! I fear for our souls! Where is our guiding light?!"

MacGreinne saw weakness in his brother. He had no questions. He was strongly on MacCuacht's side. "You must harden your resolve brother! Our mission is to repel an invasion force that arrives on our Western shoreline. Never lose sight of that! We must conquer or be vanquished!"

MacGreinne saw in MacCuill the same questioning zeal that he had seen in Eiru. The same inability to trust in and connect with MacCuacht... and look what happened to Eiru!

There was an incessant, unrelenting assault on the senses as they marched further into the Woodlands of Derwydd, the impenetrable forest, the mind altering amber mist. MacGreinne watched his brother becoming more and more unsettled, "Another traitor in our midst?" he thought to himself. As he pondered this the witch Banba came to his side, "I sense your disquiet MacGreinne. You have doubts about the loyalty of my husband?"

Turning to face Banba, "Of course, her clairvoyant skills, she knew his mind!" She nodded in response to his thoughts. Banba was perhaps the most mysterious of the three Witches of Hawardden. She too was blessed with incredible beauty, as were Eiru and Fodha. Her resolve to the dark cause was without question. MacCuill's weakness and questioning would be intolerable to her.

Eiru had deserted, would MacCuill be next? "I will talk to my husband, and I will concoct a potion to strengthen his resolve. But we must be vigilant. We are dealing with the forces of the Light. Once his heart is taken, his soul will follow ..."

The mysterious Banba, dressed in her silver cocooned fabric, pressed her cheek to MacGreinne's and gripped his hand in a comforting, but still disconcerting, gesture. Her hand was so cold!

As MacGreinne turned, Banba was already quietly fading into the mist with shapeshifting ease. As her spectral form drifted away, MacGreinne momentarily questioned his own mind. Her otherworldly presence and mind probing abilities and the coldness of her body made him shiver. Her beauty was beguiling, but she was pure evil. The depths of her possession shook him to the core.

MacCuacht marched on deeper and deeper into Derwydd. Progress slowed but his resolve unwavering. He still felt his power growing, he fed off adversity.

Suddenly without warning, the wall of conifers thinned, became more and more sparse and the last vestiges of the western light shone diffusely on to a grass covered clearing. A sentinel standing stone stood in the middle of the clearing, pointing heavenwards, a conduit between the spirit world and the first flickering stars of the evening. A cooling north-easterly breeze swept down from the icy mountains and swept away the amber mist. The stone pointed the way, aligned with Polaris and gently tilting in the direction of their path. This was the lay line that will take them to the portal of Machlleth.

MacCuacht, once at Machlleth, will commune with the spirit world and unleash the fury of the dark Sidhe upon the Western Province. He stared heavenwards, he saw the clearing skies to the west, and was pleased to see that in the East, above the line of conifers, and above the ice capped summits the ever building and brewing thunderhead, the storm front following their every move."Here we will make camp for the night! Gather your strength my dark brothers and sisters. Tomorrow we will take the Portal of Machlleth!"

With every passing hour the forces of the dark were growing stronger, the giant standing stone leaning in the direction of the layline connecting the great portals of the Western Province. MacCuacht could feel the energy coursing into the stone and along the layline.

The layline followed a natural fault line that descended deeper and deeper into the ancient deciduous woodlands and Oak groves of Derwydd. MacCuacht conspired with the two Witches of Hawardden, and his brothers MacCuill and MacGreinne. They had all been regaled with the tales of magic and spiritual encounters, "The Oak groves of Derwydd are in the power of

The Guardians of Light, their power from the spirit world radiates through the Portal of Machlleth. We must expect all kinds of strange and dangerous experiences as we descend through the ancient Woodlands of Derwydd."

MacCuill awoke before the first strains of the dawn chorus and before the weak rays of light could percolate through the ancient trees. But this day would be different. The rolling brewing turmoil of the thunderheads and storm front had arrived over night, bringing a cold, dank, dense, forlorn, all consuming mist. The grass meadows and clearance were drenched in a deluge of misting, morning dew. The massive standing stone stood stark and defiant pointing to The Portal of Machlleth.

MacCuill wakening in the smothering mist had reached crisis point. He could take no more! He would desert his dark brothers this very morning! He would go before the masses stirred.

He would go to warn the enlightened ones and go to join them in the cause of the Light.

He feared the journey through the ancient woodlands on his own – but he feared the retribution of his evil, dark, merciless brother even more. MacCuill ventured forth in trepidation, but with the lion heart of the legendary warrior he was destined to become...

He stealthily made his escape under the cover of the condensing mist. He had no reason to remain. He loathed the creature of the dark that his brother had become. He dreaded becoming one of the army of lost souls. Even his witch of a wife conspired against him, the wild, wicked and most mysterious of all the witches.Banba, could be MacCuill's greatest threat. She had confided with MacCuacht about his traitorous intentions. If he stayed her witchcraft would be his undoing.

Banba had power over MacCuill. She was in his blood, in his mind and his psyche. He must leave and put distance between him and the witch.

The dawn was upon them, new light sifted through the swaying tree tops. The distant ridges and mountain tops lit up. MacCuill heard the shrill song of the sonorous Song Thrush, sat atop one of the great, twisted and contorted ancient Oaks on the fringe of Derwydd. Morning was breaking, time was precious. He took a moment, standing under the spreading umbrella of a thousand year Oak.

Even here he was in the clutches of the damp shrouding mist. The moment was fleeting. He anxiously studied the slumbering camp for signs of any movement. Conscious of the perils of Derwydd, knowing the alarm would soon be raised, he must go...

With each step he went deeper and deeper into the depths of Derwydd. The dawn chorus became louder and louder. He felt he was being drawn and guided through the mysterious Woodlands.

He was confused and was in total wonderment at this divinely beautiful, unearthly place.

His path was clear, a trail of floral abundance mazed through the dense woodlands. The air heady with the scent of wild Garlic, Bluebells covered the ground, Foxgloves colonised the hedgerows. All thrived in the patchwork of spotted sunlight that pierced the canopy of deciduous trees of all kinds. Ash, Birch, Elder, Beech the original ancient trees, a dendrinologists dream, in a magical, mystical place...

MacCuill anticipated strange life threatening magical encounters... the stuff of fireside tales and legends...

The truth, the reality, could not have been different! Why!

The dawn chorus was in full crescendo. Every song bird known to man, and many not, gave full vent, a performance on an operatic scale given in a verdant, high vaulted cathedral created by ancient Oaks and the whole deciduous Woodland. MacCuill pressed on... by now the alarm would be raised, the army of lost souls would be in pursuit.

The Woodland continued to welcome MacCuill. The dawn chorus continued to entertain as the first soothing rays of morning light filtered through the Woodland canopy. Life was abundant, Woodland animals peered and gazed from everywhere, acknowledging him and welcoming him and then blithely going on their way. They were no threat to him, and he to them, kindred spirits all.

The giant Oaks, the Woodland animals, all sensed why he was there. He felt coaxed and nurtured... a far cry from the travails he expected...

The lush green carpeted path wound onwards, further into the Woods... the further he went the lusher and greener it got. Greens of every hue, lit up by rays of light bursting through the canopy of an ancient Oak grove with trees so massive, so ancient, so wondrous that MacCuill's mind struggled to grasp the size, their creation and their beauty.

The path twisted and wound into the verdant distance. Relieved and amazed at the ease of his journey, but still acutely aware of the hordes in pursuit, he continued to speedily press on.

He noticed a change in the topography, stranger and stranger geology and rock formations.

Limestone outcrops, rain and wind eroded over the aeons in to jagged clynts and grikes, the composition of the Woodland slowly changing. Ancient Oaks now interspersed with even more ancient Yew trees. The limestone formations had a dreamlike quality. The cover of soil became thinner and sparser as the path wound on. Oaks became rarer, soon only Yew trees could penetrate the cracks and crevices of the limestone pavement.

The Yew trees were of an indeterminate age, thousands of years at least, their roots contorting and penetrating deep into the prehistoric landscape. Land laid down when oceans covered the known world.

Before him was a raised mount of igneous bluestone, impermeable and volcanically hardened granite. The mysterious outcrop was surrounded by the most ancient of Yew trees. A pool of azure blue water gathered in the non porous rock. Stark shadowy branches reflected in water so deep that it seemed to draw MacCuill in. He was beguiled and amazed, kneeling down to dip his hands into the deep cooling water. He cupped the sparkling water in his hands and splashed and refreshed his smiling countenance. Ripples spread to all sides of the pool. As they cleared and settled, to his astonishment, he began to see forms and figures, marching and armoured, "The army of lost souls!"

The clear azure blue pool was showing his pursuers in the reflections... Banba, MacCuacht, Fodha and MacGreinne... They were leading their macabre cohort into Derwydd...

He knelt to watch the unfolding drama in the reflections. MacCuill noticed he had company!

The Woodland animals came to the water's edge, all peering into the blue depths... deer, foxes, wolves and bears watched on... the branches full of song birds, accompanied by hawks, falcons, every kind of raptor... a splendorous golden eagle perched high up in the most ancient Yew tree...

Prey and predator gathered as one... the feared and the fearless in one place. "This is the magic of Derwydd!" uttered MacCuill under his breath.

An eerie stillness descended as they watched their foe enter the enchanted Woodland of Derwydd.

Before their eyes, the nature of the place was changing...

MacCuill noticed that the sacred, ancient Yew trees were slowly oozing a blood red sap. A resin reknowned for its spiritual, magical, mind altering properties...

As the sap oozed, a now familiar amber mist began to drift in from the west. The woodland canopy was lit up, "This azure blue pool must be connected to the great Portal of Machlleth!" surmised MacCuill. He saw the threatening images of the army of lost souls entering Derwydd. The Guardians were responding, sending the lifegiving light and transforming amber mist from the spirit world.

Thiorn and his elite guard felt and saw the life giving transformative energy coming forth from the spirit world. They watched as the glowing radiance pulsed and flowed from the portal.

The all consuming, bewitching amber mist drifted through the Woodland of Derwydd.

Thiorn warned his elite guard, "The enemy enters Derwydd! Be ready!" Thiorn and his guardsmen were dug in, ready to defend the portal with their lives. They looked on as creatures of all types and shapes, of air and land, took to the wing and to the hoof. The life giving mist exuding from the portal had the power to change life forms in an instant evolutionary process. Life forms were being created purely to defend the portals, to live or die in the cause of the enlightened ones. Stags, horses, wolves morphed into deadly strange evolutionary combinations, fighting to protect the portals in the name of the Guardians of Light. Once the portals had been protected they would return to their normal forms and continue to live in peace in the enthralling, wonderful Woodland of Derwydd.

"Be witness to the magic of Derwydd my brothers!" exclaimed Thiorn, "Give your lives to the life changing powers of the Portal of Machlleth!"

With this he saw some of the elite guard transform before his very eyes! They became the legendary and mythical "Horsemen of Derwydd"! Half horse and half man armoured to the hilt, shields, swords and weaponry, with bronze glinting in the glowing radiance. Carried by the drifting, transformative amber mist they galloped towards the ancient Oak groves of Derwydd.

MacCuill watched transfixed, as he saw in the azure blue pool, how the gentle, nurturing nature of Derwydd took on its ugly defensive mantle. The azure blue pool captured vividly just how deadly Derwydd could become. A salutary thought flashed through his increasingly bewildered mind, "Lose this fight and Derwydd would be condemned to this brutal form, the gentle nurturing side gone!" This shivering, shuddering thought turned MacCuill physically cold. The bluestone pool became a conduit of his emotions, seeming to sense his concern. New images projected into the layered depths of the pool. Visions of the great Portal of Machlleth, the elite guard morphing into the legendary Horsemen of Derwydd, creatures of every kind came galloping, flying and racing towards them.

MacCuill would lead them into battle. They would go from the azure bluestone pool. They would wait for MacCuacht and his army of lost souls to penetrate deeper and deeper into the Woodlands of Derwydd... Then they would attack!

The azure blue pool revealed the size and scale of the army of lost souls. Too many to number, they kept on marching, descending into the ancient woodland. On they came...

Now they would see the real nature of Derwydd! Now they would witness the power of the Guardians! He had been told of the powers of Derwydd as a child. Vivid tales of the imagination, stories of the ancient Woodland of Derwydd. Now these mythical, legendary stories would become reality.

Thiorn looked on from Machlleth, every creature real and imaginary, normal and transmutated headed directly into Derwydd. Loyalty unbounded, he was ready to die for the cause. Eiru and Terese were already long gone, heading westwards for the distant ocean. More and more creatures, some known and others unknown, poured into the Woodland from the great Portal of Machlleth. The mysterious amber mist swirled around and permeated into Derwydd, an amber cloak bringing metamorphosised obstacles in the way of the army of lost souls.

MacCuacht marched on, growing stronger and more sinister his entourage were resolute and faithful servants to the dark Sidhe. "They are as black as black, hearts of stone, evil to the core!" he thought, "They will not be turned by the Guardians!" His own dark heart and poisoned veins pulsed in anticipation of the encounter. Banba and Fodha, his two faithful raven haired witches, warned him of the mustering forces, "Sire, we are facing danger on a scale never encountered! Derwydd is a fearsome place once awakened and threatened! The sacred Woodland is protected by the Guardians of Light pouring forth from the Portal of Machlleth... Life forms of mutated evolution will be turned against us... We will be tested as never before!"

They all gazed into the high canopy, through the strange transforming amber mist, and high, high above to the dark, brooding, menacing turbulence of the ever rolling storm front. Bringing with it the cold, condensing, cloaking, shrouding, moisture laden and drenching fine drizzle. "Derwydd awaits us!" pronounced the malevolent MacCuacht, "We shall see who prevails! We shall see how the veil falls!"

MacCuill and his gathered creatures of the Woodland, gazed into the azure pool... the army of lost souls approached the "Grove of the Druids."The perfect place for an ambush! He alerted the growing and morphing troops... an aerial assault first! Falcons, hawks, eagles, vultures, raptors of all kinds... They stooped, dropping from the skies, wings furled, talons bared... razor sharp, slicing, pecking, grabbing... Screams of shock and surprise, shrieks of pain! Pandemonium ensued! Song birds turned eye pecking bandits! Frenzied forces of transformed nature scurried and harried... biting, tearing and lacerating! Next, the assault of the land! Poison ivy wound, wrapped and smothered.Thistles flicked blinding barbs. Twisted, contorted roots of giant magical Oaks erupted out of the soil, constricting and squeezing their prey... Low lying branches whipped and thrashed, flinging their foe to the ground, roots crushing them, while rodents bit and gnawed... The soil soon running red with with blood... Ranks in disarray, the army of lost souls ran now, but with nowhere to go...

Thundering into the Woodlands next, came the rampaging stampeding, rutting and baying, magnificent red deer stags. Many pronged antlers scything and skewering the panicking dark forces.

The army of lost souls being out thought and decimated... this was the sign for MacCuill to lead the Horsemen of Derwydd into battle. Armed to the teeth and with the trampling strength of galloping stallions, they struck at the cold hearts of the army of lost souls. Designed to take out MacCuacht, "This was an onslaught full and furious, massed and dangerous, and with the element of surprise, surely no one, nothing, not even the dark one MacCuacht can resist this?"

MacCuill reckoned without the intervention of the dark Sidhe. The veil between the spirit world and the mortal realm ebbed and flowed.

The strange magic of Derwydd and the black magic of the dark Sidhe in mysterious confrontation, attack and retaliation! The power of Machlleth, the malevolence of MacCuacht!

The army of lost souls visibly shaken and on the backfoot... then the shape – shifting, silver cocooned, raven haired witches colluded with

MacCuacht, summoning the full fury of the dark Sidhe. The veil was temporarily torn, a rift through which the darkness poured. They cast occultish spells, calling the dark forces from the spirit world.

Not even the Portal of Machlleth could offer protection now. MacCuill and the creatures of the Light could not resist the combined conjurings of MacCuacht and the two Witches of Hawardden.

Thiorn and the elite guard sensed a change in the energy of the portal...

MacCuill, the Horsemen of Derwydd and the creatures of the Light, charged into the fray once more. They were fearless. They struck swiftly and forcefully...

Still there was a sense of the amber mist dissipating and the portal weakening...Time seemed to be standing still, the tide was turning...

MacCuill looked down the advancing lines of Horsemen and creatures of the Light... They were making no headway, the sounds of battle quietened...

He saw MacCuacht and the Witches beckoning to the sky, arms outstretched, they were summoning the rolling, brewing storm front to earth...

The Horsemen, the stags, all the creatures of the Light, were moving in slow motion, running in quick sand. They made no headway now... The dark Sidhe had been summoned...Pouring from the skies, the rolling tormented storm front enveloped the Woodland of Derwydd, the dank, cold, dense, shrouding mist, drenching and covering every living thing.

Then the ambushers became the ambushed. The element of surprise lost, the momentum reversed.

The moment had gone... MacCuacht channelled the demonic storm into the depths of the Woodland. Down through the canopy, down through the Oak groves, down came the demented, turbulent storm front... Tree by giant tree, life was sapped out. The verdant, emerald green turning to a lifeless grey...

The mist cloaked everything in a smothering, suffocating, stillness...

MacCuill watched in horror as MacCuacht and the raven haired witches channelled the full fury of the dark Sidhe... He sounded the retreat... They must escape into the spirit world, through the Portal of Machlleth...

Meeting no resistance, the floodgates were open. The mist became a squall of monstrous intensity, driving, horizontal, cold and freezing, a weather front of such violent intensity! Ancient Oaks, anchored and secured over the millennia, were cast to the ground, roots flailing and branches cracking.

Living entities now became debris hurtling through the void...

Then the mother cloud arrived... even darker and more menacing, descending Derwydd into a hellish world. The storm wall twisted and turned. Violent vortices touched down. Dark tendrils turning the myriad shades of green to a lifeless grey, as they consumed old and newly evolved life in a murderous moment!

Instincts in survival mode, MacCuill and the Horsemen of Derwydd and the creatures of the Light fled from the Woodlands, making for the sanctuary of Machlleth. They chased ahead of the demonic storm front and the twisting, tumultuous tornadoes. Many perished and were turned to the dark.

Thiorn and his elite guard stood resolutely to protect the Portal, but MacCuill warned him of this futility! They must all pass through the Portal while the life giving light still radiates!

The storm front was around them now, and as the army of lost souls arrived, they went beyond the thinning and dissipating veil. MacCuacht and the raven haired Witches of Hawardden threatened to pierce the veil... but they were too late! The Portal took in the frantically galloping Horsemen, the transforming creatures of the Light, and finally Thiorn and his elite guard and MacCuill.

The great Portal of Machlleth, the giver of Divine Light to the Western Province, closed. The veil once close to the mortal realm, returned deep into the spirit world. The enraged dark one had been thwarted! For the moment!

All those entering the spirit world will remain there until enlightened beings unlocked the Portal with the keystone...

CHAPTER TWELVE:
SOURCE OF THE DIVINE

On the fringe of the Northern Ocean, many days march from the Portal of Machlleth, Amergin meditated by the Temple of the Sun. He was acutely aware of the dangers the Milesian tribes were facing. His fellow sea voyagers recuperated, enjoying the rich abundance of this glorious part of the world. They fished the ocean and the rivers. Shoals were so plentiful they appeared to jump on to hooks and self impale on spears. Hunting parties replenished the larder with game and foul.

The estuary was full of migrating geese at this time of year, just arriving from more northerly breeding grounds. They arrived in great rafts, squadrons in formation, seeking out these plentiful feeding grounds. Wild horses galloped and cantered along the sweeping beaches.

Amergin revelled in the spectacular beauty of this pristine coastline. In transcendental meditation he began to compose the lyrics of a poem, to capture the sheer unadulterated beauty of this place for posterity. In writing he began to slip into an amber cosmos, communing with the ancients and the Guardians of Light and with the beautiful enlightened being of his destiny, Sceine...

"Sea Horses and Winter Geese "

Roaring gales, raging surf, mountains to oceans, heights to depths,
Senses alive, sea sounds, wind overtures, ozone, seaweed and salt,
Minerals encrusted, sea salted, tidal surge and ripping currents,
Living, breathing, ocean alive, harsh, rich, full of life,
On the edge, shoreline of plenty, sea geese picking,
Sea birds flocking, dipping, tasting, brine, weed and hoppers,
Sun light, shafts, searching, riding contours, cloud breaking,
Bursting, beaming, filling the bay, rising over Temples of the Sun,
Weather forming, lifting, Mist pouring, summits peaking,
Breaking, squall driven, light filled, rainbow arching,
Salted geese, sea horses galloping, chasing oncoming waves,
Racing the tide, hooves hammered, sand beaten, foam blown,
Water running, water lying, waters of life, everywhere...

Amergin sensed that the Great Spirit was with him. The land and the ocean of this fabled island welcomed them. He felt the gentle caress of his destined Sceine. She was always with him now, guiding him, comforting him...

That evening he would lead his priests of the Chapter of Mystics in prayer at the Temple of the Sun. They would commune with the Guardians of Light and open the portal.

This was the last great portal before the ocean. Potentially this could be the place of a last stand for the Milesians. They would need all there resourcefulness, energy and spirit in the battles to come...

Amergin gazed out over the ocean. He sensed the presence of the remaining Milesian fleet offshore. Somewhere near the shimmering offshore islands would be Scota and Milidh. Waiting for his sign to join him... Then the Milesian tribes would march south to meet his destiny...

He heard a clamour as the scouting party led by his loyal brother Eiremhou returned.

His gaze was taken by the natural sweep of the bay, over the meadows and coastal marsh land, along the meandering river and inland to the distant woodlands and high conifer forests. He was disturbed that the mountain summits were no longer visible. The storm clouds had enveloped them and were rolling ever downwards through the forests and beyond the foot hills... now they cloaked the verdantly green woodlands... He shivered. He sensed malevolence at work...

His attention was distracted once more, this time at the rivermouth, "What on earth?!"... Into the estuary swam a silver backed shoal of wild oceanic salmon. They were running with the tide, leaping high and plunging deep! "Grab the nets we are going fishing!" Amergin bolted down to the riverside and jumped into one of the landing boats. Tying a net to the stern, he rowed for all his worth, making a wide arcing course into the estuary ahead of the living, seething shoal, in a race to cut off their escape.

Amergin strained with every stroke of the oars to get ahead of the shoal. A huge silver scaled Salmon pushed upstream, leading the shoal into the narrowing channel. His furious rowing made the shoal pause, they turned in panic. They thrashed and splashed in the shallows at the opposite bank. The escape route narrowing, stroke by stroke, they would soon be trapped! The king Salmon flexed and flicked its silver shimmering body, and with a thrust of the tail was through the gap.

Amergin in frustration turned up river. In that instant the net ballooned out into the tidal stream, the shoal were through, swimming free with the pushing tide. The adrenalin of the chase still in his veins, he was determined to follow the king of the Salmon.

The building tidal flood pushed him back into the mainstream of the river. He untied the net and signalled to those on shore to regather it. A few straggling Salmon were caught by the gill net as they recovered it. The sea drift swept him upstream in the wake of the shoal. The tell tale inverted "V" of the king Salmon as it pushed upstream into the calmer waters. Amergin was still drifting with the tide, giving an occasional stroke and a guiding dip of the oars. His faithful mariners were lost out of sight as he rounded bend after meandering bend.

The wandering river curved and bent deeper and deeper into the back waters, through marshland and rich pastures. Slowing all the time, past lush meadowlands, drifting on and on with the tide.

Amergin still followed the "V" of the shoal and king Salmon, as the flooding briny tide met the flowing freshwater river. Where tide and fresh water met, the denser saline stream flowed up river along the river bed. The lighter fresh water flowed downstream towards the ocean.

Slowly, a whirlpool started to turn, forming, growing in strength. Surging tide and flowing fresh water eddied and circulated. Stronger and stronger it turned. Amergin's boat was caught, trapped in the swirling river. The fisherman, become bait... He had no control now. Despairingly he pulled at the oars, but to no avail... spinning and spinning in the vortex of tide and river, brine and fresh water. Black bog water and aquamarine sea water, fresh mountain water and silty tidal flow.

A kaleidoscope of streams and flows...

Amergin felt the boat rotating and revolving downwards. Soon the boat became immersed, and he was under the surface... but he could breath! Clear water currents and thicker denser saline solutions trapped and warped sunlight. Amergin floated weightless in a strange oxygenated watery world... Through a watery veil he saw the silver scaled king Salmon. The layers of water became crystal clear, and in the transparency he heard a voice gently sounding in his head. He was transfixed by a piercing gaze, "I am here to give you the knowledge you need, and the wisdom you deserve..."

Drawn in to a hypnotic trance, he stared into the amber eye of the king Salmon. He was taken deep in to an amber cosmos, beyond the veil between watery realm and the spirit world, "Amergin you are welcome to the Promised Land. I have sent enlightened beings to help you, to guide you. The dark Sidhe approaches, you must be ready! Do not be fooled by them, they will come in guises you do not recognise! Be careful my love... I am waiting for you!" This was Sceine speaking through the king Salmon. She gave him the knowledge of the ancients...

Amergin was drawn in even deeper, in to a dark fleck in the amber eye of the king Salmon... and in an instant, in a blink of the king Salmon's eye he was ejected to the surface and was swimming for his life. The whirlpool held him, he was now gasping for air! He was back in the mortal realm! He swam for the light, the whirlpool span him around a few more times. Just as the pushing tide reached its height, the eddying slowed and the vortex was gone...

A few breathless moments later, the tide turned and he was being taken down stream. He drifted with the ebb, rounding familiar bends, floating back to the estuary...

One last bend, and a few gentle kicking strokes and he landed on the shoreline, back with his waiting faithful... They were anxious for Amergin's safety, but were oblivious to the encounter with the spirit world.

His brothers were aware of the commotion, had seen Amergin row upstream chasing the king of Salmon, and now they arrived at the estuary to check his wellbeing. Even the Machiavellian Eimbear seemed to appear genuinely happy at his safe return... a good charade thought Amergin!

Eiremhou raced to the shoreline and gave a genuine bear hug of an embrace, "My brother, you swim back to us! What became of your row boat?"

Amergin smiled, "I will tell you later brother, but first what of your scouting party? Tell me what you have found in this strange and beautiful land!"

Eiremhou recounted their tale of reconnaissance... they had discovered the workings of an ancient bluestone quarry and evidence of recent workings and evidence that this is the sacred quarry where giant standing stones are hewn and then transported to sacred sites throughout the land.

Amergin was intrigued as to how the stones were cut and transported, some kind of ancient technology presumably. Eiremhou told of how they were witness to an explosion that echoed around the quarry. The sound ricocheted and rebounded around and a fine bluestone dust settled on the ground. Through the airborne particles appeared three forms. Rubbing the dust from their eyes they looked on in disbelief. Three of the strangest looking beings they had ever encountered, pulled and heaved at ropes connected to the huge precisely hewn bluestone monoliths.

Another three prised and levered and pushed the bluestones over oak rolling timbers.

Slowly, oh so slowly, the monstrous bluestones were rolled into a clearing. The six muscle bound, one eyed individuals securely tied leather slings around each of the bluestones. From the slings, heavy ropes were tied to six carefully designed and positioned harnesses.

Eiremhou took a breath, obviously still in awe of what he had seen...

The six Cyclops stood back and signalled to someone standing high above the bluestone quarry on a rocky escarpment. This white haired, elegant being, dressed in a gold and amber robe, raised an ornately carved oak staff into the air in response to their signal.

Another intake of breath as he told his story, Eiremhou told of six birds of prey of enormous scale, with huge wingspans flying from the distant woodlands. The white haired one descended into the quarry to greet them, and to oversee the moving of the bluestone monoliths. The Cyclops turned away to continue the excavation of the next massive bluestone. Eiremhou studied the leather harnesses, just as the giant avians landed on the escarpment overlooking the quarry.

The white haired one gestured with the carved oak staff. The avians took off once more, giant wings beating. The birds circled the clearing. They were akin to Golden Eagles, but at least four times the size.

Gusts from the down beats tried to push them off their feet, away from the Bluestones. Feathering wing tips brushed past them, soft and deceptively powerful. Sentient beasts of the air, one by one they alighted by a given harness, designed to be gripped by curling talons. Another wave of the carved Oak staff and they were airborne again. Gently rising, taking the strain on the rope ties.

Slowly, wing beat by wing beat, the rope stretched, the leather slings and harnesses creaked and gripped. Tension built the strain increasing. Slowly, the Bluestone lifted!

The brothers Eiremhou and Eimbear were staggered at the power. They looked on as the giant Eagles lifted up and were airborne. Soon they were high over the escarpment, heading eastwards to the Woodlands of Derwydd, and beyond...

"Welcome to the Quarry of Izion!" declared the white haired one, "I am Endinou, the Guardian of the Bluestones. "Eiremhou quizzed him as to the destination of the Bluestones, "To far off portals, across all the Provinces. To re-energise and strengthen all the portals that have been compromised by the dark Sidhe!" clarified Endinou, "The Bluestones here are the purest in the land, they are formed at a convergence of lay lines from the Magine Islands and the Temple of the Sun, and Hushinish and the great Portal of Machlleth. "Endinou continued, "As the Druid of Izion, and the Guardian of the Bluestones. I am empowered by the enlightened ones to send my winged carriers to places that are under threat, in order to strengthen the portals of the land. And you?" He turned to Eimbear, "What is your mission?"

As Endinou asked this question of Eimbear, he became visibly agitated, becoming pale and introverted. Endinou was shaken by the response and the energy of Eimbear. He now turned to Eiremhou, "Forgive me I am needed by the Cyclops. We are sourcing the purest Bluestone for the Portal of Machlleth. It is being infiltrated by the dark one MacCuacht as we speak!" He averted his gaze from Eimbear and grabbed Eiremhou's hand, "Go! Return to your tribes. Tell your leader that the Portal of Machlleth is falling! The Temple of the Sun may be next! Be aware, very aware that the dark Sidhe is here! They come in many forms and many guises!" Endinou turned accusingly towards Eimbear and strode purposefully away to the Quarry of Izion... Eimbear flinched uncomfortably...

He had been found out!

Eiremhou studied his brother's response. His blood ties had distracted him, disguised the real person that stood before him, "We must go brother!" he urged. As they left the clearing and the Quarry of Izion, Eiremhou was only too aware that Endinou had said too much, he had exposed the sacred Quarry of Izion to his traitorous brother.

Eiremhou hurriedly back tracked, he must warn Amergin that the Portal of Machlleth was in danger!

The Temple of Sun appeared before them, the estuary, the escarpment, and the giant Bluestone standing stones in perfect alignment. Here the lay lines converged, connecting with Machlleth and way offshore the Portal of Sceilge on the Magine Islands. Eiremhou felt the brooding presence of his brother beside him... he must warn Amergin!

Only now did they see the significance of the Portal of Machlleth and the Temple of the Sun. After the meeting with Endinou, the power and the potency of these portals became abundantly clear.

Amergin was standing, staring and searching the eastern horizon for a sign of any indication of the dark Sidhe. Eimbear turned away. He searched for someone, presumably Gonne of the Chapter of Mystics. This gave Eiremhou the chance to be alone with Amergin. Together now, they climbed the steep escarpment, using footholds and handholds carved into the track. Amergin helped Eiremhou up the track, he was glad to be with his loyal sibling again. He had listened intently to his tales of adventure and the meeting with Endinou.

They neared the awe inspiring Temple of the Sun. They surveyed the beautiful land and noticed a gathering at the estuary... Eimbear met with Gonne... the connivance continued...

Amergin and Eiremhou were chilled by this alliance. Eiremhou repeated the warning given by Endinou, the Guardian of the Bluestones, "Beware! The dark Sidhe are amongst us, they will come in many forms and guises!" Amergin recollected the warning given by the king Salmon, channelling the enlightened ones and his destined one Sceine, "they will come in forms you will not recognise!"

Amergin led his brother along the track towards the Temple of Sun, weaving their way around a confusion of twisted and contorted granite slabs. They edged their way carefully to the tip of the last lichen covered outcrop, ancient geological formations hewn and strewn in any and every direction.

One last boulder strewn length of track and they were there... high above the estuary, the glistening ocean and the peaked Magine Islands to the west.The vast and wide sweeping expanse of the bay, the coastal marshlands and verdant meadows catching the last of the radiant sunlight. To the east, darkening and stretching shadows fell over the woodlands and high conifer forests, meeting the darkening, descending cloud cover plunging ever down from the shrouded distant peaks.

"From there our adversary comes!" pointed Amergin, "See how the darkness descends and envelops all before it!" Anxiously they both observed the broiling, blackening, wall of weather that crept ominously closer. "Our adversary is already amongst us!" replied Eiremhou, looking down at the conniving duo of Eimbear and Gonne.

The magnificent Bluestone standing stone alignment was before them, "This sacred place must be preserved at all costs. This Temple is one of the last pure bastions of the Guardians of Light on this emerald isle. Here we will make a stand against the encroaching dark forces.To the death if necessary!" As he said this Amergin was all too aware of the tales that the great Portal of Machlleth had succumbed, and was potentially compromised, "Let me show you brother! I will open this portal, and unleash the powers of the Guardians of Light! Then we will travel to Machlleth to free our good people!"

Together they walked to the base of the largest Bluestone.Elegantly carved engravings, hieroglyphic messages and pictograms depicting the setting sun, a portal of radiant light and mysterious life forms emanating forth. "The Guardians of Light have come to me in my dreams. They have given me instructions... See how this crevice is sculpted to the shape of a human body... My body Eiremhou!

"I am the key!" Amergin went on, "Only I can open this portal! Only I can unleash the powers of the Guardians from this portal!"

Amergin prayed and meditated in isolation, waiting for the sun to set in the West, only then can he become the key. In the quiet of the evening he reflected on his encounters, the messages from the spirit world, and his connection with the beautiful Sceine... He travelled back in time, contemplating his upbringing, his training, his life as a royal prince... a privileged life, a life rich in experiences...

His mind drifting, he remembered in vivid memories the days as a young prince, long before the Prophecy was a consideration, long before the burdens of the destiny of Milesia were on his broad shoulders, and long before he would become the potential saviour of all enlightened beings.

He remembered those carefree days with fondness. Days of wild abandon in the hills and mountains of Northern Galicia, days of riding on bare back stallions through the wilderness of Asturias, days of swimming in the pristine rivers flowing from the snow capped mountains to the turquoise blue Northern Ocean. The dreams and memories poured forth... body surfing the powerful beach breaks of Bascais, climbing the high mountainous interior to gather the fragrant wild thyme honey... he was there now... the intensive, combative training camps, where he and his siblings were put through gruelling routines to hone their fitness and battle skills. They were groomed and moulded into warrior princes by their father King Milidh, who had a reputation as a fiercesome warrior.

Throughout the Mediterranean his conquests were legendary. He valiantly and bravely, led Milesia into battle as the conquering tribes swept through the countries of the Mediterranean to the Northern shores of Galicia. Here the

Milesian tribes settled, waiting for the legendary journey of the Prophecy to commence, across the limitless Northern Ocean.

Amergin remembered those training days with a mixture of anxiety and exhilaration... As teenagers he and his siblings would gather on a clearing on the banks of the River Douros. Milidh would measure out a combat area. This was their training battleground. Milidh would put them through their paces until they dropped with physical exhaustion. They wrestled, they boxed, they fenced... they learned the skills of the warrior and the strategies of the leader.

Amergin remembered the day that he and his siblings were tested to the limit. Milidh had set a sporting challenge. The winner would challenge Milidh himself in an armed wrestling match.

A smile spread over Amergin's face as he recalled how he and his sibling princes, all young and raw, laughed and roared and cheered and jeered at one another in youthful, competitive exuberance.

They raced and wrestled each other. High spirited, yet mindful of the seriousness of their training.

Amergin proved himself then, as in the later ordeals, a supreme athlete and fierce warrior in the mould of his father Milidh. He out ran, out raced and out swam his brothers. He was nominated champion and there he was, stood face to face in the fighting ring with his armour clad father.

A combination of hardened warrior and young pretender, Amergin's brow furrowed as he remembered the encounter. He knew Milidh would give no quarter, whether in training or in battle. Amergin fingered the scar he sustained on his upper arm, sustained in the first moments of their clash.

Milidh loudly declared, "Be on your guard my young prince!" His siblings winced, empathetically, recoiling from that blow. Crimson drops of fresh blood from the gash, hitting and discolouring the dry, silty sand. At that moment he became galvanised and alive, conscious of the time and place and the moment in the universal continuum! He saw the expressions on his brothers' faces. In the distance, on the coast, the high tower under construction, currently clad by wooden scaffolding.

In front of him, his father, the great King Milidh, his dear father, ready to give him the lesson of his young life. Amergin fought as if his life depended on it. He gave as good as he got, using all his attacking and defensive skills, thrusting and parrying. In close engagement, shields clashed and armour battered, swords sliding to the hilt. For a split second Amergin felt on top. Then with a subtle shift of weight and a deft slight of hand and sword, Milidh threw Amergin off balance. In an instant he was crashing to the floor on his back, Milidh's elbow resting forcefully on his windpipe and his sword flicked from his grasp to the edge of the clearance. Amergin's brothers roared and cheered in approval, in recognition of the finely honed skills of Milidh and the tigerish efforts of the young prince. There was also an element of relief that the heir apparent, Amergin, had come out relatively unscathed! They had all learned important lessons that day...

Back to the quietness of the Bay of Sceine, Amergin returned to the present... He looked out to the Magine Islands, beyond the precipitous headland, the channel and the offshore reefs... he sent his thoughts and prayers to his mother and father, Scota and Milidh, who waited patiently for his signal for them to join him at the Temple of the Sun. He knelt before the giant Bluestone, his shadow cast by the setting sun over the shaped cleft in the great standing stone. He prayed for the gathered tribes of Milesia...

When the moment is right, he will become the key! When the reflective light of the setting sun shone over the bay and alighted on the Temple of the Sun, he would slip into the cleft and unleash the magic of the aligned Bluestones. The portal would be opened and the might of Milesia would be joined by the divine presence of the Guardians of Light! Together they would confront MacCuacht and the dark Sidhe...

The time was nearing... once more the brooding darkness was approaching from the mountains of the East. Amergin wondered at the fate of the great Portal of Machlleth. He thought too of Endinou at the Bluestone Quarry of Izion and the warning he had given of the imminent danger. It was too much to contemplate! The dark Sidhe cannot be allowed to prevail! If either the Portal of Machlleth or the Quarry of Izion were taken by the dark forces then the lifeblood of the sacred Western Province would be cut off at source...

The lengthening shadows, as the scarlet, red and orange sunset reflected across the Bay of Sceine. Increment by increment, second by second the alignment with the setting sun gets closer.

Amergin's attention was drawn down to the encampment where his faithful tribesmen and women waited in anxious anticipation.On to the riverbank where the poisonous Gonne and the deceitful Eimbear continued to scheme. His gaze swept around the bay and along the meandering river flowing to the sea in a ghostly dwindling light. Onwards through the marshlands and meadows now covered in slowly condensing dew. The tidal ditches filling with thickening mist. The occasional flickering of the marsh gas "will o' the wisp" burst in to life.

The alignment approaches, ticking moment by ticking moment, the sunlight shimmering gold and silver and orange across the ocean.

His gaze continued up the misting valley, where waning light met darkening horizon. Only now did his heart begin to race in the realisation that the dark Sidhe were so close! The cold, steel grey clouds and black storm front rolled remorselessly towards them, consuming all before them...

What of Machlleth? What of Endinou and the Quarry of Izion?

In the cascading roseate light at the end of the day the giant standing Bluestones aligned with the setting sun... Amergin stepped into the shaped, womblike cleft carved into the greatest of the Bluestones. A voice came to him from the ether, "I am with you Amergin! Bring the powers of the Guardians of Light to the mortal realm, bring them to my Province!" In the glowing light of the sunset he saw a vision of a familiar and comforting form, "Sceine!" his beloved, his destined one... a spiritual and uplifting presence as he began to journey beyond the veil, communing with the Guardians of Light, bringing them into the mortal realm...

Once more, he felt his body being gently caressed. Sceine was massaging him, manipulating him, moving him into the cleft carved into the Bluestone... Finger tip by finger tip, muscle by muscle, limb by limb he was moulded into position. He was becoming the key to the enlightened universe. As the palms of his hands connected with the cold, highly conductive Bluestone, he began to feel the universal life force tingling and surging through his outstretched body and the radiant Light of the Divine warming his soul as it poured out of the portal into the mortal realm.

His torso twisted and turned as he was massaged and manipulated by Sceine as she took him through the veil. He became one with her. Sceine was holding him, feeling him, nursing him sensuously through the veil.The back of his skull, the nape of his neck and the small of his back, every chi point resting gently against the womb shaped cleft, each point energising and conducting.

Amergin's body flowed with the universal life force. His head filled with kaleidoscopic visions.His heart raced climactically. Gentle hands moved down his body, caressing and nurturing. Amergin gasped as Sceine pressed him into the perfectly shaped, folded rock formation. She pushed him hard into the shaped Bluestone. He fitted exactly. Sceine was before him...

She smiled, "I am with you. I will always be with you... come! ..."

Energised, he forcefully thrust into the cool Bluestone. Gliding, soft, gentle hands brushed against his body. From head to curving spine, torso arching, "You are there my love! The world of enlightenment is yours! Enter the spirit world! Come to me!" Overwhelmed and overcome, Amergin gathered himself, "Come to join me! Let the Guardians of Light pour forth! May they defend us, and bring us all to safety!

Organic form met crystalline Bluestone. Pulses of amber light surged through the Bluestone, pouring into his flexing, orgasmic being. The amber energy raced through and circulated around his outstretched body, bursting from every extremity. The porcelain surfaced Bluestone tore and ripped. Another universe came, another dimension, the Light of the Divine poured forth...

Everyone watched in wonderment... The Temple of the Sun glowed with pure, radiant light, god given and beautiful... Amergin was the key, the Temple the conduit. The champion of Milesia, the poet warrior, their Sea Druid journeying beyond the veil and bringing them to their destiny...

The enlightened ones confronted the dark Sidhe now, the prophecy nearing fulfilment. The destined one has arrived. He and the Guardians of Light face MacCuacht and the dark Sidhe...

Radiant beings poured through the portal, earthly and unearthly forms morphing in the luminescence. All kinds of weird and wonderful creations came forth...

In awe and spellbound, the Tribes of Milesia were ready. They had seen the forces of the Light unleashed...

Ominously, beyond the Temple of the Sun, their deadly foe arrives. Falling out of the skies came the rolling, turbulent, dark storm front... sweeping through the ancient Oak grove of Derwydd, past the now compromised and darkened Portal of Machlleth, beyond the abandoned and unprotected Quarry of Izion and down the misting, ghostly river valley. Rolling ever towards them...

From on high, from the escarpment of the Temple of the Sun, Amergin could clearly see his foe... the dark, brooding, deadly cloud formations... an evil shroud from which the denizens and demons of the dark would emanate

CHAPTER THIRTEEN:
THE TEARING OF THE VEIL

A few hours to the east, in advance of the marauding dark Sidhe, Eiru and Terese had met with the wizard Endinou, the Guardian of the Quarry of Izion, the source of all the Bluestones. The Bluestones are the keystones that open and energise the myriad of portals throughout the land, some are known, many unknown.

Accompanying Endinou were the giant Cyclops, the quarrymen of Izion, a fiercesome sight in the gloom of the encroaching storm front. Endinou informed Eiru and Terese how the Portal of Machlleth had been overwhelmed, and of how MacCuill and the defending elite guard had to flee deep into the portal, taking refuge beyond the veil. They were trapped, in limbo, in the spirit world.

They would wait in limbo, until a keystone is placed in the entrance of the Portal of Machlleth by an enlightened being... Endinou impressed on them how important the Quarry of Izion was to the land of the Prophecy.

MacCuacht and his hordes could inexorably infect each portal. In time as more and more portals were breached and converted to the dark, the veil becomes more impenetrable. To protect the enlightened world, the Bluestones must be protected.

Terese of the Xantha still struggled in the aftermath of her capture, but she offered to stay with the Cyclops quarrymen to protect and defend the Quarry of Izion. It was agreed that Eiru should take flight and find the Milesian Sea Druid Amergin, who has arrived on the Western shores at the Temple of the Sun. Eiru can bring him to the Quarry of Izion. Together they will go to battle for and reopen the great Portal of Machlleth. The enlightened Amergin can put the purest of Bluestone keystones in place... he can release MacCuill and his guardsmen from their limbo beyond the veil.

The plan was fraught, riddled with uncertainty... In an instant, Eiru the changeling witch, morphed into her alter entity. Giant wings beat downwards, and she was aloft, soaring westwards into the diminishing light of the day, seeking out the Temple of the Sun.

Terese of the Xantha, Endinou, the Guardian of the quarry of Izion, and the the giant Cyclops made their way back to Izion. They would defend the Bluestone source with all their combined might. They would wait for the Sea Druid Amergin and go to reopen the Portal of Machlleth.

Eiru was now a dimunitive winged form disappearing way over the distant western horizon. Endinou prayed for her, "May the Guardians of Light guide you safely to your destination!" and added thoughtfully, "May they bring protection to Izion, the Portal of Machlleth and this sacred Isle."

Before long Eiru was way out of sight. The light of the day almost gone, Endinou instructed the Cyclops to make haste and gather all the carved Bluestones, placing them in alignment with the lay line connecting the Temple of Sun and the Portal of Machlleth. The Western Province is the last bastion of the enlightened ones. Endinou knew that only together would they stand a chance of protecting this enclave of light...

Eiru with her avian super senses, saw and felt the amber radiance and pure white Divine Light glowing and pulsing from the energy source of the Temple of the Sun. Occasional sweeping shafts of silver white energy bursting over the horizon. Strange kaleidoscopic, hallucinogenic creations sped towards her. "The Temple of the Sun must be open already!" Soon she was surrounded by the strangest anthropomorphic life forms she had ever seen.

The creations of the Divine Light sent by the Guardians sensed a friend in the arriving airborne changeling. She was a kindred spirit in support of the cause of the Light. The strange shapes and forms encircled her and guided her to the Temple of the Sun. Amergin saw the creations bringing this avian wonder to him. He was curious as to who this amazing white tailed transformation really is...

The Cyclops worked long into the night. Muscle bound giants straining and grafting. They dragged, rolled and levered the purest Bluestones from deep within the Quarry of Izion. They worked and toiled, breaking their bodies. Gradually they were able to position these purest of Bluestones into preparation for alignment. Endinou, a universal conductor, stood high above the quarry, with a panoramic view. He could see the darkening horizon in the direction of Machlleth. He sensed the glowing radiance of the Temple of the Sun over the western horizon. He orchestrated the giant servantile Cyclops with his ornately engraved and decorated staff. Orchestrating them in an otherworldly labour of endurance, using all their ancient time honoured skills, they worked unremittingly into the growing gloom. They dug the last pit, then coaxed and eased the monstrously impressive dead weight of the biggest and most impressive Bluestone into place. The rolling Oak timbers were removed and sling ropes tightened over lofty pine timbered 'A' frames. The team of Cyclops heaved on the ropes in unison... the last of the Bluestones was in place... the alignment complete.

Immediately a faint mauve blue luminescence exuded from the tip of each monolithic standing stones... a photonic connection charged through the lay line energising from the Temple of the Sun to the great Portal of Machlleth... "We have it! We must act now!" Endinou enthused, "Before the hideous MacCuacht arrives!" All of them rejoiced, even the giant Cyclops!

Terese went to join Endinou from the panoramic view point. From here she could see the blue radiance streaming over the horizons, blues of all shades from mauve to deep indigo.

Endinou read Terese's worried expression... Had Eiru found the Milesian poet warrior? Could they act in time to salvage the Portal of Machlleth? "We are in the lap of the gods! By the grace of the Guardians we will prevail!"

Amergin took a step back, in awe and bewilderment, just as the white tailed, winged avian creature alighted and morphed before his very eyes into a beautiful raven haired temptress clad in a shimmering silver fabric. "I am Eiru, the estranged wife of the dark one MacCuacht! He comes from the east! You must be the prophesied one, the Sea Druid Amergin, champion and poet warrior of the Milesian nation!"

"I am", replied Amergin, slowly regaining his composure, and the power of speech, "I am destined to be on this sacred Isle! I am destined to be with your High Priestess, the beautiful Sceine!"

Eiru nodded knowingly, "I am aware of your mission... but your priority now is to go to the Quarry of Izion, and go with the wizard Endinou to save the great Portal of Machlleth, and to release our faithful warriors!" Eiru went on to explain about the sacred source of the Bluestones, and the purest of pure keystones he, as an enlightened one, must take to Machlleth. She also explained how MacCuill, the enlightened brother of the dark one MacCuacht, is in limbo in the spirit world, and how he will be vital to the cause of the Light. She went on, "I must take you to Izion, and to Endinou, the Guardian of the Bluestones... He will then take you to Machlleth. "

Amergin studied the changeling, witchcraft or not, he implicitly believed her. He followed her graceful pointing finger along the lay line connecting the Temple of Sun with the far distant Quarry of Izion "We must go to Izion, and we must go now!"

Beyond the horizon, the storm rolled and brewed. MacCuacht and his hordes came with the tempest of darkness.

No time to question, no time to waste... Amergin looked into the darkening distance as the changeling witch morphed once more. A kaleidoscope of photons, fronded wing tips and mighty powerful beating wings... Talons gripped him and took him... his feet left the ground... he too was airborne! In a swooping graceful, skyward arc they followed the radiant lay line. Amergin looked down at the rapidly disappearing Temple of Sun, the escarpment and the Milesian tribes, mere indistinguishable dots and shapes. The lay line lit their way, intense emerald and dark indigo, all colours fused into one. Amergin continued to look back... they were being followed by a formation of the strangest, weirdest, most peculiar morphing creations of the Light... an unending stream of unending strangeness... following them, pouring out of the Temple of the Sun.

Endinou, the Guardian of the Quarry of Izion and the sacred Bluestones, sensed their coming from the west, "The enlightened one, the Sea Druid Amergin, arrives!" He was aware that he and the High Priestess Sceine have the power to reopen portals that have been infected by the dark Sidhe.

Endinou had crafted the purest Bluestone keystone in readiness for his coming. He was overcome at the prospect that Amergin in harmony with the Divine in nature will counter the scourge of the dark Sidhe. His faith was restored, his courage renewed. A tear fell on to the Bluestone, separating into a myriad of rainbows as it fell to ground.

The creatures of the Light arrived first, speeding along the lay line conduit. Endinou and Terese of the Xantha looked on in wonderment as wave after wave of living Light. Creatures from all dimensions swept in from the West. Down into the Quarry of Izion, flying in dizzying formation around the iridescent Bluestones. The unerring eye of each of the Cyclops blinked as they witnessed with incredulity the light show that unfolded around the Bluestones. They raised their hands to the heavens trying to touch and hold the elusive Light forms. The Cyclops were incongruous and ungainly as they clumsily clutched and grasped at thin air as the ephemeral beings morphed and reformed.

Terese of the Xantha smiled at the strange juxtaposition of graceful Light and ungainly muscle.

A fusion of the strangest beings! She looked back to the west, along the lay line, a winged form growing larger with every powerful wing beat, "Eiru!" Gripped in her talons was Amergin.

Terese held her breath. It seemed a veritable age since she had last seen the champion of Milesia, the Sea Druid Amergin. She had ventured forth with the much lamented Bith to the Island of Destiny. Now the Milesian prince came to their rescue... Amergin's time had come!

Way, way to the south in the lofty peaks of Sliebh Mis, Sceine surveyed the defences of her mountain fortress, built to withstand the forays of waves of invaders. Since long before the days of the Tuatha, this place has been legendary, the highest most inpenetrable bastion. For centuries the Tuatha had made this place invincible.

Legend has it that a one-eyed giant, Sliebh, protected the steep sided glacial valley from the invading Firbolg. Even the Firbolg could not overcome the giant Sliebh with their weaponry and black magic. They were driven far to the north of this sacred island. From there they launched sporadic and terrible attacks.

The Tuatha were borne of this place. They were said to be children of the land. Ancient tales told of spirit folk who would occasionally venture out from the portals of this province from the under world and seek the protection of the giant Sliebh. They lived in the high glacial valleys and over the centuries built the fortress of Sliebh Mis.

The children of the Tuatha were groomed in the teachings of the enlightened ones, divine beings that occasionally transcend the veil from the spirit world and enter the mortal realm to guide and train the children of the Tuatha in the ways of the Light. Legend also tells of the day when three children of the Tuatha ventured to the north of the high glacial valleys, a long way from the protection of the giant Sliebh. The tale tells that they were soon captured by the Firbolg.

The three children were the sons and daughters of three chieftains. The children were held captive by the Firbolg in the Northern Province. The Tuathans of Sliebh Mis called upon the spirit folk to help. They conjured a force from beyond the veil. A fiercesome force formed in the likeness of the one eyed giant Sliebh. Strong, muscle bound, battling warriors hewn out of the rock surrounding Sliebh Mis. One eyed giants who came to be known as the "Cyclops of Sliebh Mis", marched to the North to rescue the three children of the Tuatha from the terrible tyranny of the Firbolg. A bloody battle raged for a year and a day... the Cyclops were no match for the black arts of the Firbolg.

The Children of Tuatha were held to ransom. The mothers and fathers must give themselves to the Firbolg with all their secrets of the spirit world. Or they will see their children tortured and slain.

This was the day that became known as the "Tearing of the Veil."When the dark secrets of the veil became known and the dark forces of the spirit world were unleashed. The parents of the ransomed children were the first beings to be turned into servants of the dark and were controlled by the Firbolg.

From that day on the veil had been torn and even with the eventual vanquishing of the Firbolg by Sceine's father Antiem, the forces of the dark, the dark Sidhe, had entered the mortal realm. With each successive mortal converted to the dark, the dark Sidhe grew ever stronger... a terrible evil now stalked the Promised Land.

Sceine surveyed the Western Province from high up on the battlements. A view unsurpassed of the gloriously spectacular gorge to the south, a glimmer of white strand and a sliver of green in the far, far distance. To the north, the mountains gave way to the rolling hills that seamlessly fused with sweeping bays and finger like peninsulas protruding into the endless Northern Ocean. To the west, high ridges and mountain peaks ascended into the transforming, life giving Western Light. High altitude thinning air, mixed with the heady ocean ozone, energising, spirit raising and life affirming.

Sceine breathed deep... Now she stared into the east, she was disorientated, plunging into the gruesome despair of the truth that confronted her and her race and the enlightened world. She gave out a long, lingering exhalation of air as she studied with trepidation, the dark rolling storm clouds over the mountains to the east. Pondering the future of the Western Province, she knelt on the cold bare stone of the battlements, clasping her hands around the amber pendant hanging on an exquisite pure silver chain from her gracefully beautiful neck. She placed her finger tips on the apex of the Pendant of Xhara and gently rubbed and massaged it, while quietly murmuring under her breath, "Amergin my beloved. I feel your presence close now... You are in mortal danger! Be brave, be courageous! Come safely to me!" An amber radiance emanated from the pendant.

A dark fleck in the amber pendant became a point of infinite power embedded in a cosmos of amber... a gateway to the universe of enlightenment... She connected to him... She was with him, inside him... She saw what he saw... they were one! Sceine smiled... and he smiled...

Amergin was with Eiru! "Good, she had found him!" She could see the downward flight path, feel the grip of her talons, and see the ever nearing alignment of Bluestones at the Quarry of Izion. Now! Endinou, the Guardian of the Quarry of Izion! There! Terese of the Xantha!

Sceine felt the energy of the lay line guiding them to Izion, and from there to the great Portal of Machlleth! Sceine concentrated every iota of corpuscular and spiritual energy she could, sending it to her beloved Amergin! "I will be with you as you go to reopen Machlleth my love! Go! Release our brave warriors from the depths of the spirit world!"

She came back to the cold flagstones high up on the battlements, a smile on her countenance now. Sceine was fully alive, every synaptic connection firing. She was on a rolling wave of emotion, exhaling so deep with pleasure and release. She was deeply comforted, deeply happy and ecstatic to have been with Amergin, to have been entwined with him, to feel him, to have him in her universe.

Sceine returned now to the heady high altitude concoction of mountain air and oceanic ozone...

Still with him, she came back to this place where the eternal battle for the enlightened world rages…

CHAPTER FOURTEEN:
THE SHAMEN OF LAND'S END

Far, far to the north, in the ancient land of the Firbolg, Septiem marched onwards... into the realm conquered by Antiem... his mission to convert, to prosthletise, to bring the more enlightened Firbolg on their side.Sent by Sceine to bring the former servant race into the fray against their former evil masters.

This was a strange land, harsher on the eye, colder on the heart, an expansive place with huge vistas opening up over the extremities of the Northern Ocean, a land of big skies.On the western horizon an indented coastline with a myriad of beaches, promontories and islands floating offshore.

To the east, precipitous flat topped escarpments plunging into the ocean, the tops a lost world of mysterious plateaus. The topography occasionally broken by glacial valleys carved deep into the plateaus. From the high edges, waterfalls cascaded into the heavens. Water vapour hung in the air for a moment, stillness, then whipped into tumultuous vortices by downblasts of cold wind descending from the high escarpments. Whirlwinds scurried across the corrie lakes, vanishing as soon as they appeared. Violent ones swept down the valley out to sea. Sea birds and sailing vessels leant into the turbulence, before resuming their normal course.

Even further to the north and east, the end of the land, just visible with the naked eye. Sea cliffs of unimaginable heights clouds billowing up and over vertical cliff faces. A mirage, a last bastion of land that drew closer in then further away, in touching distance, but out of sight, as the shafting sunlight burst through the clouds. Veiled light in a million shades of grey. Reflective liquid, grey-silver seas and grey to white sunlit clouds and in the far distance mirages of sky touching cliffs.

A cold but strangely inviting limitless ocean, stirring the senses as each intense shaft of light swept through. The body, the mind, the heart, the soul were drawn irresistibly over the water to the far distant cliffs plunging defiantly into the sea.

Septiem and his travelling crusaders were being drawn hypnotically to Land's End. They followed the wave battered coastline under the shadow of high, flat topped escarpments. There was impending danger! The route would leave them exposed between the crashing ocean and slopes of the escarpments. There would be no refuge, but they must press on to Land's End... courageous crusaders or lambs to the slaughter!? He sent word back along the winding, marching line, "Be ever vigilant! We are entering the realm of the Shamen of Land's End!" Septiem had heard tales of this place on the northern edge of the known world, tales of magic and murderous deception, tales of innocent travellers being lured to their death, or worse taken as slaves by the cruel merciless Firbolg.

Antiem, the much lamented king of the Tuathans, and father of the High Priestess Sceine, had warned warriors and travellers alike of the Shamen of Land's End. Antiem's forays into the Northern Province were legendary. He swept through, subdued and ultimately converted the majority of the Firbolg to the cause of the Light. Septiem's mission was to rally those converted and to journey even further to the North and find the fabled Shamen of Land's End, for they had powers even the dark Sidhe could not counter. It was crucial to find the shamanic Firbolg...

The Shamen of Land's End worshipped nature, their sacred site perched on the edge of the world. The path meandering along the coast and rocky outcrops was dotted with carved stone idols guiding the welcome traveller but warning the intruder...

Ahead of them lay a rocky promontory. Volcanic igneous protrusions forced vertically out of the restless, heaving ocean. Rock carvings pointed to the edge of the world, and there a single massive Bluestone obelisk pierced the sky. The standing stone stood on a carved rock slab, teetering on the cliff edge, commanding the place where the elements of land, weather and ocean collided.

"This must be the Portal of Land's End!" he speculated. Septiem peered over the cliff edge. A tortuous path traversed down to a lower wave cut platform. Here, dark stains covered the rock surface and followed cracks and fissures to the heaving ocean below.

The Shamen of Land's End were notorious for their live sacrifices, appeasing their pagan deities with animal and human blood at the full moon... The energy of the full moon will energise the Bluestone and the veil will be close to the surface, permitting the Sidhe to pour forth, "Here is the source of the Shamanic magic!" Septiem surmised, "We must hope and pray the energy of the portal is still pure and uncorrupted!" With this Septiem turned to his crusaders, he nominated eight of them to stand guard over the portal, "We will go to find the Shamen, and return to witness a blood ceremony. Only then will we know if the Shamen can be trusted!"

Septiem marched on in search of the Shamen, following the path inland towards the flat topped escarpments. They crossed a limestone wilderness of dry river beds and yawning cavernous caves.

The march was treacherous over sharp edged clynts and grikes. Septiem felt uneasy, he could feel the veil was near and in such places was uncertain as to what might pour forth from the under world.

As darkness descended they made camp on a stretch of weathered rock that gave a panoramic view of the area. A roaring, comforting fire was lit, fuelled by storm tossed and wind dried and aged sea kelp. To the west, back from whence they had come, another fire flickered on the coast line, lighting up the darkening indigo evening. Their fellow crusaders at the Portal of Land's End...

Septiem allowed his mind to drift. Relaxing with the sound of crashing waves, surging, ebbing, receding and surging again, flowing in an endless shushing and shishing, back and forth, calming and soothing...

Then across his line of vision... a flash of orange light... broken from his reverie... he watched as the single flash became a procession... moving, swaying along the edge of the high escarpment... the procession growing all the time. Straining into the dark, his eyes focussed on figures holding swinging lanterns on tall pikes.The procession now descending and traversing the escarpment edges.

The sheer faces looked impossible to negotiate. "These beings must have descended from mountain goats. How could they scale such precipitous faces?!" quizzed Septiem. Whoever they were they vastly outnumbered Septiem and his crusaders.

The swaying line of orange lanterns grew closer and closer. The line still pouring down from the escarpment as the first of them reached the limestone carst. As Septiem feared, on this coast they had nowhere to hide... they had found the Shamen of Land's End!

From such a high vantage point the Shamen had been watching from the moment Septiem and his crusaders arrived in the Northern Province. He soon realised that resistance was futile, out numbered and strategically poorly located. All they could do was stand and watch and wait as the procession got closer. The swaying lanterns mesmerised them. Soon they were able to make out the beings holding them on the long pikes. In the vanguard, a group of fiercesome swordsmen, armed to the teeth and clad in black body armour, with a texture of compressed and woven turf.

They approached to within a stones throw of the band of crusaders, wedging the pikes with lanterns into the limestone cracks and crevices. In the eerie orange glow the next group of advancing Shamen. They could not have been more different... slender, elegant beings, male and female, tall and graceful, dark skinned and handsome. Clad in woven flax and the same black body armour. They wielded lengthy spears and carried finely crafted bows with deadly sharp flint headed arrows in quivers slung over their shoulders. They too wedged pikes and lanterns into the rugged ground.

The effect now was a wall of fiery orange light, growing in intensity all the time. Through the glare came the next group... they heard them before they saw them... hooves clattered on the hard brittle limestone... now came the legendary Horsemen of the North! Legend has it that they came from the under world, creatures sent by the Sidhe to protect the mortal realm. Half horse, half man, equine bodies with the torso and heads of man. Septiem and his crusaders gasped in awe and astonishment at these four legged, hooven warriors...

Septiem had heard the mythical tales of these warriors of the North, allegedly they could not be defeated in battle... they must be converted to the cause of the Light... they would be the most stalwart of allies in the war against the dark one MacCuacht...

Septiem stepped forward into the orange glow. He raised his arms, showing he carried no weapons. He bowed his head in deference...

"No further Tuathan!" boomed a commanding voice from the orange glow. Septiem moved not a muscle. Through the orange fiery glow he began to make out a tall physically powerful Shamen.Evidently the leader, an imposing being with a fierce stare, and equally dramatic head of silver white dreadlocks falling over broad shoulders. Porcelain white flesh ...face, arms, torso, legs covered in tribal tattoos that appeared to move in empathy with his facial expressions.

Septiem had heard of these genetic tattoos, or more accurately genetic birthmarks. They grew as the "wearer" grew and their magical powers strengthened... Natural, inherited powers honed and refined by Shamanic training and culture...

Septiem looked across at the other Shamen. All in the "welcoming" committee were impressively endowed with the genetic tattoos. None could compare with this individual's living etchings!

Septiem dropped to his knees in further deference, clasping his hands together in a sign of peace.

Sensing wisdom and genuine intent the Shamen's demeanour lightened, "I am Magire the leader of the Shamen of Land's End! Our tribes have fought long and hard through the ages. Many of us fought against your High King Antiem. Many of us and many of you were slain. Only now do we of the Shamen realise that there is a greater enemy... the dark one MacCuacht, who deceived us cruelly and slaughtered hundreds in the evil process. He enslaved many of our kind and turned them to the way of the dark! We now see that Antiem was an enlightened being!"

Septiem acknowledged the praise for his great, now departed King, "We bow to your wisdom Magire! We come in peace, hopefully to convince you that we follow the way of the Light, and in time, you may join us in the cause, may the grace of the Great Spirit be upon you and your tribes!"

Magire remained expressionless, though less threatening, "We will escort you to the high escarpment to talk further, and we will send a guard to assist you in protecting the Portal of Land's End. The Bluestone must be protected! The dark Sidhe are encroaching throughout our sacred land! I will go to the Portal of Land's End and make a sacrifice to the gods... I will join you soon... my wife Zendris will go with you to the escarpment..."

Septiem was shocked at the prospect of a live sacrifice... animal he hoped!

His shock soon abated as he was greeted by the hypnotically beautiful Zendris! She stood before him in all her glorious strange beauty. Dressed in an exquisite loose flowing silver fabric, her long white silver tresses fell over bare, ornately tattooed elegant shoulders. Grace beyond belief! Beauty beyond compare! Septiem was instantly bewitched! Entranced and under her spell...

The siren Zendris was pleased at what she saw... Septiem was a handsome being... for a Tuathan!

Zendris smiled alluringly at Septiem and gestured for him to follow... He followed willingly!

Zendris smiled, she was used to such obedience and loyalty...

CHAPTER FIFTEEN:
THE FLIGHT OF EIRU

Far, far to the west, in the lee of the Magine Islands, the remaining vessels of the Milesian fleet took shelter from the strengthening easterly wind. They waited for the sign from Amergin for them to come and join him...

Milidh and Scota braced themselves at the helm of their royal barque. They stood transfixed, staring at the distant eastern horizon. They had watched as the encroaching storm front swallowed the high altitude peaks and rolled remorselessly towards the coast.

The gusts were getting more violent by the minute, sweeping out westwards over the ocean towards the islands. Seabirds of every description flew ahead of the worsening weather seeking refuge on the precipitous slopes of the islands.

Scota sensed they must make landfall, and soon! She also sensed Amergin and his brothers were in mortal danger! They searched the base of the towering cliffs for a safe haven... a place to drop anchor and a way to scale the island. The tide pushed in, the wind rose and the swell increased.

They must find sanctuary!

The fleet sailed along the leeward side of the smaller, but still towering, island. Nowhere to make landfall! The sails filled as they nosed out into the strait between the islands. They headed for the larger island... a sea mount so huge that clouds formed high over the towering cathedral spired peak. The clouds trailed far out into the ocean... seabirds glided and swooped and swirled ever upwards towards the summit of the pinnacle. The air alive with gannets, fulmars, gulls and seabirds of every description, a raucous, screeching cacophony resounded and echoed around the pinnacles and sea cliffs.

Mid way between the islands the tidal race was so strong, wind pushed against waves creating standing waves out of nowhere. They were beaten and buffeted, pitched and pulled, tipped and tossed... then suddenly they were through, released from the tides grip and pushed into a place of relative tranquillity in the lee of the big island.

Scota and Milidh looked back to see the fleet free from the watery mayhem, out of the wind now, protected from the swell. The tidal race reduced, the fleet drifted quietly, searching for an inlet or a wave cut platform and somewhere they could alight. As they edged around a huge sea stack, there before them the entrance of a cavernous sea cave. Shafts of piercing, brilliant sunlight illuminated the cave entrance, scattering fresh crystal clear water, dripping from the roof, into a myriad of rainbows, each drop of water sounding its own note, resonating deep into the cave. The pitch black sea cave seemed to beckon them in. The currents from the eddying tidal race took them in. Booming, surging swell pushed them deep into the sea cave. After what appeared like an eternity, in the pitch black, a flash of white as the wave broke against a wave cut platform at the back of the cathedral sized cave.

Slowly drifting into the sea cave the shafts of light penetrated into the saline depths, fish, large and small, lulled and lolled back and forth in the sparkling, dappled waters. Green, brown and turquoise infused with undulating fronds and strands of seaweed and kelp, intense colour then dark as they drifted in and out of the sunlight, through the gaping mouth of the cave and to the shadowy innards.

The strengthening wind and building swell forced them deep in to the sea cave. Scota turned to Milidh, expressing her mixed and confused emotions, "I have never seen such a vast sea cave. The scale is immense, almost other worldly!" Milidh agreed the shelter was welcome, but the sea cave forbidding. Their voices echoed and resounded in the high vaulted chamber...

The water was so deep they had to tether themselves to stalagmites rising up from the wave cut platform. The black water was disturblngly deep. They were in fear of being sucked out of the entrance as set waves roared through and the tidal level dropped. The tethers were made sure and tight! This was their haven while the storm raged outside...

Two of the fleet arrived late to moor in the sea cave. They had been fishing in the lee of the island sending out long lines to the plummeting depths. Hook upon hook baited with glistening, flashing sand eels caught on their journey to the sea mount. They had slowly drifted with the tide, jigging and jagging their lines. The racing tide scoured feed from the sea bed, an endless stream of Mackerel were heaved on deck. The upwelling currents around the sea mount created rich feeding grounds. The fishing vessels now appeared through the curtain of rainbows at the sea cave entrance.

"Shelter and food!" exclaimed Milidh in delight, "Praise the Great Spirit!"

From the gunnels of their vessels, stores of dried seaweed and pine cuttings were taken to the rocky platform. They were intending to smoke the fish. Very soon the first spark lit, the bone dry pine cuttings, and the seaweed smouldered with a rich, thick, aromatic smoke. Billowing clouds of the sea weed smoke filled the cave... fresh fish was gutted, cleaned and cured in the acrid smoke within the hour, food for the feast that evening and some for the stores.

Green, gelatinous sea weed that clung to the rocks beneath the tide line was thrown into a monster cooking pot, together with limpets, sea urchins and the odd scavenging crab. The pot filled to the brim and gently simmered. The smoked fish added to make a rich, thick oceanic chowder. The crew were salivating as the almost edible pungent aromas filled the cavernous chamber.

Scota watched contentedly as the mariner's, male and female, scooped ladel upon steaming ladel in to capacious wooden bowls. Appreciative grunts, slurps and belches echoed around the sea cave as they fed their smiling, appreciative faces and now bulging bellies.

Scota watched the sawdust and sea weed smoke curl and swirl high into the cavern. Some of the thick, acrid curing smoke swept high up in to the vaulted ceiling and then was sucked out of the cave entrance by the increasingly intense and frequent gusts that roared like freight trains past the island. She noticed how some of the fragranced smoke curled away from the main stream, ascended into the blackness of the cave and was gone. No matter how she squinted and strained in to the lofty blackness, she could not make out any natural chimney or escape route. Her mind and her imagination played tricks with her... the grey plumes of seaweed smoke clung to the cave wall in regular organised shapes, "Were those steps carved into the cavernous chamber!?"

Scota called Jansis, one of her lead crewman, to her side. They both peered in to the gloom at the cave wall. Huge red sandstone slabs and massive blocks of igneous granite were jumbled and heaped at the base of the cave wall, the result of a recent rock slide. The fault line responsible for the resultant land slip had taken away half of the cave wall and any obvious access point.

Scota instantly instructed Jansis to select a group of the best climbers to scale the rock slide. They took torches with them, shedding light into the high cave. Pointing into the gloom, "Go there... I see a passage way! The smoke disappears!"

Jansis and his climbers tackled the shattered rock and jumbled slabs. They were dwarfed by the scale of the land slip. Their torches began to flicker in a strengthening updraught, the light picking the deep reds of the sandstone, and now the crystalline reflections of a vein of igneous granite. An ethereal glow emanated from the vein of quartz, "Milidh, see there! The legendary Bluestone! This sea mount must have a rich vein running through it!" The climbers went higher and the flickering torches penetrated deep in to the darkness, "There! A stairway! We are not the first to be here! These workings have the hall-marks of the ancients ..!"

Jansis and the climbers now stood on the first carved step. Milidh yelled up, "Go... show us the way! We will follow!" The flickering torches soon disappeared up a narrow winding passage, ascending in to the unknown...

Milidh and Scota led the following contingent. Scota had a powerful sense of destiny. Just as many years ago she followed her path, intent in the knowledge that she would find and meet her own destined one. Now, as before, she followed a path of the ancients, the enlightened ones, who were calling her and she knew were calling Amergin...

Far to the east on the mainland, Amergin was released from the talons of Eiru, in avian form, as she alighted at the entrance of the Quarry of Izion.

Momentarily his mind was distracted. He caught a vision of Scota, and then a vision of Sceine! Something of this place was connecting him to his beloved mother and his destined one Sceine...The Bluestones, the lay lines all connecting... The message of unity indelibly ingrained on his mind, "Together we will be as one... We will fight the dark Sidhe!"

Terese of the Xantha brought him back to the moment. She hurled herself at Amergin, emotions over riding decorum, "Amergin! My Prince! You are here!" Her Amazonian hug nearly squeezing the life breath from him. "Good to see you Terese! Good that you are still with us!" Amergin returned a heart felt embrace and looked deep into Terese of the Xantha's eyes, giving a knowing nod of acknowledgement at the ordeal she had been through at the hands of the dark Sidhe.

Amergin sensed she was still in shock after the experience. He had faith in her steely resolve. She was still the fearless, resolute, battle ready Xantha that Amergin knew and admired, when he sent her with Bith in the vanguard to the Promised Land.

Eiru had now totally transformed from the winged beast of the air to the raven haired, silver cocoon clad beauty. Energised photons zipped and zapped around her body and soon were gone. She stepped forward to greet her kindred spirits. Endinou held his hand out in the gesture of the sage... the Guardian of the Bluestones and the Quarry of Izion in alliance with one of the infamous Witches of Hawardden, the bitter sweet irony both pleased and amused him! Eiru was pleased at his acceptance of her. She sensed a powerful, magical being with the undying allegiance of the Cyclops quarrymen. His frail, white haired, ageing appearance did not deceive her. She knew the wizard had powers to match her own. His timeless wisdom alone made him a priceless ally.

Amergin, now released from the crushing embrace of Terese of the Xantha, turned his attention to Endinou. He too sensed Endinou's wisdom and purity of being. He gripped the extended hand, "My friend we are here to fight for the enlightenment, to protect the Bluestones, and go to the great Portal of Machlleth!" Endinou wisely agreed, "Together we have a chance to confront the dark one MacCuacht, who approaches Machlleth now! If we fail, the Quarry of Izion, source of the purest Bluestones will be next!"

Amergin could not countenance failure, "We will go to Machlleth! We will release MacCuill and his cohort! Together we will fight the dark Sidhe!" A rallying cry ringing in their ears, they all looked to Amergin, the Milesian champion, the Sea Druid and poet warrior to lead them on their path of destiny.

As they walked on the path to the Portal of Machlleth, the towering, boiling, blackening thunderheads clouded the horizon. Amergin felt his belt pouch for the brilliant white pearl he retrieved from the deep water oyster of Rodiles. The pearl had magical properties of clairvoyance.

Disconcertingly, a darkening veil covered one hemisphere as he held the pearl towards the eastern horizon. The tipping point where the dark would overcome the light was close at hand... Amergin kept his observations to himself...

They walked into the night, resting only occasionally, catching fleeting moments of sleep.

Time was of the essence. A thin silver crescent of a new moon emerged from behind scudding clouds... disappearing and re-emerging, casting only the faintest moonglow on the path ahead.

A strange silver-blue halo circled the lunar crescent... a poignant symbol of the approaching storm.

They rested in a glade bathed in the faint lunar glow. Amergin kept guard, he gestured for Endinou to sit beside him on a rocky vantage point. Amergin spoke in quiet understated tones, while Eiru and Terese slept fitfully on the uneven ground. He remained calm, but underneath, anxiety and worry festered. He was unsure of the effectiveness of this disparate group of beings against the legions of the army of lost souls. He was soon reassured by the Guardian of the Bluestones, "Look yonder, Prince Amergin!" he gestured towards the muscular Cyclops of the Quarry of Izion, "These quarrymen carry the purest Bluestone keystones. Only an enlightened being such as you can use these keystones to open the portal. Mac Cuill and the cohorts will be freed from the under world and will fight the dark Sidhe with us."

Amergin looked again at the giant quarrymen. They carried leather panniers, each one containing the purest of Bluestones hewn from the Quarry of Izion. Keys that can regenerate compromised portals.

Endinou's wisdom, insight and knowledge will be essential, thought Amergin, together with his insight and sense of the place and his connection to the Guardians of Light. Endinou sensed Amergin's concern, "Whenever a portal is infected we can send one of the giant Cyclops with a pure Bluestone to rejuvenate it. We will act swiftly! We will avoid any portal staying under the influence of the dark Sidhe for long!" Amergin was reassured at this. He added advisedly, "We must use our insider knowledge of MacCuacht to counter his dark powers. Eiru will be the key, as will MacCuill when he is freed from Machlleth!"

Amergin went to Eiru and gently stirred her from her fitful slumber, "Eiru come and sit with us!"

He and Endinou agreed that the raven haired Witch of Hawardden, the estranged wife of the dark one MacCuacht, will be a powerful player in attempting to undermine him. She could be his nemesis! Even MacCuacht will be vulnerable to her beauty, guile and magical powers. Surely no red blooded male could resist her. The question was how many red corpuscles remained in his blood? How black, how dark, how cold is the malevolence that is MacCuacht?

Amergin spoke quietly and calmly to Eiru, "We will send you ahead in your avian splendour. You will reconnoitre and appraise the way ahead to Machlleth. Once you have signalled that the way is clear for us, you will continue to the Woodlands of Derwydd. You will meet with Erhombu, the Guardian of the Woodlands. He can summon the spirit beings of the woods, to at least slow MacCuacht and the army of lost souls, while we go with the Cyclops of Izion to open the Portal of Machlleth and free MacCuill and Thiorn and the defending cohorts.

Eiru smiled, pleased that Amergin had such faith in her... This was tempered with the knowledge that she would be returning to MacCuacht's realm. She was only just able to resist his powers at their last meeting. Now! He would be wise to her...

"There is just one more thing!" he trod warily, "You must go to MacCuacht! You must convince him that you are turned, converted to the dark Sidhe! You must risk all to become an insider again. You will plant the seeds of deception, the seeds of doubt. Give him disinformation about our intentions."

Eiru's smile was long gone, swept away by a wave of reality. She was being sacrificed! She was to become a martyr for the enlightened cause. She knew that this was the final throw of the dice for her. She enters MacCuacht's realm on a mission of persuasion and bluff. Eiru's eyes met Amergin's. They both knew that in reality she would ultimately be turned to the dark. The probability, no certainty, that the next time that they met they would be mortal enemies...

Amergin grasped her hand, "You are the only one able to do this. You are the only one who knows MacCuacht's weaknesses."They embraced in the poignancy of the moment. Eiru stood proudly before the Sea Druid Amergin, champion of the Milesians.

Terese of the Xantha stirred now, Amergin sensed her confusion and explained, "Eiru is the key to our survival through these testing, dark times. I have asked her to return to MacCuacht, to use her guile and magical powers to deceive him. We will not see the enlightened Eiru again. When she transforms and flies to reconnoitre the way to to Machlleth, from that moment on she will be gone from our lives forever!" he went on to make it clear to Terese, "As the woman he once loved, only she can hope to distract MacCuacht. There is no doubt that once in his company again, she will not be able to resist. His power is so strong now she will be lost, unable to turn as you once did..."

Terese of the Xantha understood. Eiru's heart and power will be the key. Amergin held Terese's hand in his, "You too are a key to our success! Your strength of will and physical prowess brought you through unimaginable adversity. You have been in the presence of MacCuacht. You have seen how he operates. You will fight by my side. You will warn me of dangers that I may not be aware of... dangers from a realm that I have much to learn about!"

Terese was motivated by the Sea Druid's words. She went over to the now subdued and sanguine Eiru... nothing could console the raven haired witch. She embraced and kissed her ivory white forehead, "I am resigned to my fate Terese. I do this for the cause of the Light. I go now. I have my instructions from Amergin. Remember me well Terese, for the next time we meet I may well try to kill you! Fight for Amergin Terese... defend him with your life..."

She stepped away from Terese. The silver cocoon of a dress began to shimmer and transform. Light particles exploded and collided, the physical becoming metaphysical, the changeling turning from human to avian. From a vortex of light, giant wings beat powerfully downwards. This magnificent feathered creation rose into the air above Amergin, Endinou andTerese. The Quarrymen of Izion watched in one-eyed mute amazement. "Go safely Eiru, may the Great Spirit guide you and be with you!"

Amergin had given her instructions to fly high, and when reaching the Portal of Machlleth, if all was clear, for her to fly high towards the crescent new moon, circling three times. If all was clear she would fly on to Derwydd. Erhombu the Guardian of the Woodlands awaits her.

She would see a pale green aura in the Woodlands, go to him. In the ensuing conflict with MacCuacht she will be captured... Eiru will sow the seeds of confusion and doubt...

"Go Eiru! The cause of the Enlightenment relies on you!"

A few more wing beats and Eiru was gone... silhouetted against the crescent moon...

Eiru flew on alone. She flew higher than she had ever flown before, to see the lay of the land.

Even in the diminishing light, with the faint moonglow and her sharpened sense of sight, she could clearly see from horizon to horizon. She flew even higher, to a height where the atmosphere thinned. She could see the entirety of the majestic Western Province. She saw the faint glow of the Milesian camp fires on the coast, where they guarded the Temple of the Sun. She could follow the geography of the rivers, and the path where Amergin, Endinou and Terese awaited her signal.

Eiru looked to the far western horizon where the magical, mystical Magine Islands floated like shimmering mirages. Just a glimpse of these islands raised her spirits. Instinctively she knew these were sacred places and would be one of the last bastions in the battle against the dark Sidhe.

At this height she was keenly aware of the alignment of the Magine Islands, the Temple of the Sun and way below her the great Portal of Machlleth. Beyond this nothing stirred, no light shone. No encampment, no fires, only dark. A darkness noticeable in the Western Province as usually an ethereal glow radiated from the portals. From beyond the Portal of Machlleth another world prevailed. The encroaching storm front, hiding MacCuacht and the army of lost souls, had rolled insidiously over half of the Woodlands of Derwydd. Eiru began to feel the high altitude turbulence of the storm. Her wing tips feathering in the increasing winds, she began her descent, soon to give the signal to Amergin. Eiru stooped in a wide arcing dive. She saw the pale green aura in the heart of Derwydd. Disturbingly she could also see the lifeless and lightless banks of all consuming mist rolling through the Woodlands, crabbing to the North and South in a deadly pincer movement.

Erhombu and the wood spirits must be warned! Firstly she had to signal to Amergin that Machlleth was clear...

Eiru swept down into the thickening atmosphere. She sensed the oncoming storm and dense, dank carpeting mist. The visibility was reducing as she made three circular flights in the eyeline of the crescent moon. The sharp eyed Terese spotted Eiru first, gesticulating to the others...

"Good our way is clear, we must act swiftly!" and with this Amergin asked Endinou, "Who is the swiftest, fastest and strongest of the Cyclops? He will come with me and Terese of the Xantha, carrying the purest of the Bluestones with him. We will be moving quickly and stealthily to the Portal of Machlleth. The path is fraught with danger, our return is not guaranteed!"

"Him, Sethse, he is the one you need!" pointed Endinou, "May the Great Spirit be with you and guide you safely! We will follow. We will join forces with MacCuill, Thiorn and his cohort once they are released from the spirit world."

Sethse, the strongest of the muscle bound Quarrymen of Izion took up the pannier with the weighty keystone, as if it were a featherweight. He slung the pannier on his back and strode out along the path. He was fully aware of the danger of the mission. He lengthened his stride and quickened his pace. Amergin and Terese of the Xantha had to hurry to stay with him. Sethse was like a rampant bull Elephant crashing through the low undergrowth on the rarely travelled path. Amergin and Terese broke into a steady jog. They estimated two hours to Machlleth. Terese went before the Sea Druid Amergin. She was there to defend him. Her vigilance would be crucial. She sensed the dark Sidhe were near. Her spiritual, warrior senses told her that they were not the only ones targeting Machlleth on this fateful night.

Eiru saw Amergin and the others moving towards Machlleth. She knew her job was done here.

She flew low between hillock and meadow, over crags and down ravines, following rivers and streams coursing their way to the ocean. She flew upstream to the source, and finally into the Woodlands of Derwydd.

The woods were ancient and mysterious, wrapping and enveloping the foothills of the distant mountains. She could go no further these were the lands overwhelmed by the dark Sidhe. Their malevolence was in evidence as the rolling storm front gathered and brewed...

Fleetingly, Eiru flew high again, she needed to find Erhombu. Sure enough at the heart of Derwydd was a pale green aura shining forth from the deepest and most inpenetrable swathe of Woodland. Her sharpened avian senses detected the aura in the dwindling light of day. The aura was formed by light reflecting from an oasis of green iridescent, lush, verdant vegetation surrounding a river, forcing over a mighty waterfall, sending clouds of spray high into the air. The light was trapped and reflected as the river reformed, filling a shallow lagoon, then refracted and reflected again by a vein of crystalline bedrock veined with the purest Bluestone.

"Bluestone!" exclaimed Eiru, "The heart of the Woodlands of Derwydd is another portal!"

Ambient light came deep from within the Bluestone, from the other side of the veil between the spirit world and the mortal realm. Here was Erhombu's realm! Erhombu was the Guardian of the Woodland of Derwydd, leader of the wood spirits, the beings who channelled the very life energy into the Woodlands!

Eiru alighted at the side of the pool where the crystal clear water fell from a great height in a roaring, deafening crescendo, eventually flowing into and quietening in the shallow waters of the lagoon.

Still in avian form she sipped the water, noticing how clear and how calm the pool was.

In the rippling reflections Eiru caught sight of an ephemeral being. As the ripples cleared, so the being disappeared! She surveyed the thick vegetation surrounding the lagoon. An ancient Oak grove and ancient limestone rock formations covered in pale green lichen, dripping wet in the moisture laden air. There again! A movement, and in an instant was gone! It was virtually impossible to distinguish shapes and forms against a backdrop of contorted and twisted trunks, branches and roots. But she knew she was being watched! Whatever they are, whatever realm they are from, they were studying her... "Who are you?" A loud resonant voice came from the other side of the lagoon, "What do you want here?" A magnificent, muscular red deer stag, camouflaged against the roughly textured bark, now postured and posed in the open, presenting pointed antlers that would put the fear of the Great Spirit in to any interloper, "Answer quickly, before it is too late!" The stag strutted threateningly into the shallows, evidently coming straight at her... "I am Eiru, sent by the Sea Druid Amergin, to warn you that you are in grave danger!"

The antlered form was gone, consumed by the crystal clear water... and now rippling and reflecting in the lagoon...a silver-scaled, rainbow coloured salmon hurtling across the shallows towards her, "A changeling, like her!" The speed of transformation shocked Eiru. The thrashing, silver-scaled Salmon and its thousands of reflecting scales swam effortlessly into the lagoon. The shallow, clear water over the golden brown and green pebbles erupted in a wall of liquid. Instantaneously, a tall slender, pale, spirit of the woods stood before her, "I am Erhombu!" whispered a quiet, calming, soothing voice, "I come to you as the Guardian of the Woodlands of Derwydd... tell me your message ...!" Before Erhombu could continue, Eiru transformed from her avian form into the raven haired, silver cocoon clad witch. As the energised photons and atoms settled, Erhombu spoke again, "You are Eiru, one of the notorious Witches of Hawardden, estranged wife of the dark one MacCuacht!"

All around her, Eiru sensed other spirits of the Woodlands gathering, but the mood had changed. Her infamy had travelled before her. Her former life in league with the dark Sidhe threatened to be her undoing. How could she convince them?! "Erhombu... let me show you the danger you are in! Allow me to take one of your trusted spirit beings... I will fly high over Derwydd and you will see ..!"

"You will show all of us!" roared Erhombu... The wood spirits metamorphosed as one, into one of nature's greatest wonders, a huge collective of starlings, a murmuration. Shape shifting and morphing, they flew higher and higher...

Eiru was stunned in amazement, for a moment... then she transformed and followed.

For the observer, this was a high altitude natural phenomena, unusual but explainable. Just as well, as there were sinister observers on the edge of the Woodlands of Derwydd, cloaked and hidden by undergrowth and dense, dank mist.

Higher again went the white-tailed eagle, supposedly hunting the flock of morphing Starlings. Then they were gone! The murmuration swooped down at break neck speed and disappeared in to the depths of Derwydd. Eiru was alone again, flying on towards the eastern edge of Derwydd. She knew this part of the mission was complete. Erhombu and the wood spirits of Derwydd had been warned. They will confront the dark one MacCuacht and his army of lost souls. This will give Amergin time to reach the great Portal of Machlleth, and free MacCuill and Thiorn and his cohorts from the limbo of the spirit world.

Erhombu looked on from the sacred Oak groves of Derwydd, he saw Eiru flying on alone. He sent a prayer out to her. He was aware of her mission, "Be brave Eiru, you do this for the greater good, for the cause of the enlightenment... We thank you!"

Now the sinister observers on the edge of Derwydd watched again... the word was out, "A white- tailed eagle flies alone and is entering our realm. It flies in to the mist!" MacCuacht craned his neck gazing upwards, "This is no ordinary eagle!!" He could hardly contain his rage. His darkening veins bulged and pulsed. His eyes were as black as coal, "Eiru!!!" he screamed from deep within his stone cold soul. He was usually incapable of such expressions of humanity. But she sparked memories that still stirred faint echoes of a former existence.

Eiru would have to rely on that sliver of memory to keep her alive, for more than a heart beat, when she touched the ground. The future of the Promised Land, the fulfilment of the prophecy of the destined one Amergin, the enlightenment of this Island of Destiny, all relied on her ability to outwit and her guile to deceive the dark one MacCuacht.

Wing tips feathering as she made her silent descent. Eiru had no doubt that she was being watched and a welcoming committee despatched to greet her. The dank, dense, demonic mist clung to her flight feathers. She had to push ever harder to stay airborne, barely skimming the high canopy tree tops of Derwydd. Eiru looked for an opening, a clearance where she could safely land.

Her avian senses tingled alarmingly, the woods below were alive. Not with the ethereal spirits of the Woodlands, but the otherworldly beasts and demons of MacCuacht's dark army. They lurked in the shadows, waiting for her to get too close...

Eiru's wing tips brushed the branches of a mighty Oak. Where were the spirits of the Woodlands now? She focussed on her mission now. Guile and deception would be the key!

Eiru felt the mesh of a fine netting touch her cheek, she had flown headlong into a trap! With a crumpling of wings and a crashing of branches, Eiru fell to the ground... She heard hoots and hollers of her captors revelling in her plight. She lay trapped and entwined in a feathery heap on the ground.

Immediately she began to transform, cascades of light illuminating the dark recesses of the woods and the enveloping mist. No sign of MacCuacht yet, but assuredly he would be there soon! Eiru prepared herself for the encounter. She was filled with dread, nervous with apprehension and fearful for her life...Deception was the key! She feigned unconsciousness. Her limp body was subjected to prods and pokes by creatures of the dark. She could only hear and smell them. But the awful jeering and the foulness of their stench turned her stomach. They continued to pull her raven black hair, and scratch her ivory white skin, the dark souls cackling in their coarse, grating voices as they rejoiced in her demise.

"Go away with you!" Eiru recognised the voice of her estranged partner. She stayed quiet and limp. "Damage her and you will answer to me!" Was that concern she detected in MacCuacht's voice? Eiru would prey on that. Eiru did not move as MacCuacht disentangled her silver cocoon clad body from the fine mesh netting. Remarkably gently, she felt his hands on her. He picked her up off the ground and carried her to their encampment at the edge of Derwydd. The further they walked the colder the air and the thicker the mist. More concerningly as MacCuacht cradled her in his arms Eiru felt vestiges of emotion that she thought had long gone. Emotions from before the time she flew from the battlements of the fortress of Hawardden.

Emotions long before the moment she began to despise the beast that he eventually became ... "This cannot be!" panicked Eiru, "I am already losing myself to him and to the dark Sidhe!" The inexorable process of convertion was irreversibly happening. She instinctively used all her powers to cocoon her mind, to protect her sanity... her faculties, her thoughts, had to be the last to darken.

A vision of Amergin flashed through her mind, it was as if he was before her, "Fight Eiru! Remember your mission! We rely on you!" MacCuacht barked an order to his minions. Had he sensed her thoughts, her vision of Amergin? She had to focus. She had to concentrate... if he read her thoughts she was doomed! They had arrived at the encampment on the edge of Derwydd. Eiru hoped and prayed like she had never hoped and prayed before. She would need all her super natural powers and the blessing of the Great Spirit to endure, to resist MacCuacht and to remain in charge of her faculties. There must be hope yet, or MacCuacht would have incarcerated her or worse!

Lying on fur rugs laid out on the rough ground, she slowly stirred, opening her eyes gradually, letting the scene slowly unfold. What she saw disturbed her immensely! The face she knew so well, the features that had once entranced her had changed menacingly. Darkening tracks that once were veins, black as coal eyes that once were searing blue. Hands, once elegant and artistic, were claw like, with swollen joints and discoloured nails, "MacCuacht, where have you gone?!" Eiru found herself nearly weeping. She felt sympathy for him. Somewhere deep inside, a sense of allegiance stirred... "No!!" The process of convertion continued. She closed her mind even tighter... she must remain immune to his influence! Amergin flashed through her mind's eye again. He knew she was in peril!

MacCuacht whispered in his now distorted, dissonant voice, that she barely recognised, "Eiru! I thought you were dead... You left? Why? We have so much to do together ..."

"That voice, it is drawing me in!" thought Eiru in desperation, "I have little time!"

"I had to leave. I needed time to reflect, to consider. I saw changes that I found overwhelming. You were changing so fast! I did not understand, all of life was out of balance!" Eiru chose every word with great care. She could not falter. This was the performance of her life! All the time she was being drawn to him... "I was captured, held against my will by the Milesians. There I met Gonne, the high priest of the Chapter of Mystics. He persuaded me, convinced me that there was only one way... your way! He released me, but not before I had discovered the plans of the one they called Amergin." The plan... Eiru must tell him soon! She was being drawn deeper and deeper and more quickly than she thought possible. She closed her mind... probably for the last time! "The Sea Druid Amergin's plan is to travel south to the high mountain fortress of Sliebh Mis, to meet with Sceine, thus the prophecy will be fulfilled!" She felt herself sinking deeper, "Together, their destiny will be complete and the Guardians of Light will prevail, the enlightened beings will rule the realm!"

The deception done! Eiru had hopefully thrown MacCuacht off Amergin's real mission to the Portal of Machlleth. She watched his expression to see...

Shouts came from the heart of Derwydd! The spirits of the woods were attacking! They would delay MacCuacht as well. The story told, the lies woven, the deception in place, Eiru waited nervously for his response. "Your words ring true my raven haired witch. Gonne of the Chapter of Mystics has told me of such a tale. The Sea Druid Amergin you talk of is the prophesied one! All of the dark Sidhe know this. All of the lost souls, the "Others", tell this tale consistently. Until the moment of convertion they live and breathe his name. You are right Eiru! I will hunt him down!"

With this, MacCuacht caressed Eiru's weakening and submitting body. He twisted and entwined his malformed fingers through her raven black hair. Her words received, her task done. Fading visions of Amergin, Erhombu and the spirits of the wood, her will breaking, her memories disappearing, the Light of her soul going. Finally she was gone, lost to the dark Sidhe. She was now in MacCuacht's power... again... and for eternity...

Eiru had finally succumbed to the evil that is MacCuacht once more. Unbeknownst to the others Amergin had cast a spell on Eiru. All memory of previous conversations and meetings would be erased. Her loyalty to Amergin, as if it had never been. Once infiltrated, no memory of her deception would remain. She would become the wife of MacCuacht again, one of the Witches of Hawardden again. Under the spell of MacCuacht she would become the darkest of all the Witches. She was the most dangerous and deadly of foe now, intent on slaying Amergin and all enlightened beings.

Amergin and Terese mourned the loss of Eiru. The pain of losing such a good soul cut deep. Her resistance had been futile. They felt the moment of her demise, akin to the bending and the ultimate snapping of a sapling. They felt her pain, but they knew her enlightened time was at an end. The enlightened spirit had gone...

Terese of the Xantha empathised more than anyone, only she had experienced the pain and anguish of being converted to the dark. She grasped the hands of Amergin. They were deeply conscious of having lost a brave friend, who now had potentially become their most dangerous enemy. Amergin prayed for her dark soul, "Eiru will always be remembered. Her name will become synonymous with the Island of Destiny, by the blessing of the Great Spirit!"

They embraced, enlightened beings given precious time by Eiru's sacrifice.

MacCuacht prepared to move to the south. He will take on the spirits of the Woodlands of Derwydd and then go to the high mountain fortress of Sliebh Mis to intercept Amergin before he meets Sceine, "Never will the Sea

Druid Amergin meet his destined one! Never will the Guardians of Light rule this Island!" MacCuacht looked around him... the three Witches reunited, his brother MacGreinne, the army of lost souls and the demons and denizens of the dark Sidhe, "Who will prevail against these?!"

In a moment of bitter irony he then sent Eiru in her avian splendour to search for his traitorous brother MacCuill, for she knew this territory, and in her changeling form she could trace him in hours, where as his ground troops would take days. She now threatened the mission to release MacCuill, Thiorn and his cohorts from the limbo of the spirit world. She instantly flew on a route to the great Portal of Machlleth. She could sense his life essence... Eiru was saviour turned predator!

Amergin knew that time was of the essence. They pressed on for Machlleth. There he would place the pure Bluestone keystone into the Portal... The keystone in the hands of mere unenlightened mortals would be powerless... the portal would remain closed and prone to intrusion by the dark Sidhe. In the hands of Amergin or enlightened beings such as Endinou, the Bluestone was pure unadulterated magic. Machlleth would align with the other great portals of the Western Province, the Temple of the Sun, where the rest of the advance party of the Milesians were based and unbeknownst to Amergin, the Magine Islands, where the mariners under the command of Scota and Milidh waited for his signal.

Amergin and the good spirits assembled with him, forged ahead on the trail to Machlleth. Soon they began to feel the damp, dense mist smothering the life out of the Woodlands of Derwydd. With the Portal of Machlleth closed, there was no way to counter the dark Sidhe. The inexorable suffocation of the Divine in nature continued. Only the opening of the portal would help to change the balance, reinstate the equilibrium, giving the forces of the Light a way back. They must hurry!

They strode on faster and faster, eventually they arrived in the clearance in front of Machlleth.

Before them stood Sethse, holding aloft a Bluestone of incredible beauty and perfection. The Cyclops gave them an endearing blink of his huge eye. The portal gaped dark and mysterious. Bearly no light emanated from within.

"We have come just in time!" the veil was shifting, slowly converting to the dark Sidhe...

CHAPTER SIXTEEN:
VISIONS OF SCEINE

Amergin pondered on the fate of Eiru. They had been given time by her sacrifice.If she has been successful MacCuacht would be marching south.Marching into an ambush layed by Erhombu, the Guardian of the Woodlands of Derwydd. Erhombu will give his life to protect the Woodlands.

Would MacCuacht see through their deception?

Amergin wondered how many of the spirits of the Woodlands would be lost in the ambush. The loss of Derwydd would be a huge price to pay for attempting to save Machlleth. The cold mist drifted in the air. He was brought to his senses!

Machlleth must be liberated at all costs.

Erhombu and the spirits of the Woodlands of Derwydd waited in the densest Oak grove.

Beyond them the Clearance of Conwyl and the path towards the distant mountains of the Iveare range and in the southern peaks the high mountain fortress of Sliebh Mis.

All the wierd and wonderful spirits of the woods gathered in wait, laying their ambush. Erhombu had taken up the form of the mighty red deer stag once more. He bellowed loudly through the Woodlands, calling for all to defend Derwydd with bravery and valour. Erhombu shredded the bark of an ancient yew tree with his many pronged antlers, allowing the rich, red, aromatic resin to flow freely.

The sap of 2000 year old yew tree is a potent potion with qualities that give the wearer a cloak of invisibility. Once the tips of the antlers touched the resin, everything slowed and was still.

Erhombu could travel back into the woods, seeing without being seen, an ephemeral being, just a whisper through the trees. In no time, he was among the hordes of MacCuacht. They were oblivious to Erhombu's presence. He moved among them as they travelled south. In the vanguard of the marauding hordes was MacCuacht, together with his vengeful brother MacGreinne and the raven haired Witches of Hawardden, Banba and Fodha. But where was Eiru?

What he saw in the Woodlands made his skin crawl... the verdant green now grey and stultified, emerald green turning to burnt umbers and ochres, akin to an early autumn. Withering leaves fell to the ground, life given, now lifeless. Was this the fate of all of Derwydd? The enveloping mist clung to everything, a deathly shroud sucking the very life essence from the Woodlands.

Erhombu soon realised that even with his cloak of stealth, he was not immune to the insidious infection of the dark Sidhe. The Woodland was his realm, but beyond the pall of rolling mist he too was being converted to the dark. This was MacCuacht's realm now! Hurriedly he scoured the Woodlands looking for Eiru, and at the same time seeking out weaknesses of the marauding hordes. He found no sign of Eiru. She must have deceived the dark one, for they were marching south and more importantly away from the Portal of Machlleth. He must listen to the conversations of MacCuacht and the Witches... he stealthily approached them... closer and closer he approached them. Erhombu was risking his life, one sound, a snapped twig, would mean the end! He was close enough to see their breath hanging in the mist. MacCuacht reacted as if he sensed something amiss.

He beckoned to the Witches to come closer... "Your sister should be back with us soon. She will surely have caught up with MacCuill!" He turned again, he was sensing something! He strode towards the cloaked and now very nervous Erhombu. MacCuacht peered into the gloom. Erhombu could clearly see the darkened features now, and how they shocked him! Dark veins on a petrified white complexion. He oozed evil. He stepped closer ...Erhombu was making ready to fly!

My Lord, you see something? Banba and Fodha, in unison, stepped up beside MacCuacht.

They all peered into the gloom. The shrouding, swirling mist had picked out Erhombu's form.

"There! A deer in the mist! A great stag to feast on!" yelled MacGreinne. Erhombu, his faculties already slowed by the numbing mist, was at first slow to react. MacGreinne had surprised Erhombu, coming in from the darkened side of the enclosure. His sword unsheathed, he swung at Erhombu's form, but his flight instincts had kicked in, he reacted far too quickly for the cumbersome MacGreinne. Erhombu was gone just in time, saved by the very mist that betrayed him and now consumes his realm. MacCuacht was enraged, "Go! Catch that stag my brother! Do not come back empty handed!" MacCuacht was perplexed, how could such an animal have got so close without detection? He suspected magic at work! Maybe the spirits of the woods ...What did they hear?

Erhombu was way too fast for the chasing marauders. He had learned enough! Eiru had done her work and the hordes are travelling south. But she looks for MacCuill. Surely the deception will eventually be uncovered... Amergin could be in imminent danger! The ambush must work!

The ambush had been set in the dense Oak grove of Bendigedig. Beyond that the long track to the high mountain fortress of Sliebh Mis...

…High, high above the Woodlands of Derwydd and high above the encroaching storm front, Eiru soared revelling in the freedom of her avian form. Riding the air currents and covering vast distances searching for MacCuill. She recognised the features and tracts of land... she had been here before... she knew the significance of the Portal of Machlleth! Eiru circled higher and higher.No sign yet!

Far, far to the west she could see a glimmer of intense, pure light. The light travelled along a lay line dotted with Bluestone standing stones. Eiru stalled and then stooped at break neck speed! Wings feathering hard, she swooped over the still dark and quiet Portal of Machlleth. She gathered height again and flew westward into the lightening sky. She saw the light being channelled towards Machlleth. Machlleth was the epicentre, the place where the veil was the closest to the mortal realm. This was where MacCuill was to be found and the place where Amergin travelled to!

Amergin is on a mission to re-open Machlleth and save MacCuill, then to connect all the portals of the Western Province, bringing the Guardians of Light through the veil!

Eiru was the slave of the dark one completely now... she must return to tell him all! She flew high again on the late evening thermals, soon meeting the turbulence of the encroaching storm front. Here she descended, back now in the all too familiar damp, dense mist pervading the Woodlands of Derwydd...

MacGreinne chased Erhombu into the depths of Derwydd. Like chasing a phantom, only when the clinging particles of mist outlined Erhombu, could he be seen. MacGreinne relied on his trackers, but Erhombu was far, far quicker than his hunters. The hunters were in fact the prey. They fell directly into the ambush set in the dense grove of Bendigedig. Here the creatures of Derwydd waited...

The first sign of MacGreinne arriving was the cool, dense mist sweeping through the grove. Then the trackers arrived falling head long in to a deep pit. MacGreinne and his hordes were stopped dead in their tracks. They were surrounded by spirits of the Woodlands, creatures of every shape and form. The hordes were pelted by sticks and stones. Poison darts tipped with a ground up paste extracted from bella donna, caused instant paralysis. MacGreinne's marauders were routed. But they were merely the advance party. MacCuacht, the Witches and the army of lost souls were expected to follow... but they did not...

Eiru had arrived back in the Woodlands, transforming from the eagle back to the raven haired witch in a maelstrom of photonic particles. Her dark beauty could still reach the core of the malevolent MacCuacht, "Tell me what news of MacCuill!?" Eiru related her story of Machlleth, the lay lines,the

Guardians of Light and the coming of the destined one Amergin, "You have been tricked my lord, the great Portal of Machlleth is the key, not here, not Derwydd! You must not go any further south! Erhombu the Guardian of the Woodlands of Derwydd waits to ambush you!"

MacCuacht grimaced, "MacGreinne! He must be warned!" He knew as he said this, that it was too late. The hunting party had been lost!"

Eiru continued, "Once the Portal of Machlleth is re-opened, the Guardians of Light will pour forth. The Woodlands of Derwydd will be revitalised and the power of the enlightened ones will strengthen!" With this MacCuacht snarled into the thickening mist... the army of lost souls and the demons and denizens of the dark now marched to Machlleth...

Amergin knelt before the great Portal of Machlleth. He sensed that the veil between the spirit world and the mortal realm was closer and thinner than ever, and more vulnerable to intrusion by the dark Sidhe than ever. The rolling, brewing storm front and the coming of the army of lost souls had forced Machlleth to be closed. MacCuill, Thiorn and the elite guard were caught in limbo, beyond the veil, in the spirit world.Now MacCuacht comes again to Machlleth! Amergin must hurry!

He has the power to re-open Machlleth. He is one of the enlightened beings, he can position the purest of Bluestone keystones to ensure that a true connection is made. Should he fail, then MacCuacht will tear through the veil and MacCuill and Thiorn will be taken and the dark Sidhe will pour forth.

Amergin gave thanks to the Great Spirit that Eiru's deception had worked! They had been given time by her martyrdom. He was sure that MacCuacht was aware of the deception now, and was on his way! He had seen a White-tailed Eagle soaring high above the Woodlands of Derwydd...

He knew that this time Eiru was under the influence of MacCuacht and he would be here soon!

Amergin conversed withTerese, "All the elements have to be aligned... I have to be at one with the Promised Land, only then can I go beyond the veil and re-open the portal!" He held the pure Bluestone, praying before the dark and mysterious portal. He soon found himself‚ being enveloped in a rich amber radiance. He was transported, his spirit left his mortal body and he journeyed deep in to the spirit world... his body was being caressed in to a state of blissful ecstacy. This was the place of his destiny... he travelled deeper and deeper in an amber vortex... he was joined by Sceine, "I am with you my love! Come to me!" His spirit joined with Sceine's. His love was unbounded... he saw a shimmering vision beside him... She spoke softly, "You have the blessing of the Guardians of Light, you can journey beyond the veil with me... I will help you to open the Portal of Machlleth!" the beautiful, divine being continued, "Beware! MacCuacht arrives. We will guide you!"

Amergin stared in to the amber cosmos of her eyes. He was soon drawn hypnotically to the dark fleck in her eye. "I am yours Sceine. I will be with you soon!" He fell deeper and deeper. In a wakeful moment he had returned to the entrance of Machlleth. He was being guided now. He picked up the Bluestone key. He noticed the quartzite veins in the shape of a palm. One by one he placed his fingertips in position. A charge pulsed through his nervous system, consciousness and awareness raised to new heights visions of Sceine flashed through his mind. The veil thinned, the Guardians of Light reached out to him...

Suddenly! From nowhere, a bolt of earthing lightning rooted him to the ground! He could not move!

In his peripheral vision he saw dark rolling clouds. It was as if MacCuacht controlled them, sending storm squalls tearing at the veil. The dark Sidhe tried to distract him. One wrong move, one indiscretion and they would pierce the veil.

Amergin focussed, closed his mind... one last connection... he tried to exclude the storm. He thought pure thoughts... a vision of Sceine... she was guiding him... his heart raced... his mind opened... his body released... the final placement complete...

From within the still dark, mysterious portal came Light. A fine tendril at first... reaching, flowing and finding a way through the veil. A faint glow from within the giant gatestones illuminated the dark, then a pulse of plasma travelling through the veil. A strange and wondrous light bathed the Western Province and the Guardians of Light poured forth. The great Portal of Machlleth was open once more. The Woodlands of Derwydd began to green again. The rolling cold mist that stultified the growth in Derwydd began to vaporise.

Through the portal came MacCuill, trapped in limbo and now released, soon to be followed by Thiorn and the elite guardsmen. A constant source of Divine Light poured forth, the threat of intrusion by the dark Sidhe allayed... for the moment at least...

Deep within the Woodlands of Derwydd, MacCuacht and his army of lost souls were being driven back by Erhombu and the spirits of the Woodlands. Creatures of all species and transformations pestered and harried the demons and denizens of the dark. The grip of the life extinguishing mist was loosened and every organic thing turned against the malevolent intruders.

MacCuacht, the three raven haired Witches and the much depleted army of lost souls retreated Eastwards, they made for the Pass of Brachlan, en route to the high mountain fortress of Hawardden where they regathered and licked their wounds and considered the consequences of this ignominious defeat. MacCuacht cursed his sister Sceine, and his deceased father, the High King Antiem! The Western Province yet again proving to be a thorn in his ever darkening side! He was enraged and vowed to avenge this defeat. His sister will pay dearly! Once Sceine is slain, MacCuacht will be ruler of the

Western Province. The island of Destiny and the mortal realm will be his!

He summoned the three Witches. His brothers had failed him. MacCuill had betrayed him, and the foolhardy MacGreinne had been captured... "We have failed to take the Portal of Machlleth. The Sea Druid Amergin has foiled us! We have failed to take Hushinish, the Princess Sceine denied us! They are the culmination of the prophecy that says they will rule over this land together. It seems simple to me... so clear... We kill Sceine and all will be ours!"

The Witches nodded in agreement. The mountain fortress of Sliebh Mis in the Iveare mountain range came in to their vision. Sceine was their target! They walked with MacCuacht to a ridge overlooking the Woodlands of Derwydd. Further to the South and West, the distant peak of Corran Tuathail, and beyond that Sliebh Mis. Eiru pointed to the mountain peaks famous as the home of wild White-tailed Eagles. "I will go tomorrow to join them, to survey the high mountains and find our best route. We must not be seen! Sceine is waiting for her destined one. She will not move until he arrives!"

MacCuacht agreed, "We will send our strongest warriors from all the Provinces to battle Amergin. I will return to the fortress of Hawardden. The message will be sent throughout the land for them to gather there. From there I will lead them to the Temple of Xhara. We will take the temple and with the help of the priesthood of Xhara, drive the Milesian mariner in to the ocean!" his horribly distorted features twisted in a semblance of a smile, "You, my raven haired beauties will go to Sliebh Mis and kill Sceine!"

They all agreed that this was an irresistible deadly pincer movement! Sceine will succumb to the witches! Even the great portals of the Western Province will be no match for them, once the priesthood of Xhara fall under the influence of the dark Sidhe! MacCuacht confirmed, "Xhara Is key to the fall of the great portals! The death of Sceine is paramount to thwart the prophecy! With these combined strategies, the balance will soon truly be shifted!"

The following morning in the shadow of the mountains and the still rolling and brewing storm front, MacCuacht took the army of lost souls to Hawardden. Eiru, once more, took flight in an explosion of photons. She flew to the mountains and the kingdom of the eagles. Banba and Fodha waited for her return... The final dice is being thrown...

The intertwined roots and branches of the Woodlands of Derwydd spread the news, "MacCuacht is leaving for Hawardden!" The woodland grapevine sending word as fast as sap could flow. Erhombu transformed in to the magnificent red deer stag and bounded over mountains, streams and rivers and through woodlands and forest to get to Machlleth, to be the bearer of the good news. A days journeying later he arrived at the portal. His heart stopped as he witnessed the pure radiant Light channelling along the lay line towards the Quarry of Izion and way over the horizon towards the Temple of the Sun. Heartened by this and the rejuvenation of the Woodlands, he fell to his knees, bowing his mighty antlered head and giving thanks to the Great Spirit. A tear glistened in the radiant Light and fell to the ground...

Erhombu transformed to spirit form and was greeted by Amergin, "The Guardian of the Woodlands of Derwydd I presume!"

"I am, and you must be the Sea Druid Amergin!" replied the proud leader of the wood spirits. Smiling appreciatively, no need for words, as they both were aware of what they had achieved. They studied one another... Amergin, the athletic, princely Milesian, tall and proud, a shock of sea bleached, golden brown hair falling over powerful broad shoulders. Erhombu, a tall, slender, willowy stature, a complexion ash coloured, with sharp angular elphine facial features. They embraced each other. "My lord, the Sea Druid Amergin, I am honoured to be in your presence! I come with the news that the dark one MacCuacht is driven from Derwydd, and at this moment returns to the high mountain fortress of Hawardden!"

"This is the best news you have brought, Erhombu!" He introduced him to the gathered throng, "We are all one in the eyes of the Guardian of Light! They are with us always. The Western Province is the last bastion of the enlightened ones!"

There was one who Amergin had not introduced him too...MacCuill, standing next to one of the giant Bluestones. Amergin sensed Erhombu's nervousness. He seemed to recognise MacCuill... "Forgive me Erhombu! I did not introduce you to MacCuill. Do you know him? Do not be afeared!"

MacCuill stepped forward. Amergin held both of them by an arm and formally brought them together. "It seems you have met MacCuill's siblings, and see the resemblance! MacCuill has seen the Light, he is with us!" Erhombu was relieved to hear this. Amergin continued, "MacCuill deserted his brothers MacCuacht and MacGreinne. He defended the Portal of Machlleth and was forced to go deep into the limbo of the spirit world when Machlleth closed. The portal is open once more and he, Thiorn and the elite guard are released!"

Erhombu spoke directly to MacCuill, "I have your brother MacGreinne captive! He was paralysed and put in to a deep coma in an ambush in the sacred Oak grove of Bendigedig. I believe your dark brother MacCuacht, thinks him dead!" MacCuill held Erhombu's hand, he was still nervous... "You have my assurance that I am with you. You must watch MacGreinne carefully! Once conscious he will have the ability to commune with MacCuacht and the Witches of Hawardden! Your position will be given away and he will send demons and denizens to find you!"

Erhombu reassured him, "He will remain in a deep coma until the antidote is given! Only the Physicians of Myddfai can administer the antidote."

"Be careful Erhombu!" warned MacCuill, "The infection of the dark can take the most pure and the most honest of beings!" A shudder ran down Erhombu's willowy spine, reminding him of the foe they were up against. Even the Light from the Portal of Machlleth could not comfort him. He realised that this was only the start of the long war against the dark Sidhe. A war led by MacCuacht in the mortal realm.

Amergin realised that Erhombu had been at the vanguard in the battle with MacCuacht. Many of the spirits of the Woodlands of Derwydd had fallen in its defence. Many had been taken and were now one of the legions of lost souls. Amergin too, felt that same shiver running down his spine...

Amergin broke this moment of reverie, "We are in the ascendant my brothers and sisters! We must rejoice and give thanks for that!" Amergin gave the orders for a ceremony to take place. To give thanks to the Great Spirit. To welcome the Guardians of Light to the mortal realm and to remember the fallen.

That evening in the light of a red, crimson dusk, and the radiant light pouring through the veil from the great Portal of Machlleth, they all gathered to give their thanks and their prayers to the Great Spirit. Communally they prayed for the fallen and for the lost souls. They prayed for their eternal peace ...

Later that evening Amergin conferred with Terese of the Xantha. He needed to find out from Terese her version of events, as one of the faithful Milesians who had confronted the dark one MacCuacht.

"Give me your thoughts Terese. You are one of the most valiant of Milesian warriors. You have seen the darkness that we confront. I need your perspective to help us keep the Island of Destiny pure."

Terese nodded, she knows Amergin well. She knows his powers, his bravery, his honesty and his integrity. However the attritious confrontations with the dark Sidhe have tested him, worn him down. She will try to guide him, "My Lord Amergin, you must not lose sight of your destiny, the Prophecy must be fulfilled! You have brought our nation here. Milesian destiny is here! You have won many battles, lost many souls. Still we are with you! You lead us! Your way is our way! You must trust your judgement, trust your heart and trust the love and guidance of the one you are destined to meet. We must head south to meet the High Priestess Sceine."

Amergin was in awe of the beauteous Amazonian warrior, statuesque, powerfully athletic, all with elegance and style, and blessed with magical, clairvoyant powers. Terese had given him the reality check he needed. The destined meeting with Sceine, as given in the pronouncements of the ancients, is the true path... The unabating confrontation with the dark Sidhe has clouded his judgement. The truth is that he must go to find Sceine. Meanwhile he feels the connection with Scota and Milidh, who wait for his sign offshore, and his Milesian mariners who wait for him at the Temple of the Sun.

The great Portal of Machlleth is safe for the moment. The Guardians of Light have journeyed through the veil and are in the mortal realm. The Light of the Divine radiates through the Woodlands of Derwydd. The lay line connecting the Bluestones of the Western Province is energised. Faith is restored, for the moment at least...

Amergin thanked Terese. She has grounded him. He looks at the amazonian beauty, trained by his mother, Queen Scota, in the arts of war and of the mind. Months of travelling and endurance and lonely nights... if he was not betrothed to Sceine...They parted, he kissed her delicately on the forehead...

That night his sleep was in a constant dream state. Lying so close to the portal, the connectivity charged his synapses, thoughts, impulses, emotions surged through him... Sceine journeyed through the veil... she was with him... just a touch and they came together. Amergin kissed her for seemingly hours, their bodies entwined, wrapped and inseparable.Dream or reality? They were in rapture. Time was meaningless. They journeyed together beyond the veil. Visions of her beauty and the Western Province raced through his mind.Visions of offshore islands, pinnacle spires and the Milesian fleet. All the great portals aligned and they travelled back in time... dream or reality?... the connectivity so intense... Sceine overwhelmed him. Her beauty, her touch... their bodies in rapture once more... they came together... they travelled back to the present... he journeyed alone back through the veil... and just as quickly, the dream was over...

Terese was shaking him by the shoulders, "My lord! There is news from Derwydd... you must come and talk to Endinou and Erhombu!" Amergin was back with a jolt, his head still full of Sceine's beauty, and full of questions... the lay line, the alignment, the islands, a secret portal, time travel?

All these questions had to be answered... but another time...

Endinou spoke with the wisdom of the ages, "My lord Amergin, the path of your destiny evolves!

There is no time to dwell here! You must leave! The dark one MacCuacht marches to hunt you down!" Erhombu explained further, "The time has come for the Sea Druid to bring salvation to this island of destiny. MacCuacht rallies at the high mountain fortress of Hawardden. He takes the army of lost souls from the lands to the east, where the portals are infected and compromised by the dark Sidhe. He brings a dark army to hunt you. He intends to drive you into the ocean and away from the Promised Land!"

Erhombu was so certain. Amergin looked at him questioningly. "The spirits of the Woodlands of Derwydd risked their lives to confront the army of lost souls and get this information ...By the great spirit we must go to sea!" his expression hardened as he explained why, "MacCuacht goes to the Temple of Xhara. He intends to tear the veil, to corrupt the portal and bring forth the dark Sidhe.

Should the High Priests of Xhara be taken, then the Temple of Xhara will be infected and the great portals of the Western Province will be threatened. The army that hunts you will then have enough power to corrupt Machlleth and the other great portals. You must go to sea, circumnavigate the island of destiny and get to the Temple of Xhara before MacCuacht. You must prevent MacCuacht from tearing the veil at all costs!"

Amergin was in a state of shock now. Only moments ago he was with Sceine in rapture! Endinou encouraged Amergin, "No one can match you at sea! You are Sea Druid of the Sea Kingdoms.The sea is your highway, even circumnavigating the island you will travel faster than MacCuacht. He will have to traverse the island, crossing mountain ranges and meet tribes averse to intrusion.We will contact the Aganti who will use their notorious guerrilla tactics to slow the dark one. All of the enlightened beings will pester and harry him. You will travel around the Northern Province and the sea god Manannan willing, get to the Eastern Province and the Temple of Xhara before MacCuacht!"

Stunned at the news, and even more horrified at the prospect of MacCuacht reaching the fabled Temple of Xhara, Amergin braced himself to the reality that he will soon be embarking on a sea journey even more perilous than that from the Tower of Galicia many lunar cycles ago.

How can that be? He was readying himself to journey south to meet Sceine! Now he sails north!

This time it was Terese who spoke. She had been quietly listening, "There is one thing you have not been told my lord Amergin! The witches Eiru, Fodha and Banbha go to Sliebh Mis as we speak...

Sceine is in grave danger!"

Terese of the Xantha knew what was coming next. Amergin implored her, "Terese you must take your most valiant warriors and journey to Sliebh Mis! Go with all haste, waste no time!"

The dice had certainly been thrown... Sceine in danger! The Temple of Xhara under threat! Reality had certainly come with the dawn.

The rapturous, sensuous encounter with Sceine filled his head, made his heart race and his spirits soar. That morning the Western Province was at its most glorious! New life breathed in to the Woodlands of Derwydd. Verdant energy charged in from the ether. The new dawn crackled with life giving force. The land was bathed in other worldly radiance. Yet the first step on the path to the coast seemed the longest he had ever taken. He should be heading south to his beloved Sceine...

Amergin travelled with MacCuill. He picked his brains. He had a rich local knowledge. He sensed that MacCuill would become a great leader and a maker of legends in his own right. Like Amergin, he had a streak of wrecklessness and eternal optimism. Heartened by his presence and glad to have him as an ally, even so, his familial line was still disconcerting...

Amergin's resolve grew, the closer he got to the coast. The sea was infused in his blood. Salt water in his veins... the Sea Druid came to the fore, he was ready for the voyage...

His mind was now consumed with the logistics of a marathon sea voyage, the race against time and the arrival of the dark one MacCuacht.

He had already made his farewells to Terese. She travelled south with her amazonian Xantha to intercept the Witches of Hawardden. The Xantha would die for her, their loyalty legendary, their physical prowess fiercesome, and their magic powerful. "They will need all their strengths!" thought Amergin. The forces of the feminine were on their way to help Sceine and perpetuate the Prophecy.

Time was of the essence. His stride lengthened. His resolve strengthened. He was focussed and determined. His eternal love affair must not cloud his judgement. "To the coast!" rallied Amergin.

They marched past the Quarry of Izion, leaving Endinou and the Cyclops Sethse there to protect the source of the Bluestones.

They marched to the Temple of the Sun to meet their loyal Milesian mariners. They marched in to a darkening dusk, and towards a rising crescent moon. In the east the still threatening thunderheads rolled and brewed. To the west, where the sun set over the distant silver ocean, the evening star Venus rose slowly over shimmering, mysterious islands.

Amergin turned to MacCuill, who knows these lands, "What can you tell me about these mysterious Islands on the Western horizon?"

"Very little my lord Amergin," replied MacCuill, "The Magine Islands are steeped in legend. No one has gone there in recent times. Legend has it that the ancients worshipped there. There are tales that this is the home of the sea god Mannanan. Sailors tell of sea monsters that defend the islands. It has become a place of taboo and myth!" Amergin listened carefully. He had become strangely drawn to these islands. He had seen how the light from the Temple of the Sun channelled towards the largest of these islands. The lay line from the Great Portal of Machlleth appeared to connect with these islands, "The home of the sea god Mannanan maybe.The site of a sacred temple more likely!"

Amergin stared at the crimson red sunset. Venus rising above the horizon pointed the way. The planet of love and harmony shone like a sparkling emerald hovering above the Magine Islands.He was being drawn there by the enlightened Guardians of Light.

In the dead of the night, the planetary beacon shone even brighter. A thin silver crescent of moon rose and traversed the kaleidoscopic heavens, following the milky path of a myriad stars that exuded an ethereal glow over the Magine islands, "Heavenly!" whispered Amergin in to the cool, clear night air. His mind too, was crystal clear... he knew his mission. He was being guided by the stars, the universe, and Sceine...

CHAPTER SEVENTEEN:
THE TEMPLE OF SCEILGE

The morning light lit up the Temple of the Sun high on the escarpment.The three giant Bluestones guiding their way. Pure radiant sunlight poured over the pristine shoreline of the Western Province.

Golden sands met surging ocean. White cresting waves broke powerfully on to miles and miles of deserted beaches. From the mountains to the east, to the verdant Woodlands of Derwydd, to the fringing shore, marshlands and meadows, then to the mighty ocean and on the horizon, the shimmering Magine Islands, "Breathtaking!" Amergin was taken aback by the beauty of the place...

Following the river around the final few bends, they came across the silty, estuarine anchorage where the Milesian vessels had been hauled up to a safe point above the high water mark. Amergin spotted his trusty helmsman Xomas on the prow of the flagship. He hailed him, and he and the rest of the crew jumped to shore and sprinted to meet Amergin. They hugged and embraced the Sea Druid, delighted their leader and champion had returned! "Anything strange?" interjected Amergin in the customary Milesian greeting. "Plenty my lord!" responded Xomas, "In this strange and mysterious land!" Amergin smiled... Yes, he knew there was always something strange in this land!

The crews of the rest of the fleet soon joined them. His brother Eiremhou was overjoyed. He dropped to one knee and bowed in delight and deference at the pleasure of seeing his long awaited brother. Amergin greeted Eiremhou and looked around in anxious anticipation... Eiremhou read his mind, "Eimbear and the High Priest of the Chapter of Mystics, Gonne, are away on a scouting mission with their crew," he informed him, "They will return at dusk." Amergin nodded, thankful for the warning. No more was said...

"We have much to organise my brother!" throwing his arm around Eiremhou, "Come, I will explain... Firstly, you must join me in prayer at the Temple of the Sun. All will become clear to you then!"

Together they scaled the escarpment, in complete wonder at the views of the Western Province unfolding before them. Amergin talked to Eiremhou as they walked and climbed. He was brutally honest with him. Amergin pulled no punches as to the immensity of the challenge that faced them.

Amergin was animated, galvanised and resolutely dedicated to the cause of the enlightenment. He inspired and instilled that same fervent belief. As they continued walking, deep in conversation, they were unaware of the arrival of Gonne and Eimbear. Amergin's traitorous brother was more and more closely in league with the sinister High Priest of the Chapter of Mystics.

Amergin and Eiremhou arrived at the entrance to the Temple of the Sun. He showed his brother the cleft where he had moulded perfectly in to the stone. He had become the key, the conduit. He was able to open the portal and bring the Light of the Divine and the Guardians of Light into the mortal realm. He was able to journey beyond the veil in to the spirit world.

Now he felt a sense of déjà vu... the hackles raised on the nape of his neck... he looked down at the base of the escarpment, to see the malevolent Gonne staring up at him. Amergin was aware of his powers of clairvoyance and mind reading. He immediately stopped talking to Eiremhou. The eyes and ears of the dark Sidhe were watching and listening. Eiremhou too sensed their presence. He was particularly disturbed by his devious brother Eimbear, "Come Amergin! We must go to make ready the fleet for sailing. We will sail at dawn. You will show us the way my brother. You are our Sea Druid and champion of the Milesian nation!" Amergin embraced his brother. Eiremhou's loyalty was heartening, their bond stronger than ever. As they descended from the Temple of the Sun, Amergin was intensely conscious of the sea journey that lay ahead. The dangers, the race against time... his mind drifted... he visualised the encounters... he would soon be confronting the dark Sidhe... firstly in his realm on the ocean ...and ultimately in MacCuacht's realm in the Eastern Province...

And what of Terese, where was she now? The beautiful, powerful Xanthan was marching to help his beloved Sceine. His spirits rose as he thought of the meeting with Sceine. Scota and Milidh waiting for his signal offshore... As he descended the track down the escarpment, he came to a place where it turned east. He saw the great mountain ranges on the Eastern horizon. Even if he could not see it, he was aware of the high mountain fortress of Hawardden, the lair of the dark one MacCuacht and the raven haired Witches of Hawardden. Stretching far, far to the south, the Iveare Mountains rose imperiously. Here was the high mountain fortress of Sliebh Mis where his beloved Sceine waited for him... The pain of having to sail away from her was almost too much to bear...

The tortuous track wound downwards, he looked to the east again. He saw the threatening storm clouds reaching new heights above the eastern mountain range. Descending to the base of the escarpment, he came face to face with Gonne of the Chapter of Mystics, and a few paces behind his brother Eimbear. Amergin realised in an instant that these two must not be allowed to travel with the fleet. Gonne was most certainly in league with the dark Sidhe, and he was shocked at the appearance of his brother Eimbear. He appeared changed. There was certainly something of the night about him now.

Eiremhou went to make ready the fleet. He must not give away their thoughts and plans. Amergin must deceive Gonne and Eimbear, "Gather your most loyal men!" he said pointedly to Gonne, "You and Eimbear will be the defenders of the last resort. The dark one MacCuacht comes with the army of lost souls. You will defend the Temple of the Sun with your lives! The Western Province depends on you!" He talked matter of factly, closing his mind to the probings of Gonne, "We go west to bring the rest of the Milesian fleet to join you in the battle for the cause of enlightenment!" Amergin said nothing of the circumnavigation of the Island of Destiny. He had given Eiremhou strict instructions not to divulge their destination. Speed and stealth would be the key in this marathon sea voyage to the eastern Province.

Gonne of the Chapter of Mystics questioned Amergin, "Where do you propose to do battle, at sea or on land?" This was a malevolent game of cat and mouse, "Once I have joined forces with Scota and Milidh, we will decide. I feel at this moment, that we will sail south and then march to the high mountain fortress of Sliebh Mis, and there we will make a stand ..."

For the moment, Gonne and Eimbear were oblivious to the machinations and deception afoot.

The dawn cannot come too soon... the fleet must sail!

Through the night, the master mariners of Milesia made ready. Provisions and weaponry were stored. Sails furled and vessels made sea worthy. At dusk, Amergin inspected the fleet. Impressed, but not surprised at their efficiency, he gave the order to weigh anchor and set sail! He rallied and motivated them all with a rallying cry, "We sail for the cause of the enlightenment and the fulfilment of the Prophecy! May the Great Spirit bless you and the sea god, Manannan, protect the fleet!"

Only when at sea would their destination be divulged. Now they go to the Magine Islands to meet with the rest of the fleet. Once launched, a signal beacon was lit and the giant conches sounded.

One by one they slipped out of the silty harbour. Vessel by vessel they left the safe haven of the estuary and made for the open sea. In the early morning half light, visibility was limited. They could hear the roaring breakers on either side of the channel. The tide was ebbing, the vessels sped along, the crews occasionally dipping their oars and pulling in unison. Sometimes the oars were used as punting poles as the spring tides were beginning to expose sand banks. Sharp, piercing orders broke the early morning silence, as captains and watchmen navigated their way past sand bars and cresting waves. "Bring her around! Straighten her up!" were the cries, as prows were pointed into the channel. Swell on tide created turbulent, chaotic conditions, a tidal race in a confused sea state.

Oars dipping and helmsman pulling, they sped onwards and out of the estuary and in to calmer, deeper waters of the bay beyond. They soon left behind the sound of the pounding breakers. In the early morning calm and coolness, all that was heard was the dipping of the oars and the shushing of the swell on the prow.

The sun announced its imminent rising with a streak of roseate crimson over the far mountains. The rolling storm clouds were backlit, looking even more threatening. Then a sunburst of radiant light filled the bay. Plumes of vaporised spray from the breaking surf and clouds of white ozone mist filled the air. Rainbows formed and disappeared as the breakers reared up, formed and dissipated their energy into the bay. In the far distance the Temple of the Sun became sun dial and prism, the giant Bluestone standing stones reflecting, refracting and diffracting the natural sunlight.

A pure white ethereal light was channelled along the lay line over the ocean. A burst of Divine Light rushed over the sea surface, and in an instant enveloped and irradiated the now shimmering Magine Islands. A looping circuit of plasma and Divine energy rushed and raced back and forth along the lay line. Once again, the entire Western Province lit up with Divine life giving Light.

This supernatural Light show occurs at every sunrise and sunset once the great portals of the Western Province became aligned and energised.

Amergin was awe struck! There was no doubt a great portal existed on the Magine Islands! Perhaps the greatest of all!?

He went to confer with MacCuill who was installed as cartographer on board. His local knowledge and experience is going to be invaluable for interpreting signs and giving directions between land marks. He was able to create living maps, giving guidance in the present moment. "You know of the portal?" quizzed Amergin.

"Yes my lord, in legend at least. The Portal of Sceilge is said to have the greatest supernatural powers of all. Not only channelling the Divine, radiant, life giving Light from beyond the veil, but when aligned with the other great portals of the Western Province can warp time itself!" he went on to explain further, "Tales of the ancients tell of enlightened beings that are empowered to travel in time!"

Amergin was rarely speechless, "Such power!" he was able to utter. Here was the greatest portal aligning with the purest of Divine Light, "You say, none of your race has ventured here!?"

"Not to my knowledge my lord, the tales of sea monsters guarding the islands have kept all at bay! No one has had the courage or the seamanship to venture here in recent times. No one in our history has ever attempted the crossing!" he pontificated.

"So the Portal of Sceilge remains a legend, a mystery?" suggested Amergin. MacCuill understood the thread of his questions, "No one, not even the dark one MacCuacht has knowledge of the Portal of Sceilge,"MacCuill reassured him, "The portal has remained steeped in the mists and legends of time, real but not real, purely a creation of the imagination!"

Amergin smiled inwardly... this sea journey is paying dividends already!

Now well away from land, Amergin gave the instructions to light beacons atop the mast, and for the watchmen to periodically sound the conch. This was to be the signal for the rest of the Milesian fleet, should they be within range. Hours passed, they drifted gently in the breeze. The oarsmen could rest now, the sails were unfurled. The fleet began to make steady progress to the islands. A few more hours and they would be near the Magine Islands.

Hour by hour, they drifted ever closer. The ebbing tide that took them out of the bay and in to the open ocean was slowing and slackening. A strange turbulence began to eddy around the vessels.

Cold, green vortices of slick water churned and boiled – the tide was turning... The breeze now in the south began to strengthen. The vessels of the Milesian fleet were rising and falling in a building swell. "Bring out the oars!" ordered Amergin. The oars were essential to keep the forward momentum going, to keep the prows pointed in the direction of the islands. The north to south tidal race on their journey out began to turn with the pushing tide. Within the hour it felt like the entire ocean was pushing northwards, pushing between the mainland and the Magine Islands.

Soon the tidal race was going at the speed of a galloping horse. The swell was rising exponentially as it met tidal race and strengthening wind. The turbulence became more and more chaotic.

Amergin took over from Xomas at the helm. With these sea conditions it was critical that he steer this vessel and lead all the other vessels on a true course for the islands. He checked with the watchman aloft, "How wide is this tidal race? Can you see the clearest way through?!" They were caught in the midst of the mayhem. The reply came back, "By my reckoning another three miles, my lord!"

They were being swept on a north-westerly trajectory away from the Magine Islands, into the vastness of the Northern Ocean. Amergin realised that the tidal race would eventually weaken, but they could be miles off course by then! He leaned hard on to the tiller and demanded, "More sail!"

He was trying to turn the prow into the south-west, sails and tiller bringing the vessel about. It was crucial to break out of the tidal race, and soon! They could lose a days sailing, waiting for the next tide to bring them back to the Magine Islands. The urgency of their mission weighed heavy on Amergin's mind.

Now, to exacerbate matters the wind was veering in to the north. Amergin felt the squall and wind change before he saw it. Almost too late! He released the tiller and let the sail slacken. "Tacking!" he bellowed as the mighty oak boom cracked into position, nearly decapitating some of the crew on the way. The prow pointed straight into the tidal race. Amergin with Xomas the helmsman put their combined weights on the tiller. The vessel slowly resumed its south-westerly course. Now though, they had wind on tide!

The tidal race and prevailing swell going into the teeth of the North

Wester! This caused the rolling 4-5 foot swell to rear up and become 10 foot monsters and increasing! The vessel was taking a real hiding. They could not sustain this for long! "How far to the other side of the race?" he anxiously quizzed the watch man, who was hanging on to the rigging for dear life, atop the violently undulating mast. He assessed the distance, "Another mile my lord!"

"More sail!" Amergin was gambling everything! Speed was of the essence! They must ride out the chaos! Surf the swell! It was finger tip control now, the tiller responding to every cresting wave and rearing swell. "The sea monsters of the Magine!" shouted Amergin to his helmsman Xomas, "No wonder the Tuathans haven't ventured out here!" This was nature in the raw. "Half a mile!" shouted the watchman. Amergin could see the other side of the race ahead. Clear water, but at first the chaotic turbulence must be negotiated. A green-silver monster reared up ahead of them, "Brace your selves!" He turned the tiller. The prow pointed in to the cresting set wave, riding up and over in to the trough. Another followed and another... The localised swell and turbulent chaos gave them no time to react. They were sailing by instinct and their years of experience. Amergin feared for the less experienced helmsman and crew on the other vessels. He had no time to look, full concentration was required. Only when they were out of the tidal race could the damage be assessed. Punching and forcing through each and every wave, keeping the speed and momentum going. Skill and instinct, the master mariner's of Milesia had their work cut out. The Sea Druid Amergin led the way. Rolling, riding, surfing and sailing, one last giant set wave and they were through! Free from the clutches of the river of the ocean. The sails billowed, the rigging strained and the vessel sped onwards in relatively clear water...

Amergin could now turn to watch his fellow Milesians. The tail-enders still fought furiously to be free from the tidal race. One by one they all reached the clear water! "Mighty sailors indeed!" roared Amergin in approval. He embraced Xomas, "To the Magine Islands helmsman! Make all haste!"

The freedom of the clear water, made sailing a joy, the North Wester pushed them along, the billowing sails now fully unfurled.The mysterious Magine Islands pinnacled and magnificent.

A cry came from aloft, "There my lord, a beacon!" Sure enough on the mightiest of the islands a beacon burned! They had found their fellow Milesians! In the blustery wind they could hear the sound of a resonating conch.

They rounded the first volcanic ridge that plunged into the oceanic depths. The fleet slid through green-black aqueous brine and a miriad sparkling organisms in a soup of life. An occasional Mackerel, shimmering, silvery scaled, surfaced, fed and was gone, sea life richer than the wildest imagination. Shafts of light penetrated deep into the oceanic universe.

Amergin and his fleet silently drifted through the slick, oily waters, oarsmen dipping occasionally.

The only sound was of breathing and the deep intake of ozone rich air. From mayhem to the sublime, each and every crewman gave their thanks to the Great Spirit for bringing them through. An occasional diving seabird was startled and sped off in a fury of frenzied wings and webbed feet... skipping across the surface and diving deep.

In the lee of the wind and swell, and the shadow of the igneous spires, with the gurgling, surging, breathing sounds of a heaving ocean in the deep, dark sea caves, each and every one of the Milesian mariners was lulled and mesmerised into a trance state. The sound of a conch broke the hypnotic silence. The oarsmen instinctively pulled as one in the direction of the signal sound. Beyond the sea stack, through a natural arch of rock, and around one more precipitous sea cliff... a sea cave the size of a cathedral, a massive high ceilinged chamber. Waters so deep. The cave walls immersed into the ocean and disappeared in to the depths.

The sound of the conch echoed in the cavernous space, the vessels drifted on and on, oars dipping here and a dip there. The sound of voices! A beacon lit up their way, the outline of moored vessels and the silhouette of busying people. Firelight and beacons illuminated the dark cavern and reflected off wavelets and dripping water. Amergin was mesmerised by the ethereal blue reflections from veins of quartzite. "Bluestone!" seams of Bluestone lined the high vaulted cavern. A passageway vented the drifting acrid smoke from the burning kelp. "There was a way through!"

One by one the vessels drew alongside the moored fleet. Tied and lashed together tightly. The entirety of the Milesian fleet together again in an enormous floating, gently heaving raft.

Amergin, Xomos, MacCuill and the rest of his crew leapt from boat to boat. Amergin's heart raced at the prospect of meeting his parents... "My son!!" bellowed King Milidh, his booming baritone voice echoing repeatedly around the sea cave. Amergin laughed out aloud and embraced Milidh, "Father!" Scota grabbed his hand, "Mother ...so good to see you both!" He kissed her cheek and knelt in homage to the royal blood line. "We have much to talk about, but first you must tell of this extraordinary place!" Scota sensed that her brave son would be leaving them soon. Saddened by this but overjoyed at being with him now... "We took refuge here during a storm, "Scota explained, "Fate, destiny, serendipity or however you might have it, brought us here to this incredible sea cave. We were able to land and fortuitously found the entrance above. "She pointed to where the smoke spiralled upwards." Scota continued, "We naturally explored, and discovered an entrance, a gateway to an ancient temple! Workings that go back a thousand years and may not have been visited by anyone since that time!"

Amergin turned towards Milidh. They acknowledged the importance of the find. Amergin's assumption that this place had never been visited by a Tuathan, in recent generations at least, was correct...

By the time Eiremhou had arrived and embraced both his mother and father, he had listened to the account of their experience. He held Scota's hand and she kissed his forehead, "Eimbear, what of Eimbear!?" She knowingly sensed the truth about his alliance with Gonne. Eiremhou replied, "He is safe mother... but he is not with us... We will explain later mother. Please go on ..."

Scota sensed the urgency of this meeting, "The workings are of the purest Bluestone. From this stone a temple has been constructed. A temple that radiates the purest of Light! There are otherworldly forces at work here!"

"This place is known as the Portal of Sceilge!" Amergin interrupted his mother. Amergin proceeded to the passageway with Scota and Milidh. Eiremhou and MacCuill followed closely. They climbed a hundred and more, narrow, carved steps, hewn into the igneous rock.

Amergin explained all about the journey that he must embark on. He told them of Eimbear's allegiance with Gonne and the mission that Terese of the Xantha was on. He then told them of his connection with Sceine, and how he must go to the Temple of Xhara to confront the dark one MacCuacht, Sceine's traitorous brother. This sea voyage is key to the salvation of the Island of Destiny and essential for the fulfilment of the Prophecy...

They soon arrived at the Temple. The architectural workings of the mysterious ancient ones amazed Amergin. A ledge carved into the igneous spires of this magical island, the roaring, crashing ocean over two hundred feet below. On this ledge were five Bluestone standing stones of the purest quality, purer even than those of the Temple of the Sun, and the great Portal of Machlleth.

Pure, radiant Light warped and wrapped around the Bluestones. He too sensed the presence of the Guardians of Light and the closeness of the veil. Amergin told Scota and Milidh of the tales of the magical powers of this portal. He emphasised that this portal was perhaps the most powerful of all and must be guarded at all costs...

Amergin then announced, "I have to go now my dear parents. I ask you to stay here with the royal elite guard to protect this place..." He was struggling with his words, "I will take the rest of the Milesian fleet north and circumnavigate the Island of Destiny to get to the eastern shores before the dark one arrives at the Temple of Xhara. He will try to turn the dark Sidhe against the Priests of Xhara. Should they fall to the dark one and become in league with the army of lost souls, they will march on the Western Province and the great portals will be taken and the forces of the dark Sidhe unleashed from the spirit world ..."

Amergin asked to be left alone at the Portal of Sceilge for a while. He needed to meditate, to reflect on the events that had passed, and to focus on the sea journey to come. He knelt in front of the Temple, facing outwards to the infinite Northern Ocean and eastwards to the Island of Destiny.

He turned to watch Scota and Milidh descending into the narrow passageway, back to the cavern where the vessels were tied up. Scota saw him watching her and smiled knowingly. Her strength would be his strength. Amergin smiled back and raised his hand in a symbolic farewell.

A sense of foreboding came over him, intermingled with nervous anticipation and even excitement at the prospect of his sea adventure. An adventure with potentially a deadly outcome...

His gaze swept panoramically from horizon to horizon... the ocean, the coast and far beyond the mountain ranges of the Iveare and Sliebh Mis. He tried to visualise the high mountain fortress of Sliebh Mis through Sceine's eyes...

The connectivity with the spirit world and the mortal realm was intensely strong here. Two hundred feet above the ocean, and the Bluestones of the Portal of Sceilge channelling along the lay line to the Western Province. Amergin felt at one with the spirit world... the veil came closer... he was able to pass in and out at will... he felt the Guardians of Light in his soul... guiding him, nurturing him... and then she came to him..."Sceine!" Her image shimmered before him. He felt the Light of the Divine wrapping around him. He felt her caress, her tender finger tips touching him, her breath softly over his face, his eyes closed in ecstacy. "I am with you my love..."She caressed the contours of his face, his body... She knew how to take him to a place of the deepest, purest joy. His senses were overwhelmed... he opened his eyes, staring in to an amber cosmos, he was falling again in to the dark fleck in her eye... deeper, deeper, deeper... he came back to the mortal realm...

Amergin was overcome with desire and emotion... Sceine was gone! He felt comforted, but somehow naked and exposed on a ledge two hundred feet above the boiling ocean. He breathed deep, taking in the rich ionized ozone. He was recharged, reenergised and reinvigorated. Her name was on his breath, "Sceine!" he shouted out for all to hear... her name echoed and resounded around the island temple..."Sceine! Sceine! Sceine!" her name was on all their lips...

CHAPTER EIGHTEEN:
THE NORTHERN OCEAN and THE PIRATES OF GRANNH

The weather perfect, the moon high in the night sky, the constellations shining bright, the sea as calm as he had ever seen it...

Amergin hugged his dear mother, Queen Scota, and shook the strong hand of his father, King Milidh.

He wiped the tears from the royal queen's cheek and embraced and hugged her, giving a message from the heart. "Protect yourselves, protect this place, and we will meet again soon! I give you my love and may the great spirit be with you always!" With this he stepped on board the flagship and signalled for the oarsmen to take them out to sea.

He and the rest of the Milesian fleet drifted out to sea, the entrance of the sea cave silhouetted in the moon light. Amergin gave the orders to unfurl the sails. He helped his crew tension the rigging.

He felt the coolness of the ocean breeze. The sails started to fill. He turned to give a final salute and a wave farewell to Scota and Milidh, "To the return my dear parents... to the return ...!"

Once again the rigging took the strain, the sails billowed and the vessels of the Milesian fleet tacked away from the islands. The south-westerly wind pushing them ever onwards this time they would sail outside of the line of the islands, avoiding any possibility of getting ensnared by the "sea monsters of the Magine Islands."

The tide had turned again, filling from the south. "Perfect!" exclaimed Amergin, "We shall follow Polaris, the Northern star!" He looked up in to the constellations. The portents seemed good, the Great Spirit was smiling down on them, and the sea god Manannan was giving them his blessing.

He surveyed the ocean, a low sea state, perfect for sailing, "We will make good headway tonight Xomas!" speaking in the direction of his helmsman, who agreed, "It is ideal my lord, by the Great Spirit and the sea god Manannan, may that continue to be so!" Amergin in turn spoke to MacCuill in his role as cartographer, "We will need your services this night. You must tell us of the landmarks that we must make for and the perils that might await us!" MacCuill looked up in awe as the universe unfolded before them. He had never seen such a sky! Starlit and moonlit, the milky edge of the galaxy stretching to infinity. A shout came from the watchman on high, "Look!!"

A meteorite of such brilliant Intensity arced over the north-eastern horizon, lighting up the ocean as it fell. "A sign my lord!" Xomas speculated, "The meteorite came from where we must go!" Amergin agreed and ordered his helmsman to make the necessary adjustment to their course.

In the stark moonlight Amergin could make out each and every one of his fleet, "Magnificent, he mariners of Milesia on course, and in perfect harmony once more!" Amergin felt the excitement of the adventure coursing through his veins. He knew only too well, that his enthusiasm must be tempered with the reality of the dangers that lay ahead.

Turning to Xomas, "We will take shifts, four hours on, four hours off. You take the first shift, but do not hesitate to call me." Amergin placed a comforting hand on his helmsman's shoulder, "Good work Xomas, my faithful helmsman. I will see you in a few hours."

Xomas nodded and smiled. Such praise from the Sea Druid Amergin! Their bond strengthened through the adversities of recent times. Xomas would follow Amergin faithfully. He would die for Amergin if necessary. Amergin sensed his loyalty and turned to retire below deck. He felt a wave of relief coming over him. He fell in to his quarters and was asleep before his head touched his hammock.

The events of the day and the journey beyond the veil sparking his dreams and consuming his consciousness, his slumbering body and his dreaming mind fell in to a fitful sleep. He fell in and out of kaleidoscopic dreams... he travelled through and beyond the veil, communing with the spirit world.

Returning to the mortal realm as a wave crashed on to the prow and was left in their wake. Sleeping, drifting again, into a deep dream state, and beyond the veil once more... The more he journeyed through this land and sailed the ocean, the more he felt as one. He was finding the unity he searched for... the unity of mind and of the spirit, the unity of national consciousness and a sense of destiny, the unity of creativity and imagination. Increasingly he felt unity between the mortal realm and the spirit world. Increasingly through his deep dream states, he was living beyond the veil, communing with the Guardians of Light and travelling to the spirit world. The network of portals across the land became his medium and the conduit. Through his dreams he could see events unfolding. He could see the glorious Western Province and the energised and life giving portals. He was one with the veil now. He was learning how to control his dreams. Now he could organise his subconscious and enter dream states of his choosing. The only place he could not journey was where the portals were infected. He sensed that the Eastern Province was darkening all the time, the dark one MacCuacht strengthening...

Amergin's thoughts and dreams took him deep beyond the veil that night. The proximity of the Portal of Sceilge gave him a spiritual connection to the portals of the Western Province...

He travelled to the fringes of the Woodlands of Derwydd and on to the high mountain fortress of Hawardden... here was the evidence that Amergin needed... he saw the army of lost souls marching remorselessly on. The dark forces were gathering and soon they would travel to the Temple of Xhara...

The veil warped and thinned again. He was losing the connection... his mind was becoming numbed and anaesthetised... A cold mist encroached in to the fringes of his dreams, darkening the technicolour, hallucinogenic qualities of his inner visions. Someone somewhere was influencing his dreams and intruding beyond the veil. In the recesses of his subconscious mind, he became aware of a shadowy spectre..! He was awake and back to reality, swinging gently in his hammock, deep in the gunnels of the vessel...

He blinked hard trying to focus... peering in to the dark recesses of the cabin... did that shadow move? He fell out of the hammock dagger to the ready... his vision became accustomed to the low light... He knew he was alone... just the vestiges of his dream. Amergin realised though that in his journey beyond the veil, he was not alone! The spectre must have been MacCuacht! He must be more careful next time! If he went too far, got too close, then the entire mission could be jeopardised. The spirit world was not a realm exclusive only to the enlightened ones...

Amergin had much to learn still... the realms of a dream world could easily turn to nightmare.

Uncontrolled, the world of his dreams could become the world of his nightmares... he could draw the demons and denizens of the dark Sidhe through the Veil. Without more care he could be the one to channel the dark forces to the mortal realm.

Amergin was suitably chastened. He must learn to calm his mind before sleeping. He must learn to connect with the Guardians each night. His position of power and spiritual enlightenment must be harnessed and used for the good of his people. He must not be complacent. He vowed to pray to the Great Spirit each night, to meditate... and for the sake of his sanity he would connect with Sceine each night...

Awake now, but not yet time for his watch. He lit an oil lamp at the navigation desk. He carefully studied the maps that MacCuill had drawn. They were works of art, with detailed descriptions and drawings of each day's events. More importantly he would take all the meteorological signs and the sea state of the day and attempt a map projection for the following day. Amergin would then draw on all his years of marine experience to make a judgement on the course and planned progress for the coming day. MacCuill's local knowledge has its limitation, but was essential as a basis for Amergin's judgement calls. Amergin as a master mariner, with a sense of the bigger picture, was aware that tides, lunar cycles, and weather systems would make the real time decisions for him.

The druidic powers vested in him by the ancients of Milesia and the training given to him by his father Milidh and the Queen Scota, combined with the otherworldly and magical powers of the spirit world and his destined one Sceine, will hopefully give him the wherewithal, the ability and the skill to navigate a safe and speedy course around the Island of Destiny. He would need all his powers to counter the malevolent intrusions from beyond the veil by the dark Sidhe...

Still an hour before his watch, but unable to sleep, Amergin took a quill and some parchment paper.

He opened his mind letting his creativity flow and his imagination take charge. He began to write poetic verse. Automatically he wrote, channelling his imagination, the words were his mantra. He was channelling universal poetry to guide him and calm him...

"There is no path, only a walk in your own direction,
A place to go, a way to be, a sense of reinvention,
A spirit's release, a mind's eye belief, some inclination,
To see the world, with love in your heart, imagination,
Discover yourself be free of life's regime, a proclamation,
A journey to you, the greatest distance travelled, an explanation,
Suffice it to say, your path is your way, your inspiration,
Heart felt, sublime, in nature Divine, an incarnation"

Amergin had found a sense of unity once more... unity with his nation, with the Great Spirit, and with the Island of Destiny.

Unknown to Amergin, the dark one MacCuacht could manipulate the veil at will, but only in the Eastern Province where the portals were compromised. Here the dark Sidhe of the spirit world could penetrate the veil and enter the mortal realm. MacCuacht happened to be conspiring with his dark mentors when Amergin came through the veil to spy on him. Amergin was far from the safety of the Western Province when he was discovered. MacCuacht instantly countered, determined to prevent Amergin finding out his intentions... at that moment he read Amergin's mind and he discovered the Sea Druid's intention to make the sea journey north, circumnavigating the Island of Destiny... meanwhile the army of lost souls gathered in strength. Lost Tuathans and lost Firbolg joined the demons and denizens of the dark Sidhe...

MacCuacht looked on in satisfaction, "Tomorrow we will begin the march to the Temple of Xhara!"

Amergin had been mistaken to try to attempt to infiltrate his realm. That night MacCuacht would summon the dark Sidhe and send his demons and denizens to the Northern Ocean to slow his progress...

Amergin took his turn at the helm, taking over from Xomas at the tiller. He checked the position of the fleet in relation to the constellations of the night sky... they were on course, a fleet to match any adversary. The prevailing south-westerly pushed them on steadily. Five degrees east of the Northern star Polaris, two days sailing before they would tack to the east, according to MacCuill's map.

Good visibility, a following wind and a continuing good sea state. He thanked the Great Spirit and the sea god Manannan, and lashed the tiller firmly in to position. Hour upon hour of perfect sailing, they were making good progress to the North of the Island of Destiny. The moon traversed the sky, slowly setting over the mountain ranges of the Western Province, silhouetted across the silver-black sea.

Unfamiliar outlines now, as they began to sail past the landscapes of the Northern Province. A feature of barren lunar limestone carst glowed white in the stark lunar light. Sea cliffs of monumental scale rose out of the deep ocean. Massive swells crashed on shallow jagged reefs at the base of the sea cliffs. A myriad sea birds wheeled on the updraughts and divers plunged deep in to the green black ocean, moon light danced on the waves, lighting up luminescent spray. Raucous calls of gulls echoed around the natural amphitheatre.

They sailed with the pushing tide, pushing them effortlessly along the coast of this magnificently strange land.

The south-westerly eased in the cool crispness of the early morning, the air heavy and dense at this hour. A mile offshore, a safe distance from currents eddying and boiling at the base of the cliffs and well away from the ferociously breaking surf. Amergin watched as a four hundred foot sea stack came in to view. From this vantage point, the Western silhouette of this massive sentinel, lit up by shafts of moonlight, was threatening and haggardly. "The Sea Hag of the North!" exclaimed MacCuill. He turned to Amergin to explain the significance of this hideous landmark. "This sea stack is steeped in the mythology of the ancient Firbolg. Tales of ancient mariners who had come to grief in the storm bound seas off this coast, tales of wreckers and pirates. Legend has it that beyond this sea stack are many islands with deep water anchorages, haven for the infamous "Pirates of Grannh."

The coast line soon began to shelve more gently, limestone reefs shaped in to sharp and jagged, tortuous formations by waves and weather, a vast bay opened before them. Amergin turned to MacCuill, "Which route do you suggest, map maker?" The choice was to sail directly in to the vast bay, potentially risking the deep water havens in the lee of the islands, favoured by the Pirates of Grannh or to risk the seaward, open water route exposed to the storms of the Northern Ocean.

Before MacCuill could answer, a watchman cried out, "Beware! A squall arrives!" A down blast from the six hundred foot sea cliffs caught the entire fleet by surprise. Too late! They tried to batten down the hatches.The cool calmness of the dawn had been shattered by this violent vortex descending like a freight train. This phenomenon was normally associated with storm conditions, when wind sheer and sea cliffs produce damaging gusts of sail ripping force. Amergin was fearful now! The pushing tide and drifting current had taken had taken them rapidly inshore. Far too close for safety!

He called to the oarsmen to take up position, "Row for your lives!" he cried. The mainsail had already been shredded by the violent down blast. He saw the rest of the fleet tipping and spinning as the vortex tore through.

Xomas the helmsman grabbed the tiller as Amergin took over as lead oarsman, pulling for all his might. All the crews were rowing for survival. They were directly under the Sea Hag of the North now! They were being taken by the strengthening drift towards a reef that funnelled and channelled deep water swell into massive waves of serious consequence. Currents, wind and swell pushed them towards the reef where jagged limestone formations pierced the white water with venomous intent.

"Row Milesia, Row!" yelled Amergin. He and Xomas knew that this was going to be too close for comfort. The tide and current had them in its grip!

From the green-black slickness of the ocean, roared powerful deep water waves, crashing with almighty force. The avalanche of white water pounded the reef and the dagger like rocks. Rolling and violently crashing on to the reef and the base of the cliff. The white water turbulence, with nowhere to go now rebounded and pushed back out to sea. A white water rapid swept out and beyond the breaking waves. A current of spume, foam and ozone... Amergin's vessel was caught! His crew rowing for their lives!

Another keel length closer and they would be taken in to the death zone and smashed on to the reef to become a mass of splintered timber and wreckage "Row...Row for your lives!"... Half a keel length closer ... Amergin crouched as a wall of white water crashed over the deck, the vessel pushed through as the emptying surge and tidal race grabbed them and took them clear.They were free! They were back in to the green oily black slickness of the deep water.

His crew slumped over in utter exhaustion. Behind them the next white water monster crashed on to the jagged reef. Now they all turned. Amergin, Xomas, MacCuill, the crew, they all watched helplessly, as they slowly drifted away to safety and out of harms way. They all watched in shocked silence as two vessels came to grief. They were that boat's length too far in! The white water rapids of emptying surf drew them in to the death zone. They were sucked in and up the face of the heaving waves... they were turned and sucked over the falls and smashed in bone crunching, timber snapping violence on to the dagger reef. Debris and bodies were beaten against the reef and then against the base of the cliff and finally sucked out in the emptying rip. Amergin and his crew could not watch, as they feared for the rest of the fleet. They breathed a collective sigh of relief as one by one vessels of the fleet were pulled over walls of white water, their crews frantically rowing for their lives, and were carried by the tide and currents in to the slack water of the deep ocean beyond...

Thankfully, with no more casualties, the diminished fleet now drifted out and around the Sea Hag of the North... They had been caught unawares! They had learned an appalling lesson. Amergin questioned where that violent down blast came from, at that time of day, in these conditions? He talked at length with his comrades... they could only come to one conclusion... the dark Sidhe...

Amergin ordered the fleet to drop anchor in the serene and surreal quietness of the vast bay beyond the forbidding Sea Hag of the North. Was it his imagination, as they drifted out from the scene of death and devastation, did he see a twisted smile on the Sea Hag's silhouette? Surely that cannot be!

They anchored all the remaining vessels of the fleet and gathered to hold a memorial ceremony for the crews of the fated vessels. Amergin knew both captains well. He was at sea school with Yorath. He was a fearless, intrepid master mariner. A family man and adored by his crew. Eizac was a captain known for his heart, strength and integrity. His seamanship skills were legendary. He had competed with and pushed Amergin close in swimming marathons and the ocean games, a dear friend and a loyal compatriot.

Amergin blessed the captains and their crews and sent prayers to their loved ones left behind in Galicia. Families and loved ones who waited with great excitement and anticipation, to be the first of the next wave of Milesians to sail to the Promised Land of the Prophecy, now, only the news of tragedy and devastation awaits them. Amergin cursed the dark Sidhe. He looked out over the vastness of the Northern Ocean. He felt deep down that this sinister deadly event had been orchestrated by MacCuacht...

Xomas stepped up beside Amergim, "My lord, we have a critical decision to make now. Do we go in to the bay or risk the storms of the open ocean?" Amergin was snapped out of his reverie... the mission must continue! Milesia must prevail! This was Amergin's judgement call now... the safety of the fleet and the success of the mission depended on him... He pondered and reflected... Taking MacCuill's warnings in to account and the wind, tide and weather... "We will go to the open ocean! Make ready Xomas! We will go where our marine skills will be optimised, where we will be strongest and we can fight on our terms!" Xomas agreed with Amergin. The judgement of the Sea Druid was never in doubt. Amergin was the greatest mariner the Milesians had ever seen. It was he who had brought them to the Island of Destiny...

Instinctively the open ocean felt good, even though they would be exposed to the elements. Rather that, than being trapped in the bay with no way out.

As they sailed away from the precipitous sea cliffs, they could see figures gathering, soon to begin their descent down a seemingly impossible track. They carried burning torches to light the way. Still a good hour to sunrise, the lee of the cliff was still in shadow. Like mountain goats they descended.They obviously knew the cliff well. To the unacquainted eyes there was no path...

Before long they arrived at the base of the cliff. A storm beach with debris from the wreckage of the two Milesian vessels washed up and wedged in to the rocks. They must be wreckers! On this occasion the wrecking had been done for them. No need to lure unsuspecting vessels on to the reef this time. MacCuacht had perpetrated the foul deed. They were purely scavengers of the marine debris. Amergin cringed at the thought of these vultures going through the pockets of his dead crew and plundering their personal possessions.

"We must away from here!" The crew sprang in to action, anxious to get sailing. They were soon planing on the freshening Southerly breeze. Half a days sailing, Amergin estimated, and they would be rounding the distant Southerly tip of the outer islands. Now, the first chink of sunlight! Sunrise! A glorious reddening sky and an orange silver mackerel cloudscape reflected across the ocean undulating in a long distance swell. A red dawn and a mackerel sky indicated a weather front... the portents were not the best, and they were headed for the open ocean! In his balanced judgement Amergin still considered the potential worsening weather conditions at sea, to be the lesser of two evils. The Pirates of Grannh were a much greater threat if MacCuill's tales were to be believed!

Amergin called a meeting with MacCuill. He needed to know more about his foe. They talked quietly in Amergin's cabin, the vessel gently rolling in the still low sea state, the breeze from the South West steadily strengthening as they reached the open ocean. An occasional set wave sent white water flying past the porthole on the starboard side, obscuring the occasional view of the outer islands.

MacCuill continued with his tale, "The Pirates of Grannh are ancient descendants of the original Firbolg, an invasion force from Thracia. Many generations ago the Firbolg became land bound, their sea skills obsolescent. But this tribe thrived on the ocean, becoming guerrilla warriors of the sea, attacking all comers, even their own kind!" He had Amergin intrigued and concerned, MacCuill continued, "Even Magire and the Shamen of Land's End, far to the north of here had been troubled by the Pirates of Grannh. They were free spirits, serving no one and plundering all."

"How far does their sea kingdom stretch?" asked Amergin.

"Allegedly around the entire Northern Province even as far as the Maum Mountains in the north-east!" MacCuill speculated.

"And what of the war with the Tuathans, how many have survived the forays of MacCuacht?" Amergin was well aware of the treacherous sorties made by MacCuacht, against the wishes of the High King Antiem.

"The sea my lord, the sea is their salvation! As the army of lost souls forayed northwards they took to their vessels. They took great losses when MacCuacht summoned the dark Sidhe. They were scattered to the winds. The survivors rallied and used the outer islands as their sea base." Amergin thanked MacCuill for his invaluable insights. The Pirates of Grannh were evidently a force to be reckoned with. They must be vigilant!

Amergin was concerned for the safety of the fleet and the success of their mission, but heartened that the Pirates of Grannh, another warrior tribe, had survived the insurgent forays of MacCuacht. Like their shamanic brothers from Land's End they may become allies? And what allies they would be...

In a ploy to test the water with the Pirates of Grannh, Amergin decided to send one of his vessels back to the Bay of Spideal. From there the crew would march north to meet Magire and the Shamen of Land's End. They had seen the good heart of the High King Antiem and the malevolence of MacCuacht. Amergin had faith in his captain Forsien. If there was diplomacy to be done and alliances to be made, then he was the man. MacCuill provided a map for the most direct route. The crew, hand picked and hardened warriors. They must sail south, avoiding the islands at all costs. They could be mistaken as insurgents by the Pirates of Grannh. Their demise would be swift... When they see the Maum Mountains on the horizon, they must strike north and from there, march to Land's End.

Meanwhile, Amergin and the rest of the fleet sailed on swiftly. They had already reached the outer islands. They tacked and turned directly north, once again being pushed by wind and tide. Amergin was delighted that such good progress was being made. He stood at the helm with Xomas as they rounded the most southerly point on the most southerly of the outer islands.

Exposed reefs and pounding surf came in to view. On one of the reefs stood a wreck, one of the poor victims of this storm bound coast or maybe one of the victims of the Pirates of Grannh?!

The coast changed now, from the low but rugged windswept limestone carst to precipitous cliffs rising two hundred feet sheer out of the ocean. The island was a mirror image of the topography of the main land. The fleet sailed at a rate of knots now. The tide and the ever increasing wind pushing them on and on...

The limestone cliffs rose higher and higher. A few miles to the north, the cliffs at least four hundred feet, an edifice had been carved out of the seaward side of the vertical rock face. Amergin took the helm from Xomas, "We must take a closer look at this!" As one, the entire fleet sailed towards the base of the mighty cliffs and directly under the structure. The swell from the west was steadily building. They would not get too close this time! The encounter with the violent down blast and the disasterous experience on the reef at the Sea Hag of the North, made Amergin and the entire Milesian fleet very wary. A good half mile out, in good visibility, they could clearly see the extraordinary edifice hewn out of the rock, clearly the work of an ancient civilisation.

They could see a rock platform, some kind of altar, a place of worship and possibly sacrifice. Beyond, high defensive walls made of massive, square blocks of limestone. This was an impregnable fortress, from the ocean at least.

Amergin peered upwards, squinting in to the now rising sun, but found it difficult to focus with the rolling motion in the building swell. He began to feel the turbulence from the swell reflecting and rebounding from the base of the cliff. He handed the tiller back to Xomas so he could get a steady positive look at the fortress. As he feared! The defences were manned! Armoured soldiers were on watch! They marched with pikes and spears along the perimeter wall. They were on watch and the fleet had been spotted! They hurried and scurried in to action! A beacon was lit on the rock platform and the sound of conches resonated around the cliffs. This must be the island base, the head quarters and fortress of the Pirates of Grannh! And they would be coming for the Milesian fleet!

Amergin was confident that with the element of surprise, and the fact that they sailed with the wind and the tide, that the fleet would be safe. Then another beacon and another beacon lit up the coast line. For miles, from promontory to promontory, more beacons... they were not safe! "We must head for the open ocean! We must be battle ready!" This time the Milesian conches were heard. The alarm sounded and all the crews manned their positions. The fleet tacked hard and turned away from the coast. The open water and deep ocean would surely be their salvation.

The further out in the ocean they sailed, the more islands that came in to view. On each island a beacon was lit! "There must be a hundred islands along this coast!" Amergin shared with Xomas, "The stronghold of the Pirates of Grannh!" Soon a network of beacons lit up the entire chain of outer islands, as far as the eye could see.

"Disasterous!" Amergin despaired, "We must take our advantage and sail deep in to the Northern Ocean! This strengthening south-wester could save us!" Xomas agreed, the fleet should out run the Pirates of Grannh with this kind of start.

Within minutes twin masted pirate vessels were launched and under full sail. They edged out of the channel between the islands. Their distinctive red sails and high prowed design, perfect for ocean sailing. The Pirates of Grannh in full force, twenty vessels, now there were thirty... more and more appeared from isles and islets stringing out to the North.

The Milesian fleet sailed for their lives! Surely the master mariners of Milesia would out sail these pirates. Amergin, Xomas and MacCuill watched as the vessels at the head of the fleet were out running the pirates. They were all distressed at the sight of the vessels in the rear guard slowly losing distance. The Pirates of Grannh were on an intercept course! The turning ebbing tide forcing out between the islands were projecting them directly in to their path. "We cannot stop! Our mission is our priority! We cannot fight and defend the others! We must press on!" this was most unlike Amergin, but the circumstances dictated this, it was a case of every vessel for them selves! His compatriots looked on. This was the toughest of decisions. Usually he would fight to the death...

On cue the wind strengthened. To compound their woes the coming storm! They were under full sail and were racing through the building seas. Spray and spume filled the air. The fleet desparately reaching for the deep ocean, the sails, rigging and sheets finely tuned, taking the strain. They were flying, at a breathtaking rate of knots! So too were the Pirates of Grannh. Their hydrodynamically shaped hulls sliced through the water. The back runners of the fleet were in peril!

The Milesian fleet were strung out in a wide sweeping arc, forcing ahead, surfing the swell, riding the gusting squalls, no matter how they pressed on, the Pirates of Grannh were catching!

Amergin estimated that the intercept line would put at least ten of the Milesian vessels in jeopardy.

"They will have to take up a rear guard action! There will be enough to make a stand!" he coldly expressed to his helmsman Xomas. They were both aware that these few will be like lambs to the slaughter. The sacrifice of the few for the greater cause! And so the scenario unfolded, a slow motion naval battle, an unbalanced engagement with a deadly end...

The lead vessels pressed on and on, in to the deep water of the Northern Ocean. They kept tacking in to the north-west for maximum advantage, away from the Pirates of Grannh, the passage around the Northern Province still their mission... This was a sea borne chess game, the fleet on an escape route and the Pirates of Grannh on an intercept course. The straggling rearguard the pawns, sacrifices to the end game...

More twin masted, red sailed ships appeared in the channels between the islands. They would soon be vastly out numbered! Amergin stood at the helm in a proud gesture of defiance. They sailed for the horizon, the only place of safety! Closer and closer the intercepting pirates came! Given the line and distance, the sea state and wind strength, now eight vessels were at risk! The captains of these vessels soon realised that their flight was futile. They could not out run the Pirates of Grannh!

They started to close ranks, take up defensive lines. On a hell for leather, escape run they would be picked off one by one. Their training, master mariner's one and all, and their experience in battle made even these eight ships a formidable foe. Eight ships gathered in formation. The remaining fleet still fleeing for the safety of the deep ocean, two of them were intercepted. A barrage of flesh and leather armour piercing arrows took down most of the crew. Grappling hooks and ropes tethered the vessels and they were both boarded. The remaining few were slaughtered, either spiked by eight foot pikes or sliced by slashing swords. These Milesians were hopelessly outnumbered, but they were valiant in defeat. Amergin could not look. He had to turn away. Milesians were being sacrificed and slaughtered and he could do nothing...

His strategy of sending Forsien to negotiate with the Shamen of Land's End and perhaps to form an alliance with the Pirates of Grannh had failed, too late for these brave souls. Amergin fell to his knees. He prayed to the Great Spirit. He prayed for the remaining eight vessels about to engage in a deadly battle. He prayed to the Guardians of Light. He used his Druidic powers to commune with the enlightened ones and most of all he called to Sceine to use her powers to save the desparate crews of the beleaguered vessels. Amergin felt the connection with the spirit world. Even here in the deep ocean, far from the portals of the Western Province, he was able to manipulate and penetrate the veil between the mortal realm and the spirit world. He felt the energy of the Guardians of Light and he could feel Sceine's presence, "My love, look around you! We are with you!" Amergin gazed up towards the heavens. He felt the rapturous presence of his destined one... he looked across the ocean as a pure radiant light filled the air. A radiant, brilliant, lifegiving, energising light poured from the site of the ancient fortress carved into the precipitous cliff. He felt the veil wrapping and enveloping him, bringing the spirit world in to the mortal realm. The altar was a portal!

The fortress carved out of the rock by an ancient race had become the stronghold of the Pirates of Grannh. This was a portal of great power beyond the realm of the dark one MacCuacht. Amergin heard the soothing encouragement of his beloved Sceine, "Go my love! You must sail northwards! Your crew will soon join you in your intrepid journey. Go!"

Amergin watched as the Pirates of Grannh, in shock and awe, put their weapons down and fell to their knees. As a man they prayed with hands clasped, dropping their heads in the direction of the ancient portal. They prayed to this new and powerful deity. They had been touched by the Light of the Divine, like the Shamen of Land's End far to the north they had been in the presence of the Guardians of Light. The Pirates of Grannh felt the life giving and this instance, the life saving force.

The defensive lines of the eight vessels broke formation, and they sailed free! The Pirates of Grannh were converted to the cause! Amergin smiled broadly, should Forsien have managed to strike an alliance with the Shamen of Land's End, they will be preaching to the converted here!

The eight vessels fully rigged sailed to join the Milesian fleet once more.

Reality soon returned with the oncoming weather front and the strengthening, backing wind. Xomas alerted Amergin, "A storm is brewing my lord! The wind is backing to the south-east! A gale is coming!" Amergin nodded in agreement, "We must head back to the coast. Maybe now we can take the route inside the islands! There we can find some shelter!" Xomas took the helm, gladdened to be making for calmer waters, and together with the eight rescued vessels.

They were all saddened and consumed with a bitter sweet emotion... they had lost two of their vessels and their crew, but the mission was still alive as were the crews of the eight vessels...

Amergin's attention was drawn to the islands and the distant portal. He still felt Sceine's presence...His mind drifted... Amergin knew Sceine was still in mortal danger...

CHAPTER NINETEEN:
THE DEITIES OF DUBH

"The connection grows stronger!" Sceine whispered under her breath. Her bond with Amergin was otherworldly, spiritual and verging on the Divine. But oh so sensuous, so real! Rapturous!

Sceine was overcome with emotion. Amergin was safe! She sensed he was sailing north once more!

She also sensed that MacCuacht was on his evil way. He marches to the Temple of Xhara. All she could do now was to pray for Amergin's safe journey and for him to come safely to her...

Should MacCuacht prevail... all was lost!

Sceine stood on the battlements of the high mountain fortress of Sliebh Mis in the panoramic beauty of the Iveare Mountains and the spectacular glory of the Western Province.

This day she would travel to the great Portal of Hushinish with some of her priests. She felt heartened by the connection with and help sent to Amergin. This was a day for communing with all the enlightened beings of the mortal realm, a day for bringing the Guardians of Light through the veil and in to the Western province and a day for ensuring that all her loyal subjects were safe. Sceine was cognisant of the dangers that could yet befall them.

Her party would travel light and quickly, half a day's journey to Hushinish. They would make camp for the night and return to the fortress of Sliebh Mis the following day. Sceine had already had the foresight to send a troop of elite guard to Hushinish. The great portals of the Western Province must all be protected at all costs...Sceine could not be away from the fortress of Sliebh Mis for long, she would be in grave danger away from the protective battlements of the mountain fortress. Sceine revelled in the march to Hushinish, a route of unimaginable beauty. She and her group, comprising of her priests and elite guard would take the high mountain ridge from Sliebh Mis.Then they would descend in to the Valley of the Mad.

Legend has it that an ancient race of invaders met predecessors of hers in a great sea battle. The invaders were then driven to this valley to lick their wounds and heal their despairing souls. Sceine could always feel a sense of desperation and loss in this place. The beauty and tranquillity of the valley could never appease the scale of losses incurred in that great battle. Sceine felt the despair again this time. Now though there was another presence, the evil emissaries of MacCuacht were approaching! She could not tell exactly, but she knew they were near. Whoever they were, they are able to cloak themselves from her clairvoyant powers. They must be strong!

Who are these beings!? Questions now about the journey to Hushinish running through her mind, should she return to Sliebh Mis? From here they would ascend to the Ridge of Thormond. To Sceine this ridge was an earthly representation of the veil. On the southern and western sides, views that swept on forever.Transcendant light shows as the sun illuminated distant mountain ranges and forests, then sweeping bays, golden beaches and the infinite ocean. On the northern and eastern side, a precipitous drop in to the glacially carved corrie, the dark mysterious depths of a mirror surfaced fresh water lake. Cold, frigid water as clear as crystal, only touched by sunlight at mid day and in the winter months always dark.

This lake, known as Dubh to the ancients, was a place of pilgrimage and sacrifice. Beside the lake was a slab of ancient, weathered red sandstone. Here, ritual ceremomies took place at the Summer Solstice to deities of harvest, fertility and abundance. The same slab was a site of gruesome atrocities and sacrifice at the Winter Solstice, appeasing the harbingers of death and disease. Trace memories of the ancient Winter Solstice rituals made Sceine's skin crawl. She questioned how any being, enlightened or not could possibly commit such atrocities. Animal and human sacrifices to appease dark deities! Her body shivered...

This time, as she walked to the knife edge Ridge of Thormond, the symbolism of the veil was even more poignant. A wrong step and she could tumble in to the depths, lost forever. Sceine and her priests took particular care on this journey, placing one foot at a time, carefully and meticulously, the ever changing, transforming light shows to the south and west guiding and enlightening them.

Soon they were across the ridge and were in the high wilderness of heather and moorland. They stopped at prehistoric boglands to cut turf in a time honoured ritual, a tradition for those on a pilgrimage to the Portal of Hushinish. Sceine and her party would have sufficient turf cuttings for a night of prayer and meditation. Pilgrims leave surplus turf cuttings in mounds of stacked and wind dried sculptures. This high and wind swept plateau was no place to be without fuel to burn, to warm the soul and ward off the creatures and demons of the night.

Two hours march, gently climbing to the highest outcrop, a rocky protrusion standing high and mighty, rugged and spectacular with panoramic views to elevate the soul.

Sceine felt she could touch the heavens at this place. She stood transfixed in front of the giant bluestone gatestones and capstone of the miraculous Portal of Hushinish, the most southerly of the great portals in the Western Province.

Sceine recalled her previous battle here with MacCuacht. This time the outcome could be very different. This night she would commune with Amergin, to strengthen him, to support him, to give him her undying love on his journey to intercept MacCuacht. Only together will they possibly be strong enough to match MacCuacht's dark powers. Should the priesthood of Xhara be corrupted the future of the Island of Destiny will hang in the balance!

She reached out to touch the gatestones. She could feel her powers strengthening, her connection with the Sea Druid Amergin growing. Tonight she will commune with him... her pulse raced... going beyond the veil with him was so real, so sensuous and so rapturous! She touched the gatestone, a charge of earthing pulsing energy surged through her very core. She was becoming one with Amergin... she felt him inside her..."Tonight my love!"...she came too as one of her priests took her hand...

The priest Diarmuid brought her in to a human chain surrounding the Portal, "The sunset arrives, my lady! We must be ready!" Diarmuid was the gentlest, most loyal of her priestly servants.

Sceine came back to the mortal realm momentarily. He stared in to her dilated eyes, her shallow rapid breathlessness... he had seen this state of bliss in her before. Her bond with Amergin was so strong! Diarmuid was being drawn in to an amber cosmos as the priesthood and the High Priestess Sceine chanted sacred, ancient verse. They felt the veil drawing closer. He tightened his grip on Sceine's hand, "We must contact the enlightened ones of the Western Province my lady! We must be united and ready for the onslaught of the dark one from the east!"

Sceine led the ceremony. As the orange and crimson red orb descended to the Western horizon, she chanted the ancient verse, her priests chanting in chorus. They all started rhythmically beating ceremonial bodhran. The wooden frame of the bodhran was carved from the sacred Rowan tree that grows from igneous outcrops in the Iveare Mountains. Each tree had its own unique grain and conductive, resonant qualities. The Rowan tree is the tree of true poetic inspiration. Stretched across the frame is the skin of the Sliebh Mis Mountain goat. The finished instrument of hypnotic timbre was beaten with a stick carved from the ancient Oaks of Derwydd.

The rhythm, the chanting, the slowly setting sun... they could all feel the veil drawing ever closer... radiant, pure light pouring forth from the portal as the glowing sun touched the distant shimmering horizon of the infinite Northern Ocean. The alignment with the setting sun produced a pulse of radiant, lifegiving energy that bathed the entire Western Province. The veil between mortal realm and spirit world touched all the great portals of the Western Province synchronicitously.

The High Priestess Sceine was able to go beyond the veil, travelling to all the portals at one and the same time. All the enlightened beings saw her ephemeral form emanating from the portals across the realm...

The rhythmic beating of the ceremonial bodhran called them to prayer and to commune with the High Priestess. Across the realm they joined in with the chanting chorus... Sceine spoke to them from beyond the veil... the Guardians of Light were amongst them...

As the sun slipped over the horizon, a hundred shades of roseate red and crimson pink exploded in to the heavens and over the ocean. They heard Sceine's words, "My loyal and enlightened subjects. My brothers and sisters, my priests and my brave warriors... I speak to you in the name of the Guardians of Light... I come to you with a message from beyond the veil... I urge you to be strong and faith ...the Guardians of Light are with you all. Be strong, be courageous! Use your wisdom and your powers to take on and defeat the dark forces that surely will arrive from the Eastern Province. I give you my love. I will be with you all as you battle for the cause of the Light! The Western Province shall prevail! The Guardians of Light will endure!"

Sceine inspired and motivated all her realm. That night the veil will remain close. The spirit world will be amongst the mortal realm.

The bodrhans continued to beat into the night. The turf fire burned brightly and intensely, generating heat and light and an occasional cascading galaxy of sparks in to the darkness of the clear, cool mountain air, the priests chanting their sacred verse to the enlightened world. The bodrhan beat hypnotically. One by one, the gathering fell in to a shamanic trance, communing with their ancestral spirits, seeking their wisdom and Divine guidance.

A mischievous gust of wind scattered sparks and turf ash high in to the night sky, momentarily a new constellation that drifted rapidly in to space. Sceine looked to the western horizon. The vestiges of the clear day that had gone, lingered there... a pale light in the sky. Now, a wall of grey cloud encroached towards them, imperceptibly at first, but steadily growing, steadily increasing in altitude and crabbing diagonally towards the north east. She was all too aware that this weather front was heading directly in to Amergin's path as he sailed around the outer islands.

Sceine stepped from the fire and into the darkness of the mountainside. She sensed a presence, but could not place it... a few more strides in to the darkness... there it was again! A powerful down beat of air... an indeterminate shape high above the radiant glow of the portal and the cascading sparks of the turf fire. Then a flash of white and further powerful down beats... an avian form disappeared in to the darkness... a white-tailed eagle?!

These high mountain ridges were the home of the magnificent white-tailed sea eagles, often seen cruising the thermals and the updraughts forcing up the mountain sides from the ocean. They would plummet to the earth in a violent high speed stoop, opportunistically grabbing their prey, an unsuspecting rabbit or scavenging on carrion.

Occasionally they would descend to the coast, particularly at the time of the salmon run, plucking the silver scaled kings of the ocean out of the blue. Viscious talons grabbing and never letting go.

Sceine had observed these splendorous birds of prey for a life time, but had never seen one at this place at night! Strange behaviour!

Stranger than even Sceine imagined... this was Eiru in search mode ...and she had found her prey!

Sceine was right, no normal White-tailed Eagle would venture here at night... but the shape shifting Witch of Hawardden would! Eiru soared at great speed along the Ridge of Thormond and soon alighted in the Valley of the Mad. Here her sinister sisters Fodha and Banba waited for her return.They heard her before they saw her.The pulsing beating wings and then a flash of white tail. Flesh ripping talons gripped a branch. Piercing eyes of the raptor flashed in the moonlight, a glimpse of the threateningly hooked beak and now a burst of photonic light transforming in to "human" form.

The three Witches of Hawardden were back together in their treacherous raven haired beauty.The three, clad in their cocooning silver dresses had intended to infiltrate the defences of the high mountain fortress of Sliebh Mis... this was for the better! Sceine was isolated with very few guards.This was surely the opportunity to take her!

Sceine's sixth sense warned her of the intruders... the avian incursion, "This must Eiru and her witches!" Unimaginable! Here so soon!

Sceine went to her loyal priest Diarmuid, stepping back in to the fire light, flickering forms still chanting in time to the hypnotic beat of the bodhrans. Diarmuid was transfixed in his shamanic trance, the veil between mortal realm and spirit world still merging and warping around the portal.

She must talk to Diarmuid! This could not wait! He was disturbed from his trance state, "My lady, why so anxious?!" He was still only half alert, he beckoned her in to the fire light. He had never seen her so troubled! "Sit, tell me please..."Sceine appreciated the concern of this good man, "We are in dire trouble Diarmuid!" She explained clearly and succinctly, "You will no doubt have heard of the Witches of Hawardden, the dark coven related to MacCuacht by blood."He nodded worriedly, as she continued, "This night they have tracked me down! Eiru in her shape shifting avian form was here! Only an hour ago I saw her! I felt her wing beats! She has surely gone to tell her raven haired sisters!"

This prospect scared Sceine, "We have been found Diarmuid! We are all in grave danger!" Sceine confided in Diarmuid. "In retrospect it was foolhardy and rash to come to Hushinish... at a time when so much is in the balance... when so much is at stake! To be caught here, away from Sliebh Mis and its mountain defences, how could this have happened!?"

Diarmuid comforted her, placing his hand on her shoulder, "Do you know if they are on their own? Have they come with the army of lost souls?"

"I sense only the three witches, but they are clever, they are cloaking their thoughts! Their magic is strong... there may be more of them... I cannot determine!" Sceine informed Diarmuid, "Now they have discovered us, they will send for the dark forces! They will realise this moment of weakness, while away from Sliebh Mis... they will come to take me!"

"Come with me my lady, you are the High Priestess of Xhara! You must pray with us at the Portal of Hushinish. We will commune with the Guardians of Light. They will surely come to your defence!"

Sceine realised this was her only chance! Without reinforcements, these few elite guard, and a few priests would be vulnerable to the dark forces that confront them. She remembered again the earlier confrontation with MacCuacht. At that time she was able to mobilise all the defences at her disposal. She had caught MacCuacht offguard and was able to drive him away from Hushinish. This time she had been caught offguard. She felt the awful presence of the dark one getting closer and closer...

The raven haired Witches of Hawardden, Eiru, Fodha and Banba, contrived to take advantage of this weakness. Eiru told her witches of the lake known as Dubh on the Northern side of the Ridge of Thormond, "The lake Dubh has been used by the ancients to summon the pagan deities of this land." She continued, "Deities of the Light during summer and harvest time. However, once the equinox has passed, the lake is in perpetual shade, and its deep, dark, lightless waters become the source of foul demons that bring only death, disease and destruction! The equinox is in two days time. We must go there and prepare for the time when the sun does not rise above the Ridge of Thormond. We can then release these harbingers of death upon Sceine and her loyal priesthood!" Pleased at her demonic plan she took the witches to a place where a rushing mountain stream carved a steep sided valley. This gorge led them to the lake known as Dubh, this mythical lake where the mirrored reflective surface was known by the ancients as a place where the veil was thin and easily manipulated. Depending on the season and the moods, either forces of the Light or the dark could be drawn through it...

That night, the night before the equinox, Sceine prayed and meditated with the priests. They descended in to an induced trance state, the veil between the mortal realm and spirit world surging back and forth. The Guardians escorted her through the portal. She travelled to be with her beloved and destined one. She saw him sailing for the protection of the outer islands, the encroaching weather front now begun to whip the tops off the cresting waves. She witnessed Endinou standing guard at the Quarry of Izion and Erhombu at the great Portal of Machlleth. There were other beings waiting offshore at the mysterious Magine Islands, Milidh and Scota waiting for the signal from Amergin. Others were defending the Temple of the Sun. Terese of the Xantha and her fearless warriors had been sent by Amergin to warn her of the oncoming Witches of Hawardden...

She journeyed back to Hushinish... the Witches of Hawardden were most certainly among them now.

She must commune with Amergin... night time now and he will soon be dreaming... he will soon descend in to the all familiar amber cosmos... she will guide him, caress him... she went to him beyond the veil... once more they shared a moment of blissful communion... their bodies wrapping, surrendering, giving, loving... this was their destiny... "Amergin my love!" in breathless rapture, "I come to you now! I need your wisdom!" Amergin stared in to her rich amber eyes... he was with her... "You have sent warriors to Sliebh Mis to warn me and help me. I fear it may be too late! The Witches of Hawardden are already here! They have me trapped! I am away from Sliebh Mis, at the Portal of Hushinish. We are nothing compared with the powers of the Witches of Hawardden and the forces of the dark."

Amergin understood, "I have sent Terese of the Xantha with a troop of amazonian warriors. Terese has magical powers of untested strength. She and her warriors possess unrivalled battle skills and guile and immense physical power. They have the element of surprise! They will surely tip the balance for you!" Sceine, comforted by this, returned to Hushinish, once more in the mortal realm ...

The amber cosmos dissipated... a voice from the mortal realm intruded... "My lord Amergin, the weather front arrives! We need your assistance! We are navigating through the islands and our watchman has seen a twin masted vessel with red sails on the horizon, and it closes on us all the time!"

Amergin began to come back to the mortal realm... thankful for the connection with Sceine... she now knows there is hope... Terese of the Xantha will be there soon! He returned back through the veil, back in to the mortal realm, he fell deep in to the amber cosmos, deeper and deeper in to the fleck in his beloved's eye... for the moment the connection broken...

Sceine was back at Hushinish... Where was Terese of the Xantha? Would their combined powers be sufficient to thwart the Witches of Hawardden?

Diarmuid gripped her hand tightly... the Portal of Hushinish glowed gently in the radiant Light...

Sceine had journeyed beyond the veil... How long had she been gone? It felt like an aeon, but the fire still burned brightly. Showers of sparks cracked and crackled in the gusting breeze. The priests still chanted sacred verse. The bodrhans beat on...

She unclasped her hand from Diarmuid's. The trance state was broken... Diarmuid could see she was somewhat reassured, but was still nervous and anxious... "You must tell me all, my lady! You have been beyond the veil for only seconds!" Sceine sat by the warming fireside, the strengthening breeze waffed a cloud of pungent and evocatively scented turf smoke in her and Diarmuid's direction. The weather front that disturbed Amergin from his dream was arriving here too! She covered her watering eyes with her hand... then she gripped Diarmuid's hand, "I have much to tell you!"...

CHAPTER TWENTY:
THE CURSE OF THE SIREN ZENDRIS

Amergin's decision to take shelter in the relative calm of the leeward side of the islands was the right one. The notorious Northern Ocean was living up to its reputation. A storm of significance headed their way... the open ocean would have been too perilous.

Amergin studied the Milesian fleet as they safely navigated the channel between the islands. He sent his blessings to his comrades lost at sea. His emotions running high, he tearfully turned to his helmsman, "We have lost many brave souls already on this journey Xomas... how many more, in the name of the Great Spirit, how many more?" Amergin pointed to the twin masted, red sailed vessel now entering the channel. "Even now the threat continues!"

"I have been watching them for a good while my lord," replied Xomas supportively, "They are tailing us, but making no headway. I think the Pirates of Grannh wish us no harm now. They have learned a salient lesson. I believe they are over seeing our safe passage now." Amergin was gratified to hear this. Even the Sea Druid's nerves were raw and exposed after what had befallen them. Only last night Sceine had come to him, distraught and fearful for her life. The distance across the Northern Ocean widened between them, when it should be narrowing!

Xomas deliberately interjected, breaking his leader's train of thought, "We require provisions my lord, fresh water at least," pointing towards the waterfall tumbling from a high escarpment in to the sheltered bay, "this would make for a perfect anchorage."

Amergin agreed, this place was very beautiful, soothing on the eyes and the mind. His mindset had been changed. The mission must continue and they must eat and drink! He thanked his helmsman Xomas for his constructive thoughts...

Amergin picked up the conch, giving three short sharp blasts. A message to the fleet that they were dropping anchor here, "We must take some time here Xomas. We must rest for a few hours. We will fish, hunt, collect water, recharge and rejuvenate. I will ask for the representatives of the Chapter of Mystics to hold a ceremony in honour of our comrades lost at sea. I will ask them to bless our fleet and pray for our safety on the journey to come." The fleet safely moored, Amergin noticed the red sailed vessel again, patrolling at a safe distance. Were they waiting for a moment to attack? He barked an order for the crew to make for the shore to gather provisions. Xomas helped in organising the landing parties. They were soon rowing away from the flagship. The word was spread. Soon many boats rowed to the shore...They would feast, meditate and pray that night. Watchmen were kept on high alert, just in case!

No sign of the Pirates of Grannh, Amergin began to relax. He joined his priest Xesu in meditation that evening. He was joined by the other priests of the Chapter of Mystics in the blessing of the boats. They all gave thanks for a plentiful source of fresh, pure water and a plentiful catch of mackerel.They all prayed for the souls lost at sea and prayed for distant friends and loved ones.

Amergin reflected on the situation, asking searching questions. The fiery embers of the newly lit fire sparked in to the night air. What of Eimbear and Gonne, the Machiavellian duo that would no doubt be forging a strong alliance with MacCuacht? He wondered at his decision to leave them at the Temple of the Sun. What of Scota and MIlidh at the great Portal of Sceilge on the Magine Islands? What of Endinou at the the Quarry of Izion? What of Erhombu in the ancient Woodlands of Derwydd? How far had MacCuacht marched on the path to the Temple of Xhara? He was consoled that his beloved Sceine would soon be joined by Terese of the Xantha and her amazonian warriors. So many questions, so few answers!

Xesu, the priest of the Chapter of Mystics took Amergin to one side. Amergin's perturbed expression told its own tale, "My lord, Sea Druid of Milesia, you must calm your thoughts, gather yourself and focus on your mission. You must have faith in your powers and faith in your fellow enlightened ones! The Guardians of Light are with you on your mission. The Island of Destiny relies on you being strong! The tribes of Milesia believe in you and your cause!"

Amergin smiled at Xesu, the priest doing what he was naturally able to do, "Thank you Xesu! I have been distracted!"They prayed and meditated together in silence, kneeling to face the ocean and the journey to come. The infinite Northern Ocean awaits them and beyond that the unknown perils of the Eastern Province...

The meditative silence was shattered by a yell from one of the watchmen perched high atop one of the masts of the vessels, moored in the gently undulating swell of the bay.

Xomas spotted the next vessel, "There my Lord! Another pirate approaches!" Sure enough, a second twin masted, red sailed ship appeared out of the gloom on the eastern side of the bay. Amergin and Xomas launched in to action, "Man the boats, return to your vessels! Make battle ready!" Within seconds the crews were launched and rowing furiously for their respective vessels. Amergin and Xomas were on the first boat to leave the beach, rowing as if their lives depended on it. Then something strange occurred... the incoming pirate ship took down their sails. They dropped anchor and raised a white flag... a universal symbol of peace. Amergin turned to Xomas, "They come alone. They are not attacking! They appear to be coming in peace!" Amergin was dumbstruck, the Pirates of Grannh! In peace! The encounter off the islands must have affected them. The presence of the Guardians of Light must have transformed them, questioned their whole belief system. But they were here so soon?! There has to be more to this...

They watched from the Milesian flagship as the pirates lowered a boat in the water... Amergin responded, "Come with me Xomas, select four rowers, we will go to rendezvous with them!" and he added advisedly, "wear armour, bring weapons, we must be prepared for treachery!" Xomas agreed, the reputation of the Pirates of Grannh was fiercesome. They are legendary for their trickery and guile.

In the quiet of the bay, the two clinker built row boats dipped their oars, silently sliding closer and closer to their rendezvous. Amergin too, had a white flag flying on the single mast of the rowing boat. Too much was at stake to let this unbelievable moment of appeasement pass by. Only a few hundred yards now... Amergin stood on the prow. He was barely able to make out who it was... Who were these people? Why do they make peace now?

In the gloom, a fiery beacon was lit on the approaching boat. A crucible holding what was probably whale oil burst in to flame. The flickering, intense flame cast a stark white light over the crew. Amergin could make out four people rowing, three standing. Amergin ordered for their storm lantern to be lit. Xomas lit the wick that dipped in to Sperm Whale oil. Oil that been rendered down from the liver of a stranded monster of the sea, that had beached on the Galician coast over a year ago now.Now giving them a flickering and slowly intensifying light. This meeting must be in the light, totally transparent, no skulduggery, no deception... Xomas strained his eyes, he could not believe what he was seeing, "My lord... there is Forsien!" Amergin was completely taken aback, now he understood!

"Our emissaries have done their work Xomas! Forsien returns with the Shamen of Land's End!"

Forsien was one of the rowers. The leader of the Pirates of Grannh stood on the prow. A fiercesome individual dressed in full battle dress, armed to the teeth, as were the other three rowers. They were clad in armour that seemed to have the texture of compressed and woven turf, an impenetrable fabric that absorbed all the ambient light. They were hard to see in this subdued light, they were so camouflaged. Their attire was an eclectic mix of acquired jewellery and assorted headwear, typical attire of pirates. Any exposed flesh was adorned with tattoos. They were fiercesome looking individuals! Their appearance was capped by matted dreadlocks coloured in natural dyes, wode and henna, sea dulse... all of which gave a chameleon appearance.

The clinker built wooden rowing boat came closer... they glided silently towards each other... the oarsmen pulled in the oars. The rowing boats, made of aged and seasoned oak, caulked with bitumen, touched each other.

Amergin spoke directly to Forsien, "You have returned! Welcome back!" he smiled appreciatively, "You have brought guests! You are all welcome too!" It was then that he caught sight of the leader of the Shamen of Land's End... and more noticeably, the presumed wife...

Amergin tried to remain diplomatic, but he could not take his eyes of this creature... a beautiful, beguiling female with long silver-grey dreadlocks, sweeping off delicately sculpted shoulders. Her porcelain flesh adorned with mesmerising tattoos that seemed to move and shimmer in the flickering light. Her gaze met his. He was totally entranced... "I am Zendris, the Queen of the Shamen of Land's End." She smiled, for she knew the power she had over men... "This is Magire, King and mighty leader of the Shamen of Land's End." Amergin had to tear his gaze away from her...He must compose himself...

Magire spoke directly to Amergin. He understood the powers of his wife, the Siren Zendris, who has swept many a powerful man off his feet and in many cases, swept them to their doom! "You are Amergin, Sea Druid of the Milesian tribes I presume!" boomed Magire, "Your emissary Forsien has told us of you and your nation's prophecy. I have met Antiem, the father of the one you are destined to be with...Sceine. She too has sent emissaries to negotiate with us. We have much to talk about... but first you must meet our host... meet Senet, the illustrious leader of the Pirates of Grannh."

Amergin strode forward to the side of the boat. Senet too stepped forward, and leaned over, offering his hand. Amergin shook his hand in a strong man-bonding fashion. Only hours ago they had been in mortal conflict. Two of the Milesian vessels and many of the crew had been intercepted, trapped, slaughtered and lost at sea. The vessels sunk without a trace and sent to a watery grave. He too had fled for his life and only the intervention of the Guardians of Light had saved him and the entire mission.

Now they shook hands... Senet too recognised the incongruity of the moment... until the arrival of Magire and Amergin's emissary, Forsien. He had been dead set on intercepting and taking Amergin.

This, even with the encounter with the Guardians of Light.Now, thankfully, with the wisdom offered by Magire, he saw the Sea Druid Amergin and his Milesian mariners as potential allies. The way of the Guardians of Light was perhaps their way...

This was a pivotal moment for Amergin's mission, but time was still their enemy, a poignant and apocryphal meeting in the context of the salvation of his nation and of the Promised Land and of his destiny. He must remain focussed, his resolve strong and undistracted...

Amergin was hypnotically drawn again to the sheer beauty and magnetism of Zendris... the words "And so it is written... and is in the stars" floated around and around in his mind... he must be strong... she drew him in... Her siren powers beguiling him... he heard himself speaking... "This night we must all gather. You must come to my flagship. We must negotiate and strategise... the dark one MacCuacht goes east... in the morning we sail..." Amergin was being drawn helplessly in... "We meet... tonight ... to bring our tribes together... until tonight..." Xomas pushed off, the boats disengaged. He felt the Siren's powers too... She smiled at both of them... "Until tonight ...!"

Forsien, their emissary, returned with them to the flagship. The rest of the cohort would join them later. Amergin was delighted to see his brave comrade in arms back. He will be invaluable on the journey ahead. His knowledge of the terrain useful... he instructed Forsien to meet with MacCuill, to pool their knowledge of the Northern Province and in particular the Shamen of the North. Amergin felt a strange draw to the Northern Province now. Unusually his steely resolve became unfocussed. His meeting with Zendris on his mind...

Xomas noticed the change. He felt the chemistry Amergin had with the Queen of the Shamen of Land's End. Xomas decide to join Forsien and MacCuill in their meeting... he too needed to find out about the Shamen of Land's End. They would soon be sailing in to their domain. The mission will depend on an unobstructed journey, clear in mind and clear in deed.

Xomas went to join Forsien and MacCuill. They were deep in discussion. "There was something very strange about Forsien's demeanour!" thought Xomas. What he heard positively disturbed him!

Forsien was trying to convince MacCuill that they should sail to Land's End and stay a while, to get to know the Shamen and the Northern Province, "Magire and Zendris are desirous of a pact with Milesia. The Northern Province could become a stronghold against the dark Sidhe!" he continued, "the Queen of the Shamen of Land's End desires a meeting with you personally, she would like to discover more about Sceine... plot a course for her MacCuill... take the fleet to Land's End and there all the forces of Milesia and the Shamen of Land's End can join together ..."

This was dangerous talk by Forsien! From one that is usually so loyal and would not normally do anything without first contacting Amergin. Xomas left the cabin without interrupting them. He had heard enough! He must inform Amergin! The moment had already come and gone... Amergin was not at the helm.

One of the twin masted, red sailed vessels had quietly pulled up alongside the Milesian flagship. Senet of the Pirates of Grannh was already stepping on to the gang plank. With him came the remainder of Forsien's cohort. It was so good to see them safely returned from the mission to the Northern Province. They stepped on board and made way for Magire and Zendris. These two made quite an impression with the dark silver-grey dreadlocks and their attire of woven fabric, with the texture of turf and its light absorbing, chameleon properties. Magire towered over most of the crew.

His physicality was impressive. His body was covered with startling tattoos. He intimidated most on first meeting. Zendris gracefully swept on to the deck of the flagship, a tall, elegant stunningly beautiful creature. Her long silver-grey locks captured and reflected the torchlight, her delicate porcelain complexion and the genetic tribal markings adorning the nape of her neck and shoulders... her life story and that of her ancestors covering her body. Some faded and discrete, others bold and new as if they were just forming. This meeting was at the behest of Zendris, she controlled the agenda. She appeared to control the warriors who came with her and the crew that she was newly meeting...

Xomas watched as Amergin greeted Senet, Magire and Zendris. He watched as the Sea Druid of the Milesians kissed the hand of this beauteous siren and knelt before her, "My lady!" Amergin could barely stutter the words... her power, her presence...

Xomas deliberately stayed away from the gathering. Someone had to remain clear headed! He suspected witchcraft at work... no male was safe in her presence... Xomas watched from a distance, he saw every one of his crew come under her spell. He must stay conscious and alert, clear headed and matter of fact. Once the defences were down, weakened by beauteous deception... you were hers! Like an infection, she would enter your bloodstream and suppress your resistance. No male was immune from her feminine essence and wiles. Only those aware of her witchcraft would stand a chance...

Once Amergin had kissed her hand and his lips touched her skin, he was taken, infected, obsessed by her. Zendris now controlled his mind, he was enslaved...

Magire looked on... this was so easy! The great Milesian Sea Druid entrapped! The Milesian forces and the Island of Destiny would surely be theirs! With Amergin on their side even the dark Sidhe might be subdued!

That night, the future of the Promised Land changed... potentially forever! Zendris had Amergin entrapped and enslaved. He could no longer commune with the Guardians of Light, without her consent. He could not commune with his beloved Sceine. Zendris controlled his emotions and his soul. She controlled his ability to journey beyond the veil. She had strategised and conspired with Magire and the Shamen of Land's End to undo the wrongs reaped by Antiem, the High King of Tuatha and his cruel and darkened son MacCuacht. MacCuacht had slaughtered many from the Northern Province who had come in peace to negotiate and form an alliance with Antiem.

Magire passionately gripped the hand of his siren wife, "revenge will be served cold and will be sweet!" Zendris smiled once more, her work was only just beginning!

Under the cover of darkness, Xomas climbed down the stern of the flagship and slipped in to the cool waters of the bay. Even the oceanic drift was cooling at this time of year and particularly at this time of night. Xomas swam strongly and quietly, breast stroking towards the other vessels in the fleet, moored to the south. He shivered not from the cold, but at the prospect of the fate that was befalling his leader and marine comrades. The mission was under threat, the Milesians were under threat! He must swim to the others! They must be alerted! The representatives of the Chapter of Mystics will surely know how to reverse the witchcraft at work?! He prayed to the Great Spirit that this would be done. He must act quickly! The siren Zendris will surely entrap and enslave others... she will soon be able to journey through and infiltrate the veil!

Xomas grabbed the anchoring rope of the first vessel and called to the watchman, "Throw me a line! I am Xomas, helmsman on the Sea Druid Amergin's flagship.Quickly!" He could not shout too loudly. The sound would travel in the cool of the night and his absence would be noticed. He soon found himself on the deck, shivering uncontrollably. He had been too long in the water! This was Eiremhou's vessel, Amergin's loyal brother, "Bring me your representative of the Chapter of Mystics... we have little time!" Eiremhou promptly ushered the priest Veryan to join Xomas and himself.

Whilst Xomas was being given dry clothes and a reviver of steaming hot dulse tea, he told them his story... Eiremhou had heard of the legendary, magical Shamen of Land's End, "It is not surprising to hear that they want this island for themselves, particularly with the horrific slaughter of their tribesmen, perpetrated on them by the dark one MacCuacht!"

Xomas agreed, slowly warming, his mind clearing, "However, they do not realise the potential danger of their actions! They believe that with Amergin under Zendris's spell, they will have the power to confront MacCuacht and the dark Sidhe... they are gravely mistaken!"

The priest Veryan stepped in to the light cast by the storm lantern, "They do not understand the significance of Amergin's destined meeting with Sceine... the veil will be compromised and weakened by their actions, the dark forces of the spirit world will have free reign! The siren Zendris must be stopped!" They all ardently agreed, Veryan asked, "What of Xesu, the priest of the Chapter of Mystics on board Amergin's flagship?" Xomas could not answer certainly, "I believe he is still of his own mind and powers. The siren Zendris is obsessed with Amergin... but others will surely follow...!"

"There is hope then... We must all pray that Xesu can take Amergin beyond the veil!" Veryan continued, "He must commune with the Guardians of Light in the spirit world. Only then can the spell of the siren Zendris be broken!" Veryan implored them, "Join me in prayer! Xesu will hear us. He will know what to do! This is Amergin's only hope!"

The crew of the Milesian flagship slowly fell under the spell of the siren Zendris. Her ancient magic was overpowering them, one by one. She purred at her conquests, "With Amergin in our power the Milesian destiny will become our destiny!" Later that night, Amergin drifted in and out of a tormented sleep. His ability to journey beyond the veil weakened. He saw his beloved Sceine, but could not reach her... he felt his destiny slipping away... he touched her fingertips, but she kept drifting away from him. Like a drowning man, clutching at the safety of dry land, but always falling back in to the ocean. "Sceine my beloved, where are you!?"... He felt his hand being caressed, his brow being kissed, gentle fingertips touching him... the breath of an angel. Her elegant, graceful body wrapping around his... taking him to ecstacy... they came to an orgasmic climax together.

"Open your eyes my beloved... I am with you now!" The voice! Under her spell... he stared in to the eyes of the siren Zendris! He was enslaved, under her power, "Take me beyond the veil with you Amergin! Take me ...!"

Amergin came too... someone was vigorously trying to waken him! "My lord, wake up! You are under the spell of the siren Zendris! You must resist!!" Xesu knew that once Amergin had taken Zendris beyond the veil, it would be too late for him. Amergin would be under her powers forever!

The dream was ending... the face of Zendris disappearing in to the mist. His eyes open, the vision was gone. Amergin was back in the mortal realm. A split second later and he would have been taken through the veil with Zendris, enslaved forever..."My lord Amergin! Hear me! Come back to us!" Xesu now placed the palm of his hand on Amergin's forehead, "Great Spirit hear our prayers bring back your faithful servant Amergin! Bring him back to the powers of the Guardians of Light, for he is the chosen one, the Sea Druid Amergin. Destined to meet Sceine, the High Priestess of Xhara, the Princess of the Western Province, together they are destined to bring the Guardians of Light to the mortal realm! Hear us Great Spirit! Hear us ...!"

Amergin was slowly returning, his soul drifting in an amber cosmos. Gently he was coming back to the mortal realm. A familiar voice this time, "Come back to me Amergin... I am yours!" He opened his eyes... a vision of Sceine! He was awake and back in the mortal realm, "Xesu! How! Where am I?" Confused and in a state of unreality... he began to understand, "Zendris, the siren?!"

"She has bewitched you my lord, entrapped you!" Xesu explained, "You must protect your mind! You are still in danger most of the crew are still in her power! Come with me... we will take a rowing boat, we will return to the fleet!" Stealthily they crept to the stern. Mac Cuill met them there. He had already descended the rope ladder and waited for them in the boat. Dipping the oars quietly and surrupticiously in the calm, dark ocean, they glided away from the flagship. No watchmen saw them. Amergin reticently pulled on an oar... he was abandoning his own ship! The last resort of any captain! With each stroke, new blood coursed through his veins. His mind clearing... he knew he was doing the right thing... the mission depended on it. But abandoning his own crew galled him? Have they all been bewitched?!

"Fifty boat lengths to the starboard,"Xesu called quietly in to the darkness, "The fleet!" They had escaped the clutches of the siren! Now they must free their crew!

Eiremhou greeted Amergin, "My brother, you are safe! Praise the Great Spirit! Throw them a line!"

Xomas went to Amergin, "My lord you are back, how…what of the siren?!"

"No time to explain my faithful Milesians! We must act! Our crew relies on us!" he retorted "Call for all the priests of the Chapter of Mystics to gather!" Veryan on Eiremhou's vessel raised the sacred conch to his lips and sounded a low resonant note, calling all the faithful to prayer. The storm beacon was lit, a sign that this vessel would be the place for the gathering.

Very soon boats were launched. Many priests in their long flowing robes came on board, to be greeted by their Sea Druid Amergin, "We go to the flagship. Prepare your minds! Magire and Zendris will be waiting for us. We go to free our crew!"

The priesthood prayed and meditated. They called on the spirit world and the Guardians of Light to protect the fleet and the crew on the flagship. Amergin could feel the veil drawing closer. He felt the radiant energy wrapping around Eiremhou's vessel. They sailed with a cloak of Divine protection.

Amergin looked on in wonderment as the vessel began to move in a current of Divine origin. The wake of the boat left a stream of glowing phosphorescence.

Magire and Zendris had heard the resonant blast of the conch, calling the priesthood to prayer. They were waiting for the Milesians. Zendris was enraged at her crew for allowing the Sea Druid Amergin to escape. They all feared the wrath of the siren Zendris. They had seen even the most rational, reasoning being turned in to a gibbering, demented fool, when the full force of her mind altering magic was unleashed upon them. Zendris knew her deception was done. She doubted whether she could match the combined powers of the Chapter of Mystics and the Guardians of Light. "Someone will pay for this!" even Magire shrivelled in the presence of his enraged Queen, "Bring the Milesian crew to me!"

One by one they were tied to the mast and lashed mercilessly. The "cat of nine tails" cut them to the bone. They were whipped to an inch of their lives. They cried out in to the night for mercy. "We will take this ship and its crew hostage!" exclaimed Zendris, "We will not submit to these Milesians!" Magire prepared the flagship for battle. He feared they would be boarded, "We must make an example of one of their own!" At random, one of the tortured and now demented crew was selected. He was forced to climb the rigging and go to the extreme limit of one of the cross spars. Here he was tied, bound and gagged and a noose placed unceremoniously around his neck.

Magire and Zendris of the Shamen of Land's End, waited expressionless and unfeeling. They showed no fear, no emotion and no compassion. The crew all watched on in horror.

The Milesian fleet drifted serenely closer in a current of luminescence. Zendris sensed they were immune now from her ancient magical powers. The vessels were cloaked in the Light of the Divine drawn through the veil by the priesthood of the Chapter of Mystics. "They are immune to our sorcery!" Zendris observed, "but are they immune to our reign of terror?!"

Magire could see the boarding parties preparing. They were armed to the teeth. They were completely outnumbered! "We shall see my Queen!" and with this he signalled with a downward gesture for the terror to commence, The poor hapless Milesian crewman was doused in whale oil, a highly flammable and noxious substance. A naked flame ignited the oil and he was pushed from the top most cross spar. His necked snapped in mid scream and he was left a dangling, twitching human torch.

"No!!!" a collective expression of utter horror and condemnation swept through the crew on the flagship and the oncoming fleet. They were all shocked and appalled!

Before Amergin could react, he saw the next of his crewmen being ushered mercilessly to the crow's nest and out on to the top most cross spar. Then bound and gagged and a heavy rope noose placed around the exposed flesh of his neck. He recognised Jonnh, one of his most able seamen. Ironically, he was always the one to rely on when the storm sails had to be unfurled, and someone had to scale the rolling and pitching rigging in the teeth of a gale. "Jonnh!" was now the collective cry from his fellow mariners. All eyes turned to Amergin... he knew at that moment that this awful human blackmail could not continue. This was stalemate! Leadership required now...

Amergin called to Xomas, "Drop anchor! Lower the sails! Tell the boarding parties to stand down!"

The priesthood of the Chapter of Mystics ceased chanting and meditating. There was an awful silence, a terrible dread that Jonnh, now doused in pungent and flammable oil, would be next...

Time elapsed, and more time... nothing happened... was Jonnh safe?

Amergin gave his instructions. He realised that a bigger sacrifice was required, "We must leave this place Xomas! Prepare to sail!" Amergin had acted, he must leave the flagship, leave the crew and they must sail on... the mission demanded it, the prophecy demanded it, his humanity required it...

The only way to save the crew of the flagship was a tactical retreat. This battle was lost! There would be many more to be fought...

CHAPTER TWENTY ONE:
THE KILLING MOON

One day, and one night and the equinox will be upon this land. The time when day equals night, a time when the growing season ends and the season of the dark begins.

One more night and the track of the autumn sun would dip behind the Ridge of Thormond, casting a perpetual shadow on the deep and mysterious lake known in the Annals of Tuatha as "Dubh."

Legend has it that all the pagan deities of the dark could be summoned after the equinox. Eiru understood the significance of the equinox. It was the moment when the veil touched the mortal realm. Certain places, certain portals could be used to transcend the veil, to go beyond and commune with the spirit world. The lake "Dubh" was such a place. One day and one night and she would go beyond the veil to summon the demons and denizens of the spirit world.

In league with the Witches of Hawardden, the dark forces would be irresistible. Sceine with her diminished force would be no match. Sceine has been careless. Away from the impregnable battlements of the high mountain fortress of Sliebh Mis, she is vulnerable, without reinforcements and without the destined one they call Amergin. She is as good as taken...

Eiru confided in her raven haired coven, "The Portal of Hushinish is in the control of the Guardians of Light. Soon we will be able to overcome Sceine and the demons and denizens will pour forth from the portal!" The three witches looked on as the tracking sun scraped slowly along the Ridge of Thormond, only hours now before the equinox. Eiru, Banba and Fodha stepped out on to the weathered ancient red sandstone slab... the place of ceremony and sacrifice. The festival of harvest time, a celebration of abundance and plenty, had come and gone. Now was the fallow time, of die back and retrenchment, a time when live sacrifices were sent to their doom in the eerie, reflective depths of Lake Dubh. A ritual perpetuated through the centuries to appease the pagan gods of winter.

"You can almost touch the veil now!" thrilled Eiru, "The time is close!" She thrust her arms aloft as if channelling from the depths of the mirrored lake, "I go now to find our live sacrifice!" With this, pulses of photonic light vibrated and swirled around her silver cocoon clad form. Banba and Fodha stepped back, away from the red sandstone slab to watch their sister transform. Waves of energy pulsing and morphing in the gathering gloom, Eiru became airborne, once more a mighty raptor and fierce predator. With a few wing beats, she circled the lake and followed a steep sided glaciated valley to the north and was out of sight. She flew high on the end of the day thermals, looking for her prey, watching for movement. Live animal sacrifices had been forbidden in the Western Province under the reign of Antiem. His daughter, the High Priestess Sceine, had continued with the tradition.

"The pagan gods of Dubh must be very hungry!" thought Eiru mischievously, "What can we find to appease them and summon them at the Equinox?!" She flew higher and higher, spiralling in the updraughts, covering huge distances in a wing beat. Where the high sided valley opened out in to rolling grassland, surrounded by ancient deciduous woodlands... She saw movement! Human prey!

"Even better!" rejoiced Eiru, "The pagan gods of Dubh will feed well this Equinox!"

A thousand feet below on a track winding along the edge of an ancient Oak grove, Terese of the Xantha and her troop of amazonian warriors marched steadily on... they were in a strange land, looking for land marks described to them by Erhombu, the Guardian of the ancient Woodlands of Derwydd. The high glaciated steep sided valley in the distance was such a land mark. Terese of the Xantha looked upwards, scanning the horizon... She too saw movement!

In the gathering dusk, the sun cast its final glowing remnants on to the far side of the high glaciated valley. The golden rustic glow on the high mountain ridge slowly disappeared in to shadow. Terese was aware of the poignancy of this sunset, "Tomorrow the equinox!" she informed her sisterhood of Xanthans. They had all been trained by Scota, the Queen of Milesia and the High Priestess of the Xanthans, mother of the Sea Druid Amergin. Scota had given them the knowledge of the occult and the wisdom to interpret the signs in nature. They knew that at the time of the equinox the veil was at its most vulnerable, when the dark forces of the spirit world fought to intrude in to the mortal realm. In the last glimmers of Light on the far side of the valley... a movement! A flash of white!

Terese pointed, "Look yonder! High over the ridge! A Sea Eagle spiralling in the updraughts! All the Xanthans watched now... here was an apex predator at work... the ultimate hunter!

The Xanthans too had finely tuned hunting and battle skills. They had all been trained by Milidh the King of Milesia, father to the Sea Druid Amergin. Each of the Xanthan warriors had been scrupulously selected for their physical and mental strength. Generation upon generation of training had turned the Xantha in to a feared and respected force. An iconic mixture of legendary power and strength combined with stunning beauty. The troop of Xantha stepped onwards, along the meandering track.

They kept gazing upwards as the magnificent bird of prey swooped and glided in the evening thermals. The sea eagle flew so high now that it became a speck in the gathering dark. The shadows finally consumed the mountain ridge and the raptor vanished out of sight. Terese shared her concern with Syra, her faithful and loyal second in command, "We must be vigilant! This raptor is no ordinary predator... the wing span is massive... woman nor beast is safe!"

The track steepened, progress became slower. Their number stretched out. Communication became more difficult. The path meandered in and out of thinning deciduous woodlands. The ground was strewn with moss and lichen covered boulders, limestone rock formations made their progress even slower. The line thinned out even more...

This was the moment Eiru, in ultimate predator mode, had been waiting for!

The line of marching Xanthans had spread out even more. In the evening gloom she was invisible. She came in fast over the ridge. Feathering wings, now furled, she fell in a free falling stoop. She fell from a dizzying height at break neck speed, targeting the last in the line of the marching Xantha. The last one, the straggler, just out of view from the others, skirting a massive moss and lichen covered limestone boulder.

The timing, the moment, perfect! Executed with precision! No one saw her coming! No one heard the attack until it was too late! A feather muffled thud and a shocked yell, the Xantha Nesta had been knocked unconscious and was taken...

Far too late, they saw the White- tailed Sea Eagle climb over the tree line, powerful wings beating and carrying the forlorn, drooping form, higher and higher in to the darkening sky.

"Nesta!" they cried out collectively. Terese recognised the distinctive wing beats and the avian form, "Eiru! It can't be!" The one that had saved her from the clutches of her evil partner MacCuacht now turned predator.

All the Xantha watched as Eiru flew back along the steep sided glaciated valley. Encumbered now by the weight of a living being, ready for sacrifice at the equinox, she flew lower. Nesta came round.

She was struggling to breath in the grip of the tightly clasped talons. There was no escaping, but her movement was seen, "She lives!" one of the Xanthan warriors yelled. "We must follow her! We will march through the night!" Terese commanded, "We will find her, whatever it takes!"

They marched quicker now... Terese was sure of a connection to the coming equinox. She was equally sure that Sceine was in imminent danger.

Eiru flew above the tree line and the steep sided valley, the weight of her prey taking its toll. The lake Dubh came in to view. Her wing beats more laboured now. Once more, she could feel the veil getting closer and thinner as the Equinox approached. She flew low over the mirrored surface. Eiru could see her own reflection and marvelled at the winged predator she had become! She swooped and dipped the tips of her wings touching the water, sending ripples across the lake.

Banba and Fodha saw Eiru, her prey drooping helplessly from her gripping talons, "She has the live sacrifice!" hissed Banba, "Only hours now until the Equinox!"

They lit the fire on the red sandstone slab, to greet Eiru on her return. The reflected firelight guided Eiru. She landed gracefully with her prey in tact. "A prize specimen!" drooled Fodha, as Eiru released the Xanthan from her grip. Nesta was tied and bound to a stake driven in to the sandstone slab.

"She is one of the Xantha!" Eiru clarified, "They march towards the lake now!" Eiru morphed back in an avalanche of photons…the three raven-haired Witches of Hawardden back together, "Terese of the Xantha marches to rescue Sceine... but she will be too late!"

The full Equinox moon now rose over the Ridge of Thormond. This was the time when the celestial orbs were in alignment. The time when day equals night and the season of the dark begins.

Sceine sensed that the Witches of Hawardden would use this day to try to intrude through the veil, to bring the demons and denizens of the dark in to the mortal realm. She could not return along the Ridge of Thormond, the route was too exposed. She would stay at the Portal of Hushinish with her priests and summon the Guardians of Light. Sunset would be the tipping point, the time when the season of dark would prevail, the time when the spirit world was at its most vulnerable to intrusion by the dark Sidhe. She instinctively knew this would be the time... the time known in the Annals of Tuatha as the "killing moon." The next time the moon rose over the Ridge of Thormond could be the time they meet their nemesis.

Sceine and her few loyal priests gathered around the Portal of Hushinish. They were trapped here and they were all aware of the dark powers mobilising. Sceine, the High Priestess of Xhara and Princess of the Western Province began the ritual incantations. She called to the spirit world beyond the veil, "Here us Great Spirit! Bring your Guardians of Light to protect us from the evil that arrives!"

Diarmuid, the most loyal of her priests and good friend, took up the ceremonial bodrhan, beating it rhythmically. All the priests repeated Sceine's chant, calling beyond the veil. They would chant all night, summoning the Guardians of Light... Way below in the contours of the high glaciated valley, marched Terese and her Xanthan warriors.

They all saw the aura of The Divine spilling down from the Ridge of Thormond, pouring from the Portal of Hushinish, pouring like an ethereal waterfall in to the darkness below."Sceine! We have found her!" Terese was heartened. They were still a good few hours away... and they must first rescue Nesta! She called to her Xanthans to keep moving, time is of the essence!

The track kept rising, becoming more and more arduous, boulders strewn everywhere. Ahead of them rose a seemingly impassable barricade of misshapen and jagged boulders. Water gushed through every crack and crevice. The stone surface was incredibly slippy. They struggled to find handholds and footholds. Occasionally one would slip and whince as bone met cold, hard rock.

The barricade of sandstone boulders was the result of millennia of land slips from the steep glaciated mountain sides. There was no sunlight now, sunset long gone. Behind the barricade was a vast, cold, deep and dark body of mountain water. Terese was the first to scale the barricade of boulders. She stood on one of the ancient weathered, red sandstone boulders. The silver-black reflective surface of Lake Dubh stretched out before her.

A shiver ran down her spine. She could feel the presence of evil. The tipping point was nearing...

The brooding lake...heaven in the summer months, hell in winter, dark, dense cold water, deep and mysterious, ice melt from thousands of years ago. Over this dark, cold layer, flowed clear, fresh mountain water energised and sparkling as it tumbled down the steep mountain sides. This fresh mountain water flowed in silver streams over the body of dark aqueous.

Terese helped each one of her brave and beautiful Xanthan warriors over the last slippy boulders.

Now, they all stood on a giant, weathered ancient red sandstone boulder, a remnant of the Ice Age, wedged in to the barricade by the force of ancient glaciers. They were dwarfed by the high ridges and steep slopes plummeting in to the dark depths of Dubh. Across the silver-black surface of the lake, a flicker of firelight, way over on the other side... the light beckoned them and teased them.

"This is the lair of the Witches of Hawardden!" Terese and her sisterhood searched for a way across the mysterious lake. There appeared to be no way! No path and the mountain sides too steep! How will they rescue Nesta?! They were so close...Terese sensed the connection with the Equinox. She had been told of the tales of the killing moon.

Nesta was priority, then to Hushinish to help Sceine. This moon rising over the Ridge of Thormond could be Nesta's last! She could be the live sacrifice! "But how do we get there, how do we save Nesta from an awful end?!"

Erhombu, the Guardian of the Woodlands of Derwydd, had told Terese of the spirits that live in the mountains near Hushinish, spirits that could be summoned on a full moon by prayer and the sounding of the hunting horn. The killing moon was a full moon, "This is our only hope!" despaired Terese. She confided with her faithful, explaining their predicament. The distant firelight burned brighter...

The Xantha collectively fell to their knees. They prayed to the Great Spirit. The radiant glow of the Portal of Hushinish, and then an ethereal mist poured endlessly down the steep mountain side from the Ridge of Thormond. The mist crept quietly over the dark water...

The Xanthan warriors still in deep prayer, Terese took hold of her hunting horn given to her by Erhombu. She pursed her lips and with all her breath sounded the hunting horn. The piercing, echoing sound resonated through the gloom. Filling her lungs, she blew again. A wall of sound reflected and reverberated off the steep mountain sides. The ethereal mist floating over the lake thickened and was now pouring like a river towards them. "The veil is so close now!" thought Terese.

The sound of the hunting horn pervaded the mountain air. Sceine turned to Diarmuid at the Portal of Hushinish, "Terese of the Xantha?! It must be!" Diarmuid agreed, "We must pray to the Great Spirit!"

On the far side of Lake Dubh, the three Witches of Hawardden waited for the killing moon to rise above the Ridge of Thormond. Through the pitch black gloom they heard the sound of the hunting horn, "Terese of the Xantha!" they cackled in unison. They stoked the fire that burnt more brightly on the ancient weathered sandstone slab. Sparks and smoke rose in to the cool night air. Flickering light cascaded over the silver-black lake. Nesta, the Xanthan hostage, had to turn her head away.The heat of the fire was too much for her to bear. The sparks burned her eyes, smoke nearly cauterised her windpipe and seared her lungs. At the sound of the hunting horn she managed a smile, "Terese, I knew you would come!" Nesta twisted her body towards the sound, but the ropes binding her cut deep in to her flesh. The binding around her neck was so tight she could barely breath.The friction of the rough hemp rope rubbed her skin away, "Come soon Terese!" she coughed in to the thickening smoke.

The three witches were oblivious to the river of mist flowing across the lake. The raging inferno signifying the coming of the killing moon blinded their night vision.

The veil gets closer...

Under the blanket of ethereal mist the Guardians of Light sent their messenger, "the ferryman of Dubh." The ancients used the ferryman to journey beyond the veil, to appease the pagan deities of Lake Dubh. Hooded in a white shroud, his face is never seen. Legend has it that if you happen to gaze upon the ferryman's face then you will journey beyond the veil, never to return...

Terese of the Xantha watched in wonder as the high prowed vessel, made of aged, blackened bog Oak, decorated with exquisite carvings and ornamentations, sailed out of the ethereal mist.

The white shrouded ferryman remained silent as he punted the vessel to shore. He gestured serenely to the Xantha to get on board. Under the blanket of ethereal mist, they would be punted across the silver-blackness of Lake Dubh...

The river of mist poured slowly, drifting over the silver-black surface of Lake Dubh. Silently, effortlessly, the ferryman punted them towards the now raging ceremonial fire, each dip of the punting pole keeping them in pace with the camouflaging blanket of mist. They could see, but were not seen, the intense fiery glare of the sacrificial pyre effectively blinding the witches.

Slowly, Terese and the Xanthans began to make out three sinister figures tending to the blaze. The three raven haired witches in silver cocoon dresses, shimmering and reflecting in the flickering flames. They chanted and swayed in a ritual ceremony communing with the pagan deities and summoning the demons and denizens of Lake Dubh. The killing moon nearly in position. Nesta's time in the mortal realm coming to an end...

The veil now thinner than ever, Sceine and her priests prayed to the Great Spirit. They sent messages beyond the veil to all the enlightened ones. Their message to Terese of the Xantha giving their support and telling her to stop the live sacrifice at all costs...

Terese sensed the presence of Sceine and knew she had sent the ferryman to help them save Nesta.

The concealing mist still poured over the lake. The wind gusted down from the Ridge of Thormond and in that moment as the mist cleared Terese caught a glimpse of Nesta, tied to a stake on the ancient red sandstone slab. The vortex of wind and ethereal mist sucked hot ashes and embers in to the dark night. Sparks and cinders enveloped the witches, stinging and burning them, singeing their raven locks and discolouring their silver cocoon dresses. Nesta too took the full brunt of this vortex of fire. She cried in to the dark, "Terese! Help me! I beg you!" Nesta sensed the closeness of Terese and her sister Xanthans...

Terese was helpless though, she could not go in boldly and brazenly, the powers of the witches were too great. She would have to wait and hope for a moment of weakness...

The ethereal vortex of wind went as soon as it came. The three Witches of Hawardden restoked the fire. Eiru glowered at Nesta as if to say "Your time has come!" In that moment the full equinox moon seemed to be brighter than ever. The full, rotund orb appeared to perch on the distant Ridge of Thormond and follow the track of the ridge towards the Portal of Hushinish. "The killing moon, the time is nigh! When the moon is directly over the Portal of Hushinish, we shall give our live sacrifice to the deities of Dubh!"

Terese observed the witches from the obscurity of the mist. They were cloaked from the senses of the witches whilst in the mist. They dare not venture closer. She watched as one of the raven haired ones untied the binding around Nesta's feet, then her hands and lastly her neck. Nesta crumpled in to a heap. Her circulation had slowed, and her limbs had no sensation. She was a Xanthan though. She soon rallied as blood circulated through her body. As soon as she was able to stand, she was taken at knife point to the edge of the ancient red sandstone slab.

Nesta looked at the mirrored siver-black lake. She could see her own reflection in the fresh mountain water circulating and eddying like mercury on glass over the blackness of ancient glacial melt water. The killing moon tracked remorselessly on... her demise was nearing.

Terese watched helplessly, "How could she save Nesta?!"

The moment was now... the sacrifice...

On Eiru's instruction, Banba took the dagger held at Nesta's jugular vein and in one swift downward and then slicing motion severed her Achilles tendons. First the left, and then the right, Nesta screamed in agony... Terese turned away in horror... not before she saw Nesta again crumple, and in a forward rolling motion fall headlong in to Lake Dubh. The moon was now at its zenith. The mirrored surface of the dark depths of the lake, the veil between the mortal realm and the spirit world, was broken. Shapes and forms began to appear from the deep dark aqueous...

Nesta's Achilles tendons were sliced cleanly. Bright crimson blood mingled with the fresh, surface mountain water. She could not swim with her tendons severed. She sank quickly, the cold, dark glacial waters consuming her. The deeper she sank, the colder and denser the water became, the slower she sank. Nesta was able to use her own buoyancy to flounder to the surface, gulp a lungfull of oxygen and sink for the last time through the highly oxygenated surface, mountain water. Her hand stretched out above the surface in a final gesture of helplessness. She was returning back to the denseness. As her fingertips disappeared beneath the surface... Terese stripped off her weaponry and armour and dove in...

A powerful swimmer, she was soon at the place where Nesta's hand had waved helplessly. In a shallow dive through the silver-black surface, she saw Nesta sinking in slow motion in to the denseness. Time stood still, the dark Sidhe gathered beyond the veil...

All of the Xantha held their breath with Terese as she dove deep, through the now blood red surface and down in to the cold blackness. The raven haired witches smiled at each other in firm belief that Terese was too late...

The signs were in alignment, the live sacrifice made, the hungry deities of Dubh fed. The veil between the mortal realm and the spirit world shifted. The demons and denizens began to awaken.

Even the mirrored surface of Lake Dubh grew darker and darker. The pure radiant light from the Portal of Hushinish began to dim. The killing moon continued on its remorseless track along the Ridge of Thormond. The ethereal mist began to dissipate, to reveal all the Xanthan warriors peering in to the depths over the side of the high prowed, black bog Oak vessel. The white hooded, shrouded ferryman pointed to the far side of the lake. He began to dip the punting pole. He was returning back beyond the veil. They all would be taken to join the dark Sidhe... never to return!

"Terese!!!" they all yelled, "Come back to us!" Deep below, in the denseness, all seemed lost. Terese could no longer hold her breath. Nesta, although still living, haemorraghed volumes of blood.

Deeper and deeper, time still in slow motion, Terese contemplated her life, resigned herself to her death and resigned to the dark Sidhe taking over the mortal realm... she felt a hand grabbing her wrist and an amber cosmos began to fill the cold, dark denseness... A brilliant shaft of radiant Light pierced the deep... Inexorably they began to rise! First in slow motion, then ever faster! A vision of beauty, an enlightened being... Sceine… and with her the Guardians of Light! Rapidly now, they rose to the surface... Terese with her amazonian strength kicked and swam to the silver, now reddened with blood, surface. The darkness below turning to a rich amber.The demons and denizens releasing them, returning back to the spirit world, going back beyond the veil...

Terese and Nesta burst through the surface of the highly oxygenated mountain water, filling their lungs with fresh, sweet, cold mountain air. Terese swam with the limp, rag doll body of Nesta, towards the high prowed, black bog Oak vessel, occasionally stopping to give the kiss of life while she swam away from the ancient, weathered, red sandstone slab. Xanthan warriors grabbed and hauled them in to the boat... warning them not to look at the ferryman! "Beware his gaze!" Terese continued with the kiss of life, whilst wrapping her warming body around the still limp and cold body of Nesta. Others tended to her, tying tourniquets around her still bleeding heels. Terese prayed to the Guardians of Light, "Bring this brave Xanthan back to the mortal world!"

With a gasping intake of air of amazonian proportions, Nesta came back from near death... the live sacrifice had failed!

Once more an ethereal mist slowly poured over the surface of the mirror surfaced lake, the dip, dip of the shrouded ferryman, punting them deeper in to its cloaking camouflage.

Three raven haired witches were left cursing their tormentors. They had been thwarted by the combined powers of enlightenment. The Portal of Hushinish shone its radiant Light even brighter than ever. The Guardians of Light, the saviours and redeemers of the enlightened ones prevailed for the moment...

The raven haired Witches of Hawardden, embattled and even more embittered, retraced their steps.They would rest that night in the ancient deciduous woodlands of the Valley of the Mad. The witches would return... their darkness knew no bounds. Each of them vowed to the core of their sinister souls, that they would reap revenge. Sceine had eluded death this time...

CHAPTER TWENTY TWO:
THE CAPE OF WRATH

In sanguine resignation Amergin took the helm once more, but it was not the flagship helm. The crew hauled the anchor in, but it was not his crew! They had been abandoned! Distraught and distressed, but he was not distracted. The mission must continue...

All the fleet up anchored and made ready for the open sea. In this quiet windless bay, the oarsmen heaved in synchronicitous strokes. The Milesian vessels edged nervously past and away from the eerily quiet flagship. MacCuacht had sown the seeds of this treachery. His conniving and deception and finally the murderous onslaught on the Northern Province had wrought this vengeance.

Xomas understood the pain Amergin was feeling, he could see it in his face. The Sea Druid will have to find the inner resolve from deep within, "My lord, have the courage of your convictions. The nation depends on you." Xomas tried to console and sooth Amergin's conscience, "We will return to retrieve the flagship. We will undo the spells of the siren Zendris! We will save the crew! Go below my lord, go and pray, meditate, find your strength again. Go! The night is long... I will take the helm."

The first stirring of an ocean breeze, flags fluttered and then straightened and the unfurled sails filled. Still the prevailing South Wester pushing them on, slowly at first and more quickly once they sailed out beyond the headlands and in to the beckoning open sea.

The Milesian flagship remained anchored, unmoving. Amergin stared out in to the half light. He was sure he could make out the deadly beauty, Zendris, standing provocatively on the prow. The siren, even now, was trying to lure him back. He still felt a strangely disconcerting connection to her...

"This must stop!" He closed his mind, shutting out her influence, "The power of that woman!"

He turned and went below. He must reconnect with Sceine! He was in denial, his feelings for the siren, had not gone, her influence lingered in the recesses of his mind.

Xomas remained at the helm. He too had seen the siren Zendris on the prow of the flagship. He too was drawn to her. He gripped the tiller more tightly. His nails digging in to the wood until the blood drained out of his fingertips. He must resist! He closed his mind to her beguiling magical ways...A gust of freshening wind filled the sails. The distraction needed to be free from her entrapment. The vessel planed in a stiff breeze and began to roll in an open ocean swell. Droplets of blood fell to the deck from an open wound on his white and straining knuckles.

They sailed on... two twin masted vessels followed. A thought suddenly struck Xomas, "What of the leader of the Pirates of Grannh? Was Senet now under the spell of the siren Zendris?" Xomas hung on to the tiller as a larger than expected wave surged through. The vessel rocked and rolled and then steadied itself. He must tell Amergin of his fears... but later...

Amergin prayed and meditated in quarters that were not his own. It took him a good while to feel at ease in these new surroundings. He lit a storm lantern that cast a comforting glow in to the strangeness. He knelt before an effigy of the sea god Manannan, "This god will have to smile on the Milesian fleet if this mission is to be successful!" he thought. He stared at the pagan idol, his mind beginning to rest. Staring again, his mind was beginning to drift... He prayed for the salvation of his abandoned crew. He prayed for his own sanity, free from the spell of Zendris. He prayed for Sceine. He hoped with all his heart that she will come to him this night... his mind drifted once more. For an hour or more he let his imagination run free. He prayed, he chanted ancient sacred verse. His mind easing and his spirit rising, he began to compose poems in his mind. He chanted the rhythmic, lyrical verse:

"Safe haven, protection, storm front chasing, shelter anchored.
Heave to, breaching, the seventh wave, spirits in accord.
Fine lines, carved in liquid, sail stretching, straining.
Fair weather, foul, sun burst, wind squall, raining.

Dulse, kelp, flotsam, jetsam, washed ashore in brine.
Sea soaked, weather worn, salted, leather faced, sunshine.
Aeons, wave crested, rolling, timeless, boundless, sublime.
Surf sodden and spume thrown, wind borne nature's rhyme."

The poems were his mantra. His soul was being soothed. His body was being gently caressed. He was being taken out of his body. He was travelling beyond the veil. He fell in to an amber cosmos. He opened his eyes... Sceine! "Come to me Amergin! I am waiting for you my beloved!" She was safe! He was drawn deeper and deeper. He fell in to the fleck in her eye. Her hands caressed and aroused him, taking him to blissful joy... "Sceine...Sceine!" He was in ecstacy... and then he was awake... his destiny confirmed, his resolve strengthened...

Amergin smiled in quiet relief, the first smile in a long time. His body re-energised. His mind rejuvenated and refreshed. He prayed for a final time, "Great Spirit I am your willing servant. We are journeying in your realm.

Bring us safely to our destination. Help us complete our mission! Bring the Guardians of Light to this darkening land."

Amergin stepped up on to the deck in the breaking light of dawn, "Xomas my good helmsman. How was your shift?" Xomas smiled, he was mightily relieved to see the Sea Druid was back! Strengthened and revitalised! "My lord, all fares well... but!" Just as he was about to express his concern, "We have company!" Amergin pointed to the two twin masted vessels on the distant horizon. "That is my concern my lord," responded Xomas, "Who are the Pirates of Grannh in league with? Is Senet in charge? Or is it Magire and Zendris?"

Amergin nodded, he understood the dilemma. His mind was racing, "We have greater duties now my good helmsman. Your shift is done now, but first bring MacCuill to me. I need his cartographic wisdom and local knowledge..."

As Xomas went below deck, Amergin turned to watch the horizon. Squinting in to the rising light of the new day, he certainly saw the two red sailed, twin masted vessels of the Pirates of Grannh. But there! Just revealing itself over the horizon was a third, familiarly rigged vessel. His own flagship!

MacCuill stepped up alongside Amergin. He too stared in to the sunrise, "Magire and the siren Zendris on your flagship my lord!" he wisely advised, "They will be making for Land's End and reinforcements. Once they are rejoined with the Shamen, they will be powerful adversaries!"

"We must get there before them!" urged Amergin, "What lies ahead of us? Give me your verdict and your judgement."

MacCuill spread out a sea chart, roughly drawn on parchment. "Here my lord, a days sailing to the north, the infamous Cape of Wrath. We will sail in the protection of the outer islands until this point,"MacCuill stabbed a dry quill pen in to the parchment, scratching an X to mark the spot, "From here, the sea god Manannan willing, we navigate around the cape. From here we will be exposed to the full fury of the Northern Ocean. Storms of inordinate strength track through. Now at the time of the equinox they are more powerful than ever."

Amergin studied the sea chart, "What of the tidal races and rip tides?"

"This is another concern my lord!" said MacCuill worriedly, "The tides around the Cape of Wrath are legendary. The tide from the south meets the tide sweeping along the coast of the Northern Province. Time it wrong and the incessant huge swells of the Northern Ocean combine with the converging tides making this the infamous mariner's grave yard of myth and legend!"

Amergin listened with quiet consternation. He gestured for MacCuill to continue, "It is critical to meet the convergence of tide and swell at slack tide. Then there is a window of two hours only. The two great bulges of ocean will then annul one another. The drift is east along the Northern Province. Time it wrong and the combined tidal races and swell are irresistible. Any vessel caught here at the wrong time, will be drawn in to the great whirlpool known as The Coirin. Even if you survive this, the strength of the rip currents and tidal races will take you further and deeper in to the track of the unrelenting storms. Any hapless sailor will be swept north-east in to the limitless ocean!"

"By the sea god Manannan, this is a fearsome place!" Amergin felt a cold, nervous sweat on his brow, just at the prospect of such a marine encounter. MacCuill left Amergin alone to ponder and strategise. Amergin was now fully aware that they will need his lifetime of marine training to survive the coming sea voyage. He turned to study the horizon. He called to his watchman, "How many vessels do you see?" "Three my lord!" came the reply. "Do they get any closer?" Amergin suspected that their knowledge of these waters will give them an advantage. "Yes my lord! They are steadily gaining on us!"

Not only was he facing the most notorious stretch of ocean and potentially the most inclement weather at this time of the autumn equinox, but he was facing a fiercesome adversary racing him to the Northern Province to gather reinforcements! "This is a race to the death!" Amergin must use all his guile...He faced in to the sea breeze, raising his arms aloft, he called out to the sea god Manannan, "I am but a child of the ocean, a messenger sent by the Great Spirit. Guide us safely through your domain. By the grace of the Guardians of Light, I implore you!"

Amergin could feel the ionised energy of the infinite. He could feel the universal life force entering him, inspiring him and guiding him... he must have faith!

Hour by hour they sailed, watching the outer islands go by and disappearing over the Southern horizon. This was the point of no return! Open ocean now... the place where Maccuill had scratched his X on the parchment. They were already rolling and pitching in the long distance swell that had travelled a thousand miles in the unencumbered storm track of the Northern Ocean.

On a fair day, a mariner's delight! Today was such a day... a following wind, a significantly large swell, rolling but not cresting. Steady progress being made...

Xomas rejoined Amergin. He rejoiced in the day, "A mighty sailing day my lord!" Amergin agreed with Xomas, glad to have the company of his faithful helmsman. He pointed to the east. A good five miles distance away, three vessels, fully rigged, were on course for the Cape of Wrath.

Xomas felt the pain endured by the Sea Druid Amergin. His own flagship manned by a crew of ghosts under the spell of Zendris. The flagship began to edge ahead. Magire and Zendris know these waters well. They know exactly where the deep water channels are, where the tide raced the swiftest and more importantly where the back eddies and whirlpools are to be encountered.

The skies were still clear, but the wind speed increased as they ventured further North. They were flying! A following wind and a tide in full flood and pushed on by large, rolling, long distance waves.

The watchman yelled out, "Land ahoy!" pointing to the north-east. Way in the distance the outline of a mighty headland. Huge sea cliffs, only the tops could be seen at this distance. Still a good half days sailing away. The Cape of Wrath already imposed itself on the horizon.

The flooding tide pushed them onwards. Amergin observed, "This equinox tide is the highest of the year Xomas! Our timing around the Cape of Wrath will be critical. This tide, with these winds and the size of the swell... when it meets the tide flowing west along the coast of the Northern Province... there will be mayhem! The whirlpool Coirin will be fed by these conditions!"

Xomas had been informed by MacCuill of the mountainous seas, rapid rip tides and the mariner's worst nightmare, the whirlpool known as The Coirin, "Timing will be key my lord! We must tack and tack again, until the tide has slackened. Only then can we risk rounding the Cape of Wrath!"

"Get this wrong,"Amergin thought, "we will either be smashed by rogue waves in colliding tides or swallowed up by the ever hungry Whirlpool of Coirin, or swept away to the north in to the storm track of the Northern Ocean!"

The entire fleet must round the Cape of Wrath, a sea window of no more than two hours. Amergin would have to show the Milesian fleet the way in strange and dangerous seas...

Amergin and Xomas conferred. They discussed the state of the tide and sea, and the distance to the Cape of Wrath. These and many more questions needed to be considered before the strategy could be put in place. Amergin soon made his first decision, "We will tack to the north-west for ten nautical miles, and tack back south-east after that. Then we will reassess our position, check our drift and gauge the tide!"

Xomas agreed with this nautical strategy. He immediately organised for a message to be sent to the fleet. He asked the watchmen to let him know of any course change by the three other vessels. Soon enough they all tacked to the north-west. The race of death was on. Timing was all!

Thankfully, the weather was remaining kind to them. Amergin prayed to the sea god Manannan and the Great Spirit, asking for a safe passage around the cape. The swell was building! Long distance storm swell, of mast height now, rolled ominously through. Sometimes even the distant headland of the Cape of Wrath disappeared out of sight as they dropped in to trough after trough.The waves were not cresting out here in the deep ocean. This swell meeting the opposing tide flowing from the coast of the Northern Province would bring catastrophic sea conditions.

Ten nautical miles to the north-west they tacked back again. Amergin and Xomas estimated the time to slack tide, "We have been sailing with the flooding tide for a good three hours now my lord. One more hour and the tide should slacken!" Amergin agreed, "Bring us down wind my good helmsman!"

The following wind, the still flooding, but slowing tide, the fleet should be at the Cape of Wrath in one hour. The cry of the watchman, as if to confirm this, "The three vessels are sailing down wind too! They sail on a route that will take them closer to the Cape of Wrath!" thought Amergin out aloud, "Risky!" There again, Magire and Zendris know this ocean, but Senet and the Pirates of Grannh do not! The margins will be finer, the sea window reduced, the closer to the Cape of Wrath they sailed.

The Cape of Wrath was a magnificent spectacle, the highest cliffs in the entire land. Mountainous and steeply sloping at first, becoming precipitous and sheer for the last eight hundred feet. "An extraordinary place!" enthused Xomas. The headland created its own weather. Orographic rain clouds swept up the face, creating rain and mist on the windward, top slopes. The clouds built and accumulated over the three thousand foot summit, piling skywards before being scattered and dissipated in a streaming banner in the lee of the cape.

Now with the final stages of the flooding tide, the next hours sailing would be critical. The fleet seemed akin to jockeys riding temperamental stallions. They were on a wider ocean downward course. The three vessels of their enemy had tacked again, to go as close to the headland as they possibly dare.

Amergin assumed that here the affect of the tide flowing from the Northern Province would be minimised, giving a prolonged window of slack tide and more time to round the Cape of Wrath. Otherwise why risk such a route? Fine for those familiar with these waters, but the long distance ground swell, now over mast height created unimaginable hazards. The twin masted vessels sailed by Senet and the Pirates of Grannh had never sailed these waters before and were in real peril.

The ground swell hammered in to the headland in a slow motion white water fury. The three vessels had jockeyed in to a position where normally the effect of slackening tide would make for a quiet zone under the headland. But with the mast high intensely powerful swell, the waves were reflecting and rebounding, creating damaging interference patterns. The three vessels including Amergin's flagship, under the control of Magire and the siren Zendris, were heading for the demented backwash. "Still an hour to go to absolute slack tide!" reckoned Amergin, "Xomas we must tack again and let our drift coincide with slack tide!"

Xomas barked instructions to his well trained seamen, "Bring her around one more time!" and they headed out in to open ocean... the entire fleet followed. They were all soon drifting in an ever reducing tidal race. Jockeying and holding their ground, tacking to slow their arrival at the Cape of Wrath. The Milesian fleet now five miles out to sea in deep water. The rolling ground swell picking them up, but gently putting them down, the fresh south-westerly pushing them on...

Towards the headland it was a different scenario! Still a while off slack tide, the tidal races from the south-west and the north collided! The deep ocean rolling swell powered in to a maelstrom of confused and clashing tides, compounded by the violent backwash, reflecting and rebounding off the base of the Cape of Wrath. "They have their timing all wrong!" Amergin feared for the wayward vessels, "Get out of there!" He willed them to safety. Enemies or not, he could not watch any vessel go to an awful watery grave and certainly not the crew of his flagship!

The flagship tacked first, his comrades still under the spell of the siren Zendris. They had realised their mistake, they had misjudged the tides and the size of the swell. They sailed for their lives!

The twin masted, red sailed vessels followed suit, but their reaction was slower. Senet, the leader of the Pirates of Grannh did not know these waters. They underestimated the power of the tides and the huge volumes of bulging ocean at the time of the autumn equinox, driven on by the conveyer belt of intense Northern Ocean storms.

The Cape of Wrath was like no place they had ever encountered. They were at the edge of the death zone. Magire and Zendris had sensed that and reacted, they were tacking away just in time!

Senet responded too late! Their twin masted sister ship even later! Little did they know, that for the sake of one more tack, the tidal race would have slackened, the collision zone quietened! Such are the margins of the sea...

Amergin watched from a deep water channel as the two vessels careered in to the tidal maelstrom. Both vessels fully rigged, battling to escape the grip of the tide. They leaned in to the strengthening South Wester funnelling around the Cape of Wrath. An endless battering ensued. Waves from all directions caught and swamped them, pushing them towards the Whirlpool of Coirin. Rudderless, directionless, they were out of control!

Amergin and the fleet still waited for the tide and weather window. They drifted, they waited. They were in control... Even with the ground swell, double mast high now, they were in charge of their own destiny. Unlike the poor wretches on the two twin-masted, red sailed vessels which were being assaulted by incessant, chaotic waves. Senet had never known such aquatic hell! Unbeknownst to him, beyond the collision zone, where the tides began to merge and synchronise, lurked the deadly immensity of the infamous whirlpool known as the Coirin... feeding now at full intensity, at the full height of the combined flood tides. Soon, both red sailed vessels were being swept along, drawn by the unifying currents, straight towards the watery singularity of the Coirin. This singularity was a dark sea of brooding salinity, consuming everything, ejecting huge spinning eddies of turbulence in to the Northern Ocean...

Senet, the leader of the Pirates of Grannh, was resigned to his fate. His vessel swept on faster and faster in to a spinning, spiralling current of death.

The Whirlpool of Coirin feeding, consuming, feasting... these few unfortunate mariners were joining the hundreds of lost adventurers taken to their watery doom over the millennia.

The oceanic vortex sucked everything in, Senet's vessel drifting in to a spin, towards the violent eddying turbulence. Then! With a surge of tide they were shot in to the spiralling vortex. They were in the wall of the whirlpool as the next pulse of burgeoning tide plucked them out and shot them towards the northern horizon, like a comet escaping the sun's gravity... they were free! Masts and rigging had been destroyed, sails shredded, they were destined to drift for days in the conveyer belt of storms in the Northern Ocean...

Senet, paralysed with shock, turned to see their twin masted, red sailed sister vessel disappear in to the Coirin. Sucked down, consumed, the whirlpool had been fed...

Amergin and the entire Milesian fleet watched on in horror. They had been so close to the same fate! Even now they were being drawn in by the Whirlpool of Coirin, its deadly gripping, watery tentacles pulling them in...

But the tides were slackening. A few more minutes and the turbulence had dissipated. The death zone of colliding tides quietening, just the rolling deep water swell remaining. This was the window of relative calm they had been waiting for. Xomas climbed to the lookout position, to get their bearing. He saw calm water in all directions, "We have a good sea and weather window now my lord!" The Sea Druid Amergin stood resolutely at the helm. Today he had earned his title as the Champion of Milesia, "What of the flagship Xomas?" The helmsman scanned the horizon, "They round the Cape of Wrath now!" Amergin was pleased to see that they had a good lead on Magire and Zendris.

The fleet pressed on, all were safely away from the dizzying, vertigo inducing sea cliffs of the Cape of Wrath. "We must keep that lead Xomas! The race is still on! We must get to Land's End first. Before the Shamen of Land's End have a chance to prepare for us!"

CHAPTER TWENTY THREE:
THE CYCLE OF XUSTRA

Far, far from the extremities of the Northern Province and its majestic headlands jutting out in to the limitless Northern Ocean, in the Mountains of Iveare, the dark forces were stirring. The army of lost souls had begun to march east from the high mountain fortress of Hawardden. The dark one MacCuacht watched from the impregnable battlements as his battalions crossed the draw bridge.

"We finally go to the Temple of Xhara in the Eastern Province!" he sneered to the captain of his elite bodyguard, a select group that was always at his side. Daxid replied with venom, "The High Priests of the Temple of Xhara will submit to the dark Sidhe... then nothing will stop us! Any who try will perish!" MacCuacht grimaced with his inimitable twisted smile, a contorted expression oozing bedevilment. He was pleased, he had chosen well! Daxid is a loyal servant of the dark Sidhe with a ruthless and uncompromising character. Woe betide any mere mortal that crossed him, his black arts, though not yet a match for MacCuacht's dark skills, would deter the most zealous of adversaries.

The army of lost souls, more than a thousand strong, numbering one for every year of darkness that would fall over this land, should the High Priests of Xhara be taken and the High Priestess Sceine, the Princess of the Western Province, be slain...

MacCuacht revelled in the horror that his mission will bring to the Island of Destiny, the sending of the whole of this land, including the Western Province, in to a winter of a dark cycle. In particular he revelled in the notion of the demons and denizens of the dark Sidhe pouring forth from the portals, protected by his oh so pure sister Sceine, in the Western Province. He would avenge the pain, the indignity and the humiliation foisted upon him by the recently departed High King Antiem. All the provinces of the land would be his... his reign over the darkened realm shall commence and the dark Sidhe will endure for the next thousand years.

Xustra is an epoch of time discovered by the ancient ones. A cycle during which the planets Saturn and Jupiter are in the closest orbit to earth, and the earth is on a trajectory that takes it furthest away from the sun. The combined effects of the proximity of the gas giants, Jupiter and Saturn, and the increased distance of the earth from the sun, bring the veil between the mortal realm and the spirit world precariously closer, a time when the veil is more vulnerable to intrusion and corruption by the dark forces. A time, the ancients identified, that will continue until the sun returns on its trajectory a thousand years on.

This equinox not only represents the annual cycle from light in to dark, as days shorten and the balance between light and dark tips, but in this astral year it signifies the commencement of the epoch of time named by the ancients as "Xustra." The High Priests of Xhara and the Chapter of Mystics are acutely aware of the commencement of this epoch. Sceine, the Princess of the Western Province, became aware of the significance of the commencement of this epoch on her initiation as High Priestess of the Temple of Xhara.

The High Priests of Xhara and the priests of the Chapter of Mystics are sworn to secrecy during the annual ceremony at the Tree of Life in the Inner Sanctum at the Temple of Xhara. They all gather in secrecy at the equinox in a ritual ceremony, when the veil is at its closest and thinnest, permitting them to journey beyond the veil and commune with the Guardians of Light. This ceremony aims to maintain the equilibrium between the mortal realm and the spirit world.

MacCuacht knows that the High Priests of Xhara are gathering at the Temple now. Gonne, the High Priest of the Chapter of Mystics, Machiavellian orchestrator, who has turned to the dark Sidhe, has informed his dark master of this. The priests of the Chapter of Mystics are scattered to the four provinces of the Island of Destiny, very few are present at the Temple of Xhara. MacCuacht is aware of the imbalance in the equilibrium between the spirit world and the mortal realm at this time. He intends to catch the High Priests of Xhara offguard when they journey beyond the veil, and the balance will tip towards the dark Sidhe.

MacCuacht, in league with Gonne, delights in the prospect that the time of Xustra commences and the land will be condemned to a thousand years of rule by the dark Sidhe. That same twisted grimace of a smile spread across his countenance. He was pleased at his work. Nothing will stop him and his army of lost souls from reaching Xhara. He watched as the last of them crossed the draw bridge and marched in to the desolate high mountain wilderness of the Shadowlands that lay to the East of the mountain fortress of Hawardden. MacCuacht gestured to Daxid and the elite corps of bodyguards to follow him…As the light of the day dwindled they yomped in to the gloom of the Shadowlands. They would march through the nights and through the days to reach Xhara. The army of lost souls did not need sleep. They lived off the dark energy of the spirit world. MacCuacht observed contentedly, "An invincible army, on a terrible mission!" This pleased him even more…

The Shadowlands felt like a familiar universe to MacCuacht. This was how he imagined the future.

This was a dark, inhospitable, alien land devoid of radiant Light. Most of the portals of the Eastern Province were now infected. The further east in to the Shadowlands they marched, the less the radiant Light could penetrate. Not even the pure, radiant Light of the great portals of the Western Province could penetrate this nightmarish place. If MacCuacht could be happy in any place, then this was that place...

MacCuacht was satisfied in the knowledge that nothing could challenge his mission. Satisfied too, that the three raven haired Witches of Hawardden were on a mission to slay his beloved sister, the High Priestess of Xhara and the Princess of the Western Province, Sceine!

He was satisfied to the core of his demonic being that the so called "destined one ", the Sea Druid and champion of Milesia, Amergin, was nowhere to be found on this island. His spies have reported that he was driven out to sea in the direction of the Magine Islands. Word has it that his fleet had been consumed by the silver scaled monsters of the Magine Islands...

Replete with sinister satisfaction, MacCuacht marched on through the nightmarish Shadowlands.

In this reducing and diminishing light, the storm clouds brewing and boiling over the Iveare Mountains and the high mountain fortress of Hawardden looked even more threatening.

Once more the storm front, with a wall of cold, dense, dank, condensing mist was rolling inexorably down the mountain sides, encroaching in all directions, in to all provinces. "The epoch of Xustra is upon us!" snarled MacCuacht with his twisted grimace.

The High Priests of the Temple of Xhara had gathered for the equinox. They had prepared their religious rituals for the week of the "killing moon" as it was known in pagan circles. They were very aware of the significance of this lunar event. The alignment of the planets and the trajectory of the sun meant the veil was at its most vulnerable. They were also conscious of the fact that they were far too few to resist the army of lost souls, led by the dark one MacCuacht.

Most of the Priesthood of Xhara were deliberately spread around the land, trying to protect the portals, the High Priestess Sceine was at Sliebh Mis, knowing that it was too dangerous to travel east.They were exposed and vulnerable. The army of lost souls will be amongst them in a few days.

MacCuacht will arrive in time to influence the rituals at the commencement of Xustra. Disaster!

The priesthood realised they were defenceless! The priesthood prayed at the Inner Sanctum. They knelt before the Tree of Life, looking for answers. They chanted sacred verse and began to fall in to a meditative trance. They communed with the Guardians of Light and journeyed beyond the veil. Soon, the priesthood would unveil their plans to slow MacCuacht and the army of lost souls.

A few of the priesthood journeyed through the network of portals to find Amergin. The news that he had gone to sea to arrive in the Eastern Province before MacCuacht, encouraged them. They visited the Temple of the Sun, only to find Gonne of the Chapter of Mystics under the influence of the dark Sidhe. They were heartened to see the great portals of the Western Province still radiating their pure Divine Light.

On returning they communed with the Guardians of Light, searching for a solution. They were given an answer by the Guardians, "We will send our emissaries to delay the dark one. The army of lost souls is growing all the time... only if the destined one, Amergin, arrives in the Eastern Province in time, will you and the Temple of Xhara be safe..." Then they gave the priesthood a salutary warning, "Beware of the Witches of Hawardden! Sceine is in great danger. The destiny of the promised land will be in Sceine's and Amergin's hands!"

The select few priests returned to the mortal realm. They spread the word to the rest of the priesthood. They all continued to pray at the Tree of Life. They prayed for the success of the Guardians in delaying MacCuacht. They prayed for the safe journey and the arrival of Amergin and the Milesian fleet. They prayed for the safety of the High Priestess of Xhara, Sceine. All prayed that Sceine and Amergin will meet and the ancient prophecy will be fulfilled...

On the edge of the Shadowlands lived a remote tribe descended from the first wave of invaders in the time of the ancients. They were the Aganti, living independently on the edge of the Shadowlands. They were mountain people, survivors able to eke a living out of the harshest wilderness, renowned as fearsome guerrilla warriors. No one stepped foot in to this land without their permission.

An emissary of the Guardians of Light visited the leader of the Aganti in one of his dreams.

He was told of MacCuacht's journey. The Aganti were throwbacks from the ancient times. They believed that when their warrior chiefs died, their spirits entered the giant stones strewn all over the Shadowlands. The megalithic stones were organised in shrines to the pagan gods. Only the Aganti were permitted to enter the most sacred of the shrines on the high plateau of the Shadowlands, shrines that comprised of a circle of twelve stones, each stone representing a lunar cycle.

The chieftain of the Aganti, Lutha, saw in his dreams, the dark one known as MacCuacht approaching. In his dream he saw him march straight through the shrine, pushing sacred stones over as he went, in an act of senseless vandalism. Lutha was apoplectic with rage!

The Aganti were firm believers in the power of dreams. They straightaway formed a band of guerrilla warriors, armed to the teeth with stone-age weaponry, axes, bows and arrows, daggers and spears.

They stalked MacCuacht and his army of lost souls.

The masters of guerrilla tactics, they would harry and pester MacCuacht and the army of lost souls, like wasps stinging the backsides of grizzly bears. The Aganti could not stop them, but they certainly would slow their advance. Lutha knew the Shadowlands like the back of his hand. The track MacCuacht took to go to the Temple of Xhara passed through some of the most inhospitable country. This would be to the advantage of the Aganti.

Beyond the Shrine of Bealach and its ring of twelve standing stones was the Gorge of Dunlar. The perfect place for an ambush! Lutha and fifty of his fiercest warriors scaled the sides of the Gorge, exactly at the place where it constricted to its narrowest. They dislodged and loosened giant granite boulders, ready to be launched in to their foe.

Lutha, still enraged at the desecration of the sacred Shrine of Bealach, yelled out with great delight as he gave the order to send the avalanche of boulders in to the midst of the oncoming army of lost souls. MacCuacht and the army of lost souls wound their way through the meandering and tortuous track at the base of the Gorge of Dunlar. Lutha's yell echoed around the gorge. MacCuacht looked up, but too late! The avalanche of granite descended with almighty force, crushing some of the elite bodyguard. MacCuacht hurled himself in to a fracture in a massive glacial boulder at the last second…

He watched helplessly as the avalanche smashed in to the advance party. Dozens perished.

Devastation in a place of desolation! The granite dust settled.

MacCuacht heard the jeering tormentors high up on the side of the gorge. He prised himself out of the protection of the massive fractured glacial boulder. He seethed with rage. Undeterred he barked commands at his deathly cohort. They soon retrenched and marched on with serious intent. They were so many and the Aganti so few. The army of lost souls had only been distracted and slowed.

Indeed, to MacCuacht this was nothing more than an inconvenience. There would soon be many more lost souls to join him…

Lutha of the Aganti was overjoyed at the mayhem and destruction he had inflicted upon MacCuacht. He watched as the army of lost souls continued in to the ever narrowing gorge. This section was only passable at times of low rainfall. The path was the river bed. No other way through, but to wade along the shallow torrent cascading from rapid to rapid. The Gorge of Dunlar was so narrow, so steep, that very little daylight could percolate down.

Wading and picking their way over the slippy, rock strewn river bed their progress was painfully slow. MacCuacht pushed his army on, "This is taking too long!" They picked up their pace, some fell on the angular, protruding rocks. One of his elite bodyguards fell headlong, splitting his head open. Blood darker than pitch spilt from his scalp, mingling and staining the river. The colour of this dark infected blood was shocking. The Aganti were oblivious to the infection that swept downstream... Any person, or beast, coming in to contact with the contaminated water would be poisoned with the infection of the dark Sidhe.

MacCuacht was oblivious to the strategy of the Aganti. Lutha had sent a band of his guerrillas upstream, to go behind the ranks of the lost souls to the Lake of Serpents. Many hours ago now, they had created a blockage at the point where the stream exited the lake. These Aganti had created a land slip of mud and boulders that plugged the waters. Hour by hour, the waters of the lake had risen. Now the Lake of Serpents was primed, ready to burst. Slowly the waters eroded away at the earth and stone dam.

MacCuacht noticed the waters of the stream reducing in volume. "Strange!" he thought, but he put it down to the naturally drying and receding head waters. The further they descended in to the narrowing gorge, the more he worried about the water level. The precipitation from the building and brewing storm clouds in the high Iveare Mountains would surely feed this river?

Lutha watched and waited, and waited some more, until the advancing army of lost souls reached a place in the Gorge of Dunlar where the sides of the gorge had been polished smooth by repeated floods. Here, the riverbed was strewn with particularly jagged and treacherous boulders. At this point, and at his signal, a flaming arrow was fired skywards... the signal for the Aganti upstream to send loose boulders crashing in to the manufactured plug damming the river... A poignant pause as the head waters slowly undermined and undercut the blockage. In a watershed moment, the dam burst! Deep lake water poured violently in to the gorge. The pent up fury of the Lake of Serpents crashed and roared down the gorge, sweeping all before it...

MacCuacht heard the low distant rumblings, before he saw the flood waters. He instantly recognised the danger, "Get to the sides of the gorge! Climb for the high ground!" The flood struck at the speed of a cobra. A wall of water, well over overhead, surged and boiled, creating white water rapids and a raging turbulence, where before there was a shallow torrent. Hapless victims could get no purchase on the smooth, polished sides of the gorge and were sent at breakneck speed in to the jagged river bed. Over a hundred lost souls were swept downstream. Lutha rejoiced at the sight of the army of lost souls in complete disarray. As the Aganti celebrated, the dark oozing blood of the lost souls contaminated the flood water and swept downstream through the villages of the Shadowlands and onwards in to the tributaries and rivers of the Eastern Province...

MacCuacht was momentarily non-plussed. He had watched many of his army of lost souls being swept away and dashed to pieces on the rock strewn riverbed. He clung like a drowning rat to an outcrop on the side of the gorge, "Maybe a hundred lost!" but he was still undeterred and with the twisted grimace, "There will be many more to be converted to the dark Sidhe!"...as he watched the flooding river, stained with the dark infected blood of his lost souls, flow across the Shadowlands and to the sea...

Lutha of the Aganti and his guerrilla warriors felt avenged for the desecration of the Shrine of Bealach. More importantly they had slowed the progress of MacCuacht. In the universal scheme of things, delaying MacCuacht was critical. Lutha and the Aganti guerrillas moved out of the Gorge of Dunlar, leaving MacCuacht and the remaining army of lost souls to regather and restrengthen.

Unscathed they marched back to their tribal villages on the edge of the Shadowlands. They followed the river, and the aftermath of the flood. The waters were receding now and every now and then they came across a body of one of the lost souls washed up on the silted river bank. Open wounds from the collision with the jagged riverbed, still oozed the dark infected blood. Lutha and his tribesmen were oblivious to the black peril they had unleashed. The flood waters from the Lake of Serpents contaminated with the dark virus had flowed through the hinterland and through their own village. Even now, as they marched back to their homesteads, some of the villagers washed and bathed in the infected river water, and children played in the shallows.

A plague fell upon Lutha's own village, a plague unlike any others. By the time they had marched back to the village, members of the tribe and even his own family began to show the awful signs of the infection, symptoms of delirium, anxiety and depression. The flood waters had flashed through at the worst conceivable time, when families gathered after the evening meal. They all chatted whilst washing cooking utensils in the river water. More than a hundred were infected. That night they could not sleep and as the dark one marched through the Shadowlands, they gave their allegiance to the dark Sidhe. Without so much as a backward look towards their own village, they joined the legions of the army of lost souls marching with MacCuacht.

The Aganti tribe awoke to find their numbers decimated. "The sleepwalkers of the Shadowlands" as they became to be known, left in the dead of the night, never to see their loved ones again.

Lutha took the rest of the village that were uninfected, to the Shrine of Bealach, the next day. He and the tribal elders did not fully understand the evil that had befallen their tribes. But they did suspect the rotting corpses of the army of lost souls littering the banks of the river between their villages and the Lake of Serpents.Instinctively, Lutha had taken his people to the headwaters above the Lake of Serpents, to the Glade of Siveen near the sacred shrine of Bealach. Here they would make camp until they were sure the evil had passed.

MacCuacht had marched on. His legions were now on the edge of the Shadowlands. Their numbers swelling as the water borne infection flowed in to the tributaries and rivers of the Eastern Province.

The word was out... the dark one marches on! The High Priests of Xhara and the gathering of enlightened beings at the Temple of Xhara joined in prayer. The Temple of Xhara was one of the few portals in the Eastern

Province still pristine and pure. So far, the infection of the dark Sidhe held at bay by the power of prayer.

The High Priests communed with the Guardians of Light. They knelt in meditative prayer at the Tree of Life. The veil was the closest they had ever known. This time was the commencement of the cycle of Xustra, the time when the mortal realm was at its most vulnerable. Now, the Divine was amongst them. A pure radiant Light enveloped the Temple. The Light of the Divine at this time of the commencement of the Cycle of Xustra was known as the Aurora Gahallen. This was a time of empowerment, enlightenment and illumination. The High Priests celebrated the Divine in nature.

The oldest and longest serving High priest of Xhara, Seanach, approached the Tree of Life. He celebrated the presence of the Divine at the Temple. His celebration was tinged with fear and a sense of foreboding. The commencement of the Cycle of Xustra was being overshadowed by the arrival of the dark one MacCuacht.

Seanach was wrapped in the Aurora Gahallen. Unearthly, illuminated spirit beings shone before him. They communicated telepathically to all the priests gathered in the Inner Sanctum of the Temple of Xhara. *"We rejoice with you. We come to celebrate the commencement of the Cycle of Xustra. We bring you the Aurora Gahallen to bathe your land in the Light of the Divine."*

At that moment the radiant Light shone even brighter. The Tree of Life shone intensely with the Divine in nature. The High Priests of Xhara were in awe. They knelt in deference to the Guardians of Light. They were heartened. Their spirits rose. Even in this time of great adversity, they must be strong. Their faith must endure…

The tales of horror that were befalling the faithful in the Eastern Province were turning the weak minded amongst them in to doubters. To raise their spirits the Guardians of Light sent a message throughout the land. The Aurora Galhallan lit up the land. A radiant ethereal Light travelled across all boundaries, reaching out to the faithful and reassuring the doubters. A subliminal message was wrapped in the Aurora, available to only the believers and enlightened beings of the land, "There comes the destined one to this land. He travels to the Temple of Xhara by sea. He is the Sea Druid Amergin, champion of the Milesians. He is destined to meet the High Priestess of the Temple of Xhara and Princess of the Western Province, Sceine. He has sailed over the Northern Ocean, and now he sails around the Island of Destiny. He comes to join us at the Temple of Xhara. He meets with great adversity, natural and unnatural. The dark Sidhe will become aware of his sea voyage, and they will send dark forces to fight him. MacCuacht draws the dark Sidhe through the veil. With Amergin we will be strong. We will open the portal at the Temple of Xhara to stop the dark Sidhe pouring forth. Pray for the destined one, the Sea Druid Amergin. Pray for his safe passage and arrival at the Temple of Xhara. Pray for his destined meeting with Sceine…"

CHAPTER TWENTY FOUR:
THE SEA JOURNEY OF THE NORTH

Amergin hauled at the sheet to tension the foresail, relieved to have rounded the Cape of Wrath. He busied himself with routine matters. The fleet is still together, still in tact... More than could be said for the Pirates of Grannh! Their vessels had felt the wrath of the cape. Senet's vessel set adrift at the mercy of the incessant equinox storms of the Northern Ocean. The other twin masted, red sailed vessel sunk, fodder for the Whirlpool of the Coirin, lost without trace, the wreckage only now surfacing. Most consigned as flotsam in the Northern Ocean drift, some became salvage for the Firbolg wreckers, scavenging the shoreline of the Northern Province.

Amergin stood on the prow, feeling the ocean breeze, refreshing and reinvigorating. He turned to face in to the freshening South Wester, the salt air stinging his eyes, his mane of golden brown hair encrusted with sea salt. The long distance groundswell was only mast high on this coast, the disappearing Cape of Wrath awarding some protection now.

Amergin watched as an alien landscape unfolded. The mighty cliffs of the cape were giving way to flat- topped escarpments with steep but negotiable sides. Then narrow fertile coastal plains leading to jagged, angular coastal cliffs, with the strangest formations he had ever seen. Pillar upon pillar of hexagonal shaped igneous rock of all sizes and dimensions, emerging from the ocean. The hardened, volcanic substances glistened and glinted in the evening light. Crystals sparkled and veins of quartzite shone brilliantly. The powerful ground swell crashed in to the formations, hardly a sound resulted. The hexagonal pillars absorbed all the energy, reducing the breakers in to vaporised brine. As a result the entire coastline was unusually quiet. Hardly a seabird broke the slience.

MacCuill stepped up to join Amergin. He pointed eastwards along the coast of the Northern Province, "Observe the furthest flat-topped escarpment my lord. The highest with its summit shrouded in cloud," he went on, "You can just make out a fortress set high up on the mountain's flat top. This fits the description, brought back after the Tuathan forays in to the Northern Province, of the headquarters of the Shamen of Land's end."

"Another tides sailing will bring us to it!" interrupted Amergin, "We must make haste and get there before Magire and Zendris!" Amergin continued, "Our mission is to the Eastern Province. The equinox is upon us and the veil is ever nearer and ever thinner. MacCuacht is nearing the Temple of Xhara! We have little time! If we can get to the portal at Land's End first, then maybe there is hope for the crew of our flagship!"

Amergin looked back towards the ever diminishing Cape of Wrath, disappearing on the western horizon. The fleet sailed with the wind, fully rigged and making steady progress. Still the flagship was catching them. Magire and Zendris knew these waters. They were navigating the currents and tides more skilfully than the Milesian fleet. Amergin called to Xomas, "Send an order to the last two vessels of our fleet. Tell them to hinder the progress of the flagship." Immediately Xomas mirror messaged the vessels. Straightaway two vessels of the fleet veered away, tacking directly towards the flagship, causing it to veer. The captains were under instructions to spend no time near the flagship... the spell of the siren Zendris is powerful, her attraction fatal...

Amergin guided the fleet towards the high flat-topped escarpment. Satisfied, the flagship was already falling behind. The tactics were working! Valuable time gained. A window of opportunity presented itself to Amergin.

In the dwindling light, the fleet would anchor a mile or two out from Land's End. The closer they came to the peninsula of Land's End, the features became clearer. The watchman called out, "I see a harbour hewn in to the cliffs! There is sufficient room to moor two vessels." "Perfect!" replied Amergin, "Do you see any sign of a temple? Standing stones or such like?"

"Ay my lord, there is!" came the watchman's response, "A semi circle of standing stones on the cliff edge, a mile from the harbour."

The window of opportunity was now! "Drop anchor!" the fleet followed suit. Amergin and Eiremhou's vessel then made for the harbour under the cloak of darkness. The representatives of the Chapter of Mystics had been readied for this moment. They joined Amergin and Eiremhou on their expedition to the portal...

Barely twilight to navigate by, the equinox moon not yet risen over the eastern horizon, they edged towards Land's End under reduced rigging, the long distance ground swell reducing all the while only half mast height now. Half a mile to the harbor, they could make out the sheer carved walls. The harbour entrance was very narrow. This was going to require some precision navigation.

Amergin left Xomas at the helm. He oversaw the oarsmen as they dipped gently towards the harbour wall. They edged in, sails furled, under the cloak of darkness. They must not be discovered.

There was no sign of the flagship...

The oarsman dipped quietly in to the slick black sea, just as the equinox moon rose full and large over the eastern horizon, casting long shadows, illuminating the crystalline, igneous rock face.

The hexagonal pillars, volcanic protrusions comprising rare minerals and veins of quartz, sparkling and glistening in the intensifying moon glow.

These natural sea defences turning powerful set waves in to phosphorescent white sea-spray, vaporised and hanging in the cool night air.

Beyond the harbor, lit up in a stark moonscape, Amergin could just make out the hemisphere of giant bluestones standing defiantly and precariously on the edge of the world. Amergin stared and blinked in the brightening moonlight, "We must not be seen!" Nearing the harbour, a few gentle dips of the oars more and they would safe, secreted under the high walls...

But they were too late! High up on the flat-topped escarpment, a beacon lit up, illuminating an imposing fortress... MacCuill yelled out in alarm, he had heard the tales of this place, "The Shamen of Land's End! They come!" Sure enough, within minutes, a trail of lights began to wind down the side of the escarpment.

The Milesian vessels softly shunted in to the harbour wall, the crew were instantly clambering up rope ladders. Mooring ropes were being lashed to bollards. Amergin, Xomos, Eiremhou, MacCuill and the representatives of the Chapter of Mystics soon followed.

"Still no sign of the flagship, thank the Great Spirit!" Amergin led the way towards the Portal of Land's End. He, with the Chapter of Mystics would summon the Guardians of Light. The peninsula would feel the Light of the Divine. Those under the influence of the dark veil would become enlightened. The spell of the siren Zendris would be broken and the crew of the flagship would be free of her curse!

The equinox moon had risen full and bright now, the immense bluestones stood dark and mysterious. This was Land's End, the edge of the world and portal to the spirit world...

The trail of lights traversing the escarpment were brightening and getting ever closer... "We are outnumbered! We have no time to confront these Shamen, we must get to the portal!"

Amergin stretched his stride, quickening towards the portal. A rough track hugged the precipitous cliffs. They soon left the steep sided harbour walls and were on their hurried way to the tip of the peninsula. The rock strewn trail was difficult to negotiate in the moonlight. They jumped from rock to rock on the limits of haste and safety.

The trail angled diagonally along the peninsula now. The hexagonal igneous pillars were convenient stepping stones. They nearly broke in to a sprint. Soon they reached the heather clad, thinly soiled point. Now they sprinted as fast as their armour and weaponry would permit!

The procession of lights coming down the escarpment flickered and flashed. The vanguard were already on the coastal plain and appeared to be moving ever closer, ever faster. Amergin could hear the sound of distant hooves. The fabled horsemen of the north were coming!

To compound their woes, a dark silhouette moved on the silver streaked, quietening ocean. The flagship with Magire and Zendris arrived! Lights flashed in code from the Milesian vessels warning them of their arrival. This was the moment Amergin feared! The Shamen of Land's End had a fearsome reputation. Now Zendris and Magire joined them! They were in their own land. Who knows what terror they could unleash!

This was too close for comfort! The Milesian crew under the spell of the siren Zendris depended on Amergin and the priests of the Chapter of Mystics reaching the portal first...

Finally! On the edge of the cliff, on the promontory jutting out in to the moonlit Northern Ocean, the silhouette of the giant standing stones... Now, Amergin danced from hexagonal pillar to hexagonal pillar... soon he stood beneath the gatestones and gathered the priests around him... the equinox moon shone full and bright above the portal... He touched the capstone and was instantly connected to the spirit world... the veil so close now... so thin... and so vulnerable! The priests of the Chapter of Mystics stood next to Amergin. Linking their hands and in turn touching the gatestones. "There is extraordinary power here!" shouted Amergin, as he earthed between the mortal realm and the spirit world. The priests chanted sacred verse of the ancient ones. They too felt the energy... the spiritual connection...

Amergin closed his eyes. His senses became one with the enlightened ones. He was drawn in to a golden amber cosmos... the veil wrapped and morphed around him. He felt a gentle caress of his hand, gentle fingertips touching... the energy flowed... tresses of golden hair, soft and sensuous, brushed his face... delicate, tender lips kissed his... he slowly opened his eyes... he was lost in her beauty... lost in her power... he was falling in to the universe of her rich amber eyes... he fell and fell in to the dark fleck in the iris of her right eye... "I am with you my love! I come with the Guardians of Light, to join you, to help you!"
Sceine! Amergin was taken beyond the veil... so close and so thin now...He was one with Sceine... and as one with the spirit world... their bodies wrapped and entwined… they came as one...

Their senses so connected, so alive... an explosion of radiant Divine Light poured from the spirit world, from beyond the veil and entered the mortal realm... the priests of the Chapter of Mystics knelt in awe of the Divine in their presence...An aurora of Divine radiance spread over Land's End, the portal at the epicentre...

The Shamen of Land's End were stopped in their tracks. They were god fearing pagan beings... their gods were communing with them! They fell to their knees in prayer and began chanting. They had seen the Milesians arrive and with their own eyes had seen the Divine Light! To them, the Milesians were the messengers of the Light... and they bowed before them...

Amergin returned from beyond the veil and back to the mortal realm. He emerged from the portal and walked back to his priests...

The Shamen of Land's End looked on from a distance. They saw the one they recognised as the Milesian, surrounded and enveloped in radiant Light. As god fearing, pagan beings, they were converted to the blindingly evident truth, that Amergin was an enlightened one, destined to be in this land...

Magire and the siren Zendris rowed to shore with some of the crew from the flagship, just as the aurora of radiant light burst forth from the portal. The siren Zendris was mortified, "This is our land! Our deities rule the Northern Province!" Simultaneously the Milesian crew on the flagship felt the mantle of the Divine in Nature touch their souls, one by one they were free of the hypnotic spell cast by the siren.

Her powers were gone. The aurora of radiant Light cloaked her spells. She fell to the floor in despair.

Free of her insidious control, they took her to the shore, before her power returned and the crew controlled once more. Zendris tried to call the dark Sidhe through the portal but to no avail, the Sea Druid Amergin's power prevailed.

Amergin was heartened by the reaction of the Shamen of Land's End. Akin to their counterparts, the Pirates of Grannh, they had encountered the Guardians of Light and seemed to have embarked on the journey to enlightenment. However, there was still dark in the hearts of some... Magire and Zendris were on a more sinister mission...

Amergin took heart that here was some evidence that the Northern Province could be called on to join the enlightened ones when the time came to confront the dark one MacCuacht, "Come my people, we must return to our vessels, while the Guardians of Light are in our presence." He then asked for three priests of the Chapter of Mystics to stay as missionaries in the Northern Province. To work with the Shamen of Land's End to nurture the Light of the Divine once they had departed and the Guardians of Light journeyed beyond the veil. Three brave priests volunteered. They were aware of the dangers... they were potentially martyrs in waiting. "Patrice, Xavid, Colum, we shall be forever indebted to you!" Amergin offered his hand to each of them. They duly kissed his hand and bowed in deference and allegiance. Patrice, their spokesman, said "We shall be the messengers of the Light!" They all knew they were in dire peril. Magire and Zendris will soon return...

Amergin thanked them and quickly turned away and led the way back to the harbour. On the path, they the met some of the Shamen of Land's End, they were some of the strangest beings! Human and half human, real yet unreal, some were akin to the demons and denizens they had encountered on the sea voyage to the Promised Land. Amergin knew only too well that amongst the potential converts, were sceptics and deviants that have the propensity for evil... his priests and all Milesians must be wary...

The harbour was bathed in moonglow and radiant Light. They descended the steep track, stepping carefully in the half light. Scurrying shadows startled Amergin. In the corner of his eye he witnessed two figures skulking off in to the shadows. Tall, athletic figures with shocks of matted dreadlocks, wearing light absorbing chameleon- like armour. Magire and Zendris! No sooner had he seen them, they had disappeared in to the shadows. The siren Zendris was powerless while the Guardians of Light were in her realm.

Amergin's train of thought was broken as he stepped on to the harbour side. He recognised individuals and seamen... the crew of the flagship! He embraced and was embraced by the loyal crew. They had rowed Magire and Zendris to shore, just as the aurora of the Light of the Divine swept over Land's End. They were free of the siren's spell! Now they came to the aid of their Sea Druid and champion of Milesia. There was great joy and delight abounding!

Amergin, the priests of the Chapter of Mystics, Eiremhou and MacCuill were all soon rowing back to the fleet. All the vessels and the flagship had drifted slowly towards the harbour to meet them. Soon, as they got closer, cheers broke out on the flagship as they recognised the Sea Druid. Beacons were lit, flags were raised aloft and conches sounded. Amergin stood at the bow of his rowing boat with arms raised high in a gesture of greeting and joy! "Xomas, we will take our rightful place at the helm of the flagship once more!" Xomas was overcome with joy and relief, he embraced his leader. No time for protocol here, "We sail for the Eastern Province, my lord! We fight for the Promised Land and the fulfilment of the prophecy!"

As the vessels touched, Amergin climbed the rope ladder to his flagship and his joyous crew. His heart pounding and a lump in his throat, he stepped out on to the deck. Cheers and smiles greeted him. The flagship crew, free from a ghostly enslavement, shook his hand, embraced him and kissed him in a display of overwhelming delight and gratitude.

Amergin's gaze was drawn to the still glowing radiance of the Portal of Land's End, then up to the fluttering and occasionally straightening flag of the Milesian nation on the mast of the flagship... the tower, the ocean and the flagship representing the journey across the Northern Ocean and the stars guiding them to the island of their destiny...

With renewed vigour and collective spirit, the fleet once more made ready for sea. The last and potentially most arduous leg of their epic maritime voyage awaits them. An awful fate was befalling the tribes of the Eastern Province. They had little time! The Temple of Xhara was threatened!

"One more days sailing Xomas!" Amergin and his helmsman stood at the tiller, ready and watching as the crew unfurled the sails, tensioned the sheets and fine tuned the rigging of the magnificent Phoenician designed flagship. "So good to back on board!" he signalled to one of his crew, "Weigh anchor! We sail for the Eastern Province and the Temple of Xhara!"

The sea god Manannan was being good to them. Gentle seas now, with just enough swell to cause the vessels of the fleet to pitch and roll in a gusting North Westerly. This was an ideal weather window for negotiating the coastline of the Northern Province.

The equinox moon was in its final phase now. The trajectory taking it low in the western sky. Soon the night sky would be completely black, no moonglow, only the diamond bright constellations to navigate by.

Amergin watched in trepidation as the moon disappeared over the horizon. He felt in every flowing corpuscle and each sparking synapse, to the very core of his being that the time of Xustra was upon them. The time when the veil was at its closest to the mortal realm and most exposed to intrusion and corruption. The planet Jupiter rose over the Eastern horizon. This would be their bearing for the moment. Then an alignment with the stars in the belt of the constellation Orion would take them directly to the north-eastern extremity of this island. From there they would tack long and hard in to the south-east...

Amergin watched the planet Jupiter rise in the night sky, shimmering red in the low atmosphere.

"How appropriate Xomas! The planet of the god of war shows us the way! Take the helm I go to speak with MacCuill and the priest of the Chapter of Mystics, Xesu."

Complete blackness now, only the aftermath of the moon glow and way in to the distance the aurora of the Light of the Divine still pouring from the Portal of Land's End.

Xesu, priest of the Chapter of Mystics came up from the gunnels of the flagship to rendezvous with Amergin. He gazed westwards, enthralled by the still visible Light of the Divine. Touching his forehead and his heart, he sent a blessing to all of the Milesian fleet on this fearful and fated sea voyage. He sent his prayers to all of the enlightened beings of the Island of Destiny. He greeted the Sea Druid Amergin, "My lord, the Portal of Land's End still radiates pure and strong!" "But for how long will the portal be safe from the Shamen of Land's End Xesu? For how long will it shine?" Amergin replied tentatively, "Do you feel the Cycle of Xustra beginning? Do you feel the presence of the dark Sidhe?" Xesu nodded in agreement, he could feel the presence of evil encroaching in to this island. Amergin continued, "I need your guidance as a priest of the Chapter of Mystics..." At this point MacCuill stepped up to meet them...

"You too MacCuill, as sibling of the dark one MacCuacht, I need your advice and your knowledge of this island, and what we might expect to befall us. Come with me!"

Amergin led them to the prow of the flagship. No prying eyes and ears here..."By the Great Spirit! We must be strong!" he too touched his forehead and his heart and sent a blessing to the following fleet, "Look how the Milesian fleet sails! We go to meet the enlightened ones! We go to the Temple of Xhara!"

All three of them were aware of the challenge. As soon as they begin the tack south-east they will enter the domain of the Eastern Province... an unforgiving realm where most of the portals are compromised and the dark Sidhe are encroaching.

The gusting North Wester blew them steadily on... "The Mountains of Maum sire, the beginning of the Eastern Province!" They all turned in response to MacCuill's utterance. In the blackness of a moonless sky, they could just about make out, on the horizon, an even blacker silhouette of a mountain range. "This is a place to be feared my lord Amergin!" continued MacCuill, "We must stay well out to sea! The mountains are the home of the Iness. Legend tells of a race of beings that are devoid of heart and spirit, the darkest of the dark. The enlightened of the spirit world were banished from here aeons ago. The Iness have abandoned their human bodies for ghostly apparitions. The sea sprites of Iness as they are known, can turn the unwitting, by a simple touch, into cold, lifeless sea salt. Even in an encounter they can suck the very soul out of any living being!"

Amergin and Xesu shivered in unison with spine tingling terror. MacCuill had not finished, "They are under the control of the dark one, MacCuacht, now," the colour draining from him as he spoke, "and they will be waiting for us!"

The three stayed huddled near the prow. Amergin needed as much information as possible. MacCuill informed him that the ghostly apparitions of Maum, according to the Annals of Tuatha, only appeared at night. During the day they stayed in the darkest recesses of the Mountains of Maum, never venturing away from the satanic foot hills and ridges of Maum. The moonless sky even darker now! Oh for the first glimmer of dawn! Once more the beacons were lit and messages sent to the entire fleet, that they would tack south-east until dawn. A warning was given that all the crew must stay below, barring a skeleton crew necessary to sail the vessels. They were told to shutter all portholes and avoid gazing upon the ghostly apparitions.

The fleet tacked long and hard, the North Wester pushing them in to the blackness.The sea state fine, a mere head high swell wrapping in to the North Channel, pushing them along the coastline of the Eastern Province.

Still a few hours to dawn, they were directly adjacent to the Mountains of Maum. From here the black silhouettes were even more sinister and foreboding. Amergin stood next to Xomas at the helm, only he and the watchman and one of the crew were on deck. The rest remained below, "Thank the Great Spirit for perfect sailing conditions!" he mused, by way of a distraction. The rest of the crew stayed, hopefully protected, down below.

"Keep your eyes peeled Xomas!" his helmsman nodded, these instructions were unnecessary... He was fully aware of the danger...

Amergin processed the information given to him by MacCuill. The Innis would give early warning of their arrival to MacCuacht. He prayed that they remained unobserved under the cloak of darkness. He ordered for all the beacons to be doused. They must sail in stealth from now on. The sails filled in this continuous reach to the south-east. Not a sound! No voices. No activity. They just sailed and sailed in to the south-east...

Xomas was the first to notice the growing bow wave and an undulating swell from the south. He broke the silence, "The tide changes my lord! This will slow us!" Amergin nodded this time, understanding the implications. More time in purgatory... He watched as the dark silhouette of the Mountains of Maum were passing by even more slowly and slowing all the time as the tide ran faster against them. Time began to stand still. Will power and a constant North Wester against the growing might of the tide.

Barely any progress now, the black silhouettes barely moved. They were in a limbo... the tide turning and the planets revolving. Jupiter above them now, the moon long descended on its equinox track... not a glimmer of dawn... still hours to go. The life of a mariner, one minute heaven, the next hell!

The tide pushed and pushed. They were not going backwards, but certainly not forwards. There seemed to be an inevitability of meeting with the apparitions now...

From the blackened silhouette of the Mountains of Maum came an eerie tortured sound, a scream of the Banshee... a scream etched in to the psyche of all mere mortals. A collective shiver ran down the spines of all the Milesians. Someone would surely be taken this night...

Amergin watched in fear. At the first sign of any strangeness they must cover their eyes. Merely to gaze upon the sea sprites of Iness was instant death. Corpuscular bodies of their victims dessicated and destroyed, to become sea salt and returned to the ocean. Be touched by them and your soul is taken to become one of the growing army of lost souls.

They waited in the blackness of the hours before dawn, the time when the world was at its quietest.

Even the North Wester had abated. They made no headway against the surging tide. "This is a dreadful place Xomas!" He was just about to agree with the Sea Druid Amergin and make the suggestion that they put the sea anchors down, when the watchman aloft cried out, "A ghost! I swear by the Great Spirit, a ghost!" Another tortured scream and the apparitions descended from the dark... "Cover your eyes! Avert your gaze! Go below deck... quickly!" He and Xomas sprinted for the hold, leaping in and falling in a terror stricken heap through the open trapdoor. Another cry of the Banshee, followed this time by a harrowing deathly scream from the watchman. The crewman attending to the rigging responded way too late. He had covered his eyes, but the ghostly apparitions of Maum surrounded him and enveloped him. By the time he hit the deck, he knew he was doomed. Rather than his soul be taken and become one of the army of lost souls. He hurled himself overboard, the weight of his armour sinking him to the depths, way out of the reach of the ghostly apparitions of Maum and out of the clutches of the dark Sidhe.

Amergin slammed the heavy hard wood trapdoor shut, "Make sure we are shuttered tight Xomas! Check all the portholes, all the hold doors. Make sure we are sealed in from the ghosts!" Xomas scurried around in the dim light, checking and double checking, getting all of the crew to follow suit.

The dawn was still an hour away. Amergin prayed for the rest of the fleet. By the Great Spirit he hoped they had been vigilant! Crewless, rudderless and helpless in the still pushing tide, the flagship and all the fleet, drifted aimlessly. In the dimly lit gunnels of the flagship, they waited and they waited... the ghostly apparitions, the sea sprite of Iness, swarmed around the flagship, rattling trapdoors and shutters in vain, an occasional ear piercing cry shattering the silence. For minutes that seemed like hours, the ghostly apparitions of Maum searched for a weakness. They impatiently swarmed around the drifting fleet. Amergin and the crew of the flagship shuddered with each scream of the Banshee, and the desperate yell of defenceless Milesian crewmen attacked by these demonic apparitions.

Amergin knelt in prayer in the gloom of the hold. Xesu, the priest of the Chapter of Mystics joined him. One by one the crew fell to their knees. They all chanted sacred verse. They called to the Great Spirit to bring the Guardians of Light forth, through the ever nearing and thinning veil, to help their fellow Milesians. Another yell came from a distant vessel, another soul taken or worse, another mortal body dessicated in to grains of sea salt. With each distant cry, another prayer was given... "Deliver us from this purgatory Great Spirit, may the Guardians of Light bring the new light of day. Save us from the limbo of this night. Help us! We beseech thee!" Xesu delivered his most heart felt prayers to the captive gathering, they responded in unison, chanting to the Great Spirit...

Soon, they could hear chants from the other vessels of the fleet. They kept drifting helplessly with the tide, still pushing but weakening.The sacred chanting lifting their spirits. They chanted louder and louder... so loud they drowned out any cries from the banshee ghosts. This helped to shield them from the shock and terror of when any of their hapless crew were being taken. The chanting spread and came to a crescendo. A gospel of Light raising their sprits... the veil so close now...

Amergin fell in to a shamanic trance, induced by the heartening chants and spiritual prayers. His eyes tightly closed, he shut out the terror of the moment and found himself drifting in to an all familiar amber cosmos. He prayed for their salvation... he felt his body being caressed, his heart being massaged, his soul being cleansed, his spirits rising as he journeyed beyond the veil. He was in the presence of the Guardians of Light and was joined in union with his beloved Sceine...

They journeyed deep in to the spirit world, their bodies entwined... they were destined to be together... they were in rapture... they came in to the Light... In a moment of ecstacy and bliss the Light of the Divine poured through the veil... they were the conduit... they channelled the Light of the Divine in to the mortal realm...

The fleet drifting in the flowing tide... stopped! The first glimmering rays of dawn broke over the eastern horizon. There was a final terrifying cry from the sea sprites of Iness, and the ghostly apparitions returned to the Mountains of Maum. Dawn!

The first freshening gust of the North Wester drove the fleet on. The fleet continued on its long tack to the South East, away from the Mountains of Maum. Divine Light shone over the fleet.The warming rays fell upon Amergin. His eyes wide open now, "Sceine! I come to you my love!" Wide awake and galvanised he pushed the trapdoor open and burst into the broad daylight and fresh sea air…

He searched for the two crewmen, but they were gone! Amergin raised his arms in to the skies, "Great Spirit, protect the souls of our faithful mariners!" He wasted no more time. He called the entire crew, "All hands on deck! We go south-east for one more hour until the tide is fully turned, then we tack to the south-west and the Eastern Province and the Temple of Xhara!" The crews of all the vessels of the Milesian fleet took his lead once more…

Amergin stood defiantly on the prow. He was bathed in the warming sunlight. He noticed the deck where he stood was encrusted with an abnormal layer of glistening sea salt. He swept up a few grains with two fingers. He kissed the sea salt and let the freshening North Wester take the grains back into the infinite ocean, "Another Milesian mariner returning to his spiritual home! Bless your soul!"…

CHAPTER TWENTY FIVE:
THE NEMESIS ARRIVES...

The Temple of Xhara is the most ancient place of worship on the Island of Destiny. Ancient diviners who came with the first wave of invaders to this Promised Land recognised the power here. This place is a source of the Divine in nature. This is a place where lay lines of the Eastern Province converge. A place of origin, where the first shamen communed with the Great Spirit. This is the place where the Sidhe were first drawn from the spirit world, through the veil, and into the mortal realm. For a thousand years and more, the Guardians of Light have prevailed, bringing the Light of the Divine into the natural world.

Waves of invaders found enlightenment at the Temple of Xhara and the other portals on the Island of Destiny. The Sidhe of the spirit world had always found a way to coexist with the original tribes, until the war between the Tuathans and the Firbolg had brought the traitorous MacCuacht in to their midst. Against the wishes of his father, the High King Antiem, he cheated, deceived and ultimately slaughtered many thousand of the Firbolg. He unleashed a reign of terror so brutal that there was a tear in the veil between the mortal realm and the spirit world. MacCuacht's evil brought so much death and carnage, that the dark Sidhe were fed and nurtured and brought in to the mortal realm. Now the dark Sidhe and MacCuacht were in collaboration and threaten to infect the Temple of Xhara and the other great portals of the land.

Seanach, one of the High Priests of the Temple of Xhara, warned his fellow priests that MacCuacht had left the Shadowlands and that a wave of infection went before the army of lost souls. Entire villages were falling to the dark Sidhe. Tribes were being decimated. "There is an agent of evil here we did not anticipate, a pestilence that takes all before it. MacCuacht has unleashed a harbinger of death that we have no cure for, this foulness takes all that come in to contact with it. Many souls have been taken. The army of the dark grows!" Seanach fell to his knees, "Pray with me brethren!

We will take refuge in the Inner Sanctum. We will drink the water of life and send prayers to the Sea Druid Amergin. With the destined one by our side we will go beyond the veil. Together we will battle MacCuacht and his dark pestilence!"

Once more the priests of the Temple of Xhara chanted their sacred verse.

The Tree of Life pulsed with Divine radiance. The portal channelled life giving energy from beyond the veil. Light poured forth over the Eastern Province. The Cycle of Xustra was commencing. The enlightened ones must prevail...

Unbeknownst to the Priests of Xhara, the infection came from the head waters of the rivers feeding in to the Eastern Province. The fallen soldiers of the army of lost souls continued to infect the rivers and tributaries of the Shadowlands. Water that sank in to the limestone carst of the Shadowlands rose again in the springs and holy wells through the Eastern Province. The foul pestilence was being carried by stealth in the very waters of life.

As reports of infection became more widespread and the pestilence more virulent, the priests of the Temple of Xhara were beginning to resign themselves to their fate, "Amergin must come soon!"

Seanach sent two priests to the coast to keep watch for the Milesian fleet. "Bring them back with you! Go, in haste!" The priests Cos and Yanis travelled to the coast... They made good progress, climbing steadily. Cos and Yanis were men of nature. They would forage from the wild. The Mountains of Braie rose up before them. Streams of fresh unpolluted water poured from the eastern heights, fresh mountain water flowing directly to the eastern shores and the ocean.

Cos and Yanis arrived at the peak known as Beacon Summit. Here they had the perfect vantage point... eastwards to the ocean, an unhindered view for fifty miles. They could see the mountain chains of the east sweeping to the shoreline. They marvelled at the miles of golden beaches, verdant woodlands and rivermouths pouring their fresh water in to the now benign sea. The priests felt the buffeting north-west wind on their faces. They watched the horizon for the Milesian fleet... "No sign yet!" One watched while the other foraged for timber... they would light a beacon on the appropriately named summit... to speed the Sea Druid Amergin towards them.

Cos observed while Yanis scoured the hillside for fuel for the beacon. He filled the leather water carriers with the sparklingly fresh mountain water. Sipping the pure water of life, he let his gaze scan the western panorama, back towards the Temple of Xhara. He traced the trail from whence they had come... across the fertile Plain of Gobhain, over the meandering River Sieure, in full flood now.

The gathering, menacing storm clouds descending from the Iveare Mountains emptied a torrential deluge over the Shadowlands. Above the Plains of Gobhain, on an igneous outcrop, the Temple of Xhara... too far to make out features, but the visibility just good enough to make out the giant bluestone gateway and the pulsing radiance flowing in to the Eastern Province. The full Equinox moon had set hours ago. The Cycle of Xustra had commenced. As a priest, Cos knew how vulnerable the veil was now. He was heartened to see the glowing radiance emanating from the portal. For the moment, the equilibrium was being maintained. He was unaware, however, of the pestilence sweeping through the Plains of Gobhain, creeping in to streams and irrigation channels and rising imperceptibly into the springs and holy wells. Even the Fountain of Iorwerth, source of the water for the Tree of Life in the Temple of Xhara, was slowly being contaminated.

The early morning sunlight combined with the Divine radiance from Xhara... Yanis returned to stoke the beacon fire. He rejoiced with Cos, his heart warmed by the sight before him.The strengthening morning light illuminating the mountains and coastal plains of the Eastern Province. There! On the far northern horizon, the tell tale cream white sails of the Milesian fleet, "The Sea Druid Amergin arrives!"

Cos and Yanis scoured the mountain side for everything combustible. Dried bracken, lumps of ancient, blackened bog oak and even wind dried and sun bleached horns of long dead mountain goat rams. The beacon blazed, their spirits raised. Their salvation had come! Together they would stave off the onslaught of the dark forces!

Fully expectant, they continued to stoke the fires of the beacon, raiding copses of ancient original deciduous trees. The fleet edged southwards... a mighty fleet, many vessels and hundreds of battle hardened Milesian mariners.

Amergin and Xomas had long seen the beacon burning brightly from the best vantage point in the mountains. The flagship tacked towards the shores of the Eastern Province, the rest of the fleet followed. They sailed straight for the beacon, the coastline unfolded before them. A river flowed across the coastal plains, the source deep in the Mountains of Braie. A constant source of pristine, pure mountain water, the river meandered gently to the sea. A deep, navigable channel opened up before them. Very soon the fleet sailed in to the estuary. Sails were furled, anchors dropped, mooring lines tied.

The beacon still blazed brightly... this concerned Amergin... the beacon so bright, the vantage point so good... their arrival was being announced to all!

Cos and Yanis had by now left the beacon unattended. They were making for the estuary to greet the Milesian fleet. They stumbled down the mountainside like over excited teenagers, following streams until they joined the deep flowing river. They arrived just as the Milesian fleet pulled in to the estuary...

The priests of Xhara, dressed in their white, gold and amber gowns, timed their arrival perfectly. Amergin was stepping off the flagship, on to the gangplank and then the silver sands of the estuary.

Amergin recognised the attire of the priests of Xhara. The same long white tunics edged with gold braid and amber seams, the same attire that Sceine wore when she came to him in his dreams. She was their High Priestess!

Cos and Yanis bowed in deference to Amergin. They introduced themselves and told of their mission.

Almost before they had completed telling their tales, the Milesian mariners came ashore and were readying to march to the Temple of Xhara. "We will return via the Beacon Summit my lord." Cos explained, "From there you will see the Temple of Xhara, and by dusk we will march there!"

En route to the Beacon Summit Yanis and Cos regailed Amergin with the tales of the Eastern Province, they told of the coming of MacCuacht and the pestilence that swept before the army of lost souls. Amergin dipped his canteen in a crystal clear mountain stream and swigged deep the refreshing water of life.

He observed the land. This was surely an enclave of peace and tranquility, away from the trauma that awaits them over the other sides of the Mountains of Braie.

The priests of Xhara, Cos and Yanis brought them to the summit, a pile of smouldering embers the only remains of the once fiery beacon. From here they could survey the land on both sides of the Mountains of Braie. Such a panorama! To the northern horizon from whence they had sailed. Here, hills and mountains dropped down to the coastal plains that skirt the ocean and continue on to the south. Amergin basked in the warming sun. He did not face the malevolence he expected. This eastern extremity of the Promised Land was free of the dark ones influence... so far...

Before he could ask the question, his expression had betrayed him. Unless the priests were mind readers too! "You wonder about the influence of the dark Sidhe in this place, my lord?" Yanis asked curiously, "Here we bask in the Light of the Divine. We are in the Shire of the Rising Sun. Perhaps the purest land imaginable outside of the Temple of Xhara! Since the time of the ancients this land has been blessed by the presence of the Guardians of Light." Yanis swept his hand in an extravagant gesture towards the Temple of Xhara... In his flambuoyance, he was suddenly stopped in his tracks... His enthusiastic expression became one of numbed disbelief. Surely his eyes deceived him!

"My lord Amergin, I fear we may be too late!" In shock, he fell to his knees. His fellow priest Cos, soon followed. Before them, back towards the West, the fertile Plains of Gobhain, a green, verdant and almost iridescent land bathed in the morning sunlight.Beyond this to the north-west on a dramatic outcrop of igneous rock, the Temple of Xhara, still pulsing in the radiant Light of the Divine. Amergin's first vision of the Temple of Xhara was a disturbing one. The sacred place etched in the minds and hearts of all enlightened beings was being surrounded by an encroaching wall of lifeless grey mist, rolling down from the Mountains of Iveare. The verdant Plains of Gobhain were starting to be consumed. The Temple of Xhara would be next!

All joined in prayer. They called on the Great Spirit to bring salvation to the Temple of Xhara...

All the thoughts of goodwill and all the prayers were of no good to the tribes of the Plains and the High Priests of the Temple of Xhara...

The waters of life had been contaminated. Every spring and every holy well had been infected by the dark pestilence. On the very day that Yanis and Cos left for the eastern coast, holy men and women had started to fall prey to the dark infection. There was no protection! Even in the Inner Sanctum!

The Tree of Life showed signs of disease. Akin to an early autumn, leaves were being shed. Some of the priests became infected, losing their powers of prayer and meditation. They could no longer commune with the Guardians of Light...

All of the enlightened beings and priests and priestesses uninfected by the dark pestilence, gathered at the Temple of Xhara. The veil was so close. The Cycle of Xustra had commenced. The danger of the dark Sidhe intruding in to the mortal realm was real and potentially imminent. As one they stepped beyond the veil. The connection between the spirit world and the mortal realm was broken...

Amergin was only too aware that he was watching the closure of the most sacred portal on the Island of Destiny. He heard the weeping and wailing of the priests, Yanis and Cos, as they bore witness to the divine radiance weakening and dwindling. All of the Milesian mariners and warriors stood with heavy hearts, not only saddened but distraught with a sense of calamity. The priests of the Chapter of Mystics questioned their own faith. This was the greatest catastrophe to befall them on their journey of destiny.

Amergin continued to watch from this highest vantage point. He had seen verdant iridescence being consumed by a pall of grey lifelessness. He had seen the Temple of Xhara closing. His nemesis arrives! Amergin had no choice now. A lightning bolt of realisation... he must journey on... sail south in to uncharted waters... he must go to his beloved Sceine... together they must fight for the sacred Western Province!

With the gathering strength of the dark Sidhe, there was no doubt now that MacCuacht would march for Sliebh Mis. Sceine was in danger... the threat greater than ever!

The dawning of this reality fuelled his resolve. He prayed, "Great Spirit, protect us on our journey south. Give us the strength and courage to face the demons and denizens of the dark Sidhe. May the sea god Manannan look over us and give us safe passage. May the waves of the ocean and the Light of the eternal sun guide us to our destination and bring salvation to the Promised Land!"

Xomas, his loyal helmsman, Xesu of the Chapter of Mystics, Yanis and Cos, priests of the Temple of Xhara, MacCuill, the enlightened sibling of the dark one MacCuacht and Amergin's own faithful brother Eiremhou, bowed their heads in contemplation and prayer.They and the Milesian warriors prayed for the souls of the tribes of the Eastern Province and the priests of the Temple of Xhara.

There was a cold starkness about the day now. The pure radiance of the Temple of Xhara extinguished. In the quiet moments, in isolation, each and every one of them were scared, in the cold light of day, even as the sun rose to its mid day zenith, they felt exposed, vulnerable to the menace of the dark Sidhe. They were the prey now... they must leave this peaceful enclave on the eastern shores of the Island of Destiny. The army of lost souls will soon be on the march again... they must sail in to uncharted seas...

Once more the Sea Druid Amergin must take up the mantle of leader and champion. He had caught a glimpse of the cold stark truth. Xhara had been compromised, the temple grey and lifeless. He turned and marched past the smouldering embers of the beacon fire, lit with such hope and expectancy and now doused with harsh reality. He began the long march to the coast, his loyal Milesians following, subdued and fearful.

MacCuill walked next to him, his wisdom and knowledge will be much needed. They stepped carefully down the side of Beacon Mountain, all the while engaged in conversation about the journey to come.

Amergin looked down the eastern coastal plain. He wondered what might befall them on this leg of the circumnavigation of the Promised Land. MacCuill ventured to give his wisdom, "We have no choice but to sail south my lord. We have a fair wind that will take us swiftly to the Headland of Sorn, maybe a days sailing from here. We will enter the realm of the Diventii. This realm is uncharted. The Diventii are a tribe of magical Druids descended from the ancient ones."Amergin's expression changed. He too had heard of tales of ancient Druids coming to this land in the mists of time. MacCuill continued, "No one has ever entered this realm and returned to tell the tale. The Diventii give their allegiance to the water goddess Soulis... In this realm water is the Divine conduit. There are many mariner's tales of ritual sacrifice to appease the sea and water gods... the word is that to enter this realm without consent is foolhardy... for the uninitiated and unprepared it is a death sentence!"

"The Island of Destiny never fails to disappoint!" retorted Amergin, "We have fair weather as we sail south to the Headland Sorn. We must use our time well! We must become initiated! We must be prepared!"

Amergin was intrigued by the tale. It was reminiscent of the Milesian tales of the ancient ones who had travelled before them in millenia past, the same ancient ones who had arrived on the shores of Galicia and told of the Island of Destiny. These ancient ones had imbued modern Milesians with a sense of destiny and a sense of unity, a unity of spirit, a collective mythology and a sense of national identity. Legend has it that these ancient Druids, the ancestors of modern day Milesians, had sailed the infinite Northern Ocean, discovered the Promised Land, never to return...

These Diventii, Amergin wondered... were they the tribe descended from the ancient ones? The ones who had determined his own mission in life and determined his nation's sense of destiny? The ancients who communicated with the spirit world? The ones who were destined to bring all enlightened beings together and to bring him to his beloved Sceine...

The fleet sailed on a southerly course, tacking occasionally in the still favourable and constant North Wester. In the lee of the mountains, the weather remained benign, the seas calm. The land itself seemed benign, free of the influence of the dark Sidhe. The darkness pervading the rest of the Eastern Province had not encroached here yet. This was an enclave of peace and serenity. Even with the portal at the Temple of Xhara closed, there was real tranquility here. They seemed beyond the reach of the dark one MacCuacht. The dark brooding storm clouds and foul pestilence seemed a world away. The mission to reach Sceine was the ultimate priority, but Amergin was becoming increasingly preoccupied by the tale of the Diventii. "Was this the realm of the Diventii?! Were they the ancestors of the ancient Druids?!"

The tale told of their allegiance to the water goddess. Water the Divine conduit...

On reflection Amergin had never seen such clear pristine water before, than in this realm. He pondered on this... there must be a connection between the water and the pestilence! How did the Temple of Xhara fall so easily? Amergin became convinced that this realm was so tranquil and so peaceful, the link to the waters of life as the conduit of the Divine.

A days sailing and the Headland of Sorn appeared on the horizon, and what a days sailing! The fleet in all its glory planed in unison on a reach to the south, the fresh invigorating sea air and the sparkling brilliance of reflected sunlight on cresting waves.For the moment the darkness that overwhelmed the Temple of Xhara forgotten. Amergin took up his favourite position on the prow.

He lived for the sea. His veins were infused with salt water. He breathed a heady mixture of ozone and brine. His cup of natural optimism was filling once more. He revelled in the inspiration of the ocean. Ecstatic to be sailing on a voyage that takes him to Sceine. The Light of the Divine filled his soul. Amergin was inspired, lyrical verse poured from him...

Free spirit, Go beyond the wilderness and the mountains,
Soar to infinity, over streams, woods and the wild, wild sea.
Find your nature discover your truth and the peace within.
Bring your inspiration send the world your grace and beauty.
Rise above, rise and be free, soar to the headiest heights.
Bring only joy ... give the world your blessing and journey beyond.

The verse was his mantra... For blissful moments he fell in to a deep meditative trance. He journeyed out of his body, beyond the veil. He journeyed to the spirit world where he was shown ancient rituals of the Diventii by the Guardians of Light, rituals that would appease the pagan gods of the waters of life. The clear, pure water became the conduit of the Divine. He was in the presence of enlightened beings. He was in the deepest trance when his beloved Sceine came to him... she caressed and massaged him... she was in his soul... he was overcome with blissful ecstacy... for a virtual moment their bodies entwined, their souls became as one. For a virtual moment that felt like an eternity, they embraced, they touched, they kissed, they came together, "I am with you my beloved! Come to me!"... A vision of beauty, Sceine smiled, touched his fingertips, now encrusted with the salt of the ocean spray... A set wave broached the prow of his ship consuming him in a fine drenching ocean spray... he was back in the mortal realm... Amergin smiled once more...

The sailing was so good, the Headland of Sorn reared up in no time at all, the landscape so different now. The cloud-touching summits of the Mountains of Braie were well off their stern. Amergin observed with great curiosity, a line of carved totems on the cliff edge facing to the east. "They must be totems to the goddess Soulis, celebrating the sunrise," he mused. The closer to the Headland of Sorn the fleet got, the more the detail on the totems became apparent. The totems were carved Bluestone. Carved so intricately and precisely in to giant heads, each one facing to a slightly different horizon. Xomas speculated, "They appear to face sunrise at the solstices and equinoxes my lord." He pointed to one that faced exactly at the point of sunrise at the autumn equinox. Amergin agreed. He gave instructions to his crew to tack to the open ocean to avoid the inevitable turbulence at the confluence of two seas, as they rounded the Headland of Sorn.

This dramatic, spectacular red sandstone peninsula marked the end of the protection afforded to them from the long distance ground swell. A white line of spume, a thermocline, two ocean currents colliding with slightly different temperature and salinity, swept out to sea. Well offshore now, they tacked again. Predictably, out of the lee of the headland, they started to roll in a half mast high swell. A frenzied rip tide current tossed and turned them. The fleet struggled to make headway for a while, drifting further away from shore. Finally, they were ejected out of the turbulence and in to a cleaner wind. The North Wester grabbed the billowing sails and sent them swiftly in to the south-west. They had an uninterrupted view of the uncharted coast line now. The reputation of the Diventii as an ancient tribe of Druids practicing live sacrifices to appease the goddess Soulis had kept all at bay. This was certainly in the forefront of Amergin and his crew as they sailed towards the shore.

The coastline unfolded before them in its spectacular glory, the low trajectory of the evening sun bathing the hills and forests and steep sided mountains in a golden light. The red sandstone cliffs of the Headlands of Sorn gave way to a landscape of coves and beaches. Amergin stood watchfully at the prow. The entire fleet had navigated through the turbulent waters off the Headland of Sorn. His mission was to get to the Western Province by the quickest route possible. They faced in to a stronger wind which was veering in to the west. The groundswell came from the west too. These were difficult sailing conditions. Amergin went to his helmsman, "We have a decision to make Xomas. Do we sail West in to this wind and in to this building swell? There are no charts for this coast, but by our astral positioning, MacCuill reckons on three days sailing and with these conditions worsening maybe a good deal more!" Xomas gave his reckoning, "Even when we get to the Bay of Sceine, which may take a long time in these challenging and worsening seas, we have two days march to the Portal of Hushinish and then more to the high mountain fortress of Sliebh Mis... Surely the option to land at the first navigable landing place must be considered." They both pondered this... the long march through the uncharted realm of the Diventii, troubled them both...

The helmsman further considered their predicament... the endless coastline of bays and headlands and mountain ranges sweeping down to the sea as far as the eye could see. Beyond the horizon and even further still, the tops of high mountain ranges, "Going west is the long option my lord... sailing in to this strengthening westerly and no doubt building swell... time, weather and sea are against us!" He needed to say no more! Amergin announced, "We will land at the first safe anchorage and march on to the Western Province!"

MacCuill's facial expression showed his concern, "What of the Diventii? Their magic and their cruel reputation go before them!" Amergin was fully aware of their reputation for live sacrifice. He made his choice. The strategy to march to the Western Province had been made, "We will go by stealth. We will avoid confrontation. Our mission is no concern of the Diventii. I will go with an advance party to forge the way... Ours is the way of peace!"

Amergin's resolve and conviction inspired them all. They went away without question, the rest of the crew were informed of the decision and messages mirrored to the rest of the fleet.

Amergin remained at the prow, the late evening sun bathing him and the flagship in a welcome, warming reflective glow. He would find that anchorage and safe haven. As they sailed westwards he, his crew and the watchmen aloft looked to the land. Massive round topped mountains soared to the heavens. Ancient red sandstone weathered and eroded by wind and rain over time, creating a monumental landscape of stacks and ravines. Waterfalls plunged hundreds of feet and streams carved deep in to the red earthed hillsides. Crystal clear streams flowing rapidly in to a grateful ocean, "This is the land of the Diventii. Were they the tribe of ancient Druids?" Amergin's curiosity was tinged with apprehension.

He would lead an advance party. His mission to find a safe route... but he was determined to find out about the Diventii...

On the sky line, the range of massive round topped mountains was abruptly interrupted by a canyon that penetrated deep inland, a fault line creating landslips and erosion over millennia. Here was a natural gap through the mountains. He pointed the canyon out to his crew, "This could be the way!"

Amergin alerted the watchmen, "Find us the anchorage and safe haven we need! Be vigilant!"

CHAPTER TWENTY SIX:
THE REALM OF THE DIVENTII

The Diventii watched the Milesian fleet from the secrecy of woodland that fringed a sheltered bay. The Milesian fleet rounded another headland. Amergin let out a grateful yell, "We have found our safe anchorage!"

The bay, with a southern aspect, trapped and reflected the late evening sun over golden sands, surrounded by verdant woodland. Amergin noticed a dense grove of ancient Oaks in the hinterland of the beach, "If the Diventii are in this realm... they will most certainly be here!"

The quality of the light, the beach, the woodland, the backdrop of the massive round topped mountains, gave this place an ethereal otherworldly ambience. Amergin felt the hackles on the nape of his neck rise... they were being watched!

The ten men chosen for the advance party rowed to shore in two boats. They were on full alert.

They rowed strongly, Amergin leading them. Even before the first of the landing boats touched the shore, Amergin leapt in to the knee deep water, guiding the keel in to the soft, fine grained golden amber sands. Cresting waves broke gently on the shore, dissipating harmlessly after their thousand mile journey...

The plan... to make for the canyon... Once safely there, they would light a beacon to send for the rest of the Milesian mariners.

The ten and Amergin stepped purposefully through the dry, crunching sand and through the marram grassed dunes. Sea thistles and scrubby shore land plants gave way to a velvet carpet of moss and clover and the three leaved shamrock, rabbits everywhere, scattering as they marched through. The first, twisted, wind sculpted Oak marked the beginning of the dense, wooded hinterland. A startled hare bolted from its form, escaping in a bounding, mazing, elusive run.

In the shadows of the ancient Oak grove, a red deer stag twitched nervously and was gone in to the denseness. A fox barked a warning to its mate...

Amergin felt the piercing gaze, before he saw them... then from the sacred Oak grove, appeared the Diventii. He and his faithful ten drew their swords from their scabbards in a metallic instant. More Diventii, and more, appeared from the dense woodlands. Far too many to take on! Amergin and his ten men stood transfixed. They were surrounded, their escape route to the shore blocked. Quietly and without their realisation they had been trapped. Their captors stood in silence, watching...

Amergin took the initiative, fighting not an option. He carefully and deliberately replaced his sword in to the scabbard. His instincts then drove him to do something that shocked the advance party.

He dropped to one knee, proffering his sword to his "enemy", "We come in peace!" The bronze hilted sword given to him by his father Milidh, glinted in the last rays of the sun. The sword, an heirloom presented to Amergin by the greatest warrior in Milesian legend, was now a peace offering. The loyal ten took his lead. They all dropped to one knee and offered their battle sharpened swords as tokens of peace. Amergin's sense of place and time had told him that this was the right thing to do. All his instincts, all his wisdom, all his Druidic powers told him he was in the presence of kindred spirits. For all their reputation as fearsome warriors and the tales of live sacrifice, Amergin felt to the core of his being, that here were kindred souls. He wondered if the legendary tales were true. Were these the lost tribe descended from the ancients? He and his ten men were about to find out...

The spokes person for the Diventii stepped forward in all his strangeness, "I am Gerridh!" boomed a commanding yet strangely endearing figure. Amergin stood up to greet him. He was startled at the familiarity of appearance. The half shorn head, the long plait dyed in red brown henna, his costume of woven flax and armour of the consistency of dried and compressed turf. This strange other worldly figure had all the semblance of a cast of high priests still living in Northern Galicia.

"Surely, that cannot be!?" muttered Amergin quietly in disbelief. Gerridh was bedecked in ornately inscribed bronze and gold jewellery. The design was all too familiar... infinite spirals and symbols of the trinity.The trinity of truth, mythology and the destiny of a nation. Around Gerridh's neck hung an amber amulet. A twin, an exact replica of the amulet King Milidh had given to Queen Scota at their wedding at the Temple of Japhet, on the Northern shores of Galicia, many years ago...!

Here were the descendants of the ancient ones! Here were the descendants of the originators of the prophecy! Here are the descendants of the ancient tribe of Druids that imbued and instilled the Milesian nation's sense of destiny. Tales that have been told through the mists of time, passed down from generation to generation of Milesians.Tales of myth and legend that have sparked the imagination and fired the passions of him and his people. All these tales are true... and the truth stood before him!

"I am Amergin!" He sensed they knew his identity already. There was a collective nod of heads by the Diventii. In response to his peace offering, they lowered their swords and pikes. Encouraged by this, Amergin went on, "We are Milesians. I bring our tribes on a journey of destiny to this our

Promised Land. We are on a mission of life and death. I must find my destined one, Sceine! The fate of all the enlightened ones depends on it!"

Gerridh's smile told it all, "We have been waiting for you Amergin, Sea Druid and champion of Milesia!" He stepped forward and embraced Amergin, "Come with us! We will commune with the Guardians of Light... we will show you the way!"

Amergin and his ten faithful warriors followed Gerridh of the Diventii. They were taken deep in to the sacred Oak grove on the red earthed lower slopes of a vast round topped mountain. In a clearing in the Oak grove lay a deep, dark, mysterious pool of crystal clear, fresh, mountain water. The Diventii began to circle the pool. Amergin's mind flashed back to the Pool of Cerces in Galicia, where he attended his first ceremonial ritual with the Chapter of Mystics. GerrIdh took a pouch from one of his druids. This contained tablets of bronze and lead. He engraved messages and questions on the tablets and with a prayer to their goddess Soulis hurled them in to the dark, mirror surfaced pool, "Water of Life, grant us the power to see our way forward." Miraculously, no sooner had the tablets disappeared in to the depths, the reflective mirrored surface began to form images... The first of the shimmering reflections shocked them all... the Temple of Xhara being inundated by the advancing hordes of the army of lost souls, and the dark one MacCuacht revelling in the darkness of the Eastern Province. The reflections shimmered and flickered, revealing the canyon through the range of round topped mountains. A dissolving image showed a great portal in the Western Province and the high mountain fortress of Sliebh Mis and the beautiful High Priestess of Xhara and Princess of the Western Province, Sceine... the reflective images vanished and the dark, mirrored surface of the pool remained. "You have been shown your way Amergin! You and your warriors must go west. We will take you through the mountains," and he added with real emotion, "The waters of Life in the Eastern Province are infected with the foul pestilence of the dark Sidhe... and the infection spreads!"

Gerridh implored Amergin, "For the sake of this Island of Destiny find your beloved Sceine and protect the Western Province!"

That evening the signal beacon roared in to life, burning bright in the gathering dusk. "The sign!" and the Milesian mariners hurried to make the fleet fast and safe. All barring a small security contingent were soon rowing for the shore...

Whilst the Diventii gathered provisions together for their journey through the mountains, Gerridh and Amergin conversed at the fireside. This was a meeting of minds and of kindred spirits. Through the night they talked, swapping ancient tales and stories of the Milesian nation. Amergin learned how the ancestors of the Diventii tribe, Milesian Sea Druids like himself journeyed over the Northern Ocean. Their vessels were destroyed in a tempest. They were stranded and became land bound.

Slowly, the marine skills and seamanship were lost through the generations. They found sanctuary in the lands on the southern shores of the Island of Destiny. The ancestors soon became faithful servants of the goddess Soulis. The Waters of Life became the conduit through which they could journey beyond the veil. Gerridh told of how his ancestors befriended the Sidhe who journeyed in to the mortal realm as the Guardians of Light. Together they became the enlightened ones.

Gerridh explained how the salvation of the Promised Land depended on the continuation of the enlightened ones. Messages had been sent beyond the veil to the Milesian nation, to the Chapter of Mystics, to find their champion, to find the most enlightened being of their nation. Through these messages the prophecy of all Milesians was perpetuated... the enlightened champion would journey to the Island of Destiny... to meet the most enlightened being of this island... together, the Island of Destiny has a chance ... apart the dark Sidhe will prevail... "You are that enlightened one Amergin!"

Gerridh exclaimed from the heart, "You are destined to be with the High Priestess Sceine! Your progeny will inherit this land and bring enlightenment to all!"

Gerridh and select Druids gathered at the pool, named after the goddess Soulis. Amergin was invited to join them.Once more they inscribed messages on palm sized lead and bronze tablets. This was a ritual before every journey. Amergin was given a tablet. He would be the first to make an offering to the goddess...

The Sea Druid Amergin knelt beside the pool, now encircled by the Diventii. He peered through the high canopy of the great, ancient Oaks, trees centuries old, magnificent and gnarled with twisted and contorted branches spreading out over the pool, reflecting in the silver-black surface. Again his mind flashed back to Galicia, to the Pool of Cerces and his first encounter with Gonne of the Chapter of Mystics. He remembered how he was taken deep in to the sacred waters and was being drawn towards the dark Sidhe, only to be rescued by the Guardians of Light and his beloved High Priestess Sceine. Those days of the ordeal an age away now...

Gerridh took his place on the edge of the pool. He stood on a red earth platform and began the ritual ceremony with religious incantations. He gestured to Amergin to join him. The high canopy swayed in harmony with the chanting, "A storm from the West!" thought the mariner in him... Amergin was so glad he had chosen the over land path.

Gerridh channelled this natural energy... the veil between the spirit world and the mortal realm rose to the reflective surface. Amergin sensed this was his moment. He threw his inscribed tablet in to the Waters of Life. Gerridh chanted to the goddess Soulis... a familiar amber cosmos began to percolate mysteriously from the depths... strange morphing creatures of the Light swirled upwards towards the surface... a vision of beauty formed... Sceine! She came in response to his message. The journey to come would be fraught with danger... she brought her message... "Travel safely, my beloved... I will be with you always!"

Sceine was in his head now. Her voice spoke only to him, "You have chosen the path well my beloved! The Diventii will guide you through the Canyon of Sorrow. Beware the Banshee of Mordha, this is their realm! Do not travel at night!" she implored him, "From the canyon you and your tribes will travel alone. You will follow the river through the extremities of the Eastern Province. Do not drink the water here, the darkness infects it! You will come to the Lake of the Dead. From the lake you must strike up to the high ground, through the Pass of Cathsin and upwards to the Mountain of Foran in the Iveare range. Here you will find a lone standing stone on the ridge overlooking the Western Province. The stone is dedicated to Mor. The daughter of the sun, married to the sea god Manannan. From here the Guardians of Light will be with you and they will guide you to me! Until you reach the standing stone never venture off the path, the land harbours the demons and denizens of the dark Sidhe! Hurry my love! The dark one MacCuacht marches back to his high mountain fortress of Hawardden. From there he marches to Sliebh Mis to find me. His army of lost souls strengthens all the time! Hurry! I wait for you! Come to me!" The shimmering vision of Sceine began to recede in to the silver-black reflective depths of the pool... "Hurry my love!"... The amber cosmos vanished and on impulse, Amergin stripped off his clothes and dove in deep in to the frigid waters... Swimming deep and powerfully he was able to connect with her shimmering form... they embraced, her pure energy coursing through him... their love unbounded... a moment of pure bliss and he came to the surface joyously!

From the distant canyon, a mournful cry split the cooling night air. The Banshee of Mordha awaits them...

The frigid waters of the pool still dripping from him, the cry out of the darkness made him shudder uncontrollably. They must heed Sceine's warning!

Drifting in and out of a fitful sleep, Amergin rested by the fire, gratefully lit by the Diventii. Dry and warm now, they waited for the dawn... the journey would continue...

Gerridh greeted Amergin as the first rays of dawn percolated through the Oak canopy, "Your warriors have been given a bag full of provisions and water, sufficient for the two days march to the Mountains of Iveare. The sun rises, the realm of the Banshee is safe. We must go now! The march through the Canyon of Sorrow is long and arduous and the sun sets early there. Behind the round topped mountains, the light fades fast. You must lead your warriors bravely Amergin!" Gerridh handed Amergin a woven, flax bag, stuffed full of unleven bread, mountain goat cheese and strips of sea salted and dried kelp. This he slung over his shoulder together with the goat skin water carrier. "None of the natural water can be drunk until you climb high in to the Iveare Mountains!" Gerridh pointed out. Amergin told Gerridh of his experiences on the eastern shores, that there still were places free of the foul pestilence. As he related his tales, beads of cold sweat appeared on his brow. The prospect of the pestilence arriving in the Western Province was too much to bear...

The Milesians followed in the footsteps of the Diventii, the lead taken by Gerridh. Amergin walked beside him... they both revelled in the richness of the sacred Oak groves... so verdant, such a diversity of life. For two hours they walked through the woodlands. Red deer, camouflaged in the trees, the green woodpecker knocked on the ancient Oaks, ravens and crows raucously called their warnings as they marched through, golden eagles soared overhead. Every turn of the path, there was more life... a place of origin, protected by the mountains and the forebidding Canyon of Sorrow.

Already the sun climbed high in the canyon. This was such a forlorn place... what a contrast! The rich tapestry of life in the woodlands and here, desolation!

They left the green carpeted track behind... now a boulder strewn, rugged mountain track, climbing steeply. Each step was laboured and deliberate, picking their way through a minefield of rockfalls and ancient glaciations. Far in to the distance over miles and miles of treacherous terrain, a high mountain pass. Beyond this, the extreme margins of the Eastern Province, the realm of the dark one MacCuacht. At this juncture Amergin questioned his decision to go overland to the high mountain fortress of Sliebh Mis on the western side of the Iveare Mountains. As he thought this, a blast of icy mountain air hit him and Gerridh full square, making them lean in to the gale to keep their balance.

One look at the skyline and the approaching storm front reassured Amergin the right choice had been made. He was convinced now that they were on the right path, and hadn't the secret of the Prophecy been unlocked too! He turned to observe Gerridh, the descendant of the ancient Druids.

Amergin was destined to take this path. He strode on with real purpose now...

The watery sun dipping in and out of building storm clouds was on a speedy trajectory today. The boulder strewn, ever steepening track was taking forever to negotiate. Gerridh knew the way, but even so the track was virtually impassable in places. Time stood still, progress painfully slow, and still the sun tracked across the canyon. Mid afternoon now and they didn't even appear to be halfway.

Gerridh looked furtively up at the sky, checking the progress of the sun. He looked back to see the Diventii mountain guides and the Milesians stretched out for miles. He had never made this journey with so many! He and Amergin exchanged glances. No words were necessary. They just pressed on. They were beyond the point of no return. The Canyon of Sorrow was living up to its name. This was the realm of the Banshee. Night time was their domain...

The further in to the canyon, the narrower the window of daylight became. Normal calculations of time of sunset had to be dispensed with. The higher they climbed, the further they marched, the less time they had. Time until the sun dipped behind the mountains. The shadows lengthened and darkened. All too soon a line of creeping darkness began to cross the canyon. "An hour maximum!" estimated Amergin. The cold beads of sweat reappeared on his furrowed brow, even though his body was over heating with the exertion of the climb. As if to exacerbate their plight a blood curdling cry chilled the mountain air. The domain of the Banshee approached!

A race against time! The shadow cast by the mountain growing. Gerridh pointed the way to Amergin, "Go first, you must be safe!" Amergin looked upwards.The final stage, a steep scree run, with loose boulders ready to dislodge and collide with any undiscerning climber. Three steps forward and two back in the loose mountain scree. Progress so slow, the high ridge still bathed in daylight seemed an age away. The exertion, the effort, began to take its toll... impossible to track straight up the scree run. Amergin began to traverse, making more headway now, but the route longer... akin to tacking in to a strengthening head wind... slow and arduous! He stopped for a moment, a brief respite, blowing hard, his heart pounding, blood pressure maxing.The shadow of the mountain now engulfing the lower track. Many Milesians were yet to reach the scree run...the shadow creeping...Many of his countrymen becoming potential prey to the Banshee.

"Don't look back!" yelled Gerridh, "Keep moving! Stay in the daylight! The Banshee will know who you are. They come from the underworld... they are in league with the dark Sidhe!"

This galvanised Amergin, he pushed on even harder... there was an optimum speed... too fast and too much scree would slip away.Steadily with deliberate strides... on and on... upwards and upwards...chasing the daylight like a drowning man gasping for oxygen. The window of daylight receding, he gave a final last push. He was on the verge of exhaustion. Ten more traverses and he would be there! He ran now! He ran for his life! A precariously placed boulder broke free and hurtled down the slope, "Look out below!" In the corner of his eye he saw Gerridh, fellow Diventii and Milesians leap to one side to avoid certain death!

In that moment he too threw himself on to the final stretch of scree! The gradient eased and he sprinted to the top of the ridge. He fell in a collapsed heap, hyperventilating like a marathon runner hitting the wall. Blowing hard in recovery mode, a shaft of welcoming sunlight swept through, now dancing over the mountain tops, now hiding behind the burgeoning storm clouds. Gerridh arrived next and one by one the Diventii mountain guides, the Milesians were too slow... They were mariners, not mountaineers! "You must keep going Amergin! Even here on the high ridge, daylight will soon go! We must reach the Lake of the Dead, here you will be safe. The spirits of our ancestors will protect you..." Milesians now began to arrive, friendly faces...

Xomas, MacCuill, Eiremhou! "At least they are safe!" thought Amergin. He feared for the others... the Canyon of Sorrow in virtual darkness now. The shadow complete ...Amergin turned away, to continue on the path. Even here on the high ridge daylight was dwindling. The track was easier now, following a tumbling mountain stream on its downward course to the Lake of the Dead. No more than a few minutes on this track, the first of a series of blood curdling screams cut them to the core. Each scream, the loss of a good soul, another recruit for the dark army! Amergin whinced in empathetic pain, he cried out in despair at the demise of good men, Milesian mariners wanting only for a decent sea burial, whilst fighting for the cause of the Light.

Gerridh felt his pain, knowing there will be many lost in the Canyon of Sorrow that night...

CHAPTER TWENTY SEVEN:
BEYOND THE CANYON OF SORROW

The word has travelled to MacCuacht that the "destined one" has sailed south and journeys through the forbidden realm. He grimaced pleasurably at the prospect of them venturing through the Canyon of Sorrow..."more recruits for the dark army!"

His dark deeds done at the Temple of Xhara.The Waters of Life contaminated and spreading his foulness... now he marched for the Western Province. He will muster his forces at the mountain fortress of Hawardden and then march for Sliebh Mis...

MacCuacht had cut a swathe through the Eastern Province. The plague of darkness was upon the tribes of the Eastern Province. As he returned to the distant Mountains of Iveare, lost souls swelled the ranks. By the time they reached Hawardden they were thousands strong. MacCuacht schemed,

"I will send the demons and denizens of the dark to intercept the Sea Druid Amergin. He will never make it out of the Mountains of Iveare!"

The next day, the army of lost souls marched in to the Western Province... stronger than ever... the sacred Woodlands of Derwydd fall to the dark Sidhe. MacCuacht felt invincible... the plague of the dark spreads west...

Erhombu and the spirits of the Woodland of Derwydd had to retreat to the Quarry of Izion, the purest source of Bluestones on the Island of Destiny. They will make a stand there with Endinou, the Guardian of the Quarry of Izion and the cyclopic quarrymen. They will wait for the Sea Druid Amergin and the Milesian forces and ultimately fight to retake the Woodlands of Derwydd and protect the great Portal of Machlleth. They feared for their survival, but their faith was strong,

"The Guardians of Light are with us!" encouraged Endinou, "Amergin marches to meet his destined one, Sceine, at the mountain fortress of Sliebh Mis!" Both of these powerful Guardians knew that the fate of their sacred island hung in the balance...

Sceine, the Princess of the Western Province, High Priestess of Xhara, returned to the high mountain fortress of Sliebh Mis in the south of the magnificent Iveare Mountain range.

She and her entourage of priests had survived the encounter with the raven haired Witches of Hawardden. They were escorted from the Portal of

Hushinish to the mountain fortress of Sliebh Mis by Terese of the Xantha and her amazonian warriors...

Returning along the Ridge of Thormond, Sceine looked out over the glorious Western Province, the setting sun sending shimmering reflections over the infinite Northern Ocean, the Light of the Divine gently bathing her realm in life-giving energy. She found a moment of transcendent peace, while all around her was in chaos!

The emissaries of the dark were all around her. The three Witches of Hawardden skulked in the Valley of the Mad, waiting for their chance. The dark one MacCuacht had already taken the sacred Woodlands of Derwydd and threatens the great Portal of Machlleth. Now he marches to Sliebh Mis!

There, Sceine will wait for her beloved Amergin... she prays to the Great Spirit that he comes safely to her!

The impressive fortress perched high in the Iveare Mountains was a sight for sore eyes. Sceine breathed a sigh of relief as she and her escort scaled the steep mountain track and soon arrived at the massive portcullis bridging the yawning precipice between them and the safety of the battlements. Her beloved father Antiem had turned Sliebh Mis in to the most impregnable bastion, during the years of his reign.

Sceine smiled up at the heavens. She felt his presence guiding her. "The defences are going to be tested like never before!" she spoke in to the ether as if he stood next to her. "We will fight to the last! I wait for my destiny! The Western Province and the Island of Destiny shall find its salvation! The seeds of the Enlightenment shall spread throughout the Promised Land! The Guardians of Light shall prevail!" She blew a kiss out in to the ether and smiled to the universe. Looking out over the southern peaks of the Iveare, she sensed Amergin was near, "Come to me! Journey safely! I am waiting for you!"

Beyond the Canyon of Sorrow, on the descent to the Lake of the Dead, on the extremities of the Eastern Province, Amergin looked up to the heavens, towards the distant peaks of the Iveare Mountains. All his senses were heightened... he felt Sceine guiding him, comforting him...

This was as far as Gerridh and the Diventii guides would go. At dawn they would return to the "forbidden realm" on the Southern shores of this sacred island. They must protect their lands and the culture and heritage of the ancients. Gerridh dipped his hands in to the cool pristine waters of the lake, fresh water from the southern mountains of the Iveare range. Free from the poison oozing in to the Waters of Life further to the north and east.

As he splashed his face, Gerridh explained to Amergin, "Here we send the souls of the departed Diventii to the spirit world to join the Guardians of Light." He went on to vividly describe the ritual ceremonies. The funeral pyres on the rafts made of the most ancient Oaks. These rafts were floated out in to the Lake of the Dead. Burning with such intense heat, the bodies were cremated and their ash descending to the depths. The inscribed tablets of lead and bronze melted, together with the weaponry and armour placed on the raft, and they too sunk in to the depths of the Lake.

The messages on the tablets and the ceremonial rituals of the Druids of the Diventii, summoned the Guardians of Light from the spirit world. The Guardians then took the souls of the departed beyond the veil safely in to the spirit world. Amergin cupped his hands and washed his face with the pure water. He could feel the veil was near! He sensed the life giving properties of the water. This was a holy place indeed!

Through the evening and in to the night, the Milesians arrived at the lake. They were shocked and traumatised by the experiences in the Canyon of sorrow. Many had been lost to the Banshee. Some of the unfortunates were killed trying to escape the terrifying entities. The bodies of a few hapless victims were carried to the lakeside. Amergin, with Gerridh, organised a funeral ritual for the fallen.

They all gathered by the lake. Milesian and Diventii chanting sacred verse and performing ancient rituals, sending their souls beyond the veil...

With the first rays of dawn filtering over the mountain tops, Amergin and Gerridh made their farewells. They were both on the same mission now, to protect the Island of Destiny! Amergin was so thankful that his chosen path had brought him to the realm of the Diventii. Gerridh and the ancestral Druids had revealed many truths. The one certain truth was that Amergin must go to find Sceine!

The Milesian mariners began the ascent up the high mountain pass. Soon the Lake of the Dead was a shimmering reflection, hundreds of feet below them. The smouldering embers of ancient Oak rafts sending wisps of white smoke wafting around the mountain sides. The Diventii made their way back through the Canyon of Sorrow, safe in the broad daylight.

Before leaving, Gerridh had warned Amergin and his tribesmen not to venture off the path. The high pass was notorious for ambush. The bandits of the Aganti tribe preyed on any strays or stragglers.

According to Gerridh and his Druids the Aganti tribe had fallen to the horrors of the dark plague, and they along with the demons and denizens of the dark Sidhe had been sent by MacCuacht to intercept and slay the Milesian Sea Druid and his tribes...

Over the high mountain pass in the southern peaks of the Iveare Mountains... Sceine surveyed the Western Province from the allegedly impregnable battlements of the fortress of Sliebh Mis. She had called her priests to her chambers... the situation required collective minds and the wisdom of the ages. They were ushered in to the room by her Captain of the Guard. Sceine was a virtual prisoner in her own domain... guarded day and night. The priests sat around a magnificent, carved, ancient Oak table. Sceine took her place in an equally impressive, ornately engraved Oak chair... the same chair Antiem had conducted his affairs of state and war. The atmosphere was palpable, tension in the air, "The situation worsens my lady!" Sceine did not need to be told this by her priesthood, "I need solutions, not statements of the obvious! We can only fight the dark one MacCuacht from our strengths!" The reprimanded priests offered the positive news, "The Sea Druid Amergin is on the high mountain pass to the South of the Iveare Mountains. He comes to you. He is a day's march away from Sliebh Mis!" Sceine had sensed his coming, but it was good to hear the confirmation of his progress. The priest continued, "We hear that the Guardian of the Woodlands of Derwydd, Erhombu is at the Quarry of Izion with the wizard Endinou. The spirits of the Woodlands and the Cyclops of Izion stand with them to protect the source of the Bluestones and the great Portal of Machlleth."

This was the news that Sceine wanted to hear. The Guardians of Light were with them! They must have faith! The priests continued to give advice, "We have word from the Guardians of Light too, that there is a gathering of Milesians at the ancient Portal of Sceilge on the Magine Islands... they wait for a sign from the Sea Druid Amergin!"

This was even better news! Sceine was heartened at this... so far the great portals of the Western Province remain in tact. Not even MacCuacht knew of the power that could be unleashed when the portals are connected! She implored her priesthood, "Go now! Send your messengers to all those guarding the portals! Tell them the Secret of the Alignment. Tell them of the power that can be unleashed at the commencement of the Cycle of Xustra!" The secret was traditionally given only to the High Priests and Priestesses. To reveal the Secret of the Alignment to the uninitiated was deemed as sacreligious in the extreme. However Sceine and her priesthood recognised these apocalyptic times and recognised the measures needed!

Sceine walked out on to the balcony of her chamber, high in the battlements of the fortress.

She was more focussed than ever. The meeting had galvanised all. Surveying the Western Province in the bright light of a new day, all appeared normal, but how deceptive were appearances! Her mind was consumed with dark thoughts of her brother MacCuacht. He marches for Sliebh Mis now!

His army of lost souls had taken the Woodlands of Derwydd. The great Portal of Machlleth could be next! Then Sliebh Mis! She feared for her beloved, her destined one, Amergin, on the high mountain pass at this very moment...

The terrifying prospect of MacCuacht overwhelming the Western Province crystallised her thoughts. In the cold light of day, the dawning of the realisation that she must return to the Portal of Hushinish one more time! This time she would travel with full military guard. She now knew that the Witches of Hawardden lurked somewhere in the hinterland. The day of reckoning had arrived! The dark one marches! The Cycle of Xustra commences! The enlightened ones must prevail!

Sceine marched for Hushinish. She intended to meet the Sea Druid

Amergin on his route from the high mountain pass. Together they would go to the great Portal of Hushinish! Together they would summon the Guardians of Light through the veil! Together they will bring enlightenment to the Island of destiny!

So it is written....and is in the stars...

The high mountain pass zig zagged endlessly. No sign of the bandits or the demons and denizens of the dark... yet! Amergin was concerned that his warriors should stay close, stay compact. From previous experiences, the more stretched they became the more vulnerable they were to attack.

Amergin let Xomas and Eiremhou lead the way. He dropped back to liaise with his map maker MacCuill. They would need all the local knowledge available in this treacherous terrain.

MacCuill concurred with Amergin... another day's march... they would reach the summit in daylight and descend in to the Western Province as the sun sets...

He gave Amergin a further warning about the Aganti tribe, "They are a fierce independent tribe, worshipping ancient gods. They believe the spirits of their ancient ones are in the very rocks of the mountains. The Aganti hail from the Shadowlands of the Eastern Province and are battle hardened mountain men! Word has it they are in league with the dark Sidhe now!"

Ahead, Xomas and Eiremhou had halted. They peered in to a gorge that ripped through the steeply ascending track. Amergin caught up with them, just as they began to traverse the steep sided gorge... "Mariners to mountain goats!" he mused. He did not like the situation at all... loose scree and giant boulders perched precariously... a perfect place for an ambush! They had no choice! They must press on!

Amergin stepped up his pace, he took the lead again. They must move more quickly! Stand still and they were easy targets! This was easier said than done... the more Milesians that descended in to the gorge, the more bottlenecks formed... Amergin urged them on, "Move quickly! Spread out!"

Even as the words left his lips, he saw a movement way up the mountain side, "No!"...his worst fears were being realised! He watched as shadowy figures prised and levered massive, teetering boulders in to a freefalling, deadly avalanche of granite and sandstone... "Look above! Get out of there!" he frantically yelled, "Climb for your lives!" The Aganti had waited for the greatest bottleneck to form. A group of frightened and desperate Milesians became a helpless human target.

Amergin had to look away as a crushing wall of fractured rock and bombarding boulders swept straight through his paralysed and stultified fellow mariners... the granite and sandstone avalanche purged the gorge of any living flesh, leaving behind a pall of dust and a river of blood. Bodies were strewn everywhere. But this was not over! From the shadowy northern slopes of the mountains came the demons and denizens of the dark Sidhe, emissaries of MacCuacht! Rolling in with a cold condensing mist, they came to scavenge. A dank, all consuming mist that Amergin and his mariners had come to fear and loath. The lifeless bodies of the fallen Milesians now became prey to the dark Sidhe... awful pickings and converts for the army of lost souls...

Stunned and shocked, in absolute silence, Amergin watched the granite and red sandstone dust settle. The macabre battlefield revealed itself, as shell shocked stragglers picked their way through the debris and carnage, to join them on the other side of the gorge. The Aganti assassins disappeared from view, melting in to the high mountain side as quickly as they had appeared. The rolling darkness of demons and denizens of the dark Sidhe receding to the shadowy northern slopes, from where MacCuacht and his malevolence marched ever nearer to Sliebh Mis.

Amergin and his fellow Milesians were all deeply traumatised! Even his faith was being tested!

Amergin looked to the heavens... he needed a sign! The high mountain pass zig zagged before them...

The prospect of a further ambush daunted him...

From the point where the high, mountain pass met the ridge leading to the Western Province, a flash of gold! A golden eagle bathed in the late afternoon sun. The ultimate symbol of freedom! Circling higher and higher over the southern summits of the Iveare range, here was the sign! Free wheeling and free spirited! The sheer beauty of golden wings, feathering in the updrafts, gave Amergin heart...

His spirits soared with the King of the air! Here was the Divine in nature! The golden eagle was the embodiment of the truth that Amergin sought! The Guardians of Light had shown him the way! Without a glance back he led the way once more. They followed the flight path of the golden eagle to the place where the high mountain pass met the ridge descending to the Western Province...

On the familiar but now daunting track to Hushinish. Sceine paused for a moment... she felt his presence... her destined one was nearing the Western Province... she scanned the peaks and ridges of the southern peaks for any signs...

The Portal of Hushinish was a familiar place of pilgrimage for Sceine, a place of sanctuary, a place of refuge. The route had taken on a sinister dimension. Out there were the raven haired Witches of Hawardden. Lurking, lingering, predating...

Sceine's entourage bristled with armed warriors. All her priests travelled with her for this ceremony to summon the Guardians of Light. Safety in numbers. Then why did she feel so vulnerable? What was this sense of awful foreboding?

The glorious Western Province stretched out before her. The late afternoon sun dipped and chased through the ever thickening belts of rain clouds and showers. She prayed for a clear evening conducive for their ritual at the Portal of Hushinish.Estuaries and lakes reflected in the silver light, mountains dark and brooding then illuminated and verdant green. Far, far to the west, the mighty ocean, a streak of liquid silver, dotted with distant islands. The sheer beauty, the Divine in Nature... the veil so close...

On they marched, her priesthood close by. Sceine went to her loyal friend and priest Diarmuid, "Do you feel his presence?! I feel joy at his coming, but I have a deep sense of foreboding too ..."

Diarmuid empathised with the bitter sweet emotions.The joy of the knowledge that the Sea Druid Amergin was close, yet the agony of the closeness of the dark one and his army of lost souls.

They climbed higher up the narrowing and steepening Ridge of Thormond. The slanting searchlights of the late afternoon sun touched and illuminated the summits and high passes of the southern Iveare Mountains. Sceine's gaze was drawn to a golden speck bathed in the radiant glow of the setting sun, "A golden eagle!" Her spirits soared with the eagle! This was a sign... She was as one with the eagle, gliding, swooping and soaring... she saw what the eagle saw...Below! A flash! A glint of light on armour! A reflection!

"My loyal priests watch the horizon! The Milesian Sea Druid! He comes!" Sceine was so excited she nearly lost her footing on the narrow track. Her priests gathered around her, to protect her from her own exuberance and to confirm what she was seeing. Sure enough, in the low slanting light, a line of armour clad warriors descending from the high mountain pass! "We must go to meet them!!" cried out Sceine in her joy and anticipation, "We will go to the valley below! There we will wait for them! We will light a beacon to guide them and we will celebrate!" Sceine was overcome with emotion. She exuded joy and delight... her destined one arrives!!!

Her entourage of priests and armed guards followed her orders. They were soon marching back down the Ridge of Thormond... already one beacon was alight on the ridge... another would soon be lit in the valley below...

Sceine's spirits soared higher than the golden eagle now! Her mind raced. Her heart near bursting!

"This day the prophecy will be fulfilled! Together we will bring enlightenment to the Promised Land! Our progeny will spread the word and carry the faith and bring salvation to the Island of Destiny! The Guardians of Light will journey from beyond the veil in to the mortal realm! They will pour forth from the Portal of Hushinish and all the great portals of the Western Province! Together we will prevail!"

There was great joy abounding as they arrived in the wooded valley and commenced building the second beacon, to guide the Milesians.

The priest Diarmuid and the captain of Sceine's guard stood back and watched with restrained enjoyment as the beacon fired in to life. The Sea Druid Amergin will surely be with them soon!

The two sages were delighted for Sceine, but they doubted the wisdom in delaying here, for this was the notorious Valley of the Mad. "We should have marched to Hushinish and met the Sea Druid there!" declared the captain of the guard, his military antennae bristling.

As the beacon blazed, the priest Diarmuid agreed! In the heat of the moment, with the fulfilment of the prophecy nearing, Sceine's judgement may have been clouded. The sense of foreboding felt earlier, returned, descending upon him like a shroud of condensing mist...

The shadows lengthened and the signal beacon burned brighter in to the descending night. The guard was on constant alert. They should have been at Hushinish by now! They all waited, surely the beacon had been seen and the Milesians on their way.

The Valley of the Mad was living up to its name. Flickering flames sending shifting shadows in to the ether. The guards began imagining movement. Hallucinogenic forms in the darkness. The awful feeling of knowing you were being watched... they should have been at Hushinish by now!

The southern peaks of the Iveare Mountains caught the glowing remnants of sunset as the Western Province descended in to shadow.

The first beacon on the Ridge of Thormond lit up their hearts. Amergin danced for joy, "Sceine! I will be with you soon ...!" He embraced Eiremhou! All were overjoyed! They were living the prophecy!

Soon the tribes would meet, Amergin's destiny complete! A determined stretch to their stride now, they bounded along the mountain path. The second beacon lit up the western sky, located deep in a distant valley... there they would meet...

The exuberance was palpable, the joy tangible. Amergin could barely contain his excitement. He had waited so long... overcome so many adversaries... the moment had come, "An hour's march!" he breathlessly conferred with Xomas, "Send the word back to our faithful... the journey is nearing its end!"

Xomas sent messengers along the line of marching Milesians, while he watched the eastern horizon. The summits of the Iveare range were plunged in to darkness. The consummate mariner, Xomas always had a weather eye out, always looking for the unexpected. He felt the deep joy for his leader, the Sea Druid Amergin, the Champion of Milesia, but he also had a strengthening sense of foreboding. He could smell a foulness descending with the cold mountain air. He could feel the brooding presence of the dark Sidhe.

MacCuacht marches to the fortress of Sliebh Mis and then inevitably to the Portal of Hushinish. He had sent his beasts and demons ahead to ambush them on the high mountain passes. Xomas still had the nightmarish vision of his fellow Milesians being crushed by the avalanche of rock, fresh in his mind. Their souls then predated on by the ghoulish creatures of the dark. But he could feel something else... something lurked in the darkness, something unknown and totally unexpected. The sight of Amergin embracing his faithful mariners, alive with sheer joy, encouraged Xomas... but he still felt uncertain, unsure... he was distracted... what was out there?

Amergin dropped to his knees by a pool of fresh mountain water, the warning of Gerridh not to drink the water, ringing in his ears. But this was the Western Province! They were free of the foul pestilence! Amergin splashed his face with the crystal clear Water of Life. He roared to the heavens, "We thank you Great Spirit! We thank you for the life giving water! We thank you for guiding us safely to our destination!" One by one, the Milesians fell to their knees and drunk deep of the Water of Life. One by one they prayed to the Great Spirit. They thanked the Guardians of Light for protecting them on their journey.

Xomas spoke wisely and advisedly to the champion of Milesia, "My lord Amergin. We must fill our water carriers and march on! We must reach the valley where the beacon burns before the dark of night. There you will meet your princess, your destined one!" Xomas delighted in the broad smile that swept across Amergin's face at the very mention of Sceine. He continued, "I fear we are not alone my lord. We must make all haste! Even here in this bountiful province where the Light of the Divine pours from beyond the veil... even here we are not safe!" Amergin sensed this too... even with the prospect of meeting his destiny... he sensed the presence... he feared the unknown... something was waiting for them... preying on them...

The moon rose above the Iveare Mountain range at exactly the point from whence they had come, marking the track of the high pass. Amergin took a furtive glance back, fearing they were being followed. All seemed quiet. The moon beyond the fullness of the equinox now. The Cycle of Xustra just commencing. The veil was still at its closest to the mortal realm.

The path snaked down the stark moonlit mountain side. Only a faint streak of daylight remained on the western horizon. The signal fire blazed brighter and brighter against the darkening backdrop...

CHAPTER TWENTY EIGHT:
THE DIVINE IN BODY AND SPIRIT

The Valley of the Mad, verdant and lush in contrast to the boulder strewn mountain track. Amergin felt an unexpected pang of sorrow and isolation. He couldn't fathom his feelings... he recalled his earlier sense of foreboding. Xomas walked beside Amergin as they made the final traverse in to the valley. He too was wary, he sensed his leader's unease.

Amergin heard voices now! All his worries disappeared! His heart pounded! His spirits soared! Any moment now... this was the culmination of his journey! Sceine had come to him many times in his dreams and visions. She had drawn him beyond the veil, guiding him, caressing him, nurturing him...

A torch bearer came towards him and waited in the centre of a moonlit clearance. In the gentle lunar glow and the flickering torch light stood a radiant being of extraordinary beauty. All time stood still. Everyone and everything stopped in their tracks. Only Amergin and the ethereal, enlightened being were moving. They came towards each other, the veil wrapping around them, protecting them.

Amergin finally regained the power of speech, "Sceine!"
She smiled, "My lord Amergin! You have journeyed far!" Words were unnecessary... they embraced... her long golden brown tresses... her fingertips delicately touching ...her lips on his... he looked in to her amber eyes... the familiar fleck in the iris of her eye drew him in hypnotically. They journeyed beyond the wrapping and morphing veil... together finally... destiny complete! Bodies entwined... their souls as one... they travelled deep in to the spirit world. They were met by radiant, enlightened beings... they were in the presence of the Guardians of Light.From the amber cosmos, a voice... "Amergin, Sceine... May the Great Spirit bless you! May you bring peace and harmony to the mortal realm, may your children and your childrens' children serve the cause of the enlightenment for eternity!"

The other Guardians chanted in chorus,
"So it is written... and is in the stars... and is in the prophecy!"
They journeyed further and further beyond the veil. They travelled through the portals of the Promised Land... they saw the Temple of Xhara, the great Portal of Machlleth, the Temple of the Sun and even the Portal of Sceilge. They journeyed alone now...

She held him gently, caressing him, kissing him, overwhelming him... her long white tunic edged with gold fell off her body. Amergin fell to his knees, kissing her, touching her, caressing her. Sceine's beauty intoxicated him. He was entranced by her, lost in her. He kissed every part of her divine body. Touching, exciting, arousing. They embraced, bodies entwined.Their hearts pounding in rhythm, their spirits rising and their souls uniting. He entered deep in to her soul.

Time stood still. They came together in blissful ecstacy. The prophecy in fulfilment!

Sceine smiled, her divinely beautiful body knew peace like she never knew before! Amergin stared in to her amber eyes, he was drawn in to her universe... soon they travelled through an amber cosmos and journeyed beyond the veil... they were back in the moonlit clearance... back in to the mortal realm ...the words of the Guardians of Light spinning around their minds, "May you bring peace and harmony, may your children serve the cause of the enlightenment for eternity!"

They held each other. The reality of the mortal realm a cold shock to their still overwhelmed and overcome bodies. Time moved on again... voices permeating their senses... real time in a very real world...

Amergin kissed Sceine... together their mission will continue!

He raised the still burning torch in to the air, casting a light on familiar faces and strangers gathering in the clearance. This was a meeting of kindred spirits with much embracing and joy. Sceine interrupted the harmonious proceedings, "My faithful ones, at first light we journey to the great Portal of Hushinish. Stay safe this night! Enjoy this gathering..." She recognised the peril they were in and sensed the nervousness of her captain of the guard. Sceine's words fell on a hushed silence.

Her beauty and charm had them all entranced, "The Sea Druid Amergin and I bring hope and the promise of salvation to this our Island of Destiny! Our blood lines are one. Our progeny, the "Children of Light", will carry the eternal message of enlightenment to the Promised Land."

All those present knew they were witnessing a poignant moment in their destiny. Amergin fell to his knees, chanting the sacred blessing given to them by the Guardians of Light, "May we bring peace and harmony to the mortal realm. May our children serve the cause of the enlightenment for eternity! Praise the Great Spirit!" These words became their mantra. All present fell to their knees and began praying and chanting the sacred blessing...

Sceine took Amergin's hand. The signal fire still burned brightly and even more intensely against the pitch black of the night and the shifting shadows of the ancient woodland. She smiled, enjoying the moment. The many torches lighting up the clearing and the coming together of kindred spirits fighting for the cause of the enlightenment! Excited voices! Laughter! A cacophony of merriment, the like of which had not been heard in the Western Province for many lunar cycles...

"Walk with me my lord Amergin!" Sceine took a torch from one of her priests and gently grasped his hand, "I want to show you the Western Province by moonlight!"

In the noise and clamour of the tribal gathering, no one, except the priest noticed their retreat in to the ancient woodlands. In the quiet of the night Sceine took Amergin deep in to a sacred grove of ancient Oaks. The path climbed gently upwards, the magnificent, gnarled and twisted trees thinning as they ascended. The rising moon, still near fullness, cast fleeting shadows. The light ever brightening as the high canopy opened out. One last, short, steep climb up to a rocky granite outcrop and they burst through the trees and the shelter of the high canopy. Sceine doused the flickering torch and stood before Amergin, "Close your eyes my beloved!" gently placing her delicate, beautifully formed hands over his eyes, "I will turn you around to face the west, and then you can open them!" Sceine turned him slowly around, cradling her body in to his. Amergin felt the warmth of her body against his, her soft breath on the side of his face and neck. Sceine lowered her hands, touching him, arousing him, "Now my beloved! Open your eyes!"

She kissed him on his unexpecting lips. His senses nearly exploding, Amergin opened his eyes! What he saw took his breath away! Mountain range upon mountain range sweeping in to the distance, reflecting in the fleeting moon light, glistening lakes, streams and rivers flowing to the liquid silver ocean... She kissed him again... his heart nearly stopped! Heaven was on earth!

The spectacle before him was the Divine in Nature! The beautiful enlightened being beside him, the Divine in body and spirit! Overcome by her beauty, Amergin pushed her gently to the ground. In waves of passion and sensuality, they came together with all their heart and undying love...

They came back to reality once more. The clearing sky and the still rising moon cast a cold harsh light over the Western Province. In the chilling air, Amergin wrapped a robe that had been cast to the ground in the passion of the moment, around Sceine's curvaceous body, "We must go my love! The night air chills! Your guard will be missing you..." Amergin pulled her towards him. They began the descent in to the shadowy darkness of the woods, holding each other for guidance and support.

Step by step they retraced their tracks once more, much more difficult now. The torch had been doused. Clouds began to shroud the near full moon. Barely any dimming moonlight could pierce the high canopy of the dense woodland. Each step more measured and precarious. Sceine held on to Amergin's hand in the gathering dark. They helped each other, trying to avoid tripping over twisted roots or stumbling over loose rocks...

While Amergin concentrated on the placement of his feet over the rugged terrain, he crashed in to a low hanging branch that cut and scraped his forehead. Instinctively he reached for the cut, blood oozing down his face. He momentarily let go of Sceine's hand to wipe the dripping blood away. He stopped to gather some moss to use as a compress to stem the flow of blood. The scent and feel of blood in the pitch darkness sparked old fears. The sense of foreboding, temporarily forgotten, returned with a vengeance! He reached out to hold Sceine's hand... and in that moment! In the wall of darkness... a shaft of moonlight reflected in the eye of a demonic beast! Sceine was taken!

Wolves! Three of them! No!!!...The Witches of Hawardden as predating monsters...

A demented howl penetrated the dense woodland. Amergin crashed through the undergrowth and the low branches, towards the sound of the last spine chilling howl. He fell and stumbled over the twisted roots and scratching bramble. He unsheathed his sword, slashing at anything that moved and was vaguely threatening. Slashing out wildly again, he heard a whimper! He had connected with one of the "wolves." Sceine must be close! In the darkness and the shifting shadows, he could just about make out a pale whiteness, lying motionless. Amergin flailed wildly in the gloom, the razor sharp sword scything through the branches. In a shaft of fleeting moonglow, he saw three predatory demons. He flailed out again, screaming dementedly! The three predators skulked off in to the darkness, one of them whincing in pain. He had done enough to scare them off!

In the dim moonlight, Amergin found the pale white, now lifeless body, of his beloved Sceine.

It was his turn to howl "No!!!Sceine this cannot be...my beloved Sceine!!!"

Amergin fell to the ground, crying an ocean of tears.

He lay with her, his face next to hers, the blood from his cut forehead mixing with the blood from the clawed lacerations down the side of her neck. Amergin lay motionless for hours, next to her lifeless, but still beautiful body... crying until his soul ran dry... until he was found...

Diarmuid talked to the priest who was last seen in the company of Sceine and Amergin. He was mortified that they should have walked in to the woodlands without a guard. He called the captain of the guard, and he called Xomas, "We must send out search parties, they have been gone too long!" They heard the panic in his voice. They all had the same terrible sense of foreboding.

Search parties scoured the woodlands, praying all the while for their safe return... Through the night they searched...

Tired and despairing Diarmuid led a search party to one of Sceine's favourite places, the outcrop that gave the most glorious panoramas of the Western Province. He arrived just as the first rays of a new dawn broke over the Eastern horizon. Still no sign of them, but he soon found the disgarded remains of a burned out torch. He called out in to the ether, "Here! They were here!" In no time search parties gravitated to his cry. Diarmuid followed the track descending in to the dense woodlands. Evidence of turmoil was found. Broken and slashed branches. His heart missed a beat, spots of blood on the track... more broken branches... and there in the undergrowth! Amergin, the Sea Druid cradling Sceine in his arms, blood stained and pale, they both appeared lifeless... but then there was movement!

The Sea Druid lives! Diarmuid wept at the sight of his Princess and High Priestess, neck lacerated, her body limp, pale and definitely lifeless. "Sceine!" he knelt beside Amergin, "My lord, we are here for you now. Let me take her body ..."

The procession to the Portal of Hushinish, once intended as a rallying march for the enlightened ones, was now a mournful funeral crawl. The bearers carried Sceine's body on a creation of Oak branches and robes. Amergin walked in painful synchronicity with the bearers. He was followed by all his faithful Milesians... they were followed by Sceine's priests and guards. Heads bowed and hearts broken, an inconsolable sense of desolation. They had all gathered in the valley to celebrate the fulfilment of the Prophecy, but now with one grievous swipe of a wolfish claw... all was gone...

They were bereft, the Prophecy torn asunder. The Sea Druid Amergin's meeting with his destined one, destroyed! The Island of Destiny seemingly in the firm grip of the dark Sidhe...they were helpless now... the Cycle of the Dark was upon them...

From the dense woodland, way below the Ridge of Thormond, three raven haired, black hearted, witches looked on as the funeral procession crawled along the ridge, silhouetted against the cold morning light. They were transformed from the devilish beasts, back to the cold blooded ogres, clad in cocooning silver dresses. They crowed and cackled in true demonic delight. The Witches of Hawardden sensed their dark time had come. They will soon be all powerful. They will reign supreme through the Cycle of Xustra. They would wait until Sceine has been cremated at the Portal of Hushinish. In that finality, they would journey to meet the dark one MacCuacht, who marched from the mist shrouded Woodlands of Derwydd. From there they would all return to the high mountain fortress of Sliebh Mis to consolidate their demonic victory. From there, they will watch as the dark Sidhe pours forth from all the great portals of the Western Province...

The coven of corruption kept watching in smug satisfaction as the funeral procession edged along the Ridge of Thormond. Amergin, head bowed, tears streaming, followed the bearers. The Portal of Hushinish came in to view in the distance, the giant Bluestones reflecting the low morning sunlight.

Clouds raced through in the freshening westerly breeze, occasionally obscuring and casting shadows over the awe inspiring standing stones.

Amergin's heart beat faster as he raised his eyes to the horizon. He listened intently to the conversation the priests were having. He couldn't hear everything being said, but again and again he heard the words, "Secret of the

Alignment"... Sceine too had mentioned the secret, as they journeyed beyond the veil together, in those blissful moments of union.

Amergin had not fully understood, but all he knew was that as they journeyed beyond the veil, time stood still... they had been blessed by the Guardians, allowed to travel deep in to the spirit world, travel through the portals in to the mortal realm and enjoy each other physically and spiritually for what seemed to be an ecstatic age... when they returned through the veil, time had barely moved.

Amergin was beginning to understand.

The procession arrived at the Portal of Hushinish. Sceine's faithful priests came to Amergin... now he would fully understand... "You must go to the Magine Islands, to the Portal of Sceilge. You will meet the Guardians Endinou and Erhombu.Take them with you. These enlightened beings will show you the way. You must take the purest and most ancient of the Bluestone keystones to the Portal of Sceilge. You, with the Guardians, will be able to energise this most powerful of all the portals. The Guardians of Light will come through the veil. All the great portals of the Western Province, the Temple of the Sun, Machlleth, and of course Hushinish will connect with the Portal of Sceilge," their revelation almost complete, "This, my lord Amergin, is the Secret of the Alignment! The enlightened one, who connects the portals, can turn back time.You! The destined one! Will turn back time! The Secret of the Alignment will be yours to use! You will take your beloved Sceine, High Priestess of the Temple of Xhara and Princess of the Western Province, back in time. You will meet your beloved Sceine again!" Diarmuid, the most loyal and most faithful of Sceine's priests and her closest confidant, took Amergin's hand firmly in his, "Go now! We will keep Sceine here. Preserved in the aura of the Portal of Hushinish... when the moment comes... when the Alignment begins... she will return to you!"

Amergin could scarcely believe his ears, the "Secret of the Alignment"! Surely this cannot be! He had resigned himself to a new, desolate, lonely life without Sceine... He roared out aloud, shouting to the heavens,"By the Great Spirit, how can this be!?" in a mixture of rage, delight and confusion. His voice echoed loud and long, rebounding off the Bluestone sentinels and out in to the ether.

In the woodlands fringing the Valley of the Mad, the raven haired witches turned to look up at the Ridge of Thormond. They noticed with a sense of disquiet, a small group descending. They were too far away to discern who they were, but questioned, "Who would be journeying away from the portal before the funeral pyre had been lit? Why would they go?" Reading each others thoughts... no need for words... the three witches sensed this was a sea change moment... even though they could not know the real truth!

Amergin had chosen to journey with his most loyal and faithful ones, Xomas, Eiremhou, MacCuill, and of course Terese of the Xantha with a troop of her amazonian warriors, a potent group of his strongest and most resourceful Milesians. They must travel over land and over sea... they must travel quickly, avoiding the forces of the dark. They had already been observed. Their journey will be fraught with danger!

The three raven haired witches transformed again in to wolfish form. In this form they were perfectly adapted to track their prey, from a distance...

The rapidly mobilised travellers soon made their way through the Valley of the Mad. They would stay in the low valleys, foraging off the land. They would skirt to the South West of the Woodlands of Derwydd. Amergin was unsure how far the dark one MacCuacht had penetrated in to the woodlands. His group of faithful travellers would make straight for the great Portal of Machlleth.

Here they would meet the Guardians Endinou and Erhombu...

Unbeknownst to the group they were being tracked and were in mortal danger. The saving grace was the element of the unknown. The witches again quizzed, "Amergin! Terese! Where were they going? What was their mission?!"

Banba felt the open wound on her flank. Still raw and oozing dark blood... inflicted by the flailing sword of the Sea Druid Amergin, just as she clawed and lacerated the High Priestess Sceine to death! "Why is Amergin marching at this time, when his beloved Sceine lies cold and lifeless at Hushinish?" They thought collectively, but none of the witches had an answer...

Eiru was sent, once more in avian form, to find MacCuacht in the Woodlands of Derwydd.

The witches realised the track the Sea Druid was on, "tell MacCuacht to go straight to Machlleth! We will meet you there! We must discover the reason for this mission!" Eiru was airborne with an explosion of photons and powerful thrusting down beats of wings. Low at first, then climbing, looking for signs of the dark one. From soaring heights she saw the giveaway, far distant wall of dense shrouding mist... she would soon be with him...

Amergin and Terese had both heard the low thrusting sounds of powerful wing beats. Neither could see anything through the high canopy of the ancient deciduous woodlands, but they both recognised the rhythm that made their syncopating hearts miss a beat...

"Eiru!" whispered Terese, "The other witches must be close!" Amergin drew his bronze and iron sword from its sheath... still encrusted with the dark dried blood of one of the wolfish assassins.

He sharpened the blade slowly and deliberately with a piece of weathered, red sandstone. He was ready for revenge... he wasn't the only one with a bloodlust! Remaining vigilant, they pressed on. The Portal of Machlleth was a good day's march away.

Skirting the southern fringe of the Woodlands of Derwydd, they could feel the life giving energy of the Portal of Machlleth. The extremities of the woodlands were still in their lush and verdant glory.

But the dark one comes again... once more the summits to the East were shrouded in threatening storm clouds, a cold condensing mist percolated through the woodlands. MacCuacht was on their trail... Eiru had betrayed them again...

Amergin was unsettled at the thought of Eiru being with the demonic MacCuacht again. The very notion of her soul darkening and she lying with the beast, made him physically sick... particularly while his beloved Sceine lies cold and lifeless at Hushinish. The reason for Amergin sending Eiru to her martyrdom was all around... the life and growth of woodlands bathed in the Light of the Divine. Eiru had saved them once, but at what cost? Now she betrays them and grows darker and more powerful every day.

Amergin walked resolutely on... the dark forces were gathering... but he was more determined than ever. The further they walked through the southern extremities of the Woodlands of Derwydd, the closer to the great Portal of Machlleth, the stronger the life force.The travellers were joined by the many and diverse Spirits of the Woodlands, an army of enlightened beings marching to Machlleth.

From the Sacred Oak Grove of Bendigedig, Erhombu appeared. He came in the form of a magnificent red deer stag, stamping and tearing at the ground. Amergin was at first shocked, but then in a magical slight of energy, antlers and hooves transformed in to the pale, slender, gaunt Guardian of the Woodlands, "We will travel with you to Machlleth my lord Amergin!" He offered his elegant hand in welcome. Amergin thanked Erhombu. There was no need to explain his mission... Erhombu had heard of Sceine's fate and he was one of the enlightened few privy to the Secret of the Alignment.

Amergin became more and more heartened the closer they got to Machlleth. The Light of the Divine bathed everything in a wondrous glow. For the first time since the appalling demise of his beloved Sceine he began to feel a spark of hope. Until now he was on a blind mission, resolute, but unfeeling.

The beauty and the glory of the Western Province bathed in Divine Light gave him the spiritual strength that had been missing. He stepped out more confidently with his band of brave travellers. Erhombu by his side, he began to rekindle his sense of destiny, with every purposeful stride.

Machlleth next and then the Magine Islands and the Portal of Sceilge!

Eiru had found MacCuacht. He was marching towards the Sacred Grove of Bendegedig. They were closer than Amergin and his faithful realised. The dark one and his army of lost souls were soon on course to Machlleth, "Why march for Machlleth?" he asked Eiru after she had given him the news. He could not understand why Amergin would leave his beloved Sceine. She has been slain, her body remains uncremated! Surely he would take charge of the ceremony and spread her ashes across the Western Province... MacCuacht contorted his now hideous face at the prospect of the

Western Province without its Princess, and the Island of Destiny without its High Priestess, and the prophecy without fulfilment!

"This is the only unknown MacCuacht!" Eiru was distraught... if he is so powerful and in league with the dark Sidhe. How does he not know?! She thought that this showed weakness and it displeased her immeasurably! He had already lost face against Sceine at their earlier encounter at Hushinish and now he shows weakness again... "I must return to my sisters. We will meet you at the Portal of Machlleth. You must counter this insurgency. You must stop Amergin. He must not pass Machlleth. Do not fail again MacCuacht!"

She could still pierce him to the core. He was enraged at how a mere woman could admonish him so and cut him to the quick. Eiru was becoming an irritation to him... she was a threat to his power.

Eiru left feeling there had been a perceptible power shift. Her dark power grows! MacCuacht shows frailty. He had failed to intercept the Sea Druid on numerous occasions. The champion of Milesia still marches! Amergin travels in to the unknown! MacCuacht's weakness threatens their dark cause!

She transformed in to her avian splendour and returned to the coven. Banbha and Fodha greeted their sister. They sensed her rage. The Witches of Hawardden were the dominant ones now!

They had slain Sceine! All their enemies had cause to be fearful! Even MacCuacht!

CHAPTER TWENTY EIGHT:
REVELATION OF SCEILGE

The monolithic standing Bluestones of Machlleth radiated their ethereal Light, stood before the portal was Endinou, the Guardian of the Bluestones and the Quarry of Izion. He walked, or rather glided across the clearance towards them. White haired and wizard like, of indefinable age and blessed with the wisdom of the aeons. Behind him at the edge of the clearance was Sethse, the cyclopic Quarryman of Izion. Nearer to the portal, Thiorn and the elite guard.

Endinou raised his arms in his familiar welcoming gesture. His ornately carved staff raised high in the air, "The Sea Druid Amergin! Erhombu!" he surveyed the many wood spirits and Milesians that arrived, "All of you are most welcome!"

Straightaway, Amergin went to the sage, "Endinou, we journey west!" Before he could say any more, Endinou grabbed Amergin and placed his finger over his pursed lips, "Say nothing more my lord Amergin! You are being tracked! These woodlands have sinister ears!" He ushered the Sea Druid and the Guardian of the Woodlands of Derwydd, Erhombu, to the far side, nearer the Portal of Machlleth, out of the earshot of any predating forms. Endinou glanced furtively from the surrounding woodlands to the portal and back again to Amergin and Endinou, "I know your mission! I know of the Secret of the Alignment! We will travel together to the Magine Islands!" he glanced around again, conscious of a malevolent presence, conscious of the nearing army of lost souls and the dark one, MacCuacht, "You my lord Amergin! The destined one! You, with our guidance and help, shall energise the Portal of Sceilge! You shall connect the great portals of the Western Province! You, my lord Amergin, will have the power to turn back time itself... your beloved Sceine shall live again!!!" Endinou scanned the woodlands once more, "We are being watched!"

They were indeed being watched. The Witches of Hawardden in their wolfish form observed the three conversing. They snarled in frustration. The aura radiating from the portal masked the conversation. They could not read their minds. They were still oblivious to the Secret of the Alignment and even unsure of the significance of the Magine Islands.

Endinou stabbed his ornately carved staff in to the soft turf, "We must journey west now! We are in peril here!" With a rallying gesture he pointed west, "We go with you my lord Amergin! We go to resurrect your destiny!"

They were all very aware that the journey will be fraught. They were being preyed on by a hidden menace and the dark one MacCuacht marches onwards...

Amergin and the Guardians Endinou and Erhombu immediately prepared to march west to the ocean. They will travel with Xomas, Eiremhou and Terese of the Xantha with her amazonian warriors. MacCuill, Sethse, Thiorn and the elite guard, and the wood spirits of Derwydd will remain at Machlleth to protect the portal from the oncoming dark hordes. They will slow the progress of the army of lost souls. They will frustrate the progress of the dark one MacCuacht.

Endinou advised Amergin that they must visit the Quarry of Izion en route. Again he glanced furtively in to the dense woodlands as they walked westwards, "The purest Bluestone ever hewn and crafted from the Quarry of Izion is the keystone to the Portal of Sceilge, quarried, hewn and crafted by the ancients who first travelled to the Promised Land." He spoke quietly, still conscious of the lurking menace, "This keystone is perfectly designed and crafted for the Portal of Sceilge. With this stone, the enlightened being of destiny can energise the portal and the Secret of the Alignment realised!"

The weight of the Prophecy fell heavy on Amergin's broad shoulders... he thought of Gerridh of the Diventii and the tales of the ancient Sea Druids, who had originally journeyed to the Island of Destiny. They had foretold of the coming of the enlightened being, the champion of the Milesian nation. They had instilled in his tribes the sense of destiny. Amergin felt to the core of his being that the ancient Sea Druids were calling him to the Portal of Sceilge... the Secret of the Alignment was in his power...

So it is written... and is in the stars... and is in the Prophecy...

Through the night they marched. Terese and her Xanthan warriors carried torches to light the way.

An occasional flash of light reflected from the retinas of animals of the woodland causing missed heart beats in the ranks. Terese suspected an attack could happen any time. They were all on tenterhooks! Waiting... marching...

They came upon the Quarry of Izion. "Praise the Great Spirit!" Amergin was relieved, another stage of his sojourn complete. Endinou led him deep in to the minings. Terese accompanied them as torch bearer. Her Xanthan warriors would carry the keystone. A maze of tunnels took them deep in to the hillside. Without Endinou they would be lost. Soon they followed a tunnel irradiated by ethereal blue light, a vein of Bluestone of the purest quality, running deep in to the rock face. "Here my lord Amergin is the purest Bluestone ever mined!" Endinou pointed to a subterranean passage that appeared to penetrate to the core of the earth, a sink hole so deep that it connected with the underworld. "Here the ancients first discovered the power and the energy of the sacred Bluestone, the power to conduct the Light of the Divine from the spirit world to the mortal realm."

The flickering torch light revealed the keystone, hewn and crafted out of the Bluestone of the purest quality, the size and shape of a human skull. Clean, precisely cut facets reflected and magnified the torch light a thousand times.

Endinou encouraged Amergin to lift the keystone from its resting place... he could feel the Bluestone conducting the energy coursing along the lay line. The veil so close... he could feel the presence of the Guardians of Light. Here was the key to the Portal of Sceilge, the key to energise the portal and connect the great portals of the Western Province. The key to reveal the Secret of the Alignment!

Amergin presented the skull shaped keystone to Terese. She and her Xanthan warriors would protect it with their lives...

They made for the surface. The journey west must continue!

From the depths of the woodlands, Eiru and her deadly coven, still in wolfish form, watched with curiosity and increasing frustration. Eiru seethed with rage! Where was MacCuacht? The Xanthan guard never left the Sea Druids side. They needed the army of lost souls to put this venture to an end! What was this mission? What is the significance of their visit to the Quarry of Izion?

Too many questions! The frustration festered in her dark heart! Her bile knew no bounds. Her contempt for MacCuacht deepened. The further the Sea Druid marched west, the more her frustration grew and the more she placed the blame on the inadequacies of MacCuacht! Eiru could feel the pent up bloodlust coursing through her wolfish form. She would have her day!

On they marched... now to the Temple of the Sun on the western shores of the Island of Destiny. Occasional standing stones marked their route. The ancients had placed these on the lay line centuries ago. A soft spectral Light came from the last vestiges of dusk over the western horizon.

This Light was channelled along the lay line in a gentle beam of energy, guiding them to the Temple of the Sun and beyond...

Eiru, Banba and Fodha in their wolfish forms, had to bide their time. Their moment must come! The time of the dark Sidhe must surely be nearing!

Amergin marched with his brother Eiremhou. They talked of the coming journey to the Magine Islands and the inevitable reunion with their royal parents. They delighted at the prospect! In the same breath they despaired at their disloyal and dangerous brother who waits for them at the Temple of the Sun, "We must be wary my brother!" warned Eiremhou in confidence, "Remember that Eimbear is in league with the traitorous Gonne, the High Priest of the Chapter of Mystics."

Amergin did not need reminding, their deceptions on the perilous sea voyage to the Promised Land were very fresh in his mind, "You are right my faithful brother. They do not know of our mission and they cannot be trusted! We will send them to Machlleth under the pretence that they are needed to protect the great portal from their sinister overlord and master!"

Eiremhou smiled at his brother's guile. Together they will contrive to deceive the dark duo...

Eiremhou was the first to see the Temple of the Sun standing in all its monumental magnificence, overlooking the ocean. The first rays of dawn catching the monolithic standing stones.

Amergin arrived at the estuary with his faithful travellers. They were soon spotted by the watchmen on the vessels anchored in the silty river mouth. They were quite rightly hailed as returning heroes by the Milesian crews.

The word was out that they were sailing for the outer islands to meet Scota and Milidh and the rest of the Milesian fleet waiting offshore with reinforcements. They would return and take the battle to MacCuacht and the army of lost souls...

This tale seemed to appease Gonne and Eimbear. Amergin greeted them coldly and without emotion. He went on to compound the deception with the collusion of his loyal brother Eiremhou, "Go to the great Portal of Machlleth! We will join you and the resistance forces and confront the dark one!" Eiremhou looked Eimbear in the eye and was shocked at the soulless stare that greeted him, "My brother we rely on you! Go straight to Machlleth. Tell Thiorn and the elite guard, that we are on course and will join them soon..." His Machiavellian brother was completely under the spell of the sinister High Priest Gonne. He was lost to the dark Sidhe! He and Amergin endeavoured to hide the distress, the loss of their brother caused to them. They shared anxious glances with each other, understanding the cold reality of the situation. They must go, before the dark, corrupt duo read their minds and saw through the deception...

In true seamanship fashion the vessels were sea ready within the hour. The Milesian vessels were soon lifted by the rising tide. Anchors were lifted and mooring lines untied. The mainsails were unfurled and sheets tensioned. The south-westerly filled the billowing sails and keels broke free from the soft, silty estuarine sand. Amergin took up his place by his helmsman Xomas as their clinker built, Phoenician rigged vessel leaned in to the breeze. They were tacking across the estuary and out in to the bay. He watched the Temple of the Sun slowly drift in to the distance. He waved to his brother on the other vessel, satisfied that the precious cargo carried by Terese of the Xantha was safely on board. Satisfied too that Gonne and Eimbear were on their fool's errand to the great Portal of Machlleth.

Amergin's spirits lifted once more. He was so glad to be back in his element. Fresh salted ozone filled his expanding lungs... only the ocean can feed his soul like this. He felt liberated again... the weight of the Prophecy lifting from his shoulders, temporarily at least. But it was not the same... his heart kept missing a beat... his spirit could not rise to the heights he had previously known. Part of him was missing... and she lies cold and lifeless at the distant Portal of Hushinish. Sceine!! Amergin grieved for her. Waves of unbearable pain swept over him again...

By way of a distraction and a release from the constricting grief, he took the helm from Xomas. As the next gust blew through, he tacked hard, the planing vessel pushing speedily on towards the Magine Islands. "We must get to the channel before the tide turns Xomas!" he roared in to the wind, "Before the silver dragons of Sceilge show their crested, scaly backs!"

Amergin observed his crew and the crew of his brothers vessel, "Never has such a potent contingent set sail!" he thought out aloud. Sailing with him were Terese and her Xanthans guarding the flawless, skull shaped keystone with their lives.On board Eiremhou's vessel were Endinou and Erhombu, the Guardians crucial to the forthcoming ceremony at the Portal of Sceilge. Both vessels were ably sailed by the best mariners alive. Xomas, his ever present companion of the sea, fearless warrior and the most skilled mariner, will be critical to the mission.

The mysterious Magine Islands reared up out of the ocean before them. One more tack and they would be in to the notorious Sound of Sceilge, where the silver scaled dragons resided. Already the dragon was starting to show its teeth! The silver crested "scales" forming as the strengthening south-westerly blew against tide and swell. Standing waves were beginning to form, rising and falling with each surging set wave. "We are just in time my lord!" Xomas encouraged them on.Amergin skilfully controlling the tiller, keeping the prow pointing to the stunningly spectacular Magine Islands. As they got closer, Amergin passed the helm over to Xomas.

He took on the role of navigator and watchman, giving occasional guiding commands as Xomas masterfully steered the vessel through the sound.

Their vessel pushed over the last of the standing waves and they were in to calmer waters. Still, a swirling turbulence slowed their passage. They slowly sailed past the smaller pinnacle spired island, white with a myriad nesting and airborne seabirds. Looming majestically in front of them the monumental cathedral spired island, location of the ancient temple and Portal of Sceilge.

Amergin watched the assembled crew and passengers as their expression went from wonderment to disbelief as they sailed past the natural paradise of the smaller island to the jaw dropping magnificence of the larger island. The Magine Islands were truly divinely beautiful!

The vessels silently glided in to the lee of the large island, the precipitous, heaven touching cliffs alive with wheeling, raucous seabirds. Drifting ever closer to the yawning, cavernous sea cave hidden deep in the sheltered sea cliffs. Amergin's vessel silently entered in to the high vaulted cave. He lit a beacon on the prow, and put a giant conch to his lips, blowing a low resonant note in to the gloom.

Oars were at the ready to punt them off the cave walls if necessary. Slowly their eyes became accustomed to the low light. The contrast from the glare of the cave entrance to the dark of the inner recesses was striking. Shapes of moored vessels gradually came in to focus. Beyond, the flickering of torchlight and the burning embers of a fire, spewing thick, seaweed scented smoke high up in to the vaulted chamber. The acrid smoke swirled and disappeared through a vent in the cave ceiling. From here came an ethereal glow from a vein of the purest Bluestone.

The wave cut platform, to where Xomas skilfully steered the vessel, was alive with a clamour of activity and scurrying people. Through the firelight and the haze of smoke, Amergin began to make out recognisable forms and figures, "Scota!" he yelled at the top of his voice. His beloved mother stood at the edge of the platform, as regally beautiful and elegant as ever. Next to her was Milidh, the proud and majesterial King of the Milesians, "Father!" he cried out in delight.

He was soon tying the mooring ropes to the quartzite outcrops and leaping ashore to greet his loving, royal parents. Milidh and Scota were beyond themselves with happiness at Amergin's arrival.

Their son and Milesian champion was safe! They rejoiced in the reunion, but were soon under no illusion how things had changed! Milidh and Scota saw the grief oozing from his every living pore. His sadness was palpable. They could see how driven he was and how brave and courageous in the face of his worst nightmare. Amergin embraced both of them and quietly spoke of the Secret of the Alignment.

In no time, they were making for the steep, narrow stairway carved in to the gunnels of the island.

All of his faithful travellers had disembarked and followed him to the Portal of Sceilge.

No time for introductions now! Even Eiremhou barely had time to greet his beloved parents. He walked with them, telling all as they climbed the narrow, winding, claustrophobic stairway.

Endinou, the Guardian of the Bluestones and the Quarry of Izion, source of the purest Bluestone, could not contain his sense of awe and anticipation, "The legendary Portal of Sceilge! I have rarely seen such Bluestone. Only the keystone carried by Terese of the Xantha matches this purity!"He ran his fingertips over the exposed veins that followed the stairway and lead up to the Portal. He felt the energy conducting from the spirit world. He sensed the presence of the Guardians of Light. The veil was so close!

Erhombu the Guardian of the Woodlands of Derwydd stayed close to Terese of the Xantha. She struggled with the weight of the carved keystone. The carved and crafted, skull shaped Bluestone trapped and reflected all of the torch light, the precisely cut facets sending a kaleidoscopic cascade of ethereal Light in to the stairwell and beyond.

Endinou was only too aware that the ancients had hewn the keystone out of the purest vein of Bluestone. Now, here in the Temple of the Magine Islands, were the standing stones carved out of the same purest Bluestone. The Portal of Sceilge! Carved by the very same race of ancient Sea Druids!

Amergin turned to his mother Scota and smiled. She returned his smile.

Scota understood that this was her son's only chance! The Secret of the Alignment had been revealed to him... this was part of his destiny... he was one of the very few enlightened beings over the ages who had been given the power to invoke this sacred and spiritual phenomenom. Scota realised that her son's heart was breaking. If this ancient ritual, guided by the Guardians Erhombu and Endinou, did not work, then the Prophecy of the Milesian nation and the destiny of her son, the Sea Druid Amergin, would be lost in the ether of time and space.

Amergin could feel the weight of history and the destiny of the Promised Land. He studied the Temple where four massive Bluestone standing stones marked the equinoxes and solstices of the year. He walked slowly to the great stone in alignment with the autumn equinox. It was here at sunrise that he would place the skull shaped keystone in to its rightful place. He hoped they were still in time. The exact equinox had passed. The Guardians tell him that they are still early enough in the Cycle of Xustra to make the connection and unveil the Secret of the Alignment.

Amergin could feel the presence of the ancients. They talked to him that night. He knelt in prayer with Erhombu and Endinou. The three, communed with the Guardians of Light. The rituals necessary to reveal the Secret of the Alignment were unveiled. They were ready for the sunrise...

Scota gave Amergin her blessing. Of all the mortal beings present, she knew the poignancy of the time. She could feel the sense of duty weighing down on him. The culmination of the Prophecy and his destiny was here, right now! Amergin went to embrace his father, Milidh, for it was he that had given him the strength, the courage and the training in marine and battle skills. Then he went to his loyal brother, Eiremhou to thank him for his support, common sense and humour in times of real adversity. Finally he went to Terese of the Xantha. There were no words for her courage and bravery. Amergin took the sculpted keystone and thanked her for her devotion to the cause of the enlightenment.

The keystone was flawless perfection, he marvelled at the craftsmanship of the ancient Druids.

The sunrise not far away now, Endinou began chanting the sacred verse, passed down through the generations of Guardians. Amergin knelt in prayer, facing east, waiting for the tell tale aurora that preceded the dawn. The veil was all around them... visions of Sceine burst in to his consciousness...Their rapturous moments, just before she was cruelly taken by the Witches of Hawardden in wolfish guise.Then a vision of her lifeless body, cold and still, at the Portal of Hushinish.

The first hint of dawn began to illuminate the peak of Corran Tuathail in the southern Iveare mountain range. Amergin would need total composure now, total control of his mind and senses.

In a state of meditative calmness, he began to recite some of his spontaneous, spiritual poetic verse. The verse was his mantra...

He needed to remove any unpure thoughts and focus on the Divine in nature... Amergin tapped in to the realm of the spirit world... The veil wrapped around him... The verse poured forth in a stream of consciousness:

"On creaking, dipping, heaving vessels, hewn of wood, nailed and riveted.
From places maritime, sundried, wind shriveled mortals on a watery
Plain,
Spirits of the sea, born to the water, a blood and brine infusion, steeped.
No rest, no limits, the way is clear, horizon to horizon, destiny to here.
Ocean full, shimmering, sea of scales, salt liquid, ship of sails.
Ancient tradition, ageless condition, new horizons and ways of
Enlightenment"

Amergin felt the Light of the Divine coursing through his veins...

He channelled the pure energy from the spirit world...

An ethereal, ephemeral glow began to emanate from the Bluestones. They were connecting to the spirit world and the source of enlightenment.

Endinou chanted louder. Erhombu and all present followed. They chanted sacred verse descended from the ancients. The aurora of the dawn lit up the eastern horizon.

All the elements were in place... the perfectly crafted keystone fitted precisely in to the ancient Bluestone.

Amergin's hands cradled the skull shaped keystone, just as the first burst of radiant sunlight broke over the eastern horizon.

At that exact moment the Light of the Divine poured forth from the spirit world. Amergin felt the Guardians of Light all around him now. The sacred chanting rose to a climactic crescendo! The ethereal blue of the standing stones turned to a brilliant, heavenly glow as the very cosmos seemed to light up!

Then in an explosion of brilliant, pure white intensity, the Light of the Divine channelled through the massive Bluestones, energising the lay line, the conduit between the great portals of the Western Province. All around seemed to slow and stand still. One by one, the great portals of the Western Province were aligning and connecting...The Temple of the Sun, the Portal of Machlleth and then finally Hushinish.

Amergin felt, sensed and saw the Light of the Divine, exploding and pulsing from the spirit world.

He felt the connection with the soul of his beloved Sceine. Her body still cold and lifeless preserved in the aura of the great Portal of Hushinish. Amergin flushed with excitement. He could feel her spirit! He must remain focussed!

The lay line channelled more and more pure Light in to the ether.

Slowly the veil touched the mortal realm. The continuum of time and space warped and wrapped through the veil. Events began to fold in on themselves. History was unravelling. Moments in time touched and collided. Parallel universes intertwined. New universes were created... and in an apocalyptic burst of Divine Light, time began to reverse...

All the portals were fully connected.They seemed to be as one. The Guardians of Light journeyed beyond the veil to all the portals. The enlightened beings of the mortal realm were bathed in Divine Light. Time stood still once more... and in a sudden burst of radiant life giving Light, the continuum of time and space moved forward...

Natural sunlight warmed Amergin's face... a new day had begun... but more than that, new life had been given!

Amergin turned to the east once more... his heart brimming with love and life. He could feel her spirit! He could feel her life force! His beloved Sceine was alive!

Overlooking the Ridge of Thormond and the southern summits of the Iveare Mountains, Hushinish was bathed in the Light of the Divine and the light of a new dawn. The great portal was still pulsing in the final phase of the Alignment.

The priests guarding the body of Sceine, preserved in the aura of the Bluestones of Hushinish, were bemused, enthralled and amazed all at the same time! They had witnessed the Alignment, the Secret had been revealed! They felt the cosmos turning, moving... they sensed time standing still, reversing and then moving on... they were filled with awe... the universal life force... the lifegiving Light of the Divine... radiant energy pouring forth from the spirit world...

New life was being given! The pale, limp, lifeless body of the High Priestess Sceine stirred in to life!

Before their very eyes... her finger tips, her eyelids, her lips, quivered and stirred in to life... her eyes opened, the familiar rich amber glinting in the morning sun... the dark fleck drawing you in to infinity... the lips parted and a beaming smile lit up the Western Province! Sceine flexed and stretched her graceful body... her hands sweeping in an elegant arc... she thrilled in her reincarnated life! Sceine flexed her torso and massaged her body, coursing with the newly given life...

Her gracefully elegant legs trembled as she attempted to regain her balance. She stretched out her beckoning hand. Diarmuid, her loyal friend and faithful priest, with tears flooding from his eyes, took her hand and gently eased Sceine to her unsteady feet. Her newly conscious mind recalled her last living memories... her rapturous moments with the Sea Druid Amergin... she called out his name..."Amergin! My beloved! I am here!"

The priests went to her, surrounding her, protecting her, nurturing her...

Nothing would ever take her away from them ever again!

Deep in the Woodlands of Derwydd, there was a gathering of dark souls.

The Witches of Hawardden still in their wolfish alter entities, prowled the shadows. They had helplessly seen the Sea Druid Amergin, champion of the Milesian nation, sail west to the Magine Islands.

They now knew his mission! Nothing could have prepared them for this! They had witnessed first hand, the Secret of the Alignment being revealed! Radiant Light of the Divine poured forth from the great portals of the Western Province. They were at the Portal of Machlleth with Eimbear and Gonne to rally with the dark one MacCuacht, to battle there against the Sea Druid Amergin, on his return with the Milesian reinforcements.

Their clairvoyant powers had sensed the Secret of the Alignment being revealed to the mortal realm! Too late! Time had stood still, reversed and moved forward... they had felt the life giving force... Sceine lived again!

The Witches of Hawardden were enraged! They wanted blood! They had been duped by the Sea Druid Amergin! Together with the High Priest of the Chapter of Mystics, Gonne, and the traitorous brother of the Milesian, they had been sent on a fool's errand! Eiru blamed all of this on MacCuacht!

She had long suspected him of weakness. He had failed to intercept and slay the Sea Druid on numerous occasions... now this!

Eiru had lost her soul to the dark Sidhe long ago. Over time, she had become the darkest of all. Eiru was merciless, ruthless and vengeful. She was filled with hatred and contempt for her estranged partner. MacCuacht had failed her too many times... she now saw him as weak, pitiful and incompetent!

Amergin and Sceine live! The Prophecy will be fulfilled!

In her dark eyes MacCuacht was to blame!

The deep Woodlands of Derwydd were still cloaked in the dank, dense cooling mist. The dark one MacCuacht talked to the sinister Gonne, High Priest of the Chapter of Mystics. Eimbear the Machiavellian brother of the Sea Druid listened on. The army of lost souls hung on to his every word. MacCuacht was cursing them, trying to accuse Gonne and Eimbear of collusion with Amergin. "How could you have fallen for this deception?!" these were his last words... from the shadows of the woodlands cloaked in dense, dank mist... they struck without warning! The witches in their wolfish alter entities were in hunt mode! Slashing, lacerating, biting and clawing! Incisors and claws tearing in to MacCuacht's deathly white flesh. His dark, infected blood poured forth, covering them and staining the ground. MacCuacht was torn limb from limb and in no time the crazed wolfish predators had devoured him...

Bone, blood and entrails, every dark morsel was consumed!

The three were empowered and strengthened. Their darkness knew no bounds now...

In that fateful moment, they transformed from their wolfish alter entities back to the raven haired Witches of Hawardden. The three raven haired beauties, in their shimmering, silver cocoon dresses, stood on the dark, blood stained earth. The evil energy of the dark Sidhe coursed through their veins! Their power was unbounded now!

All those who witnessed the awful slaughter of the dark one MacCuacht, had no doubts as to who their new mistresses were. The darkest of all, their new leader...

Gonne of the Chapter of Mystics fell to his knees, chanting, "The dark one MacCuacht is dead, long reign the darkest one of all...Eiru!!!"

Eimbear and the army of lost souls knelt before her. They chanted her name, "Eiru! Eiru! Eiru...!"

That night under the cover of darkness and the receding cold, damp mist, Eiru and her sister witches retreated to the high mountain fortress of Hawardden. Gonne and Eimbear joined the army of lost souls. Together, they would return to their fortress to retrench and gather strength.

As dawn broke, the three raven haired witches stared malevolently out from the high battlements of Hawardden... the dark forces were gathering...

They shall return...

BIOGRAPHY:
PETER GREEN

Peter Green was born and bred in the dramatically beautiful North Wales.

In later years he lived in the stunning Pembrokeshire Coast National Park. His beautiful and talented daughter Josie was born here.

Peter now resides on the spectacular Dingle Peninsula on the West coast of Ireland. His writing, art and photography are inspired by these rugged, timeless places where ocean, weather and land collide.

A keen historian and lover of all things Celtic, he is intrigued by the history, myths and legends of the Sea Kingdoms of Western Europe.

A lifelong lover of the ocean and a keen water sportsman, Peter has surfed and kayaked at locations around the world and along the entire coast of Western Europe.

Peter is a marine conservationist, keenly promoting marine and coastal protection areas to conserve, protect and nurture the irreplaceable biodiversity and habitats along our coasts, whilst actively supporting sustainable economic activity for coastal communities.

Tales of the Milesians are plentiful on the West coast of Ireland. This heady concoction of imagination and history combined with a rich literary and artistic tradition has culminated in *"The Tales of Amergin - Sea Druid, the Journey Beyond the Veil"* This is the first novel in a series of tales exploring and illuminating the adventures of the Sea Druid, Amergin.

For more information on *"The Tales of Amergin"*, please contact -

Peter Green at: www.celtichorizons.ie

Email: celtichorizonspetergreen@yahoo.com

Tel: 00353 (0)87 2662920